"Why?" she asked urgently. "Why me?"

She hesitated, and though he didn't look at her, he was aware of her every movement. Of her restless fingers tracing the neckline of her bodice, of the flutter of pulse at her throat, of the moment she parted her lips again.

"Because," he murmured, "you draw me. Because you are kind but not soft. Because you cradle a desperate secret to your bosom, like a viper in your arms, and don't let go of it even as it gnaws on your very flesh. I want to pry that viper from your arms. To take that pain within myself and make it mine."

She trembled beside him. He could feel the quivers through the arm she kept on him. "I have no secret."

He bent and whispered against her hair. "Sweet, darling liar."

"There's an enchantment to Hoyt's stories that makes you believe in the magic of love."
—*RT Book Reviews*

PRAISE FOR
ELIZABETH HOYT'S
MAIDEN LANE SERIES

Wicked Intentions

"4½ stars! Top Pick! A magnificently rendered story that not only enchants but enthralls."
—RT Book Reviews

"Hoyt brings steamy sensuality to the slums of early eighteenth-century London...earthy, richly detailed characterizations and deft historical touches."
—Publishers Weekly

"A great book...and a wonderful start to a series...*Wicked Intentions* will make it onto my favorites of 2010 and will be reread with enthusiasm until book two makes its way to the shelves."
—SmexyBooks.com

"Hoyt brings mystery, romance, and intrigue to debut her latest series...and you are never left without wanting more...I can't wait for the next book in the series."
—TheMysticCastle.com

"Fantastic...I can't wait to read more in this series."
—TheBookGirl.net

Duke of Midnight

"Richly drawn characters fill the pages of this emotionally charged mix of mystery and romance."
—Publishers Weekly

"There is enchantment in the Maiden Lane series...the wonder of love combined with passion, unique plotlines, and unforgettable characters."
—RT Book Review

"Emotional and intriguing."
—DearAuthor.com

"Great suspense, lots of adventure, emotion-laden romances, and some serious sexiness...a deliciously dark, but romantic read."
—RomanceNovelNews.com

"An excellent historical romance."
—ImpressionsofaReader.com

"A wonderful story of passion and love...with engaging characters and intriguing story lines...a must-read!"
—MyBookAddictionReviews.com

Lord of Darkness

"*Lord of Darkness* illuminates Hoyt's boundless imagination...readers will adore this story."
—RT Book Reviews

"Hoyt's writing is imbued with great depth of emotion... heartbreaking... an edgy tension-filled plot."
—*Publishers Weekly*

"*Lord of Darkness* is classic Elizabeth Hoyt, meaning it's unique, engaging, and leaves readers on the edge of their seats, waiting for the next book... an incredible addition to the fantastic Maiden Lane series. I Joyfully Recommend Godric and Megs's tale, for it's an amazing, well-crafted story with an intriguing plot and a lovely, touching romance that I want to enjoy again and again and again... simply enchanting!"
—JoyfullyReviewed.com

"I adore the Maiden Lane series, and this fifth book is a very welcome addition to the series... [It's] sexy and sweet all at the same time... This can be read as a standalone, but I adore each book in this series and encourage you to start from the beginning."
—*USA Today*'s Happy Ever After blog

"Beautifully written... a truly fine piece of storytelling and a novel that deserves to be read and enjoyed."
—TheBookBinge.com

Thief of Shadows

"An expert blend of scintillating romance and mystery... The romance between the beautiful and quick-witted Isabel and the masked champion of the downtrodden propels this novel to the top of its genre."
—*Publishers Weekly* (starred review)

"Amazing sex scenes...a very intriguing hero...This one did not disappoint."
—*USA Today*

"Innovative, emotional, sensual...Hoyt's beautiful blending of the essential elements of a fairy tale into a stunning love story enhances this delicious 'keeper.'"
—*RT Book Reviews*

"All of Hoyt's signature literary ingredients—wickedly clever dialogue, superbly nuanced characters, danger, and scorching sexual chemistry—click neatly into place to create a breathtakingly romantic love story."
—*Booklist*

"When [they] finally come together, desire and long-denied sensuality explode upon the page."
—*Library Journal*

"With heart and heat rolled into one, *Thief of Shadows* is a definite must-read for historical romance fans! Hoyt really has outdone herself...yet again."
—**UndertheCoversBookblog.blogspot.com**

"A balanced mixture of action, adventure, and mystery and a beautifully crafted romance...The perfect historical romance."
—**HeroesandHeartbreakers.com**

Scandalous Desires

"Historical romance at its best...Series fans will be enthralled, while new readers will find this emotionally charged installment stands very well alone."
—Publishers Weekly (starred review)

"4½ stars! This is the Maiden Lane story readers have been waiting for. Hoyt delivers her hallmark fairy tale within a romance and takes readers into the depths of the heart and soul of her characters. Pure magic flows from her pen, lifting readers' spirits with joy."
—RT Book Reviews

"With its lush sensuality, lusciously wrought prose, and luxuriously dark plot, *Scandalous Desires*, the latest exquisitely crafted addition to Hoyt's Georgian-set Maiden Lane series, is a romance to treasure."
—Booklist (starred review)

"Ms. Hoyt writes some of the best love scenes out there. They are passionate, sexy, and blazing hot...I simply adore Ms. Hoyt's books for her sensuous prose, multifaceted characters, and intense, well-developed story lines. And she delivers every single time. It's no wonder all of her books are on my keeper shelves. Do yourself a favor and pick up *Scandalous Desires*."
—TheRomanceDish.com

"*Scandalous Desires* is the best book Elizabeth Hoyt has written so far, with endearing characters and an all-encompassing romance you'll want to hold close and never let go. If there's one must-read book, especially for historical romance fans, it's *Scandalous Desires*."
—FallenAngelReviews.com

Notorious Pleasures

"Emotionally stunning...The sinfully sensual chemistry Hoyt creates between her shrewd, acid-tongued heroine and her scandalous, sexy hero is pure romance."
—*Booklist* (starred review)

"Excitement and suspense."
—*Publishers Weekly* (starred review)

"Passionate and stirring...Elizabeth Hoyt at her best."
—ARomanceReview.com

"With romance, danger, intrigue, and sensuality to spare, NOTORIOUS PLEASURES is a wonderfully entertaining story from beginning to end."
—JoyfullyReviewed.com

ELIZABETH HOYT

Wicked Intentions

GRAND CENTRAL
PUBLISHING

NEW YORK   BOSTON

Grand Central Publishing
Hachette Book Group
1290 Avenue of the Americas
New York, NY 10104
www.HachetteBookGroup.com

Grand Central Publishing is a division of Hachette Book Group, Inc.
The Grand Central Publishing name and logo are trademarks of Hachette Book Group, Inc.

The Hachette Speakers Bureau provides a wide range of authors for speaking events. To find out more, go to www.hachettespeakersbureau.com or call (866) 376-6591.

The publisher is not responsible for websites (or their content) that are not owned by the publisher.

Printed in the United States of America

Originally published in hardcover by Hachette Book Group
First mass market edition: August 2010
Reissued: October 2014

10 9 8 7 6 5 4 3 2 1
OPM

For my sister, SUSAN, again, despite the fact that she regularly makes fun of my inept computer skills, and once a year finds it necessary to try and explain to me how the Internet really works, which always causes my head to nearly explode. Love ya! ;-)

Acknowledgments

To all the wonderful people who have helped me with this book: my agent, **Susannah Taylor**, who has selflessly found the very best ethnic restaurants in which to dine five years running at RWA nationals; to my editor, **Amy Pierpont**, who has yet to blink at my rather incoherent book proposals; to the Grand Central Publishing art department, especially **Diane Luger**, which has come up with my totally awesome book covers, time and time again; to the spectacular GCP sales team, especially **Bob Levine** (hi, Bob!), which makes sure my books are actually in stores to buy; and, of course, to my terrific copy editor, **Carrie Andrews**, saving readers the world over from my tragic spelling errors.

Thank you all.

Chapter One

*Once upon a time, in a land long forgotten now,
there lived a mighty king, feared by all and loved by
none. His name was King Lockedheart....*
—from *King Lockedheart*

A woman abroad in St. Giles at midnight was either very foolish or very desperate. Or, as in her own case, Temperance Dews reflected wryly, a combination of both.

"'Tis said the Ghost of St. Giles haunts on nights like this," Nell Jones, Temperance's maidservant, said chattily as she skirted a noxious puddle in the narrow alley.

Temperance glanced dubiously at her. Nell had spent three years in a traveling company of actors and sometimes had a tendency toward melodrama.

"There's no ghost haunting St. Giles," Temperance replied firmly. The cold winter night was frightening enough without the addition of specters.

"Oh, indeed, there is." Nell hoisted the sleeping babe in her arms higher. "He wears a black mask and a harlequin's motley and carries a wicked sword."

Temperance frowned. "A harlequin's motley? That doesn't sound very ghostlike."

"It's ghostlike if he's the dead spirit of a harlequin player come back to haunt the living."

"For bad reviews?"

Nell sniffed. "*And* he's disfigured."

"How would anyone know that if he's masked?"

They were coming to a turn in the alley, and Temperance thought she saw light up ahead. She held her lantern high and gripped the ancient pistol in her other hand a little tighter. The weapon was heavy enough to make her arm ache. She could have brought a sack to carry it in, but that would've defeated its purpose as a deterrent. Though loaded, the pistol held but one shot, and to tell the truth, she was somewhat hazy on the actual operation of the weapon.

Still, the pistol looked dangerous, and Temperance was grateful for that. The night was black, the wind moaning eerily, bringing with it the smell of excrement and rotting offal. The sounds of St. Giles rose about them—voices raised in argument, moans and laughter, and now and again the odd, chilling scream. St. Giles was enough to send the most intrepid woman running for her life.

And that was without Nell's conversation.

"*Horribly* disfigured," Nell continued, ignoring Temperance's logic. "'Tis said his lips and eyelids are clean burned off, as if he died in a fire long ago. He seems to grin at you with his great yellow teeth as he comes to pull the guts from your belly."

Temperance wrinkled her nose. "Nell!"

"That's what they say," Nell said virtuously. "The ghost guts his victims and plays with their entrails before slipping away into the night."

Temperance shivered. "Why would he do that?"

"Envy," Nell said matter-of-factly. "He envies the living."

"Well, I don't believe in spirits in any case." Temperance took a breath as they turned the corner into a small, wretched courtyard. Two figures stood at the opposite end, but they scuttled away at their approach. Temperance let out her breath. "Lord, I hate being abroad at night."

Nell patted the infant's back. "Only a half mile more. Then we can put this wee one to bed and send for the wet nurse in the morning."

Temperance bit her lip as they ducked into another alley. "Do you think she'll live until morning?"

But Nell, usually quite free with her opinions, was silent. Temperance peered ahead and hurried her step. The baby looked to be only weeks old and had not yet made a sound since they'd recovered her from the arms of her dead mother. Normally a thriving infant was quite loud. Terrible to think that she and Nell might've made this dangerous outing for naught.

But then what choice had there been, really? When she'd received word at the Home for Unfortunate Infants and Foundling Children that a baby was in need of her help, it had still been light. She'd known from bitter experience that if they'd waited until morn to retrieve the child, it would either have expired in the night from lack of care or would've already been sold for a beggar's prop. She shuddered. The children bought by beggars were often made more pitiful to elicit sympathy from passersby. An eye might be put out or a limb broken or twisted. No, she'd really had no choice. The baby couldn't wait until morning.

Still, she'd be very happy when they made it back to the home.

They were in a narrow passage now, the tall houses on either side leaning inward ominously. Nell was forced to walk behind Temperance or risk brushing the sides of the buildings. A scrawny cat snaked by, and then there was a shout very near.

Temperance's steps faltered.

"Someone's up ahead," Nell whispered hoarsely.

They could hear scuffling and then a sudden high scream.

Temperance swallowed. The alley had no side passages. They could either retreat or continue—and to retreat meant another twenty minutes added to their journey.

That decided her. The night was chilly, and the cold wasn't good for the babe.

"Stay close to me," she whispered to Nell.

"Like a flea on a dog," Nell muttered.

Temperance squared her shoulders and held the pistol firmly in front of her. Winter, her youngest brother, had said that one need only point it and shoot. That couldn't be too hard. The light from the lantern spilled before them as she entered another crooked courtyard. Here she stood still for just a second, her light illuminating the scene ahead like a pantomime on a stage.

A man lay on the ground, bleeding from the head. But that wasn't what froze her—blood and even death were common enough in St. Giles. No, what arrested her was the *second* man. He crouched over the first, his black cloak spread to either side of him like the wings of a great bird of prey. He held a long black walking stick, the end tipped with silver, echoing his hair, which was silver as well. It fell straight and long, glinting in the lantern's light. Though his face was mostly in darkness, his eyes glinted from under the brim of a black tricorne. Temperance could feel the weight of the stranger's stare. It was as if he physically touched her.

"Lord save and preserve us from evil," Nell murmured, for the first time sounding fearful. "Come away, ma'am. Swiftly!"

Thus urged, Temperance ran across the courtyard, her shoes clattering on the cobblestones. She darted into another passage and left the scene behind.

"Who was he, Nell?" she panted as they made their way through the stinking alley. "Do you know?"

The passage let out suddenly into a wider road, and Temperance relaxed a little, feeling safer without the walls pressing in.

Nell spat as if to clear a foul taste from her mouth.

Temperance looked at her curiously. "You sounded like you knew that man."

"Knew him, no," Nell replied. "But I've seen him about. That was Lord Caire. He's best left to himself."

"Why?"

Nell shook her head, pressing her lips firmly together. "I shouldn't be speaking about the likes of him to you at all, ma'am."

Temperance let that cryptic comment go. They were on a better street now—some of the shops had lanterns hanging by the doors, lit by the inhabitants within.

Temperance turned one more corner onto Maiden Lane, and the foundling home came within sight. Like its neighbors, it was a tall brick building of cheap construction. The windows were few and very narrow, the doorway unmarked by any sign. In the fifteen precarious years of the foundling home's existence, there had never been a need to advertise.

Abandoned and orphaned children were all too common in St. Giles.

"Home safely," Temperance said as they reached the door. She set down the lantern on the worn stone step and took out the big iron key hanging by a cord at her waist. "I'm looking forward to a dish of hot tea."

"I'll put this wee one to bed," Nell said as they entered the dingy little hall. It was spotlessly clean, but that didn't hide the fallen plaster or the warped floorboards.

"Thank you." Temperance removed her cloak and was just hanging it on a peg when a tall male form appeared at the far doorway.

"Temperance."

She swallowed and turned. "Oh! Oh, Winter, I did not know you'd returned."

"Obviously," her younger brother said drily. He nodded to the maidservant. "A good eventide to you, Nell."

"Sir." Nell curtsied and looked nervously between brother and sister. "I'll just see to the, ah, children, shall I?"

And she fled upstairs, leaving Temperance to face Winter's disapproval alone.

Temperance squared her shoulders and moved past her brother. The foundling home was long and narrow, squeezed by the neighboring houses. There was one room off the small entryway. It was used for dining and, on occasion, receiving the home's infrequent important visitors. At the back of the house were the kitchens, which Temperance entered now. The children had all had their dinner promptly at five o'clock, but neither she nor her brother had eaten.

"I was just about to make some tea," she said as she went to stir the fire. Soot, the home's black cat, got up from his place in front of the hearth and stretched before padding off in search of mice. "There's a bit of beef left from yesterday and some new radishes I bought at market this morning."

Behind her Winter sighed. "Temperance."

She hurried to find the kettle. "The bread's a bit stale, but I can toast it if you like."

He was silent and she finally turned and faced the inevitable.

It was worse than she feared. Winter's long, thin face merely looked sad, which always made her feel terrible. She hated to disappoint him.

"It was still light when we set out," she said in a small voice.

He sighed again, taking off his round black hat and sitting at the kitchen table. "Could you not wait for my return, sister?"

Temperance looked at her brother. Winter was only five and twenty, but he bore himself with the air of a man twice his age. His countenance was lined with weariness, his wide shoulders slumped beneath his ill-fitting black coat, and his long limbs were much too thin. For the last five years, he had taught at the tiny daily school attached to the home.

On Papa's death last year, Winter's work had increased tremendously. Concord, their eldest brother, had taken over the family brewery. Asa, their next-eldest brother, had always been rather dismissive of the foundling home and had a mysterious business of his own. Both of their sisters, Verity, the eldest of the family, and Silence, the youngest, were married. That had left Winter to manage the foundling home. Even with her help—she'd worked at the home since the death of her husband nine years before—the task was overwhelming for one man. Temperance feared for her brother's well-being, but both the foundling home and the tiny day school had been founded by Papa. Winter felt it was his filial duty to keep the two charities alive.

If his health did not give out first.

She filled the teakettle from the water jar by the back door. "Had we waited, it would have been full dark with no assurance that the babe would still be there." She glanced at him as she placed the kettle over the fire. "Besides, have you not enough work to do?"

"If I lose my sister, think you that I'd be more free of work?"

Temperance looked away guiltily.

Her brother's voice softened. "And that discounts the lifelong sorrow I would feel had anything happened to you this night."

"Nell knew the mother of the baby—a girl of less than fifteen years." Temperance took out the bread and carved it into thin slices. "Besides, I carried the pistol."

"Hmm," Winter said behind her. "And had you been accosted, would you have used it?"

"Yes, of course," she said with flat certainty.

"And if the shot misfired?"

She wrinkled her nose. Their father had brought up all her brothers to debate a point finely, and that fact could be quite irritating at times.

She carried the bread slices to the fire to toast. "In any case, nothing did happen."

"*This* night." Winter sighed again. "Sister, you must promise me you'll not act so foolishly again."

"Mmm," Temperance mumbled, concentrating on the toast. "How was your day at the school?"

For a moment, she thought Winter wouldn't consent to her changing the subject. Then he said, "A good day, I think. The Samuels lad remembered his Latin lesson finally, and I did not have to punish any of the boys."

Temperance glanced at him with sympathy. She knew Winter hated to take a switch to a palm, let alone cane a boy's bottom. On the days that Winter had felt he must punish a boy, he came home in a black mood.

"I'm glad," she said simply.

He stirred in his chair. "I returned for luncheon, but you were not here."

Temperance took the toast from the fire and placed it on the table. "I must have been taking Mary Found to her new position. I think she'll do quite well there. Her mistress seemed very kind, and the woman took only five pounds as payment to apprentice Mary as her maid."

"God willing she'll actually teach the child something so we won't see Mary Found again."

Temperance poured the hot water into their small teapot and brought it to the table. "You sound cynical, brother."

Winter passed a hand over his brow. "Forgive me.

Cynicism is a terrible vice. I shall try to correct my humor."

Temperance sat and silently served her brother, waiting. Something more than her late-night adventure was bothering him.

At last he said, "Mr. Wedge visited whilst I ate my luncheon."

Mr. Wedge was their landlord. Temperance paused, her hand on the teapot. "What did he say?"

"He'll give us only another two weeks, and then he'll have the foundling home forcibly vacated."

"Dear God."

Temperance stared at the little piece of beef on her plate. It was stringy and hard and from an obscure part of the cow, but she'd been looking forward to it. Now her appetite was suddenly gone. The foundling home's rent was in arrears—they hadn't been able to pay the full rent last month and nothing at all this month. Perhaps she shouldn't have bought the radishes, Temperance reflected morosely. But the children hadn't had anything but broth and bread for the last week.

"If only Sir Gilpin had remembered us in his will," she murmured.

Sir Stanley Gilpin had been Papa's good friend and the patron of the foundling home. A retired theater owner, he'd managed to make a fortune on the South Sea Company and had been wily enough to withdraw his funds before the notorious bubble burst. Sir Gilpin had been a generous patron while alive, but on his unexpected death six months before, the home had been left floundering. They'd limped along, using what money had been saved, but now they were in desperate straits.

"Sir Gilpin was an unusually generous man, it would seem," Winter replied. "I have not been able to find another gentleman so willing to fund a home for the infant poor."

Temperance poked at her beef. "What shall we do?"

"The Lord shall provide," Winter said, pushing aside his half-eaten meal and rising. "And if he does not, well, then perhaps I can take on private students in the evenings."

"You already work too many hours," Temperance protested. "You hardly have time to sleep as it is."

Winter shrugged. "How can I live with myself if the innocents we protect are thrown into the street?"

Temperance looked down at her plate. She had no answer to that.

"Come." Her brother held out his hand and smiled.

Winter's smiles were so rare, so precious. When he smiled, his entire face lit as if from a flame within, and a dimple appeared on one cheek, making him look boyish, more his true age.

One couldn't help smiling back when Winter smiled, and Temperance did so as she laid her hand in his. "Where will we go?"

"Let us visit our charges," he said as he took a candle and led her to the stairs. "Have you ever noticed that they look quite angelic when asleep?"

Temperance laughed as they climbed the narrow wooden staircase to the next floor. There was a small hall here with three doors leading off it. They peered in the first as Winter held his candle high. Six tiny cots lined the walls of the room. The youngest of the foundlings slept here, two or three to a cot. Nell lay in an adult-sized bed by the door, already asleep.

Winter walked to the cot nearest Nell. Two babes lay there. The first was a boy, red-haired and pink-cheeked, sucking on his fist as he slept. The second child was half the size of the first, her cheeks pale and her eyes hollowed, even in sleep. Tiny whorls of fine black hair decorated her crown.

"This is the baby you rescued tonight?" Winter asked softly.

Temperance nodded. The little girl looked even more frail next to the thriving baby boy.

But Winter merely touched the baby's hand with a gentle finger. "How do you like the name Mary Hope?"

Temperance swallowed past the thickness in her throat. "'Tis very apt."

Winter nodded and, with a last caress for the tiny babe, left the room. The next door led to the boys' dormitory. Four beds held thirteen boys, all under the age of nine— the age when they were apprenticed out. The boys lay with limbs sprawled, faces flushed in sleep. Winter smiled and pulled a blanket over the three boys nearest the door, tucking in a leg that had escaped the bed.

Temperance sighed. "One would never think that they spent an hour at luncheon hunting for rats in the alley."

"Mmm," Winter answered as he closed the door softly behind them. "Small boys grow so swiftly to men."

"They do indeed." Temperance opened the last door— the one to the girls' dormitory—and a small face immediately popped off a pillow.

"Did you get 'er, ma'am?" Mary Whitsun whispered hoarsely.

She was the eldest of the girls in the foundling home, named for the Whitsunday morning nine years before when she'd been brought to the home as a child of three. Young though Mary Whitsun was, Temperance had to sometimes leave her in charge of the other children—as she'd had to tonight.

"Yes, Mary," Temperance whispered back. "Nell and I brought the babe home safely."

"I'm glad." Mary Whitsun yawned widely.

"You did well watching the children," Temperance whispered. "Now sleep. A new day will be here soon."

Mary Whitsun nodded sleepily and closed her eyes.

Winter picked up a candlestick from a little table by the door and led the way out of the girls' dormitory. "I shall take your kind advice, sister, and bid you good night."

He lit the candlestick from his own and gave it to Temperance.

"Sleep well," she replied. "I think I'll have one more cup of tea before retiring."

"Don't stay up too late," Winter said. He touched her cheek with a finger—much as he had the babe—and turned to mount the stairs.

Temperance watched him go, frowning at how slowly he moved up the stairs. It was past midnight, and he would rise again before five of the clock to read, write letters to prospective patrons, and prepare his school lessons for the day. He would lead the morning prayers at breakfast, hurry to his job as schoolmaster, work all morning before taking one hour for a meager luncheon, and then work again until after dark. In the evening, he heard the girls' lessons and read from the Bible to the older children. Yet, when she voiced her worries, Winter would merely raise an eyebrow and inquire who would do the work if not he?

Temperance shook her head. She should be to bed

as well—her day started at six of the clock—but these moments by herself in the evening were precious. She'd sacrifice a half hour's sleep to sit alone with a cup of tea.

So she took her candle back downstairs. Out of habit, she checked to see that the front door was locked and barred. The wind whistled and shook the shutters as she made her way to the kitchen, and the back door rattled. She checked it as well and was relieved to see the door still barred. Temperance shivered, glad she was no longer outside on a night like this. She rinsed out the teapot and filled it again. To make a pot of tea with fresh leaves and only for herself was a terrible luxury. Soon she'd have to give this up as well, but tonight she'd enjoy her cup.

Off the kitchen was a tiny room. Its original purpose was forgotten, but it had a small fireplace, and Temperance had made it her own private sitting room. Inside was a stuffed chair, much battered but refurbished with a quilted blanket thrown over the back. A small table and a footstool were there as well—all she needed to sit by herself next to a warm fire.

Humming, Temperance placed her teapot and cup, a small dish of sugar, and the candlestick on an old wooden tray. Milk would have been nice, but what was left from this morning would go toward the children's breakfast on the morrow. As it was, the sugar was a shameful luxury. She looked at the small bowl, biting her lip. She really ought to put it back; she simply didn't deserve it. After a moment, she took the sugar dish off the tray, but the sacrifice brought her no feeling of wholesome goodness. Instead she was only weary. Temperance picked up the tray, and because both her hands were full, she backed into the door leading to her little sitting room.

Which was why she didn't notice until she turned that the sitting room was already occupied.

There, sprawled in her chair like a conjured demon, sat Lord Caire. His silver hair spilled over the shoulders of his black cape, a cocked hat lay on one knee, and his right hand caressed the end of his long ebony walking stick. This close, she realized that his hair gave lie to his age. The lines about his startlingly blue eyes were few, his mouth and jaw firm. He couldn't be much older than five and thirty.

He inclined his head at her entrance and spoke, his voice deep and smooth and softly dangerous.

"Good evening, Mrs. Dews."

SHE STOOD WITH quiet confidence, this respectable woman who lived in the sewer that was St. Giles. Her eyes had widened at the sight of him, but she made no move to flee. Indeed, finding a strange man in her pathetic sitting room seemed not to frighten her at all.

Interesting.

"I am Lazarus Huntington, Lord Caire," he said.

"I know. What are you doing here?"

He tilted his head, studying her. She knew him, yet did not recoil in horror? Yes, she'd do quite well. "I've come to make a proposition to you, Mrs. Dews."

Still no sign of fear, though she eyed the doorway. "You've chosen the wrong lady, my lord. The night is late. Please leave my house."

No fear and no deference to his rank. An interesting woman indeed.

"My proposition is not, er, *illicit* in nature," he drawled. "In fact, it's quite respectable. Or nearly so."

She sighed and looked down at her tray, and then back up at him. "Would you like a cup of tea?"

He almost smiled. Tea? When had he last been offered something so very prosaic by a woman? He couldn't remember.

But he replied gravely enough. "Thank you, no."

She nodded. "Then if you don't mind?"

He waved a hand to indicate permission.

She set the tea tray on the wretched little table and sat on the padded footstool to pour herself a cup. He watched her. She was a monochromatic study. Her dress, bodice, hose, and shoes were all flat black. A fichu tucked in at her severe neckline, an apron, and a cap—no lace or ruffles— were all white. No color marred her aspect, making the lush red of her full lips all the more startling. She wore the clothes of a nun, yet had the mouth of a sybarite.

The contrast was fascinating—and arousing.

"You're a Puritan?" he asked.

Her beautiful mouth compressed. "No."

"Ah." He noted she did not say she was Church of England either. She probably belonged to one of the many obscure nonconformist sects, but then he was interested in her religious beliefs only as they impacted his own mission.

She took a sip of tea. "How do you know my name?"

He shrugged. "Mrs. Dews and her brother are well-known for their good deeds."

"Really?" Her tone was dry. "I was not aware we were so famous beyond the boundaries of St. Giles."

She might look demure, but there were teeth behind the prim expression. And she was quite right—he would never have heard of her had he not spent the last month stalking the shadows of St. Giles. Stalking fruitlessly, which was why he'd followed her home and sat before this miserable fire now.

"How did you get in?" she asked.

"I believe the back door was unlocked."

"No, it wasn't." Her brown eyes met his over her teacup. They were an odd light color, almost golden. "Why are you here, Lord Caire?"

"I wish to hire you, Mrs. Dews," he said softly.

She stiffened and set her teacup down on the tray. "No."

"You haven't heard the task for which I wish to hire you."

"It's past midnight, my lord, and I'm not inclined to games even during the day. Please leave or I shall be forced to call my brother."

He didn't move. "Not a husband?"

"I'm widowed, as I'm sure you already know." She turned to look into the fire, presenting a dismissive profile to him.

He stretched his legs in what room there was, his boots nearly in the fire. "You're quite correct—I do know. I also know that you and your brother have not paid the rent on this property in nearly two months."

She said nothing, merely sipping her tea.

"I'll pay handsomely for your time," he murmured.

She looked at him finally, and he saw a golden flame in those pale brown eyes. "You think all women can be bought?"

He rubbed his thumb across his chin, considering the question. "Yes, I do, though perhaps not strictly by money. And I do not limit it to women—all men can be bought in one form or another as well. The only trouble is in finding the applicable currency."

She simply stared at him with those odd eyes.

He dropped his hand, resting it on his knee. "You, for instance, Mrs. Dews. I would've thought your currency would be money for your foundling home, but perhaps I'm mistaken. Perhaps I've been fooled by your plain exterior, your reputation as a prim widow. Perhaps you would be better persuaded by influence or knowledge or even the pleasures of the flesh."

"You still haven't said what you want me for."

Though she hadn't moved, hadn't changed expression at all, her voice had a rough edge. He caught it only because he had years of experience at the chase. His nostrils flared involuntarily, as if the hunter within was trying to scent her. Which of his list had interested her?

"A guide." His eyelids drooped as he pretended to examine his fingernails. "Merely that." He watched her from under his brows and saw when that lush mouth pursed.

"A guide to what?"

"St. Giles."

"Why do you need a guide?"

Ah, this was where it got tricky. "I'm searching for…a certain person in St. Giles. I would like to interview some of the inhabitants, but I find my search confounded by my ignorance of the area and the people and by their reluctance to talk to me. Hence, a guide."

Her eyes had narrowed as she listened, her fingers tapping against the teacup. "Whom do you search for?"

He shook his head slowly. "Not unless you agree to be my guide."

"And that is all you want? A guide? Nothing else?"

He nodded, watching her.

She turned to look into the fire as if consulting it. For a moment, the only sound in the room was the snap of a piece of coal falling. He waited patiently, caressing the silver head of his cane.

Then she faced him fully. "You're right. Your money does not tempt me. It's a stopgap measure that would only delay our eventual eviction."

He cocked his head, watching as she carefully licked those lush lips, preparing her argument, no doubt. He felt the beat of the pulse beneath his skin, his body's response to her feminine vitality. "What do you want, then, Mrs. Dews?"

She met his gaze levelly, almost in challenge. "I want you to introduce me to the wealthy and titled people of London. I want you to help me find a new patron for our foundling home."

Lazarus kept his mouth firmly straight, but he felt a surge of triumph as the prim widow ran headlong into his talons.

"Done."

Chapter Two

*Now, King Lockedheart was a very proud man.
For though he had been born to a small and
insignificant kingdom, he had, through courage,
guile, and daring, defeated the surrounding larger
countries until he controlled a vast and powerful
kingdom. To the north were mountains rich in
minerals and sparkling gems. To the east, fields of
golden grains and fat cattle. To the south lay tall
hardwood forests. And to the west was an ocean
overflowing with silver fish. A man could start from
the capital city and walk a month in any direction
and not leave the lands belonging
to King Lockedheart....*
—from *King Lockedheart*

Temperance caught her breath, feeling suddenly as if the
jaws of a trap had slammed shut around her. She didn't let
her gaze waver, however. Lord Caire struck her as something of a predator, and it wouldn't do to show fear in his
presence. Instead, she leaned forward and gently poured

herself another dish of tea. She noted with some pride that her hands were steady.

When she'd taken a sip, she looked at him, this exotic creature lounging in her drab little sitting room, and squared her shoulders. "Let us discuss the particulars of our arrangement, my lord."

His wide, sensuous lips quirked as if he found her amusing. "Such as, Mrs. Dews?"

She swallowed. Naturally, she'd never made a pact such as this in her life, but she did bargain regularly with the butcher and the fishmonger and the various tradespeople one dealt with when running a foundling home. And she fancied she was not such a bad bargainer.

Temperance set down her teacup. "I'll need money for living expenses."

"Living expenses?" His black eyebrows arched up his forehead.

She felt a bit brash asking for money when they'd already settled on his introducing her to potential patrons as his part of the bargain. But the truth was that the home needed the money. Desperately.

"Yes," she said, lifting her chin. "As you yourself noted, our rent is in arrears. In addition, the children haven't had a proper meal in days. I need money to buy some beef, vegetables, bread, tea, and milk. Not to mention both Joseph Tinbox and Joseph Smith need new shoes—"

"Joseph Tinbox?"

"And most of the younger Marys need new chemises," Temperance finished in a defiant rush.

For a moment, Lord Caire merely watched her with those mysterious sapphire eyes. Then he stirred. "Exactly how many children do you house in this home?"

"Seven and twenty," Temperance said promptly, then remembered tonight's work. "I beg your pardon. *Eight* and twenty with the addition of Mary Hope—the babe I brought home tonight. We also have two infants who are under the care of wet nurses at the moment outside the home. When they are weaned, they'll come to live here as well. And, of course, I live here with my brother, Winter, and our maidservant, Nell Jones."

"Only three adults for so many children?"

"Yes." Temperance leaned forward in her eagerness. "You see why we need a patron? If we had proper funding, we could hire another nursemaid or two and perhaps a cook and a manservant. We could serve meat at both luncheon and dinner, and all the boys could wear decent shoes. We could pay a good apprenticeship fee and outfit each child in new clothes and shoes when they leave the home. They'd be so much better prepared to face the world."

He lifted an eyebrow. "I can well afford to maintain your home if you wish to renegotiate my part of this bargain."

Temperance pursed her lips. She didn't know this man. How could she be certain that he'd take the position of patron responsibly? Or that he wouldn't abandon them after only a month or two?

And, of course, there was an even more important consideration. "The home's patron must be respectable."

"Ah. I see." She expected him to be insulted, but he merely gave her an ironic half smile. "Very well. I'll stand you the monies needed to pay your home's rent as well as enough for the various expenses the children have. In return, however, I will expect you to be ready to lead me into St. Giles tomorrow night."

So soon? "Of course," Temperance replied.

"And," he said, his voice dangerously soft. "I will expect you to serve me until such time as I no longer have need of your services."

Temperance blinked, feeling wary. Surely it was the height of foolishness to bind herself to a stranger for an indefinite length of time? "How long do you think your search will take?"

"I don't know."

"But you must have an end date in mind? If you don't find what you want, say, within a month, you'll give up your search?"

He simply looked at her, a small smile flickering at the corner of his mouth, and it crashed down on her—again—that she didn't know this man. She knew nothing about him, in fact, beyond Nell's ominous warning about him. For a moment, Temperance felt fear creep on little spider feet up her spine.

She straightened. They'd made a bargain, and she'd not dishonor herself by reneging on it. The home and all the children in it depended on her.

"Very well," she said slowly. "I will help you for an indefinite time. But I will need forewarning when you wish to go into St. Giles. I have duties within the home and will have to find someone to take my place."

"I mainly search at night," Lord Caire drawled. "If you require a replacement for your work at the home, I will fund that as well."

"That's very generous of you," she murmured, "but if we are to go out at night, then the children should already be abed. Hopefully, I will not be needed."

"Good."

"How soon will you be able to take me to meet potential patrons for the home?" She would somehow have to find a new dress and shoes at the very minimum. Her usual black stuff workday clothes wouldn't do for meeting the wealthy of society.

He shrugged. "A fortnight? Perhaps more. I may need to go begging for invitations to the more sedate parties."

"Very well." A fortnight was not very much time, but then again, the home needed immediate help. She couldn't afford to wait longer.

He nodded. "Then I believe our negotiations are concluded."

"Not quite," she said.

He halted in the act of raising his hat to his head. "Indeed, Mrs. Dews? You yourself have said I've been generous. What more do you need?"

The tiny smile was gone from his mouth, and he was looking rather intimidating, but Temperance swallowed and lifted her chin. "Information."

He merely cocked an eyebrow.

"What is the name of the person you are looking for?"

"I don't know."

She frowned. "Do you know what they look like or the areas where they habitually frequent?"

"No."

"Is this person a man or a woman?"

He smiled, deep lines incising themselves into his lean cheeks. "I have no idea."

She blew out a breath, not a little frustrated. "How do you expect me to find this person for you, then?"

"I don't," he replied. "I merely expect you to help me search. I'd think that there would be several sources of gossip in St. Giles. Lead me to them and I will do the rest."

"Very well." She already had an idea of who might be a good source of "gossip." Temperance stood and held out her hand. "I accept your bargain, Lord Caire."

For an awful moment, he merely stared at her out-thrust hand. Perhaps he found the gesture too masculine or simply silly. But then he stood as well, and in the small space, she had to tilt her head to look him in the face. She was suddenly aware of how much bigger he was than she.

He took her hand, a strangely frozen expression on his face, shook it quickly, and let go as if her palm had burned him.

She was still puzzling over the odd little moment when he placed his hat on his head, swirled his cape about his shoulders, and nodded. "I shall come for you tomorrow evening in the alley outside your kitchen door at nine o'clock. Until then, I bid you good night, Mrs. Dews."

And he was gone.

Temperance blinked and then hurried out to the kitchen to bar the back door. Soot got up from the hearth as she entered.

"That door was locked. I know it," she muttered to the cat. "How *did* he get in?"

But the cat merely yawned and stretched lazily.

Temperance sighed and went back to her sitting room for her tea things. As she entered the room, she glanced at the chair in which Lord Caire had lounged. There, in the middle of the seat, was a small purse. Temperance snatched it up and opened it. Gold coins spilled into her palm, more than enough to pay Mr. Wedge his rent.

Lord Caire had paid in advance, it seemed.

*   *   *

BASHAM'S COFFEEHOUSE WAS boisterously loud by the time Lazarus entered the doors late the next afternoon. He wound his way past a table of elderly gentlemen in full-bottomed wigs arguing heatedly over a newspaper and made his way to a solitary gentleman in a gray wig in the corner. The man sat peering through half-moon spectacles at a pamphlet.

"You'll ruin your eyes trying to read that dreck, St. John," Lazarus said as he took a chair across from his old friend.

"Caire," Godric St. John murmured. He tapped the pamphlet. "This writer's thesis isn't entirely unimaginable."

"Only partially? I am relieved." Lazarus snapped his fingers at one of the youths flying back and forth with loaded trays of coffee. "One here."

He turned back to find St. John gazing at him over his spectacles. With his somber tie wig, spectacles, and plain dress, others sometimes mistook St. John for a grandfather. In fact, he and St. John were of the same age—four and thirty. On closer examination, one noticed St. John's clear gray eyes, his strong jaw, and his dark brows. Only the truly perceptive saw the ever-present sorrow that wrapped St. John like a death shroud.

"I've got a translation for you to look at," Lazarus said. He withdrew a sheaf of papers from his coat pocket and handed it to the other man.

St. John peered at the papers. "Catullus? This will set Burgess's back up."

Lazarus snorted. "Burgess thinks he's the foremost authority on Catullus. The man has as much knowledge of Roman poetry as the average snot-nosed schoolboy."

"Well, naturally." St. John lifted an eyebrow behind his spectacles, looking faintly amused. "But you'll start a nasty brawl with this."

"Oh, I hope so," Lazarus said. "Can you glance at it and give me your opinion?"

"Certainly."

There was a shout at the next table, and a tankard of coffee was flung to the floor.

Lazarus looked up. "Are they discussing politics or religion?"

"Politics." St. John glanced at the arguing gentlemen dispassionately. "The newspapers are saying that Wakefield is calling for yet another gin bill."

"You'd think by now he would have learned that too many of his fellow peers' fortunes depend upon the sale of gin."

St. John shrugged. "Wakefield's argument is sound. When so many of the poor become enfeebled by gin, it hurts London's industry."

"Yes, and no doubt the fat country baron faced with either selling his excess grain to a gin distiller or letting it rot will put London's health before money in his pocket. Wakefield's a fool."

"He's an idealist."

"And, I repeat, a fool," Lazarus drawled. "His ideals do nothing but make him enemies. He'd do better pounding his head against a stone wall than trying to get Parliament to pass an effective gin bill."

"You would have us simply sit back and let London go to rot?" St. John inquired.

Lazarus waved a hand. "You ask as if there is another option. I submit there is not. Wakefield and his ilk would like to believe that they can change the course we sail, but they are deluded. Mark me well: pigs will sprout feathered wings and fly about Westminster before gin is taken away from the London rabble."

"The depth of your cynicism is breathtaking as always."

A boy slid a tankard of coffee in front of Lazarus.

"Thank you, you young imp."

Lazarus tossed a penny, and the coffee boy handily caught it before scampering back to the stall where the coffee was brewed. Lazarus took a sip of the hot liquid, and when he lowered his tankard, caught St. John examining him like an insect under a magnifying glass.

"You stare at me as if I had pox sores on my face," Lazarus said.

"Someday you no doubt will," St. John replied. "You've bedded enough whores."

"I have needs—"

"You have indulgences," St. John interrupted quietly, "and you make no effort to rein them in."

"And why should I?" Lazarus asked. "Does the wolf mourn his joy at running down his prey? The hawk the desire to soar and then dive to catch the hare in his talons? It is in their nature, just as my...*needs*...are in mine."

"The wolf and the hawk have no conscience, no soul, as you very well know."

"The women I use are paid quite well for their time. My needs hurt no one."

"Don't they?" St. John asked softly. "I wonder if they hurt you, Caire."

Lazarus curled his upper lip. "This is an old argument and one that neither one of us has yet to win."

"If I give up the argument, I give up you as well."

Lazarus rapped his fingers against the worn tabletop, saying nothing. Damned if he'd submit to St. John's worries. His needs were unusual—strange, even—but certainly not morbid.

Of course, St. John had no problem with probing where he wasn't wanted.

The other man shook his head and leaned back in his chair. "You were out last night."

"Gracious me! Have you become a fortune-teller? Or were you 'round my town house last night and found me absent?"

"Neither." St. John calmly pushed his spectacles up onto his forehead. "You wear the same look as last time I saw you, a kind of—"

"Weariness?"

"I was about to say *desperation*."

Lazarus took a sip of the hot coffee, damnably aware that he was buying time, but in the end, all he could reply was, "I didn't know you had such a flair for the dramatic. *Desperation* seems to overstate the case by miles."

"I don't think so." St. John peered absently into his own tankard of coffee. "You've worn that look since Marie's death. Do you deny that you were searching for her killer last night yet again?"

"No." Lazarus sat back in his chair, regarding his old friend from beneath half-lowered eyelids. "What of it?"

"You're obsessed, man." St. John said the words evenly, which somehow only gave them more impact. "She's been dead nearly two months, and you've spent every night looking for her murderer. Tell me, Lazarus, when will you give up the hunt?"

"When would you give up if Clara were murdered?" Lazarus shot back.

The only sign of how deeply the arrow hit was a small tic on St. John's jaw. "Never. But the cases are different."

"How? Because you are married to your woman whilst Marie was merely my mistress?"

"No," St. John said gently. "Because I love Clara."

Lazarus looked away. However much a mean-spirited part of him wanted to deny that difference, he couldn't in truth do it. For St. John was right: he did love his Clara.

Whereas Lazarus had never loved anyone at all.

"I DON'T LIKE this, ma'am. I don't like it at all," Nell said late that night in the foundling home kitchen.

"You've made your disapproval quite plain," Temperance muttered as she tied her cloak under her chin.

Nell was undeterred by the reminder. "What if he has designs upon your virtue? What if he seduces and abandons you? Or worse—what if he sells you to a whoremonger? Oh, ma'am! Terrible things could happen to you!"

Temperance suppressed a shiver at the thought of Lord Caire doing "terrible things" to her. It should have been a shiver of revulsion. Instead, the thought of Lord Caire's sexual proclivities made her unnaturally curious. That wicked wanton part of her sat up and twitched its nose, eager as ever to be let loose. *That* she couldn't let happen. Once, long ago, she'd let her base nature take control and had committed an unforgivable sin. Ever since, she'd lived every day knowing she must atone and refrain from letting her demons loose again.

Temperance yanked her hood over her head. "I very much doubt Lord Caire is interested in doing anything at all to me—terrible or not—and besides, I've brought the pistol."

Nell moaned. "He's not like other gentlemen, ma'am."

Temperance hefted the soft bag that concealed the pistol. "You've made these mysterious hints before. Tell me now—in what way is Lord Caire different from other men?"

Nell bit her lip, stood on one foot and then the other, and finally squeezed her eyes shut and said quickly, "His bedsport."

Temperance waited, but no other explanation was forthcoming from the maidservant. Finally she sighed, keeping a firm rein on the part of her that had leapt at the word *bedsport*. "The home is in danger of closing. I can't let what Lord Caire does in his bedchamber keep me from using his assistance."

Nell's eyes popped wide in alarm. "But, ma'am—"

Temperance opened the back door. "Remember: If Winter asks, I've gone to bed early. And if he presses, tell him it's a female matter. That'll stop any questions."

"Be careful, ma'am!" Nell called as Temperance pulled the door closed behind her.

A blast of wind whistled around the corner. Temperance shivered and pulled her cloak tighter, turning to go down the alley. A broad male chest loomed suddenly in front of her.

"Oh!"

"Good evening, Mrs. Dews," Lord Caire drawled in his dark, ominous manner. His cloak swirled about his legs in the wind.

"Please don't do that," Temperance said, rather too sharply.

But he only looked amused. "Do what?"

"Pop out at me like a footpad." She glared up at him, watching as his wide mouth curled at the corner. She had a ridiculous urge to smile back at him, but she suppressed it ruthlessly. Tonight his silver hair was contained in a queue under a black cocked hat. Her belly trembled and she couldn't help but wonder in exactly what way Lord Caire was *different* in the bedroom.

But he'd turned and begun striding down the alley. "I do assure you that I'm no footpad, ma'am." He glanced over his shoulder, and she saw the flash of his blue eyes as she hurried to catch up. "If I had been, you'd be dead by now."

"You're not giving me any encouragement to come with you," Temperance muttered.

He stopped suddenly and she nearly ran into him again. "You're here, are you not?"

Wretched man! "Yes, I am."

He bowed extravagantly, his silver-tipped walking stick in his outstretched hand, his black cloak sweeping the filthy ground. "Then lead on, fair lady."

"Humph." Temperance faced forward and began trotting down the alley, aware that he followed close behind her, a large dark presence.

"Where will you take me tonight?"

Was it her imagination or did she feel his hot breath on the back of her neck?

"It was rather hard to decide, since you refused to tell me much of anything about who it is you're looking for."

She waited for an explanation, but he didn't comment.

Temperance sighed. "You said only that you were searching for someone, which, I must tell you, my lord, was no help at all."

"Yet I sense you still have a destination in mind," Lord Caire murmured.

"I do." They'd come to the end of the alley, and she ducked through a crumbling archway into an even narrower alley.

"And that is?" There was a trace of amusement in Lord Caire's voice.

"Right here," she said with some satisfaction. Really she was rather pleased with herself for coming up with a source for him on such little information.

They stood in front of a building without any windows. Only a swinging wooden sign with a painted candle on it indicated that this was a chandler's shop. Temperance pushed open the door. Inside, the shop was tiny. A counter ran along one side. The goods were displayed here and there, in heaps and piles and hanging on the walls. Candles, tea, tin cups, salt and flour, string, lard, a few knives, a ragged fan, some new brooms, buttons, one little plum tart, and, of course, gin. At the far end of the counter, two women huddled over their cups. Behind the counter stood Mr. Hopper, a small, dark man who might've grown to his exact size so that he might fit inside his shop.

Selling gin without a license was illegal, of course, but licenses were exorbitantly dear and few could afford them. Besides, the magistrates relied on paid informers to bring unlicensed gin sellers to the courts—and no informer would dare set foot in St. Giles. The last had been attacked by a mob, dragged through the streets, savagely beaten, and finally left to die of his injuries, poor man.

"What might I do for you t'night, Mrs. Dews?" Mr. Hopper asked.

"Good evening to you, Mr. Hopper," Temperance

replied. "My friend is looking for someone, and I wonder if you might help him?"

Mr. Hopper squinted at Lord Caire suspiciously, but he said cheerfully enough, "Aye, I might. Who be you lookin' for?"

"A murderer," Lord Caire replied, and every head in the room swiveled toward him.

Temperance caught her breath. A *murderer*?

The gin drinkers silently slipped out of the shop.

"Nearly two months ago, a woman was murdered in her rooms in St. Giles," Lord Caire continued, unperturbed. "Her name was Marie Hume. Do you know anything about her?"

But Mr. Hopper was already shaking his head. "Don't have no truck with murder. An' I'll thank you to take this gentleman out of here, Mrs. Dews."

Temperance bit her lip, glancing at Lord Caire.

He didn't seem particularly put out. "A moment, please," he said to the shopkeeper.

Mr. Hopper reluctantly looked at him.

Lord Caire smiled. "Might I have that tart?"

The shopkeeper grunted and handed him the plum tart, pocketing tuppence in return before pointedly turning his back. Temperance sighed, feeling rather irritable. It was obvious that she'd have to find another informant for Lord Caire.

"You could've warned me," she muttered outside the shop. The wind blew her words back in her face and she shivered, wishing she were by her own cozy fire.

Lord Caire seemed unaffected by the cold. "What difference would it have made?"

"Well, for one, I wouldn't have tried Mr. Hopper."

She stomped across the street, making sure to dodge the sludge in the channel.

He easily caught up with her. "Why not?"

"Because Mr. Hopper is respectable and your inquiries obviously aren't," she said in exasperation. "Why ever did you buy that tart?"

He shrugged. "I'm hungry." He bit into the pastry with relish.

She watched him lick purple syrup from the corner of his mouth and swallowed in reaction. The tart did look awfully good.

"Would you like a bite?" he asked, his voice deep.

She shook her head firmly. "No. I'm not hungry."

He cocked his head, eyeing her as he swallowed another mouthful. "You're lying. Why?"

"Don't be silly," she snapped, and began walking.

He cut in front of her, making her come to an abrupt halt or run the risk of running into him. "It's a plum tart, Mrs. Dews, not riches or drink or any other decadent sin. What can it hurt? Have a bite."

And he broke off a piece, holding it with his fingers to her lips. She could smell the sweet fruit, almost taste the flaky pastry, and before she knew it, she had opened her lips. He fed her the bite, the plum tangy on her tongue, the syrup sugary sweet, exquisitely delicious here in the dark St. Giles street.

"There," he whispered. "Tasty, isn't it?"

Her eyes snapped open—when had she closed them?—and she stared in near horror at him.

His lips quirked. "Where to now, Mrs. Dews? Or was Mr. Hopper and his shop your only source?"

Temperance lifted her chin. "No. I have another idea."

She stepped around him and began walking swiftly, the taste of sweet plums still on her tongue. This part of St. Giles was one of the worst, and she wouldn't have dared to come here during the day, let alone at night, if it weren't for the presence of the large male trailing silently behind her.

Twenty minutes later, Temperance stopped before a crooked door, set two steps down.

Lord Caire looked at the door, his blue eyes narrowed with interest. "What is this place?"

"This is where Mother Heart's-Ease does business," Temperance replied just as the crooked door popped open.

"Out wi' ye!" a tall, gaunt woman bawled. She wore an old red army coat over leather stays so filthy they were black. Beneath was a black-and-red-striped linsey-woolsey petticoat, the hem ragged and caked with mud. Behind her, dim firelight flickered, giving her the appearance of standing at the mouth of hell. "No coin, no drink. Get out of me 'ouse, then!"

The object of her ire was a thin woman who might've been pretty had it not been for her blackened teeth and an open sore on one cheek.

The pitiful creature cringed and held up her arms as if to ward off a blow. "I'll gi' ye a penny an' a ha'penny tomorrow. Just gi' me the gin tonight."

"Go an' earn yer pennies," Mother Heart's-Ease said, and shoved the unhappy woman into the alley. She turned and propped her large, red-knuckled fists on her hips, looking Lord Caire up and down with greedy eyes. "Now, then, what're ye doin' here, Mrs. Dews? I don't reckon this's yer part of St. Giles."

"I wasn't aware St. Giles was divided into territories," Temperance replied stiffly.

Mother Heart's-Ease flicked beady eyes at her. "Weren't you?"

Temperance cleared her throat. "My friend would like to ask you some questions."

Mother Heart's-Ease grinned at Lord Caire, revealing missing front teeth. "Best come inside, 'adn't you, then?"

She didn't glance at Temperance again, her avarice obviously focused on Lord Caire. Nevertheless, he stood back to allow Temperance entrance first. She ducked inside the door and descended the steep wooden steps leading to a cellar.

The front room was low, long, and dark, lit only by a fire roaring in the rear. Above, the rafters were blackened by smoke. To one side, a warped board was thrown over two barrels to make a counter. Behind it stood a one-eyed girl, the only barmaid. Here Mother Heart's-Ease sold her namesake: gin, a penny and a half a cup. A score of soldiers in tall meter hats were laughing drunkenly at a table in the corner. Beside them, two shady-looking fellows hunched their shoulders as if trying to become invisible. One wore a triangular leather patch to hide a missing nose. Across the room, a quarrel had broken out between three sailors playing cards, while nearby, a solitary man in a too-large wig smoked serenely. A man and a woman sat together against the wall on the bare dirt floor, their small tin cup cradled in their hands. They might sleep the night here—if they each paid Mother Heart's-Ease another five pence for the privilege.

"Now, then, 'ow can I 'elp a fine-lookin' gent like yerself?" Mother Heart's-Ease shouted over the din of the arguing sailors. She rubbed her fingers together suggestively.

Lord Caire took a purse from beneath his cloak and opened it. He smiled as he extracted a half crown and placed it in the woman's hand. "I'm interested in the murder of a woman in St. Giles. Her name was Marie Hume."

Mother Heart's-Ease had lost her smile, her lips pursing thoughtfully. "That kind o' information will cost ye just a bit more, m'lord."

Did she know Lord Caire, or was the woman merely flattering a potential money source?

Lord Caire raised his eyebrows at the demand but silently fished another half crown from his purse. He tossed the coin to Mother Heart's-Ease, and it disappeared along with its mate down the top of her stays.

"'Ave a seat, m'lord." Mother Heart's-Ease gestured to an empty chair, a rickety wooden thing. "It's a murdered woman, you say?"

Lord Caire ignored the attempt at hospitality. "She was thirty years or so, blond hair, fair of face and form but with a red birthmark the size of a penny just here." He tapped the outer corner of his right eye. "Do you know her?"

"Well, now, there're quite a lot of pretty wenches about, and a birthmark might be hidden," the woman said. "Anything else particular about her?"

"She was gutted," Lord Caire said.

Temperance inhaled sharply, all of Nell's warnings flooding back. Dear God.

Even Mother Heart's-Ease blinked at the blunt choice of words. "Gutted like a pig," she muttered. "That one I remember. Fancy sort, wasn't she? Found in a bare little room in a house in Tanner's Court, the flies abuzzin' in her black blood."

If Mother Heart's-Ease's words were meant to shock Lord Caire, they failed. His expression remained curious, amused, even, as he cocked his head. "Yes. That's the one."

Mother Heart's-Ease shook her head in mock sorrow. "I can't help you with that, then, m'lord. I didn't know the wench."

Lord Caire held out his hand. "Give me back my coins."

"Hold up there, m'lord," the woman said hastily. "I don't know about the murder, but I know who might."

Lord Caire stilled, his eyes narrowing slightly as if he'd sighted prey. "Who?"

"Martha Swan." Mother Heart's-Ease smiled a twisted, evil smile and crooned, "The last woman to see her alive."

THE WIND TOOK away her breath as Temperance climbed back up Mother Heart's-Ease's outer steps. Lord Caire was behind her, eerily silent. Who was the murdered woman? And why was he asking about her murder? She shuddered, remembering the way he'd described the woman as "gutted." Dear Lord, what had she involved herself in?

"You are unusually quiet, Mrs. Dews," Lord Caire observed in his deep voice.

"How would you know what is usual with me, my lord?" she asked. "You hardly know me."

He breathed a soft chuckle behind her. "And yet I sense that you are a loquacious woman when you are with those you are comfortable with."

She halted and turned, arms crossed to hold in her heat, but also perhaps to reassure herself. "What type of game are you playing with me?"

He'd stopped as well, much too near to her. His queue was coming undone, and strands of his long silver hair blew across his face. "Game, Mrs. Dews?"

"Yes, game." She glared, refusing to be afraid of him. "You tell me that you're searching for someone in St. Giles, but when I take you to Mr. Hopper's shop, you ask about a murdered woman, and now at Mother Heart's-Ease's, you ask about a *gutted* murdered woman."

He shrugged, broad shoulders moving under his cape. "I did not lie to you. I do seek someone—her murderer."

Temperance shivered as the wind blew icy droplets of rain against her frozen cheeks. She wished she could see his eyes, but they were hidden under the brim of his hat. "Who was she to you?"

His wide, sensuous mouth curled up into a half smile. He did not answer.

"Why me?" she muttered low, a question she realized belatedly that she should've asked the night before. "How did you find me? Why did you choose *me*?"

"I've seen you about," he said slowly, "as I've searched in St. Giles. You were always hurrying, always in black, always so very...determined. When I saw you last night, I followed you to your home."

She stared. "That's it? You chose me on a whim?"

"I'm a whimsical man. You are cold, Mrs. Dews. Come."

And he set off again, this time leading the way, his steps assured.

"Where are we going?" she called after him. "Don't you want to find Martha Swan?"

He halted and turned toward her. "Mother Heart's-Ease said she frequented Hangman's Alley. Do you know the direction?"

"Yes, but it's half a mile or more that way." She gestured behind them.

He nodded. "Then we'll save Mistress Swan for another night. It's late and it's time you were home."

He started off again without waiting for her answer.

Temperance trotted after him like an obedient terrier. He'd answered her questions but in a way that made new ones crop up in their place. There were hundreds of women in St. Giles. Granted, many were prostitutes or engaged in other illicit activities. But had he wished, he could've found a dozen or more willing women to lead him about. Why had he chosen her? Temperance frowned and hurried to keep step with him. He might be a stranger with dark secrets, but she still felt safer walking these alleys with him by her side.

"I don't know that we can trust Mother Heart's-Ease," she said, gasping a bit as the cold wind snatched away her words.

"You doubt there is a Martha Swan?"

"Oh, she's probably real enough," Temperance muttered. "But whether she actually has any information is a different matter."

"How is it you know Mother Heart's-Ease?"

"Everyone knows Mother Heart's-Ease. Gin is the demon of St. Giles."

He glanced back at her. "Indeed?"

"Young and old drink it. Some make it their only meal."

Temperance hesitated. "But that is not the only reason I know her."

"Tell me."

She raised a hand to pull her hood more closely about her face. "Nine years ago, when I first came to the home, Mother Heart's-Ease sent us a message. She had a young girl of about three years of age. I don't know where she got the child from, but it was certainly not hers."

"And?"

"She offered to sell the toddler to us." Temperance paused, for her voice had begun to shake—not from fear or sorrow, but from rage. She remembered her hot anger, her contempt at Mother Heart's-Ease's mercenary cynicism.

"What happened?" Lord Caire's voice was soft, but she heard it clearly. It almost vibrated in her bones.

"Winter and Father were against buying the child. They said it would only encourage Mother Heart's-Ease to sell more orphaned children."

"And you?"

Temperance inhaled. "I hated to pay her, but she made it quite plain that she would find another buyer if we did not give her the price. Someone who would not care for the child's welfare at all."

"A whoremonger."

She glanced swiftly at him, but his face was in profile to her, cold and remote. They'd crossed into a larger lane, one in which she could walk beside him. This wasn't the way she'd taken Lord Caire to Mother Heart's-Ease's cellar. Idly she wondered if he was lost.

Then she faced forward again. "Yes, a whoremonger, most probably, though Mother Heart's-Ease never actually said the words. She simply hinted horribly." Temperance's head was down, remembering that ghastly negotiation. She'd still been a little naive then. She'd had no idea how black a woman's soul could be.

She wasn't paying enough attention to the way. Her toe caught on something, and her hands shot out as she stumbled, trying to regain her balance. There was an awful second when her belly dove, and she knew she was going to hit the ground.

And then he caught her, hard hands—painful hands—gripping her elbows but keeping her safe. She looked up and he was there, right in front of her, his blue eyes gleaming like a demon's. He drew her closer, almost into an embrace. Like a friend. Like a lover.

All her worst desires clamored to the surface.

He whispered, his breath brushing her lips, "So you bought the babe."

"Yes." She glared at him, this unfeeling aristocrat. Why did he want to hear this story? Why did he insist on ripping open old wounds? Why was he searching for a dead woman's murderer? "Yes, I paid the price. I sold the only bit of jewelry I had—a gold cross my husband had once given me—and I bought the babe. I named her Mary Whitsun for the Whitsunday on which I first held her."

He cocked his head, his blue, blue eyes asking the question.

She sobbed, fury and sorrow welling up from that place where she carefully controlled all the emotions she couldn't afford to feel. Temperance trembled as she tried to beat her passion down. Trap it and conceal it.

He shook her as if to dislodge the answer he waited for.

"Winter was right," she gasped. "The baby girl was

safe, but two months later, Mother Heart's-Ease came to us again with another baby, a boy this time. And his price was twice what the girl's had been."

"What did you do?"

"Nothing." She closed her eyes in defeat. "The price was too high; we hadn't the money. We—*I*—could do nothing. I begged, I got on my knees and pled with that witch, and she sold him anyway."

She bunched the edges of his cloak in her fists, shaking them as if to impress the awfulness of the memory on him. "She sold that sweet baby boy, and I could do nothing to save him."

One moment she was crying in fury up at him and the next he'd swooped down and caught her mouth. Hard, with no mercy. She gasped at the shock. He ground his mouth against her soft lips. She felt his teeth, tasted his hot tongue, and that part of herself, that wretched, sinful, *wrong,* part broke free and went running. Reveling in his savagery. Rejoicing in his blunt sexuality.

Completely out of her control.

Until he raised his head and looked down at her. His lips were wet and slightly reddened, but otherwise he showed no sign of that devastating kiss.

He might've just relieved himself against a wall for all the emotion he displayed.

Temperance tried to pull from his grasp, but his hands held strong.

"You are such a passionate creature," he murmured, examining her from beneath half-lowered eyelids. "So emotional."

"I am not," she whispered, horrified at the mere notion.

"You lie. I wonder why?" He raised his eyebrows in amusement and let her go so suddenly she stumbled back a step. "She was my mistress."

"What?"

"The murdered woman, the one gutted like a pig at the butcher's. She was my mistress of three years."

She gaped at him, stunned.

He inclined his head. "Until tomorrow evening. Good night, Mrs. Dews."

And he walked away, disappearing into the night shadows.

Temperance turned, her mind whirling, and saw it, not twenty steps away. The door to the foundling home.

Lord Caire had brought her safely home after all.

Chapter Three

*King Lockedheart lived in a magnificent castle
that sat on the top of a hill. In his castle there lived
hundreds of guards, a swarm of courtiers, and a
multitude of servants and courtesans. The king
was surrounded day and night, and yet none were
close to his heart. In fact, the only living thing
that was important to the king was a small blue
bird. The bird lived in a jeweled golden cage, and
sometimes it would sing or chirp. In the evening,
King Lockedheart fed the bird nuts through the bars
of its cage....*
—from *King Lockedheart*

The sun never seemed to shine in St. Giles, Silence Hollingbrook reflected the next morning. She glanced up and
caught sight of only a handspan's width of blue amongst
the overhanging second stories, signs, and roofs. St. Giles
was far too crowded, the houses built one on top of another
and the rooms divided and then subdivided again until
the people lived like rats in warrens. Silence shivered,

glad for her own neat rooms in Wapping. St. Giles was a terrible place to live one's life. She wished her elder brother and sister could find another place for the Home for Unfortunate Infants and Foundling Children. But then St. Giles was where Father had founded the home, and St. Giles was where the poorest of the poor lived in London.

She stopped before the worn stoop and knocked loudly on the thick wooden door. The foundling home had had a bell until last Christmas, when someone had stolen it. Winter had not had a chance to replace it yet, and sometimes she knocked for several minutes before being heard.

But today the door was opened almost at once.

She looked down into scrubbed pink cheeks, black hair scraped back from a wide forehead, and sharp brown eyes. "Good morning to you, Mary Whitsun."

Mary bobbed a curtsy. "Good morning, Mrs. Hollingbrook."

Silence entered the narrow hall and hung up her shawl. "Is my sister about?"

"Ma'am is in the kitchen," Mary said.

Silence smiled. "I'll find her, then."

Mary nodded solemnly and marched up the stairs to whatever work she'd been interrupted at.

Silence hoisted the flat-bottomed basket she'd brought and walked back to the kitchens. "Good morning!" she called as she entered.

Temperance turned from a huge pot boiling over the fire. "Good morning, sister! What a nice surprise. I didn't know you were to call today."

"I wasn't." Silence felt her cheeks heat guiltily. She hadn't been to the home in over a week. "But I bought some dried currants at market this morning and thought I'd bring some over."

"Oh, how thoughtful! Mary Whitsun will like that," Temperance said. "She has a fondness for currant buns."

"Mmm." Silence set the basket on the old kitchen table. "She seems to have grown another inch since I last saw her."

"She has indeed." Temperance wiped at the sweat on her temples with her apron. "And she's quite lovely, though I don't tell her so to her face. I don't want her to become vain."

Silence smiled as she uncovered the basket. "You sound proud."

"Do I?" Temperance asked absently. She'd turned back to the steaming pot.

"Yes." Silence hesitated a moment before continuing apologetically. "She's of age to apprentice out, isn't she?"

"Yes. Almost past the age, in fact." Temperance sighed. "But she's of such use about the home. I haven't begun looking for a position for her yet."

Silence took the items from her basket without comment. Temperance knew better than she that becoming too fond of the foundling children could only lead to hurt.

"You've got more than currants there," Temperance said, coming to the table.

"I brought some stockings I made as well." Silence shyly presented her workmanship—three pairs of tiny stockings. True, none of them were quite the same size as the other, but at least they matched in shape. More or less. "I was making a pair for William and some wool remained."

"Oh, my." Temperance set her hands on her hips and

arched her back, stretching. "I'd quite forgotten that Captain Hollingbrook was to return soon."

Silence felt the ripple of quiet joy spread through her at just the mention of her husband's name. William had been away at sea for months, captaining the *Finch*, a merchant ship returning from the West Indies.

She ducked her head as she replied to her sister. "He's due any day now. I hoped that when he returns, you and Winter would come and sup with us in celebration."

When Temperance didn't respond immediately, Silence looked up. Her sister was frowning down at a pile of turnips on the table.

"What is it?" Silence asked.

"What?" Temperance glanced up quickly, her face smoothing. "Oh, nothing, dear. You know Winter and I would be pleased to dine with you and Captain Hollingbrook. It's just that we're so busy with the home right now...." Her words trailed away as she looked about the big kitchen.

"Perhaps, then, it is time to hire more help. Nell works hard, but she's only one woman."

Temperance laughed, but the sound was hard and short. "If we had a patron to supply the home with money, we would. As it is, we were just able to finally pay this month's rent and last's today. If we're late again, Mr. Wedge may well evict us."

"What?" Silence sank into a kitchen chair. "I have nearly a pound left from my grocery money. Would that help?"

Temperance smiled. "No, dear. That would only help us for a little while, and I don't want to take Captain Hollingbrook's money. I know how you and he scrimp and save."

Silence colored a little. William was a wonderful husband, but a merchant ship's captain didn't make all that much, especially when he had a wife and an elderly mother and spinster sister to keep.

"What about Concord?"

Temperance was shaking her head. "Winter says the brewery has lost money since Father's death. And besides, Concord has his own family to take care of."

Silence shook her head. She'd had no idea Concord was in financial straits, but then the men of the family didn't always like to talk business with their women. Concord and his wife, Rose, had five adorable children and another on the way.

She looked up. "And Asa?"

Temperance grimaced. "You know Asa has always been scornful of the home. I think Winter hates the thought of going to him again with hand outstretched."

Silence pulled the turnip toward herself and picked up a knife to chop off the greens. "Winter is the least prideful man I know."

"Yes, of course, but even the most humble of men have just a touch of pride. Besides, even if Winter did ask Asa, there's no guarantee he would help."

Silence wanted to protest that of course Asa would help if he could, but the truth was that she was uncertain. Asa had always walked apart from their family, secret and alone.

"What shall you do?" Silence began dicing a turnip, her little pieces more odd lumps than squares. She'd never been very good at dicing.

Temperance took up another knife but she hesitated. "As to that, I already have a plan."

"Yes?"

"You must promise not to tell our brothers."

Silence looked up. "What?"

"Or Verity either," Temperance said. Verity was the eldest of the Makepeace family.

Silence stared. What secret would Temperance want to keep not only from their brothers, but also their sister?

But Temperance's expression was almost fierce. If Silence wanted to know, she'd have to promise. "Very well."

Temperance set down the knife and leaned close to whisper, "I've met someone who will introduce me to the influential and wealthy people of London. I'm going to find a new patron for the home."

"Who?" Silence knit her brows.

Their family was a humble one. Father had been a beer brewer, and on their father's death, Concord had taken over the family business. Father had believed deeply in learning and had seen to it that all her brothers were very well educated in religion, philosophy, and Greek and Latin. She supposed in that way they might be called intellectuals, but that didn't take away from the fact that they worked for their living. The kind of people Temperance was talking about were well out of their league.

"Who is this powerful friend?" Silence saw the moment when something shifted behind her sister's eyes. Temperance was a wonderful person, which was perhaps why she was also a terrible liar. "Temperance, tell me."

Her sister tilted her chin. "His name is Lord Caire."

Silence's brows furrowed. "An aristocrat? How in the world did you find an aristocrat to help you?"

"Actually, he found me." Temperance pursed her lips,

her eyes firmly fixed on the growing mound of chopped turnip roots. "Do you think anyone really likes turnips?"

"Temperance..."

Temperance poked the tip of her knife into a white cube and held it up. "They are very filling, of course, but really, when was the last time you heard someone say, 'Oh, I'm so very fond of turnips'?"

Silence set down her knife and waited.

The lid of the pot over the fire rattled, and Temperance's knife thunked against the table for perhaps a half minute before she broke.

"He followed me home the night before last."

"What?" Silence gasped.

But her sister was speaking rapidly. "That sounds worse than it is. He was quite harmless, I assure you. He merely asked me for my help in speaking to some people in St. Giles. In return, I requested that he introduce me to the people he knew who were wealthy. It's a very practical arrangement, truly."

Silence eyed her sister skeptically. The picture Temperance drew was altogether too rosy. "And I suppose this Lord Caire is an ancient gentleman, white-haired and bony-kneed?"

Temperance winced. "His hair *is* white, actually."

"And his knees?"

"I hope you don't think I stare at a gentleman's knees."

"*Temp*erance..."

"Oh, very well, he's a young and rather handsome man," Temperance said not very graciously. Her cheeks had pinkened.

"Dear Lord." Silence stared with concern at her sister. Temperance was a widow of eight and twenty, but sometimes she behaved with all the circumspection of a silly girl. "Think. Why would Lord Caire pick you in particular to lead him about St. Giles?"

"I don't know, but—"

"You must tell Winter. This thing sounds like a made-up story to entice you. Lord Caire might have dreadful plans for you. What if he lures you into debauchery?"

Temperance wrinkled her nose, drawing attention to a speck of soot at the tip. "I hardly think that's likely. Have you looked at me recently?"

She spread her arms wide as if to emphasize the ridiculousness of an aristocrat wanting to seduce her. Silence had to admit that standing in her kitchen, her hair half down, and with soot on her nose, Temperance certainly didn't look like someone particularly tempting to a seducer.

But she replied loyally. "You're quite pretty and well you know it."

"I know nothing of the sort." Temperance let her arms drop. "You've always been the beauty of the family. If a dastardly lord were to corrupt anyone, it would be you."

Silence looked sternly at her sister. "You're trying to distract me."

Temperance sighed and sank into a kitchen chair. "Don't tell anyone, Silence, please don't. I've already accepted Lord Caire's money to pay the rent—that is how we paid off our debt."

"But Winter is sure to find out eventually. How did you explain paying the rent to him?"

"I told him that I sold a ring that Benjamin had given me."

"Oh, Temperance!" Silence covered her mouth in horror. "You lied to Winter?"

But Temperance shook her head. "It was only a small lie. This is the only hope we have for the home. Think what it would do to Winter should the home close."

Silence glanced away. Of all their brothers, Winter had been the most devoted to their father and his charitable works. It would disappoint him terribly to have the home fail under his watch.

"Please, Silence," Temperance whispered. "For Winter."

"Very well." Silence nodded once. "I won't tell our brothers—"

"Oh, thank you!"

"Unless," Silence continued, "I feel you are in danger."

"I won't be. That I can promise."

LAZARUS WOKE ON a silent scream. His eyes opened wide, and for a moment he simply lay there and looked about the room, straining to remember where he was. Then he recognized his own bedroom. The walls were a dark brown, the furniture old and impressive, and his bed hung with dark green and brown curtains. His father had slept here before him, and Lazarus hadn't bothered changing anything when he'd inherited the title. He felt each muscle in his body slowly relax as he glanced at the window. The light there was a pale gray; dawn couldn't be too far away—and he never went back to sleep after a nightmare. He stretched and rose, nude, then padded to the tall dresser to splash cold water on his face. He donned a yellow brocaded banyan and sat at the elegant cherrywood desk in the corner—the only piece of furniture in the room that he'd brought with him. His father would've disapproved heartily of writing in dishabille.

Lazarus grinned at the thought. Then he uncapped his inkwell and began work on his current translation project. Catullus was particularly scathing of Lesbia in this poem. He wanted to find the right word—the *perfect* word— that, when correctly set, would shine like a diamond in an exquisite ring. It was exacting, meticulous work, and it could consume him for hours at a time.

His valet, Small, entered sometime later, and Lazarus looked up to see that the room was bright with sunshine.

"Your pardon, my lord," Small said. "I didn't realize you were awake."

"It's of no consequence," Lazarus replied, his gaze back on his translation. The words were calling him, but he hadn't quite found the right arrangement yet.

"I'll ring to have your breakfast sent up, shall I?"

"Mmm."

"And if you're ready for your toilet?"

Bah! The thing was lost now. Lazarus threw down his pen impatiently and leaned back in his chair. Small immediately laid a steaming cloth over the lower half of his face. The valet's movements were quick and efficient, his hands delicate like a woman's.

Lazarus closed his eyes, relaxing as the moist heat soaked into his skin. He remembered Mrs. Dews's light brown eyes last night. The way they'd closed in bliss when he'd fed her the plum tart. The way they'd narrowed in anger when he questioned why she wouldn't take it from him initially. For one such as he—a man who could not feel emotion—her moods were irresistibly alluring. The flare of her temper had created a heat he could almost feel. He'd been drawn to it as surely as a cat was to the warmth of a hearth. Her emotion was foreign, wild and exciting, and entirely fascinating—and she tried so very hard to hide it. Why? He wanted to spend time with the source of such powerful emotion. Wanted to experiment, poke and prod, see what else made her cheeks flush, her breath come fast. What would make her laugh? What frightened her? How would her eyes look at the point of orgasm? Would she try to hold back, or would the bodily sensation overwhelm her defenses?

The thought was oddly arousing this early in the morning. He'd never cared one way or the other about a woman's response. She was but the vessel for his own lust. But with Mrs. Dews, it was the woman herself who was the interesting part.

Small removed the cloth and brushed warm lather over Lazarus's jaw. Lazarus kept his eyes closed, refusing to flinch at the first scrape of the razor against his bare cheek. Surreptitiously he gripped the arms of the chair. To let another touch him was a ghastly physical trial, which was part of the reason he permitted this ordinary intimacy each morning. It gave him a kind of satisfaction to confront this most basic fear and overcome it daily.

The valet finished his left cheek, and Lazarus tilted his head to receive the razor on the right, repressing a shudder of revulsion. He'd had this loathing of another's touch for as long as he could recall. No. That wasn't correct. Lazarus couldn't repress a wince as Small ran the razor over his upper lip. Once upon a time, when he'd been a very small child, there had been a touch that did not cause him fear and loathing and outright pain.

But that was long ago and that person long dead.

Small wiped the last of the soap foam from Lazarus's face, and Lazarus opened his eyes. "Thank you."

If the valet had any idea of the pain he'd caused his master, the knowledge did not show in his placid expression. "What shall you wear today, my lord?"

"The black silk breeches and coat with the silver worked waistcoat."

Lazarus stood and dropped the banyan to the chair. Small handed him the clothing and he dressed himself—there was a fine point between endurance and self-torture.

"My stick as well," Lazarus said as he allowed the valet to club back his hair with a black velvet ribbon.

"Of course, my lord." Small looked doubtfully at the window. "You have an appointment so early?"

"I'm to visit my mother." Lazarus smiled without humor. "And that is a task best done as early as possible."

He took the stick that Small proffered and strode from the room without waiting for the valet's reply.

The master bedroom led out into a wide upper hall paneled in dark, intricately carved wood. This town house had been in the Caire family since his grandfather's time. It wasn't in the most fashionable part of London anymore, but it was big and grand and fairly reeked of old money and power. Lazarus descended the stairs, trailing his hand down the pink banister. The stone was imported from Italy, carved and polished until it shone nearly like a mirror. He should feel something touching the cold, smooth stone, he knew. Pride perhaps? Or nostalgia? But instead he felt as he always did.

Nothing at all.

He reached the lower hall and took his cape and tricorne from the butler. Outside it was windy, the chairmen shivering a bit as they waited for him. His sedan chair was new, especially built for his height, the outside enameled in black and silver, the inside fitted with plush crimson cushions. One of the men held the top open as Lazarus stepped between the rails to enter. The front door was shut and latched and the top lowered. The men hefted the chair, and then they were jogging through the London streets.

Lazarus wondered idly what had caused his mother to summon him. Would she ask for more money? That seemed unlikely since she had a generous allowance from him as well as a few estates of her own. Perhaps she'd taken up gambling in her waning years. He snorted aloud at the thought.

The chairmen halted and Lazarus descended. The town house he'd bought for his mother was small but fashionable. She'd complained—still complained—when he'd forced her to move out of Caire House, but he'd be damned if he'd live with the woman.

Inside, the butler escorted Lazarus to an outrageously gilded sitting room. There he sat for a good half hour, contemplating the golden curlicues on the top of the Corinthian columns guarding the door. He would've left but then he'd merely have to repeat this farce another day. Best to get it over with.

She entered the room as she always did—pausing just a fraction of a second inside the doorway to let the full impact of her beauty fill those within with awe.

Lazarus yawned.

She tittered, the sound not quite hiding the anger beneath. "Have you lost all sense of propriety, my son? Or is it fashionable now to no longer rise on a lady's entrance?"

He rose with just enough languor to make the movement an insult, and then bowed as briefly as possible. "What do you want, my lady?"

Which was a mistake, of course. Showing his impatience only gave her reason to draw this meeting out.

"Oh, Lazarus, must you be so rude?" She lowered herself to carefully lounge on one of the delicately painted settees. "It becomes tiresome. I've ordered tea and cakes and such"—she waved a hand vaguely—"so you must stay for that at least."

"Must I?" he asked softly, the edge in his voice making the two words grit.

A fleeting look of uncertainty crossed her beautiful face, but then she said firmly, "Oh, I think so."

Lazarus sat back down, conceding for the moment to his lovely, vapid mother. He watched her as they waited for the promised tea. He hated tea, always had. Did she not know or—more likely—did she serve it to him merely to provoke?

Lady Caire had been a famous beauty in her youth, and time had been gracious to her. Her face was a perfect, serene oval, her neck long and graceful. Her eyes were like his, a clear blue, faintly tilted at the corners. The forehead above was white and unmarred. Her hair was the same startlingly premature white as his own, but instead of trying to dye it or wearing a wig, she flaunted the unusual color. She favored dark blue gowns to highlight the white and wore black or dark blue caps, decorated with lace and jewels.

She had always known how best to draw the eye.

"Ah, here's the tea," his mother said as two maids entered bearing trays. Was there relief in her voice?

The servants set the repast silently and then quietly left. Lady Caire straightened to pour. Her hand hesitated over the teacup. "Sugar?"

"No, thank you."

"Of course." Her aplomb was restored. She handed him the cup. "I remember now—neither sugar nor cream."

He raised his brows and set aside the teacup untasted. What game was she playing?

She seemed not to notice his lack of enthusiasm for the tea, resuming her languid pose with her own cup. "I hear you've been seen with the elder Miss Turner. Have you interest in that direction?"

He blinked for a moment, truly surprised, and then burst out laughing. "Have you decided to matchmake for me now, ma'am?"

A line of irritation appeared between her brows. "Lazarus—"

But he interrupted her, his words quick and light, belying the edge they held. "Perhaps you'll vet and approve a select group of fillies, line them up for my inspection. Of course, it might be difficult, what with the rumors of my . . . proclivities flying about London society. All but the most mercenary families make sure to keep their virgins away from me."

"Don't be crude." She set down her teacup with a moue of distaste.

"First rude, then crude," he drawled. His patience had worn out. "Really, madam, it is a wonder you can stand my company at all."

She frowned at that. "I—"

"Are you in need of funds?"

"No, I—"

"Have you any other pressing matter to discuss with me, then?"

"Lazarus—"

"No worry over business?" he interrupted. "Your lands or servants?"

She simply stared at him.

"Then I fear I must go, Lady Caire." He rose and bowed without meeting her eyes. "I bid you good morning."

He was already at the door when she said, "You don't know. You don't know what it was like."

His back was to her, and he didn't turn to acknowledge her before closing the door behind him.

MARY HOPE WAS not improving.

Temperance watched anxiously as the wet nurse, Polly, tried once again to get the infant to latch on to her nipple. The baby's tiny, lax mouth opened about the tip of the nipple, but she lay unresponsive, her eyes closed.

Polly tched and looked up, her face sad. "She's not suckin', ma'am. I can 'ardly feel her on me."

Temperance straightened, wincing at a crick in her back. She'd been hovering over Polly and the baby for what seemed like hours now. Polly sat in an old armchair with the infant. The chair was the nicest piece of furniture in her little rented room—Temperance had given it to Polly when she'd hired her as one of the foundling home's wet nurses. The wet nurses didn't live in the home. Instead they took their tiny charges to their own homes, whatever that may be.

Since Temperance didn't directly oversee the wet nurses, it was imperative to find women she could trust, and Polly was the best. Not much over twenty, the wet nurse was dark-eyed, dark-haired, and rather pretty. But Polly had the pragmatic air of a woman twice her age. Her husband was a sailor, coming home only often enough to sire two children with his wife. In between his infrequent appearances, Polly fended for herself and her little family.

Besides the chair, Polly's room held a table, a curtained bed, and a cheap print on the wall depicting gaily dressed ladies. Over the mantel of the fireplace, a round polished mirror hung to reflect what little light there was back into the room. Polly had set her few possessions on the mantel: a candlestick, a pot for salt and one for vinegar, a teapot, and a tin cup. In a corner of the wretched room, Polly's babies played, a toddler and a child who had just learned to crawl.

Temperance returned her gaze to Mary Hope. Polly's small room might be poor, but it was spotlessly clean, and Polly herself was neat and sober. Unlike many of the women who made their living wet-nursing, she didn't drink, and she actually seemed to care for her tiny charges while they were with her.

That made her worth her weight in gold.

"Can you try again?" Temperance asked anxiously.

"Aye, I'll put 'er to the pap, but whether she'll suck or not…" Polly trailed off as she positioned the babe again. She'd partially unlaced her leather stays and pulled aside her woolen chemise, uncovering one breast.

"What if we drip milk into her mouth?"

Polly sighed. "I've made some milk flow into the wee one's mouth, but she swallows naught but a drop or two."

She demonstrated, and Temperance watched as the fresh milk dribbled out the side of the baby's mouth. If she swallowed any, it was hard to tell.

The smallest of Polly's babies had crawled over and now pulled herself up to stand against the chair, crying.

"Can you take her a mo' while I see to my own?"

Temperance swallowed, reluctant somehow to take the fragile infant, but Polly was already putting Mary Hope in her arms. Temperance held her stiffly. The baby seemed as light as a bird. She watched as Polly pulled her baby into her lap. Her child immediately went to the nipple, sucking contentedly with great gulps as she idly held one stockinged toe with her chubby fingers. Temperance looked from the obviously well-fed child to the sallow cheeks of Mary Hope. The baby had opened her eyes, but she stared over Temperance's shoulder vaguely, the wrinkles around her eyes in marked contrast to Polly's plump, healthy baby.

Temperance quickly averted her gaze, her chest clogging with some emotion she refused to identify. She would not feel for this dying baby, she would not. She'd been burned once in the past by giving her love too freely, and now she held it safely locked away in her breast.

"There, ducks, aren't you happy now?" Polly crooned to the child in her arms. She looked up at Temperance. "Let me try again with that one."

"Very well, but don't neglect your own," Temperance said, handing Mary Hope over with relief. She'd heard of wet nurses who'd starved their own children to feed a paying baby.

"Never fear," Polly said stoutly. "I've enough for all."

She suited action to word by taking down her chemise from her other breast, placing Mary Hope there while allowing her own baby to continue suckling from the first breast.

Temperance nodded. "Thank you, Polly. I'll leave a little extra this week. Make sure you spend it on food for yourself, please."

"Aye, I will," Polly replied, her head already bent to the ailing baby.

Temperance hesitated a moment, but in the end, she simply bid Polly good night and left. What more could she do? She made her way through the crowded rooms of the house in which Polly rented her room. She'd hired the best wet nurse available and had even paid the woman extra out of the home's meager funds.

The rest was in the hands of God.

Outside, the light was beginning to dim as the day fled St. Giles. Temperance shivered. A woman passed her, balancing a wide flat basket on her head that held a few leftover clams and a pewter cup for measuring. Winter had sent word that he would work late at the school tonight, but she still had to cook her own supper and settle the children before meeting Lord Caire.

A big shadow moved in a doorway as she passed, and for a moment her heart stuttered.

Then Lord Caire's deep voice reached her. "Good evening, Mrs. Dews."

She stopped, her arms akimbo in exasperation. "Whatever are you doing here?"

She could see his dark eyebrows rise beneath the brim of his tricorne. "Waiting for you."

"You followed me!"

He inclined his head, unperturbed at her accusatory tone. "Indeed, Mrs. Dews."

She huffed in exasperation and started forward again. "You must be very bored to play such a childish trick."

He breathed a chuckle behind her, so close she thought she felt his cloak brush against her skirts. "You have no idea."

She remembered suddenly that kiss he'd pressed on her—hard and hot and not at all gentle. How it had made her heart speed, her skin dampen with sweat. He was a danger to her and all the emotions she held in such tenuous check. Her voice was sharp when she replied. "I'm not a diversion for a bored aristocrat."

"Did I say you were?" he asked mildly. "Who did you go to see in that house?"

"Polly."

He was so silent behind her that he might've been a ghost.

Temperance inhaled. Any other gentleman—especially an *aristocratic* gentleman—would've given up on her at her tart words and turned and left her in outraged male anger. Whatever the game Lord Caire played, he was patient.

And besides, the home still needed a patron.

"Polly is our wet nurse," Temperance said more calmly. "You'll remember the night we met, I brought a new baby to the home. I've placed the baby, a frail child, with Polly to nurse. Her name is Mary Hope."

"You seem…" He trailed off as if analyzing the tone of her voice. "Unhappy."

"Mary Hope will not suck," Temperance said. "And when Polly dribbles milk into her mouth, she hardly swallows."

"Then the child will die," he said, his voice remote.

She stopped and whirled on him. "Yes! Yes, Mary Hope will die if she cannot take sustenance. Why are you so uncaring?"

"Why are you so caring?" He'd stopped with her, too close as usual, and the wind blew his cloak forward, wrapping around her skirts like a living thing. "Why feel so much for a child you hardly know? A child you must've known was ailing, perhaps already dying, when you brought her to your home?"

"Because it is my work," she said fiercely. "It's the reason I get up in the morning, the reason I eat, the reason I sleep—to provide for these children. To keep the home running."

"That's all? You do not love the child herself?"

"No, of course not." She turned and continued walking. "I...I care for each of the children, of course I do, but to let oneself love a dying child would be the height of foolishness. Don't think I don't know that, my lord."

"So selfless," he said, his voice deep and mocking. "Such a martyr to those poor, wretched infants. Why, Mrs. Dews, you might as well be a saint. All you need is the halo and the bloody palms."

A hot retort was on the tip of her tongue, but Temperance pressed her lips together, swallowing the words.

"And yet," Lord Caire mused somewhere close behind her, "I wonder if it is possible to stop yourself from loving a child. For some it might be easy, but for you, Mrs. Dews, I very much doubt it."

She quickened her steps in irritation. "You consider yourself an authority on emotion, my lord?"

"Not at all," he murmured. "I rarely feel anything. But like the legless man, I'm unaccountably fascinated by those who can dance."

She turned the corner, thinking. They were walking away from the home now. "You don't feel anything?"

"Nothing."

She paused to look up at him curiously. "Then why spend so much time searching for the murderer of your mistress?"

His mouth curved cynically. "I wouldn't read too much into that. A whim, merely."

"Now who lies?" she whispered.

He looked away as if in irritation. "I notice we're not going toward your home."

She was oddly disappointed at his deflection of the subject. If he truly felt no emotion, then why spend months looking for a murderer on a "whim"? Did Lord Caire feel more than he would admit? Or was he really the cold, uncaring aristocrat he painted himself?

But he was silent, obviously waiting for her reply. Temperance sighed. "I'm taking you to Hangman's Alley, where Martha Swan supposedly lives."

"Won't your brother worry for you if you don't return home?"

"If we can go and come back in the next hour, I'll say that I was checking on the other wet nurses," Temperance muttered, setting off again.

"Tsk, Mrs. Dews, lying to your own brother?"

This time she simply ignored him. Night had fallen fully now, the streets emptying as the hunters came out, and she was glad she'd brought the pistol, tucked into a bag hanging beneath her skirts. Half an hour later, they turned into Hangman's Alley, a gathering place for footpads, thieves, and pickpockets. She wondered if Lord Caire knew just how dangerous this area was. When she looked at him sideways, she noticed that he walked with a predator's grace, his ebony stick held in one fist like a club.

He caught her glance. "What a lovely neighborhood."

"Humph." But despite her dismissive tone, Temperance was relieved that he looked so formidable. "There 'tis."

She pointed to a worn sign depicting a shoe. Mother Heart's-Ease had said that Martha Swan lived over a cobbler's shop. The building was dark, the alley before it deserted. Temperance pulled her cloak closer about herself, feeling surreptitiously for the pistol under her skirts. They should have stopped for a lantern.

Lord Caire stepped forward and knocked against the door with his stick. It echoed hollowly, but no movement came from within.

"If she's a pickpocket or a prostitute, she may be out," Temperance said.

"No doubt," Lord Caire replied, "but having come so far, I suggest we at least look."

She frowned, about to protest, but over his shoulder, she saw a movement in the shadows. Her breath caught on a scream as three figures scuttled from an alley, moving fast.

Moving with obvious deadly intent.

She would've called a warning to Lord Caire, but there was no need. His eyes sharpened on her face. "Run!"

And then he was whirling, putting her behind him near the building as he faced the attackers. They spread as they came at him, the outer two men going to either side of Lord Caire, the center man raising a knife. Lord Caire hit the center man's wrist with his stick, deflecting the first blow. He withdrew a short sword from his stick, and then they were on him in a flurry of rapid blows and kicks, three against one.

It was only a matter of time until Lord Caire went down, even armed.

She had her pistol. Temperance hauled up her skirts, fumbling for the sack. She withdrew the pistol, letting her skirts drop.

She looked up in time to see Lord Caire grunt and half turn as if he'd been hit. One of the men staggered away, but the remaining closed in. She brought the pistol up, but the combatants were too close together. If she fired, she might hit Lord Caire.

And if she didn't, the assailants might kill him.

As she watched, one of the men feinted with a dagger on one side of Lord Caire while another raised a knife on his other side. She couldn't wait any longer. They were going to kill him.

Temperance fired.

Chapter Four

Once a year, it was King Lockedheart's custom to give a speech to his people. But because he was a man more used to wielding a sword than a pen, the king made a habit of practicing his speech. Thus one morning, King Lockedheart paced the balcony of his magnificent palace, declaiming his speech to the open air and the caged blue bird.

"My people," the king declared, "I am proud to be your leader, and I know that you are proud to live under my rule. Indeed, I know that I am beloved of you, my people."

But, sadly, here King Lockedheart was interrupted—by a giggle....

—from King Lockedheart

The pistol shot came from behind him. A wild fury filled Lazarus's chest at the sound. They couldn't, they hadn't the *right* to hurt the little martyr. She was *his* plaything.

He lunged in vicious anger at the attacker to his right, driving his sword deep into the other's gut. He saw the man's eyes widen in shocked surprise, and at the same time Lazarus sensed the rush from his left. He whirled, leaving his sword behind, and slammed the other half of his stick against his attacker's wrist. The man howled, cradling his injured wrist as the knife spun out of his hand. Unarmed, the attacker realized his vulnerability. He swore and skipped back, darting down an alley. He was gone as suddenly as he'd appeared. Lazarus turned to the third man, but he had disappeared as well. Suddenly the night was quiet.

Only then did he look behind him at his little martyr. *His* Mrs. Dews.

She stood still and prim, a pistol in one hand by her side.

Not hurt, then. Not killed. *Thank God.*

"Why the hell didn't you run?" he asked very softly.

She tilted her chin, damn her, in obstinate martyrish dignity. She was quite composed, not a hair out of place—and her mouth was red and inviting. "I couldn't leave you."

"Yes," he said as he advanced on her, "you could have and you *should* have. I *ordered* you to run."

She seemed completely unmoved by his ire, looking down as she shoved her enormous pistol into a pathetic sack. "Perhaps I don't take orders from you, my lord."

"Don't take orders," he sputtered like an overwrought old woman. One part of his brain was amused at what an ass he was being, while another part found it very, very important that she know that she had to obey him. "Let me tell you—"

He moved to take her arm, but she jerked it away. Pain flamed up his shoulder. "God's blood!"

Her brows knit. "What is it?"

Where his concern had driven her away, his weakness pulled her closer. Contrary creature. "Nothing."

"Then why did you cry out in pain?"

He looked up impatiently from peering under his cloak. "Because, Mrs. Dews, I seem to have received a knife wound." He could feel hot blood soaking his coat now.

She gasped, visibly paling. "Oh, dear Lord. That's not *nothing*! Why didn't you say so? Perhaps you should sit and—"

"Who's there?"

They both turned to see a crooked little woman peering from the door to the cobbler's shop. She squinted and cocked her head. "I heard a pistol shot."

Lazarus stepped toward her, but at his movement, she made as if to withdraw inside. Not damned likely. Lazarus reached around her and shut the door swiftly, cutting off her escape. "We came to see Martha Swan."

The woman shrank back at the name. "Who are you?" she cried, peering from one side to the other. She was obviously blind or near blind. "I'll have no truck with—"

Mrs. Dews took one of her hands. "We mean you no harm. We were told Martha Swan lives here."

Mrs. Dews's touch seemed to calm her, but the woman's thin chest still heaved as if she'd take flight if she could. "Martha lived here, aye."

Mrs. Dews looked disappointed. "Then she's gone?"

"Dead." The woman cocked her head again. "She was found dead just this morn."

"How?" Lazarus narrowed his eyes. His arm was soaked now with blood, but he needed this information.

"They say she was slit open," the woman whispered. "Slit from top to bottom, her innards all strewn about."

"Dear God," Mrs. Dews gasped. Her grasp on the woman's hand must have loosened. The little woman turned and opened the door, darting into the house.

"Wait!" Mrs. Dews cried.

"Leave her," Lazarus said. "She's told us what we needed anyway."

Mrs. Dews opened her mouth as if to argue, but then closed it into a flat line. He waited a moment to see if her ire would win out over her control, but she simply stared at him.

"Someday you'll break," he murmured. "And I pray to God I'm there when it happens."

"I haven't any idea what you're talking about."

"Yes, you do." He turned and placed his boot deliberately on the chest of the man he'd stabbed. With a grunt of pain, Lazarus withdrew his short sword from the body. The man lay facing upward, the light from a nearby window reflecting off his open, sightless eyes. He wore a leather patch over the place his nose should've been. Had he thought that the day might end with him lying dead in the filth of a street gutter? Doubtful.

But then only a fool mourned the death of his own assassin.

Lazarus bent to wipe the blade on the man's coat before sheathing it in the other half of his black walking stick. He glanced at Mrs. Dews. She stood watching his movements with concern in her wide eyes. "Best we get you back to the relative safety of your home, madam."

She nodded, falling into step beside him. Lazarus walked rapidly, his stick held firmly in his right hand. He had no desire to look like an easy mark to their attackers should they return—or to any other predators who might be prowling the streets of St. Giles. The night was black as pitch, clouds hiding the moon. He made his way by instinct and the inconsistent light of the buildings they passed. Mrs. Dews was a slim shadow by his side, her pace not slowing him. He had a reluctant admiration for her. She might've refused his command earlier, but she hadn't flinched at either the fight or the news that he was wounded. In fact, she'd had the forethought to bring along a weapon, even if it had been useless.

"You need to practice if you're to carry a gun to protect yourself," he said. He felt her stiffen beside him.

"I think I was quite capable when I fired."

"You missed."

Her face swiveled toward him, and even in the dark, he could sense her outrage. "I fired into the air!"

"What?" he halted, catching her arm.

She tried to jerk away again and then seemed to remember his wound. Her mouth thinned with irritation. "I fired into the air because I feared hitting you should I aim at your assailants."

"Fool," he hissed, his heart speeding again with fear. Silly little martyr.

"What?"

"Next time—if there is a next time—aim at the attackers and damn the cost."

"But—"

He shook her arm. "Do you have any idea what they would've done to you had I failed in driving them off?"

Her head cocked in disbelief. "You'd rather I shoot and possibly hit and *kill* you?"

"Yes." He let her go and continued down the alley. His shoulder was throbbing with pain now, and his shirt was growing cold from the wet blood.

She skipped to remain by his side. "I don't understand you."

"Not many do."

"My life can't possibly be worth more than yours."

"What makes you think my life is worth anything at all?" he inquired politely.

That seemed to silence her, at least for the moment. They tramped through an alley and to a wider street.

"It's very strange," Mrs. Dews muttered.

"What is?" Lazarus was careful to keep his head up, his eyes alert.

"That Martha Swan should be killed in the exact way your mistress was."

"It's not strange at all if the killer is the same person." He felt more than saw her quick glance.

"Do you think it was the same murderer?"

He shrugged, and then had to bite back a gasp as his shoulder shrieked with pain. "I don't know, but it would be very odd if there were more than one murderer in St. Giles with that particular method of killing women."

She seemed to think for several minutes and then said slowly, "My maidservant, Nell Jones, says that the Ghost of St. Giles disembowels his victims."

Lazarus laughed despite the growing ache in his shoulder. "Have you seen this ghost, Mrs. Dews?"

"No, but—"

"Then I think this ghost is merely a tale told to frighten little children on dark nights. The man I look for is of flesh and blood."

They walked in silence for what seemed like a very long time before the back door to the foundling home came within sight.

Lazarus grunted, relieved and light-headed at the same time. "There you are. Make sure you bar the door behind you when you're inside."

"Oh, no, you don't." She caught his good arm.

For a moment he froze. His sleeve shielded his flesh from her hand, but no one touched him without his permission. He usually reacted with sarcasm, with violence and rejection. With her he didn't know what to do.

While he stood there, stunned, Mrs. Dews had set down her sack, brought a key out from somewhere under her cloak, and unlocked the back door to the home. "We have to see to your wound."

"There's no need," he began drily.

"Now," she said, and somehow he found himself inside the old kitchen. He'd stolen through it the other night when he entered her little sitting room. Then it had been empty and dark save for the embers of the fireplace. Now it was lit with a roaring fire and occupied by a swarm of urchins of all sizes.

And one man.

"Oh, ma'am, you're home!" the eldest girl exclaimed.

At the same time, the man rose from the kitchen table, looking quizzical. "Temperance?"

"Winter, you've returned early," she said distractedly. "Yes, I'm home again, Mary Whitsun, all safe and sound, but I'm afraid I can't say the same for his lordship. Can you please fill a bowl with hot water from the hearth? Joseph Tinbox, bring me the rag bag. Mary Evening, can you please clear a space at the table? And *you* sit here."

The last command was directed at Lazarus. He chose the better part of valor and sank meekly into the indicated chair. Mrs. Dews's brother eyed him sharply, and Lazarus attempted to look weak, wounded, and helpless, though he had a feeling it didn't quite convince the man.

The kitchen was hot, the low, plastered ceiling reflecting the heat of the blazing fire. He saw now that the children must've been in the midst of making some type of meal. There was a huge kettle over the fire, tended by one of the older girls, and there was some type of dough on the table. All the children were busy except for one small boy who stood on one foot, staring at him with a limp black cat over his arm.

Lazarus arched an eyebrow at the urchin, and he scuttled to hide behind Mrs. Dews's skirts, cat and all.

"Who is this gentleman, Temperance?" Winter Makepeace asked mildly.

"Lord Caire," Mrs. Dews said as she helped the child named Mary Evening remove a bowl with flour from the table. The urchin mirrored her moves, always mostly hidden in her skirts. "He's wounded."

"Indeed?" Makepeace asked, only a little more sharply. "And how did that happen?"

She hesitated for a fraction of a second—so briefly that perhaps only Lazarus saw it—and darted a glance at him.

He smiled, baring his teeth. He had no urge to help her out of her obvious dilemma when her explanation might be so much more interesting.

Mrs. Dews pursed her lips. "Lord Caire was attacked but a quarter of a mile from here."

"Yes?" Makepeace tilted his head in a familiar gesture, waiting for the rest of his sister's explanation.

"And I brought him home so we could tend to him." She smiled swiftly and blindingly at her brother.

But the man was more used to her charming wiles than Lazarus. He merely raised his eyebrows. "You simply happened upon Lord Caire?"

"Well, no . . ."

Mrs. Dews must indeed be a favorite of God. The small boy she'd sent for the "rag bag" returned at that moment, saving the need for an explanation.

"Oh, good, Joseph Tinbox. Thank you." She took the bag and placed it on the table next to the steaming bowl of water the girl called Mary Whitsun had provided. Then she turned stern eyes on him. "Take it off."

He raised his eyebrows, mimicking her brother. "I beg your pardon?"

Oh, there were gods who would punish him for his delight. Her cheeks darkened to a pretty rose.

"Take off your, er, upper garments, my lord," she said through gritted teeth.

He hid a grin as he took off his hat and bent to unfasten his cloak. He threw the cloak off and had to bite back an oath at the stab of pain the movement gave his shoulder.

"Let me help." She was suddenly by his side, helping him ease out of his coat and waistcoat. Her proximity was distracting, and oddly sweet. He found himself leaning toward her as they both worked, drawn perhaps by the tender curve of her neck, the faint scent of lavender and woman.

He raised his arms grudgingly, letting her pull his shirt over his head, and then he was nude to the waist. When he looked up, a ring of curious small children surrounded him. Even the urchin had emerged from her skirts.

The boy held the cat by its upper body, its lower limbs

stretched and hanging. It looked dead, except for the fact that it was purring. "His name is Soot."

"How fascinating," Lazarus replied. He hated cats.

"Mary Whitsun," said Makepeace, "kindly take the younger children into the dining room. You may hear them recite their Psalms."

"Yes, sir," the child said, and herded her brethren from the room.

Mrs. Dews cleared her throat. "Perhaps you should oversee them, Winter. I can manage here by myself."

The man smiled far too benevolently. "Mary Whitsun will do well enough on her own, I believe, sister."

Makepeace resumed his seat across the table from her, but as she turned her back to rummage in a cupboard, he shot a look at Lazarus—one that Lazarus had no difficulty in reading. Winter Makepeace might be ten years his junior and have the appearance of an aesthetic monk, but if Lazarus harmed his sister, Makepeace would do his damnedest to send him to hell.

TEMPERANCE TURNED BACK from the cupboard with the jar of salve in her hands. She tried not to wince at the sight of Lord Caire's wound. Blood painted his shoulder and trailed in trickles down to his wrist, startlingly crimson against his white skin. Fresh blood dripped down his chest from where they'd reopened the wound when they removed his shirt. Her eyes followed the bloody trail helplessly, down over his surprisingly muscled chest, lightly sprinkled with black hair, over the shocking brown of his nude nipple, to a line of black hair that began at his navel and disappeared into the waistband of his breeches.

Good Lord.

Her eyes snapped up hastily and she turned her back, attempting to remember what she had been doing. There was a jar of healing salve in her hands. His wound. Right. She had to clean and dress it.

Temperance swallowed and bustled to the table with the jar of salve, and caught sight of Winter glaring at the aristocrat. She looked swiftly between the men, her eyes narrowed. Winter had resumed an aspect of patient innocence while Lord Caire returned her stare, his wide mouth quirked, a devilish gleam of amusement in his eyes. Had he seen her ogling his bare body?

Oh, bother. Now was not the time to be embarrassed by missish nerves.

Temperance drew a calming breath, carefully keeping her gaze focused away from Lord Caire's mesmerizing chest. "Would you like some wine, my lord? This procedure may be painful."

"Please. I wouldn't want to grow faint." His words were innocent, but the tone held irony.

She reproved him with a look even as Winter got up to fetch their only bottle of wine, hoarded and saved for a special occasion. Well, physicking a lord in their kitchen was certainly special.

Temperance found a clean rag in the rag bag and moistened it with the hot water. She turned determinedly to Lord Caire. Winter had returned and uncorked the wine. He poured a cup and handed it to Lord Caire. She dabbed at the blood around the wound as he took a mouthful of wine. Lord Caire's skin was warm and smooth. He stiffened beneath her fingers and set the wineglass down abruptly. She darted a glance at his face. He was staring straight ahead, his eyes glazed.

"Am I hurting you?" she asked in concern. She hadn't even touched the wound yet, but some people were more sensitive to pain than others. Perhaps he hadn't been jesting about growing faint.

There was a pause, almost as if he hadn't heard her, and then he blinked. "No. I'm not in pain."

His voice was cold, all humor gone from his eyes. Something was wrong, but she couldn't tell what.

Temperance turned her attention back to the wound. She had a strange feeling that he was keeping himself from shoving her away only by a great effort. She pressed the cloth over the wound itself, half expecting that he would react violently. Instead he seemed to unbend a little at the pain.

How odd.

She raised the cloth and examined the cleaned wound. It was only a few inches across, but it was obviously more deep than wide. Fresh blood seeped steadily and the edges gaped.

"I'll need to sew this shut," she said, looking up.

He was so close, his face only inches from hers. She could see a small muscle twitching next to his mouth, the involuntary movement in sharp contrast to the rest of his still countenance. Something lurked, deep at the back of his bright blue eyes. Something that looked like suffering.

Temperance drew in her breath with shock.

"I'll get your kit," Winter said from across the table.

Temperance jerked her head up. Her brother was already rising from the table, his expression serene. Had he not noticed the pain in Lord Caire's eyes? Or the look they'd exchanged?

Evidently not.

She released her breath, rummaging in the rag bag to give her hands something to do. They were trembling. She'd sewed up innumerable small cuts, tended scrapes and bumps and fevers, but she'd never caused the kind of pain that marked Lord Caire's eyes. She wasn't even sure she could continue.

"Just do it," Lord Caire murmured.

She looked at him, startled. Had he somehow read her thoughts?

He was watching her, his expression wary. "Just sew me up quickly and I'll leave."

She glanced across the room, but Winter was still searching a cupboard for her kit. She looked back at Lord Caire. "I don't want to hurt you."

His wide mouth twitched, but it was hard to tell if it was a wince or a smile. "I assure you, Mrs. Dews, that whatever you do, it cannot make my pain worse."

She stared at him and knew that the pain he spoke of had nothing to do with the wound in his shoulder. What had...?

"Everything is in order, I believe," Winter said, setting her kit on the table. "Temperance?"

"Yes?" She looked up, smiling blindly. "Yes, thank you, brother."

He glanced suspiciously between her and Lord Caire, but took his seat again without comment.

Temperance breathed a sigh of relief. The last thing she needed was Winter questioning her now. She opened her kit, a small tin box where she kept large needles, catgut, a fine, pointed pair of tweezers, scissors, and other implements useful for repairing small children who fell down quite often. She was glad to see that her fingers no longer shook.

Threading a sturdy needle, she turned to Lord Caire's shoulder and pinched the edges of the wound together. She placed the first stitch. Children often had to be held down when she did this. Some screamed or wept or grew hysterical, but Lord Caire was obviously made of sterner stuff. He drew a breath as she pierced his skin, but made no other indication that she was hurting him. In fact, he seemed more relaxed now than he had when she was wiping the wound clean.

But she couldn't think of that right now. Temperance leaned a little closer, making sure her stitches were small, neat, and firm. They needed to hold the flesh together so it would heal properly, but stitches badly placed could make a scar more misshapen.

She breathed a sigh of relief as she cut the catgut on the last one.

"There. Almost done," she murmured, as much to herself as to the man she tended.

He made no comment, sitting as still as a statue as she opened the small jar of greasy salve. But when she dabbed the salve on his wound—lightly, with one finger—he shuddered. She snatched her hand away, startled, and her gaze flew to his face.

His brow shone with sweat. "Finish it."

She hesitated, but she could hardly leave the wound undressed. Biting her lip, she spread the salve as swiftly as possible, aware that his breathing had quickened. She drew a large piece of old cloth from the rag bag and folded it into a pad, then began winding a long length about his chest. This required that she lean close to him, wrapping her arms about his torso. Lord Caire drew in a breath and seemed to hold it, turning his face away as if her proximity revolted him.

His obvious distress should've dulled her own body's reaction to his nearness, but it did not. The warmth of his skin, the pulse that beat at the side of his neck, even his male odor all combined to arouse her old demons. Temperance was trembling again by the time she tied the bandage off.

The minute she turned away, Lord Caire was up and out of his chair. "Thank you, Mrs. Dews."

She stared. "But your shirt—"

"Is a rag now for your bag." He grimaced as he swung his cloak over his naked shoulders and grabbed his tricorne. "As are my waistcoat and coat. Again, Mrs. Dews, I thank you and bid you good night. Mr. Makepeace."

He nodded briefly to them both before striding to the back door.

Temperance straightened, an odd panic in her throat. Surely he wasn't going to journey home in the dark? "You're wounded, my lord, and alone. Perhaps you should consider spending the night with us here?"

He pivoted, his black cape swirling about his legs, and touched the tip of his black walking stick to the brim of his hat. She noticed for the first time that the silver head of his cane was worked into the shape of a perched hawk. "Your concern is flattering, madam, but I do assure you that I can make it home to my own bed safely."

And with that he was gone.

Temperance let out a sigh, feeling oddly deflated.

That is, until Winter slowly turned in his chair, making

it creak. "I think I need an explanation, sister, as to how you came to know the infamous Lord Caire."

HE WAS A creature of the night, unfit for the company of humans.

The gloom of the St. Giles night enveloped Lazarus as he strode rapidly away from Maiden Lane and Mrs. Dews's innocent little home for children. He was no more suited to that place than a falcon was a dovecote. He leapt over the stinking channel that ran down the middle of the street and turned down another smaller lane, heading west. What must she think of him, a wretched twisted animal that couldn't even stand the touch of his own kind? A shadow moved in a doorway ahead and he charged toward it, welcoming the possibility of violence. But the shadow separated from the darkness about it, and a slight figure fled away into the night.

Lazarus slowed his steps to a walk again, cursing the missed opportunity for distraction. He felt a trickle of moisture tickle his side—he'd reopened the wound with his exertion. But that wasn't why he looked for diversion.

He was hard and throbbing and had been ever since Mrs. Dews had touched his bare skin with her slim, pale hands. Her touch had brought not only desperate mental pain, but also an erotic lust so intense that it lasted into the coldness of the night. He laughed silently. The little martyr would no doubt be disgusted if she knew what she'd done to him. She'd be even more appalled if she knew his preferred method for easing such bodily urges. If the blood wasn't soaking into his breeches, he'd find a female amenable to his demands. He'd take his selection to some rooms nearby and . . .

The image of his last lover pushed itself into his head. Marie. Marie was dead, her body torn into a grotesque pile of offal. She'd been murdered in the rooms he'd rented for her here in St. Giles. The place had been at her insistence, and at the time—two years ago now—he hadn't thought much about the location beyond the fact that it was rather inconvenient for himself. But now it was evident that St. Giles held the key to her murder. It wasn't only because of his wound that he didn't take the time to relieve the lust Mrs. Dews had engendered—he'd been targeted tonight. The assassin with the leather nose patch had been at Mother Heart's-Ease's last night. Perhaps he'd merely been a footpad intent on a purse, but Lazarus didn't think so.

Someone didn't want him to find Marie's murderer.

"You know Lord Caire?" Temperance stared at her brother.

He arched a brow. "I may be a mere schoolmaster, sister, but even I hear the gossip in St. Giles."

"Oh." She looked down at her hands as she automatically cleaned and put away her needle and scissors. Her mind had gone completely blank except for the thought that everyone seemed to have heard of Lord Caire save herself.

Winter sighed and got up. He crossed to a cupboard and took down two glasses. They were fragile things that had once belonged to their mother, two of what had originally been a set of six. He brought them to the table and carefully poured two small glasses of the red wine.

Then he sat and took a sip, closing his eyes as he swallowed. He tilted back his head, the lines about his mouth deepening. "This wine is atrocious. I'm surprised Lord Caire didn't dash it against the wall."

Temperance reached for her own glass and tasted, the sweet, acidic liquid warming her belly. The wine might be cheap, but she didn't care. She'd always thought it a funny quirk that Winter, the most ascetic of men usually, should be picky about wine.

"Will you tell me where you met the infamous Lord Caire?" Winter asked quietly, his eyes still closed.

She sighed. "He came to visit me two nights ago."

His eyes opened then. "Here?"

"Yes." She wrinkled her nose, setting her wineglass carefully on the kitchen table.

"Why didn't I know about this visit?"

She shrugged, avoiding his eyes. "You were asleep when he called." She held her breath, wondering if she'd have to explain *how* Lord Caire had called.

But Winter had other concerns. "Why didn't you wake me, Temperance?"

"I knew that you'd disapprove." She sighed and sat in the chair that Lord Caire had vacated. The seat was already cold. She'd known that she would have to have this conversation with Winter eventually, but she'd been cravenly putting it off. "I don't know why exactly he's notorious, as you say, but I knew you wouldn't like me associating with him."

"So you lied to me."

"Yes." She tilted her chin up, ignoring her twinge of guilt. "I made a deal with him. He'll help me find a patron for the home, and in return I'll help him find the murderer of his mistress."

"Indeed?"

She took a deep breath. "I've already paid the rent with the money he provided."

There was a shocked silence. Temperance swallowed and looked down, avoiding the awful expression of hurt on Winter's face. She was doing this for him, she reminded herself. For Winter and the home.

After a moment, her brother sighed heavily. "I'm afraid you don't know what you've gotten yourself involved in."

"Don't patronize me." She glanced up sharply. "I know that the home will close even if you work yourself to death. I know I can't sit back and let that happen. I know I can help. I know——"

"Lord Caire is notorious for his sexual perversions," Winter said, the flat, precise words interrupting her heated speech.

Temperance stared, closing her mouth. If she was a good woman, a chaste and pious woman, the words would repel her. Instead she felt a thrill, low and deep and forbidden. Dear God.

He continued. "Be careful, sister. I cannot stop you, so I will not try. But if I ever think you are in danger, I will bring this matter to Concord."

She drew in her breath but said nothing.

Winter's brown eyes, usually so calm and caring, had become hard and determined. "And mark you this: Concord *will* stop you."

Chapter Five

Now, below King Lockedheart's balcony was a
stone terrace with a door that led into the castle.
In the room inside, there was a very small and very
insignificant maid kneeling at the hearth. Her name
was Meg, and it was her duty to clean the castle
grates. It was a dirty job, but Meg did it cheerfully,
for she was glad of the work. But because Meg was
so very insignificant, the other inhabitants of the
castle never noticed her at her work. Thus she'd
overheard more than a few conversations.
So when the king from his balcony above proclaimed
how beloved he was, Meg couldn't help but giggle.
She immediately clapped a hand over her mouth, but
by then it was far too late....
—from *King Lockedheart*

Silence opened her eyes two mornings later and was
greeted by the most wonderful sight in the world: the dear
face of her husband, William. He was asleep, his full lips
slightly parted, his brilliant green eyes closed. Fine white

lines radiated from the corners of his eyes, in contrast to the sunburned skin of his face. His nightcap sat slightly ajar over his freshly shaven head. A light dusting of reddish stubble on his jaw glinted in the morning sunlight. Red curls shot with gray peeked at the top of his white nightshirt in delicious contrast to the strong column of his throat. She clenched internally at the sight. She wished she could push aside the nightshirt collar, kiss the base of his neck, and perhaps trail her tongue over his lovely, clean skin.

She blushed at the wanton thought. William preferred their bedsport at night after the candles had been put out, and he was quite right. Only a lustful creature would want to make love in the light of day on the morning after she'd been so thoroughly satisfied by her husband's enthusiastic efforts the night before.

So she rose, careful to not wake William. She refreshed herself with the pitcher of water on a chest of drawers and dressed quickly before quietly moving into the next room.

The rooms that William had found for them were not very big, but they were quite nicely appointed. Besides the tiny bedroom, they had a sitting room with a hearth on which Silence could cook. In the two years that she and William had been married, she'd made their rooms cozy with small touches: a china shepherdess holding a pink lamb on the mantel, a lidded jar in the shape of an artichoke beside it—Silence liked to hide pennies in there—and curtains on the one window, scrimped and saved for and sewn herself. True, the curtains were a bit lopsided and didn't altogether close in the middle, but they were a lovely shade of peachy orange that always made her feel like sitting down to tea.

It was a nice home and she was proud of it.

Humming to herself, Silence built the fire up again and

set a kettle of water on to make tea. By the time William emerged, yawning, from the bedroom, she had their little table laid out with hot tea and warmed buns and butter.

"Good morning," William said, sitting at the table.

"Good morning to you, my husband." Silence placed a kiss on one bristly cheek before pouring him a cup of tea. "Did you sleep well?"

"Indeed I did," he replied as he broke apart one of the buns. They were only a little burned, and she *had* scraped off the worst bits. "Amazing how much more pleasant it is to sleep on a bed that isn't rocking."

His grin was quick and flashed white teeth, and he looked so handsome it made her breath catch.

Silence looked down at her own bun, realizing she was squashing it between her fingers. She hastily set it on her plate. "What will you do today?"

"I have to oversee the unloading of the *Finch*. We'll lose half our cargo to mudlarks if I don't."

"Oh. Oh, of course." Silence took a sip of her tea, trying to hide her disappointment. She'd hoped that he could spend the day with her after so many months at sea, but that was a silly wish. William was the captain of a merchant ship, an important man. Naturally his responsibilities to his ship should come first.

Still, she couldn't completely tamp down a twinge of disappointment.

He must've seen it. William caught her hand in a rare show of open tenderness. "I should have started unloading last night. Had I not such a beautiful young wife, I would have too."

She could feel the slow heating of her cheeks. "Really?"

"Indeed." He nodded solemnly, but there was a twinkle

in his green eyes. "I'm afraid I was quite unable to withstand your temptation."

"Oh, William." She couldn't keep a silly grin from spreading over her face. They may've been married for two years now, but over half that time her husband had been at sea. Each time he returned, it was like a honeymoon anew. Would that ever change? She certainly hoped not.

William squeezed her hand. "The quicker I'm done with my duties, the quicker I can escort you to a park or a fair or even perhaps to a pleasure garden."

"Truly?"

"Yes, indeed. I quite look forward to spending a day with my lovely wife."

She smiled into his eyes, feeling her heart flutter with happiness. "Then you'd better eat your breakfast, hadn't you?"

He laughed and set to the bun and tea. Too soon he rose and finished dressing, donning a white wig in the process that gave him an air of stern authority. William kissed Silence on the cheek and then he was gone.

She sighed and looked about the room. There were dishes to wash and other chores to be done if she were to dally with her husband for a day. She set to work with determination.

Two hours later, Silence was darning a hole in one of William's white stockings and wondering if yellow yarn had been really the right color to use even if she had run out of white, when she heard running footsteps in the hall outside. She glanced up, frowning.

She'd already risen by the time the pounding came at their doors. Silence hurried over and unlatched the door, pulling it open. William stood in the doorway, but she'd never seen her husband in such a state. He was pale beneath his sunburn, his eyes stark.

"What?" she cried, her heart in her throat. "What has happened?"

"The *Finch*..." He staggered into the room, but then stood, his hands by his sides, staring wildly as if he knew not what to do. "I'm ruined."

"VERY GOOD, MARY Whitsun," Temperance said as she watched the girl place a careful stitch in her embroidery. They sat together in a corner of the kitchen while some of the other children made dinner. Mary's needlework was exquisite, and Temperance loved to help her with it when she had time. Unfortunately, there was rarely time. "Perhaps we can place you with a mantua maker. Would you like that?"

Mary bent her head lower over her work—the decoration on the edge of an apron. "I'd rather stay here with you, ma'am."

Temperance felt a familiar pang at the girl's whispered words. Her hand rose to stroke Mary's hair, but she caught herself in time and folded her fingers into a ball before withdrawing her hand. It was wrong to give false hope to the girl.

"You know that's not possible," she said briskly. "If we kept every child at the home, we'd soon overflow."

Mary nodded, her face hidden by her down-bent head, but her shoulders trembled.

Temperance watched helplessly. She'd always felt closer to Mary Whitsun than the other girls, though she knew she should not. Temperance had come to help work at the home after the death of Benjamin, her husband.

She'd saved Mary Whitsun not long after. The little girl had climbed into her lap that day, sitting there, warm and soft and comforting. At the time Temperance had needed someone to hold. Ever since then, she'd known Mary Whitsun was special, no matter how Temperance tried to fight the feeling.

"Oh, ma'am, you'll never guess," Nell cried, panting as she entered the kitchen.

Temperance looked up and arched an eyebrow at the maidservant. "No, I probably won't, so you had better tell me."

Nell held out a folded square of paper that she'd obviously already read. "Lord Caire is escorting you to a musicale this evening!"

"What?" Temperance took the paper, opening it blindly. She hadn't heard from Lord Caire since the night of his injury, and while she'd been terribly worried for his health, at the same time she hadn't been entirely sure if sending a letter to inquire would be quite the thing. "I don't..." She trailed off as she read the elegant handwriting.

He was calling for her at four this afternoon. Temperance's gaze flew to the old clock on the kitchen mantel. The hands read just past noon. She was conscious that the kitchen had become suddenly silent, all the children staring at her.

"Dear God." For a moment, she was frozen, the missive crumpled in her hand. "I have nothing to wear." She thought she'd have at least a week to find a new dress!

Nell blinked and straightened like a soldier called to arms. "Mary Evening, you are in charge of the kitchen. Mary Whitsun, Mary St. Paul, and Mary Little, come with me. And you"—Nell pointed a stern finger at

Temperance—"go to your little sitting room and take off your dress."

Nell left with her minions marching behind her.

Temperance looked down at the sheet of paper in her hands, carefully smoothing it straight. Lord Caire's words jumped out at her, bold and firm. She would see him tonight. She'd accompany him to a respectable entertainment. She'd be on his arm. Oh. Oh, goodness. She felt her cheeks flush at just the thought, and while the majority of her emotions were fear and trepidation, there was a small but very definite part that leapt in excitement.

Temperance snatched up a candle and hurried into her small sitting room. She swiftly stripped off her shawl, dress, and shoes. By the time Nell came back with her troops, Temperance stood in only shift and stays.

"I've had this for five years or more," Nell said as she entered with a bundle. "I couldn't bear to part with it even when I was at my most desperate."

She laid the bundle on a chair and unwrapped it. Shimmering red silk slithered across the chair's cushion. Temperance stared. The dress was beautiful—bright and colorful and far, far too bold.

"I can't wear that," she blurted before she could think of Nell's feelings.

But Nell merely set her arms akimbo. "And what else might you be wearing, Mrs. Dews? You can hardly go in *that*."

That being Temperance's usual black stuff dress, lying now across the back of the armchair. Temperance had exactly three dresses, and all were practical black stuff.

"I—" she began, but was immediately muffled as Nell threw the red dress over her head. She fought her way through the sleeves and bodice and emerged sputtering. Nell ran around behind her and began hooking up the back.

Mary Whitsun cocked her head critically. "It's a pretty color, ma'am, but the bodice doesn't quite fit."

Temperance looked down, realizing she'd never before seen so much of her bosom on display before. The bodice was extremely low. "Oh, no. I can't—"

"No, you certainly can't." Nell came around to examine her. "Not like this anyway." And she plucked the loose fabric at the bodice, pulling it forward to two points in front of Temperance's own smaller breasts. Nell let the silk go and it sagged in the front. "No, we'll have to take it in."

"What about down here?" Mary Whitsun asked. She'd bent to peer at Temperance's hem, which unfortunately was several inches off the floor.

Nell grunted. "That too. Ladies, we have a busy afternoon ahead of us."

And they did. All afternoon, Nell and her company tugged and stitched and cut.

Nearly four hours later, Temperance stood in the kitchen for a last inspection. In the intervening time, she'd bathed and washed her hair. Nell had set it expertly, threading a bit of crimson ribbon through her hair. The cherry-red dress almost glimmered in the firelight as Temperance attempted to yank up the neckline. It was still far too low for her tastes.

"Stop that." Nell batted at her hands. "You'll pull out the stitches."

Temperance froze. The last thing she needed was the dress to completely fall off of her.

"It's a pity you don't have proper slippers," Mary Whitsun said.

Temperance pulled aside her skirts to look at her sturdy black buckle shoes. "Well, these will just have to do. And with the addition of the ruffle Nell added to the hem, I think they'll hardly be noticeable." The ruffle was black silk and had once been one of Papa's nicer coats.

"It does look lovely," Mary said.

Temperance's mouth trembled. "Thank you, Mary Whitsun."

She was absolutely terrified. Only now did the full implication of her bargain with Lord Caire bear upon her. She was going to rub shoulders with the aristocracy—with those sparkling people, so elegant and bright they hardly seemed human. Would they think her a figure of fun?

How could they not?

Well, Lord Caire was certainly human enough. Temperance squared her shoulders. What did it matter what these exotic creatures thought of her? She was attending the musicale to save the home. For Winter and Nell and Mary Whitsun and all the other children. For them she could certainly endure one night's humiliation.

So she smiled at her audience of small children and said, "Thank you all. You've been—"

"Someone's at the door!" One of the little boys scurried to the front door.

"Joseph Tinbox." Temperance started after him into the front hallway. "Do not run. It hardly matters if—"

But Joseph Tinbox unlatched the door at that point and pulled it open, revealing not Lord Caire, but Silence.

Temperance halted. Her sister's face was pale and she wore no cap. Her lovely russet hair was windblown, her hazel eyes tragic. Silence never even glanced at the beautiful cherry-red dress.

"Temperance."

"What is it?" Temperance whispered.

Silence put her hand to the door frame as if to brace herself. "William's cargo has been stolen."

IT WAS PAST four by the time Lazarus's carriage pulled up at the end of Maiden Lane. The lane itself was too narrow for the carriage, so he descended the steps and told the coachman and footmen to wait before walking to the door of Mrs. Dews's foundling home. The sunlight hadn't yet completely faded, but he was sure to keep his fist firmly on his ebony walking stick. He caught the movement of a shadow out of the corner of his eye, a strange flicker of black and red, but when he turned, the thing—a man?—was gone.

After two nights of rest, his shoulder felt even worse than it had the evening he was wounded. It throbbed with a low, continual beat of pain. At the sight of the wound this morning, Small had broken his usual reserve to suggest that his master might do well to spend the evening abed—a suggestion that Lazarus had discarded after only a moment's consideration. He owed Mrs. Dews an event in which she might go hunting a patron for her home. In addition, he was oddly eager to see her again, a state of mind that a dark inner part of himself found vastly amusing. He'd nearly forgotten about the musicale invitation, but once remembered this morning, he knew it was one of the few events to which he might take Mrs. Dews.

Most of his invitations were considerably less benign than a musicale.

Lazarus used the head of his stick to rap upon the home's wooden door. It was opened almost at once by a small female urchin with an abundance of freckles over her cheeks and snub nose. She stood back without a word and he entered the pitiful hallway. It was empty save for themselves.

He arched an eyebrow at the child. "Where is Mrs. Dews?"

The child stared back, apparently stricken mute by his presence in her home.

Lazarus sighed. "What is your name?"

There was another awkward silence during which the child inserted a thumb into her mouth, and then they were both rescued by the clicking of advancing heels.

"Mary St. Paul, please return to the kitchen and tell Nell she must bar the door well behind me," Mrs. Dews said.

She was lit from behind by the light in the kitchen, and she seemed to come toward him in a glowing nimbus cloud. She wore a crimson frock, a startlingly bright color that contrasted to the severity of her usual attire. Her bosom was framed by a low, round neckline, the expanse of smooth white skin nearly glowing.

His groin had the predictable reaction.

He bowed. "Mrs. Dews."

"Hmm?" Her gaze focused on him as if she'd only now noticed him, and his vanity reared in disbelief.

He straightened, deliberately holding out his arm for her. It was expected, of course, the offering of his elbow to a lady, an everyday polite gesture. For him, however, with his peculiar aversion to touch, it'd always been a source of discomfort and thus avoided if at all possible. But right now he seemed to yearn for her touch. Odd, that. She placed her fingers on his sleeve. He felt the jolt, even through the stiff fabric, but whether it was of pain or some more indefinable sensation, he was unable to tell.

Interesting.

"Shall we?" he asked rhetorically.

But she seemed to hesitate, glancing back toward the home's kitchen. "I think ... Yes, I think so." She looked at him squarely for the first time, and he thought he detected a faint flush high on her cheeks. "Thank you, my lord."

He nodded and escorted her out the door. The night was chill, and she drew a thin wrap about her shoulders. The wrap was gray and coarse, obviously more her usual style, and looked even poorer contrasted to the rich red of her silk dress. Lazarus frowned, wondering where she'd gotten the dress. Had she always had it, saving it for special occasions, or had she been forced to purchase it for this evening?

Mrs. Dews cleared her throat. "Your letter said that it is a musicale we'll be attending."

They'd drawn abreast of the carriage, and one of the footmen had already jumped down to set the step. Lazarus took Mrs. Dews's fingers in his gloved hand, assisting her into the carriage.

He didn't know if he was glad to have her no longer touching him or not. "The hostess is Lady Beckinhall, a veritable lioness in London society. There should be many wealthy guests at her house tonight."

Mrs. Dews settled herself on the cushions across from him. Lazarus knocked on the roof and took his own seat.

She was frowning down at her lap. "You make me sound mercenary."

"Do I?" He tilted his head, studying her. She was nervous and distracted tonight, but he didn't think it was at the prospect of attending such a rarefied social event. What had upset her? "I don't mean to, I assure you."

She turned to look out the darkened windows, staring

at her own reflection, perhaps. "I suppose I am mercenary, but it's for the home."

"I know." For a moment, he felt an odd tenderness toward her, his little martyr.

Then she looked back at him. "How do you know Lady Beckinhall?"

His mouth twisted. "She is a good friend of my mother."

"Your mother?" Her eyebrows had winged up her white forehead.

"Did you think I emerged fully formed from my father's thigh?"

"No, of course not." She raised a hand to her bosom and then let it drop. "Your mother is alive, then?"

He inclined his head.

"Do you have brothers or sisters?"

He remembered wide brown eyes, too solemn for her age, and a touch that had never brought pain.

Lazarus blinked away the phantom. "No."

She cocked her head, eyeing him doubtfully.

He made himself smile. "Truly. I am the last of my family save my lady mother."

She nodded. "I have three brothers and two sisters."

"The Makepeaces are obviously quite fertile," he replied drily.

She pursed her lips, as if in disapproval, but continued. "I have a younger sister. Her name is Silence."

He raised his eyebrows but had the intelligence not to comment.

She leaned forward a little, the movement making her wrap slide off one ivory shoulder. He found himself wondering if she'd made the movement intentionally.

"Silence is married to a ship's captain, Mr. William

Hollingbrook. He returned recently to port. Last night the cargo of his ship was stolen."

She stopped and watched him with those odd light brown eyes, as if waiting for a reaction.

He tried to think what would be usual, were this situation usual and he an ordinary man. "I'm sorry?"

She shook her head, his reply obviously inadequate. "If the cargo is not recovered, at least in part, Captain Hollingbrook will be ruined. Silence will be ruined."

He rubbed his thumb over the silver falcon on his stick. "Why? Had he invested in the ship?"

"No, but apparently the ship's owner is accusing him of complicity with the thieves."

He contemplated that. "I don't know if I've ever heard of an entire ship's cargo being stolen."

"It is rather extraordinary. Apparently it's not unusual for a portion of the cargo to go missing, but everything on board..." She shrugged and sank back into the squabs as if weary.

He watched her, this woman from another world. He didn't know why she had chosen to confide her worries to him, but it pleased him irrationally to be the recipient of her confidence. His mouth twisted at his own idiocy.

She looked up suddenly. "I'm sorry to burden you with this."

"Not at all."

She smiled suddenly, her lips trembling. "I haven't thanked you for your invitation tonight."

He shrugged. "It's part of our bargain."

"Nevertheless, I am grateful for your kindness."

"Don't be a fool," he said curtly. "The very last thing I am is kind."

She stiffened and turned her face away from him.

Damn it, he'd spoken too rashly. He wanted to see her eyes, hear her telling him her worries again.

Lazarus cleared his throat, his voice gruff. "I did not mean to speak so harshly."

A corner of her mouth curved a little, though she did not deign to show him her full face. "Are you apologizing to me, Lord Caire?"

"And if I were?" he asked softly. "Would you accept my obeisance?"

She lowered her eyelashes. "I have no need to have you at my feet."

"Don't you?" he asked lightly. "Then perhaps it is my needs that would find me there."

He watched as a blush slowly stole up her neck.

"Or perhaps," he whispered, "you might care to kneel before me?"

She drew in a quick breath as if insulted and looked at him, her eyes wide. It was to be expected—his suggestion was crass and ungentlemanly. She should be insulted. But it wasn't insult that quickened her breath, made her sweet breasts press against her bodice with each inhale. It was something far more primitive.

Lazarus dropped his eyes as he felt the heat rise in his own body. He'd hunted like this before, sighted and circled prey before diving and catching in his talons, but this...this was far more intense than any other hunt.

"You shouldn't...shouldn't talk to me that way," she said, her voice trembling—but not with anger.

He stared at her from under his brows. "Why not? It amuses me to discuss these things with you. Does it not you?"

She swallowed. He could see the movement of her throat clearly in the lantern's light. "Don't."

"I think you do like it. I think you have the same image in your mind as I do. Shall I tell you what I see?"

She had her hand at her throat, but she was mute, staring at him, her eyes glazed.

He let his gaze drop deliberately to the upper slopes of her exposed breasts. "I see you in that dress, madam, kneeling before me, your skirts spread in a shining pool of crimson. I see myself standing before you. You look up at me, your golden eyes half closed as they are now, your lips reddened and wet from your tongue—or perhaps mine."

"No," she moaned, her voice so low he only knew her words from the movement of her lips.

"I see myself taking your hand and placing it on the fall of my breeches." His cock was hard, throbbing with his own words and her reaction to them. "I see your slim, cool fingers carefully undoing each button as I stroke your bound hair. I see—"

The carriage jerked to a halt.

Lazarus inhaled softly and parted the curtains to glance out. Lady Beckinhall's town house blazed with light.

He let the curtain fall and looked across the carriage at Mrs. Dews. Her eyes were wide, her cheeks flushed, and he'd wager his life that she was wet beneath those shimmering crimson skirts.

A corner of his mouth quirked up, but it wasn't humor he felt. "We're here. Shall we descend?" He watched as she became aware, as white teeth bit that plump, lower lip. His voice lowered to gravelly depths. "Or shall I tell the coachman to drive on?"

Chapter Six

King Lockedheart bellowed for his guards to bring him the miscreant who had the temerity to laugh at him. Within seconds, Meg was dragged before him, bedraggled and sooty.

"What is your name?" roared King Lockedheart.

"Meg, if it please Your Majesty."

He glowered at her. "And what did you find so amusing in my speech?"

The guards and the courtiers, drawn by the commotion, all expected the small maid to throw herself at his feet and plead for her life.

But Meg rubbed the end of her sooty nose and decided since she was already damned, she might as well speak the truth. "Only that you think you are beloved by your people, Your Majesty."…

——from *King Lockedheart*

He was temptation personified.

Temperance stared at Lord Caire, feeling the rapid beat of her heart, the ache between her thighs. She'd

avoided men for the last nine years precisely because of
her sinful desires. Yet here, now, she found herself seated
across from a man far more seductive than any other she'd
ever met. He knew exactly how to rouse her demons, how
to taunt and thrill until she was at feverish pitch, and
the awful, terrible thing was that a part of her wanted—
needed—to give in. To submit to the allure of his blue
eyes. To kneel before him and touch that most earthly part
of a man. To do the forbidden and open her mouth around
him in an act that in no way could be about reproduction.

An act that was purely carnal.

No.

Temperance broke contact with his mesmerizing stare,
drawing a shaky breath. "Let me out."

For a moment he didn't move, didn't blink, simply stared
at her with sapphire eyes that seemed to burn her exposed
skin. Her breath caught at the look and the possibility that
he wouldn't let her go, that he'd take her and make her do
those wicked things he'd spoken of in that deep voice.

Then he sighed. "Very well, Mrs. Dews."

He stood and opened the door to the carriage, descend-
ing first and holding out a hand to help her alight. Temperance placed her trembling fingers in his grasp, and for a
long second, his hand closed over hers, hot and possessive,
even through his glove. Then her feet touched the ground
and he let go, offering his arm again instead. She took
it, inhaling to steady herself, aware that he'd shuddered
at her touch. Around them, fashionable ladies stepped
from carriages emblazoned with gilded coats of arms.
The cherry-red dress that Nell had worked so hard on all
afternoon suddenly seemed old and too obvious, the ribbon in her hair simply gauche. She swallowed in sudden

trepidation. She didn't belong here. She was a house sparrow among peacocks.

Lord Caire leaned over her. "Are you ready?"

She tilted her chin. "Yes, of course."

"Brave even when entering a den of lions," he murmured.

Inside, Lady Beckinhall's town house fairly sparkled with white marble, gilt, and crystal. Overhead, a chandelier shone with hundreds of candles. Temperance absently surrendered her old gray wool wrap to a footman, not even caring when he grimaced and took it with thumb and forefinger. The town house was like a fairy-tale castle. She trailed her fingers on the marble banister as Lord Caire led her upward. How many servants spent their days on hands and knees to keep the white marble clean?

At the top of the staircase, they followed the stream of brightly plumed people into a long room, mirrored along one entire wall so that there seemed to be thousands of gorgeously gowned ladies escorted by innumerable dauntingly elegant gentlemen. Had she been by herself, Temperance might've fled, but Lord Caire's arm was solid and warm beneath her fingers.

"Courage," he murmured.

"My dress," she said under her breath.

"Your dress is fine," he whispered back. "I would not have let you enter otherwise. More importantly, you have nothing to be ashamed of in this crowd. You are just as well spoken as these ladies, just as quick-witted. And you have something they don't: you know how to make your way in the world."

"That's not usually something to be proud of," Temperance said.

He glanced at her. "Perhaps it should be. Hold your head high."

One of the sophisticated ladies turned at their entrance and slowly strolled their way. Her dress was a deep blue, and as she drew nearer, Temperance could see that what she'd at first taken for embroidered flowers on her skirts were, in fact, rubies and emeralds sewn into the fabric.

Dear God.

"Lazarus," the otherworldly creature drawled, "how unexpected to find you here."

She was exquisitely beautiful, like some goddess come to earth to amuse herself at the expense of mortals. This close, Temperance could see that she wore two lovely pins in her hair, diamonds, emeralds, and rubies fashioned into birds. Small diamonds on the end of delicate wires trembled whenever the lady moved her head.

It was all Temperance could do to keep from gaping, but evidently Lord Caire had no such awe for the lady. He inclined his head in a bow so brief it was insulting.

The lady's lovely lips thinned, and her gaze turned to Temperance. "And who is this . . . person?"

"May I introduce Mrs. Dews," Lord Caire said shortly.

Temperance noticed that he didn't introduce the other woman to her.

Apparently the lady noticed it as well. She stiffened. "If you've brought one of your bawds to Lady Beckinhall's home . . ."

Lord Caire arched an eyebrow. "Your imagination does you no credit, my lady. I assure you that Mrs. Dews is likely the most respectable person here."

The lady's eyes narrowed. "Careful, Lazarus. You tread a fine line."

"Do I?"

"What is this woman to you?"

Temperance felt her cheeks heat at the lady's obvious dismissal of her. She talked as if Temperance was a dog or a cat, a dumb beast unable to communicate.

"A friend," Temperance said.

"What did you say?" The lady blinked as if honestly startled at her ability to speak.

"I said I am a friend of Lord Caire's," Temperance said firmly. "And you are . . . ?"

"Lazarus, tell me this is a prank." She'd turned back to Lord Caire, dismissing Temperance as thoroughly as she no doubt did a downstairs maid.

"No prank." Lord Caire smiled thinly. "I would've thought you of all people would be happy I chose a respectable lady to escort to this assemblage."

"Respectable!" The lady closed her eyes as if disgusted by the word. Then her sapphire eyes snapped open. "Send her away and let me introduce you to one of your own rank. There are several unmarried—"

But Lord Caire had already started to guide Temperance away.

"Lazarus!" the lady hissed behind them. "I am your *mother.*"

Lord Caire stiffened and turned, a cruel smile on his lips. "So I've been told. Madam."

He sketched a bow. A fleeting expression crossed the lady's face as they turned away. Something vulnerable and unpracticed. Hurt, perhaps? And then her expression was controlled and cold again, and they were past her.

Temperance glanced at Lord Caire, aware that her cheeks had flamed. "That was your mother?"

"Alas, yes," he replied, and yawned behind an elegant fist.

"Goodness." She would never have guessed their relationship from the open hostility that Lord Caire had shown the lady. Did he hate his own mother? She frowned as she remembered something else. "Did she really think I was your—"

"Yes," he clipped. He glanced at her and his voice gentled. "Don't let it worry you. Anyone else has merely to look at you to know you would never let yourself be corrupted by me."

Temperance glanced away, unsure if he teased or not, and that was when it happened. As she placed her foot down, she felt a catch and heard a rip. "Oh, no."

"What is it?"

Temperance glanced down at her frock, hoping she wasn't too obvious. "I've torn my hem." She looked up at him. "Is there somewhere I might repair it?"

He nodded and in a moment had procured the direction to the ladies' retiring room from a footman. The room was down a short hall, and Temperance carefully lifted her skirts as she made her way there. She looked around when she entered—the room was well lit and nicely appointed with low chairs for a lady to rest on—but no one was about. She stood, nonplussed for a moment. Weren't there supposed to be maids to assist the ladies?

She shrugged and sat to inspect her hem.

"Can I help?"

Temperance lifted her head, expecting to see a maid, but a lady had entered the room. She was tall and pale, her posture as correct as a queen's, and her hair was a lovely shade of light red. She wore a splendid gown—a muted gray-green, overembroidered in silver thread.

Temperance blinked.

The woman's face became bland. "I don't mean to intrude...."

"Oh, no," Temperance said hastily. "It's just that I was expecting a maid or...or...well, not a lady in any case. My hem is torn."

The woman wrinkled her straight nose. "I hate when that happens." She glanced over her shoulder. "Lady Kitchen is having an attack of hysterics or nerves I believe. No doubt that's where all the maids have gone to."

"Oh." Temperance glanced again at the black ruffle on her hem. It sagged quite sadly.

But the lady was kneeling before her now, her green and silver skirts spread about her like a shining cloud.

"Oh, please don't," Temperance said instinctively. This woman was obviously aristocracy. What would she do if she knew Temperance was the daughter of a beer brewer?

"It's all right," the lady said quietly. She hadn't taken offense at Temperance's outburst. "I've got a few pins...."

Deftly she flipped the hem up, pinned the ruffle in place, and flipped it back again. The pins didn't even show.

"Goodness! You do that so well," Temperance exclaimed.

The lady rose and smiled shyly. "I've had practice. Ladies should stick together at these social events, don't you think?"

Temperance smiled in return, feeling confident for the

first time since receiving Lord Caire's invitation. "You're so kind. Thank you. I wonder—"

The door burst open and several ladies entered, maids fluttering about them. Apparently it was Lady Kitchen and her hysterics. In the confusion, Temperance was separated from her new friend, and by the time she made the hall outside the ladies' retiring room, the other woman was nowhere to be seen.

Still Temperance returned to Lord Caire with a lighter step, having been warmed by the stranger's kindness. She found him leaning against a wall, surveying the company with a cynical gaze.

He straighten when he saw her. "Better?"

She beamed. "Yes, quite."

His lips curved in answer. "Then let's find your prey."

They strolled to the far end of the room where gilded chairs had been placed in rows facing a beautifully painted piano. No one had yet taken a seat. Lord Caire led her to a trio of gentlemen.

"Caire." A cadaverously thin gentleman in a white, full-bottomed wig nodded as they neared. "I had not thought this your type of entertainment."

"Ah, but my tastes are diverse." Lord Caire's lips curled. "May I introduce Mrs. Dews? Mrs. Dews, this is Sir Henry Easton."

"Sir." Temperance made her best curtsy as the older gentleman bowed.

"And these are Captain Christopher Lambert and Mr. Godric St. John. Gentlemen, Mrs. Dews, along with her brother, Mr. Winter Makepeace, runs the Home for Unfortunate Infants and Foundling Children in the East End, a most Christian and charitable institution."

"Indeed?" Sir Henry raised bushy eyebrows, looking at her in interest. Captain Lambert had also turned his gaze to her. In contrast, Mr. St. John, a tall man in a gray wig, had cocked an eyebrow over half-moon spectacles at Lord Caire.

For a moment, Temperance wondered what the connection was between Lord Caire and Mr. St. John.

Then Sir Henry asked, "How many foundlings does your institution house, Mrs. Dews?"

Temperance smiled her most charming smile, intent on catching one of these fine gentlemen for the sake of the home.

"WHAT ARE YOU about, Caire?" St. John hissed out of the corner of his mouth.

Lazarus kept his eyes on his little martyr as she used all of her Christian wiles to seduce Lambert and Easton into supporting her foundling home. "I have no idea to what you refer."

St. John snorted softly and half turned so as to be heard only by Lazarus. "She's obviously as respectable as you claim, which means that you're either using her for some ends of your own or your debauchery has descended to the rape of innocents."

"You hurt me, sir," Lazarus drawled, placing his fingertips over his heart. He knew he looked ironic—jaded, even—but oddly, inside his chest, he did feel a twinge of something that might've been hurt.

St. John had leaned close to whisper, "What do you want from her?"

Lazarus narrowed his eyes. "Why? Will you play her gallant knight and steal her away from my dastardly arms?"

St. John cocked his head, his normally mild gray eyes sharpened to granite. "If need be."

"Think you that I'd truly allow you to take from me something I wanted?"

"You talk of Mrs. Dews as if she's a plaything." St. John's expression had turned analytical. "Would you break her in a fit of spoiled temper?"

Lazarus smiled thinly. "If I wanted."

"Come," St. John murmured. "You are not so lost to humanity as you sometimes like to play."

"Aren't I?"

Lazarus no longer smiled. He glanced at Mrs. Dews, discussing her charity home with earnest enthusiasm. Had she made the slightest sign of acquiescence in the carriage, she might at this moment be accepting his cock into her sweet saintly mouth. Wasn't the debauchery of a saint the work of a devil? He looked back at St. John, the only man in this world who he might call a friend. The room had grown damnably hot, and his shoulder sent sharp shards of pain down his arm.

"A word to the wise: make no wagers on my humanity."

St. John arched an eyebrow. "I'll not sit back and watch you hurt an innocent. I will take her away from you if I think she needs my help."

The anger shot through him so quickly Lazarus had bared his teeth before he realized.

St. John must've seen the murder in his eyes. He actually stepped back. "Caire?"

"Don't," Lazarus hissed. "Not even in jest, St. John. Mind your own lady. Mrs. Dews is mine to do with as I please."

The other man's glance flicked between him and Mrs. Dews. "And does she have no say in this matter?"

"No," Lazarus growled, aware that he sounded like a dog standing guard over a bone.

St. John raised his eyebrows. "Does she know your intent?"

"She will." And Lazarus turned and caught Mrs. Dews's arm, interrupting her in midspeech. "Excuse me, gentlemen. I wish to find Mrs. Dews the best seat possible."

"Of course," Sir Henry murmured, but Lazarus was already steering her away from the others.

"What are you about?" Mrs. Dews looked none too pleased with him. "I had just begun discussing the amount of fresh vegetables we buy every month for the home."

"A most interesting topic, I have no doubt." He needed to sit down, to rest a bit. Damn the wound in his shoulder.

Her brows knit. "Was I boring them? Is that why you intervened?"

His mouth twitched in amusement. "No. They seemed more than happy to listen to you lecture them on clothing and feeding urchins for the rest of the night."

"Humph. Then why did you take me away?"

"Because 'tis always better to leave the buyer wanting," he whispered into the dark hair over her ear. The silly red ribbon twined in and out of the glossy locks, and for a wild moment, he wanted to tug it free. To watch as her hair came tumbling down about her shoulders.

She turned and looked up, so close he could see the flecks of gold in her light brown eyes. "And have you sold very many things, Lord Caire?"

She was teasing him, this proper Christian woman.

Did she have no fear of him? Did she not sense the darkness that bubbled deep within him?

"Not things so much as...ideas," he drawled.

She cocked her head, those gilded eyes curious. "You've sold *ideas*?"

"In a manner of speaking," he said as he guided her toward two chairs at the end of a row near the front. "I belong to a number of philosophical and scientific societies." He seated her and flicked apart the skirts of his coat to sit beside her. "When one argues a point, one is in effect selling it to the opposition, if you understand me."

He didn't mention the other type of "selling" he did— the luring of sexual partners into performing actions they would in other circumstances never contemplate.

"I think I comprehend your meaning." Mrs. Dews's eyes lit with amusement. "I confess, I'd not seen you in the role of idea merchant, Lord Caire. Is that what you do with your days? Argue with other learned gentlemen?"

"And translate various Greek and Latin manuscripts."

"Such as?"

"Poetry, mostly." He glanced at her. Did she really find this interesting?

But her golden eyes sparkled as she cocked her head. "You write poetry?"

"I translate it—quite different."

"Actually, I would think it somewhat similar."

"How so?"

She shrugged. "Don't poets have to worry over meter, rhyme, and the proper words?"

"So I'm told."

She looked at him and smiled, making him catch his

breath. "I would think the translator would have to worry over those things as well."

He stared. How did she know, this simple woman from another walk of life entirely? How had she with one sentence articulated the passion he found in his translations? "I suppose you have a point."

"You hide a poet's soul well," she said. "I would never have guessed it."

She was definitely teasing him now.

"Ah." He stretched his long legs before him. "But then there's quite a lot you don't know about me, Mrs. Dews."

"Is there?" Her gaze skipped over his shoulder, and he knew she looked at his mother in conversation with Lady Beckinhall in the corner. "Such as?"

"I have an unnatural fondness for marzipan sweetmeats."

He felt more than heard her giggle, and the small, innocent sound sent a frisson of warmth through him. She hid her emotions so well usually, even the joyous ones.

"I haven't had marzipan sweetmeats in ages," she murmured.

He had a sudden urge to buy her a boxful just to watch her eat them. Her red lips would become sprinkled with the sugar and she'd have to lick them clean. His groin tightened at just the thought.

"Tell me something else about yourself. Something true." She watched him, those pale brown eyes mysterious. "Where were you born?"

"Shropshire." He looked away, watching as his mother made some comment to another lady. The jewels in her white hair sparkled as she tilted her head. "My family's seat is near Shrewsbury. I was born at Caire House, our ancestral home. I'm told that I was a puling, weakly babe, and my father sent me away to the wet nurse with little hope that I would live out the sennight."

"It sounds as if your parents were worried for you."

"No," he said flatly, the knowledge as old as his bones. "I stayed with my nurse for five years, and in that time, my parents saw me only once a year, on Easter day. I remember because my father used to scare me witless."

He had no idea why he told her this; it hardly showed him in a heroic light.

"And your mother?" she asked softly.

He glanced at her curiously. "She accompanied my father, of course."

"But"—her brows knit together again as if she were trying to puzzle something out—"was she affectionate?"

He stared. Affection? He looked again at his mother, now making her way to a seat. She moved gracefully, the embodiment of cold elegance. The thought of her showing affection for anyone, let alone him, was ludicrous.

"No," he said patiently, as if explaining the intricacies of the English monetary system to a Chinaman. "They didn't come to express affection. They came to see if their heir was being adequately fed and housed."

"Oh," she said, her voice small. "And your nurse? Was she affectionate toward you?"

The question sent a nasty wave of pain through him, the sensation exquisitely awful, and his shoulder throbbed in the aftermath.

"I don't remember," he lied.

She opened her mouth as if to question him further, but he'd had enough. "And you, Mrs. Dews? What was your upbringing like?"

She pursed her lips for a moment as if she wouldn't let him lead her into a different conversational avenue. Then she sighed. "I was born here in London, not far from the foundling home, actually. Father was a brewer. There are six children in my family: Verity; Concord, who runs the brewery now; Asa; myself; Winter; and my youngest sister, Silence. Father met the acquaintance of Sir Stanley Gilpin when I was quite young, and with his patronage, Father established the foundling home."

"A pretty tale," Lazarus drawled, watching her face. She'd recited the story almost by rote. "Yet, it tells me very little about you."

She looked startled. "But there isn't much to tell beyond that."

"Oh, I think there is," he murmured softly. The chairs about them were beginning to fill, but he was loath to give up this discussion so soon. "Did you work in the home as a child? Were you schooled at all? And where and when did you meet your husband?"

"I spent my childhood at home mostly," she said slowly. "Mother schooled me until she died when I was thirteen years of age. Thereafter, my elder sister, Verity, took over the chore of raising us younger children. The boys were sent to school, of course, but there wasn't enough money to send the girls. I fancy, though, that our education was quite adequate."

"No doubt," he said. "But you haven't mentioned the late Mr. Dews. In fact, I've never heard you speak of your husband."

She looked away, her face paling, a reaction he found infinitely fascinating.

"Mr. Dews—Benjamin—was a protégé of my father's,"

she said quietly. "Benjamin had studied for the church but decided to join Father in his work to help the orphans of St. Giles instead. I met him when I was seventeen, and we married shortly thereafter."

"He sounds like quite the saint," Lazarus said, irony dripping from his words.

Mrs. Dews was somber, though. "Yes, he was. He worked incredibly long hours at the foundling home. He was always gentle and patient with the children; he was kind to everyone he knew. I once saw him take off his own coat and give it to a beggar who had none."

Lazarus gritted his teeth, leaning close to hiss, "Tell me, Mrs. Dews, do you have a shrine in your rooms to commemorate your dead saint?"

"What?" She turned a shocked face to him.

It only inflamed his urge to hurt her more. To make her feel so that he could revel in her reflected emotions. "Do you kneel before his shrine and genuflect? Does his memory keep you warm in your lonely bed at night? Or do you have to resort to other, less spiritual means of satisfaction?"

"How dare you?" Her eyes sparked at his crude insinuation.

His corrupted heart crowed at the sight of the rage his words had provoked. She made to stand, but he caught her arm in a hard grip, forcing her to remain seated.

"Hush, now," he crooned. "The music is about to begin. You wouldn't want to storm out now and destroy all the progress you made earlier with Captain Lambert and Sir Henry, would you? They might think you a fickle creature."

"I loathe you." She pressed her lips together, turning her face away as if the very sight of him revolted her.

But despite her words, she remained by his side, and that was all that mattered in the end. He cared not a whit if she loathed him, even wanted him dead, as long as she felt something for him. As long as he could keep her close.

HOW DARE HE?

Temperance stared at her balled hands in her lap as she struggled not to show her rage. What had provoked Lord Caire's disgusting attack on her and the memory of Benjamin? They'd been having a simple conversation about everyday things and suddenly he'd erupted. Was he insane? Or was he so jealous of a normal man—a man who could feel kindness and sympathy—that he must lash out at merely the thought?

Lord Caire's hand still gripped her elbow, hot and hard, and he tightened it at her shiver. "Don't even think of it."

She didn't bother replying to him. The truth was that a part of her anger had dissipated when she thought of his loveless childhood.

Not, of course, that she meant to tell him that.

Temperance looked away from him, watching as the guests found seats. Lady Caire let herself be seated by a handsome gentleman in a bag wig. The man was obviously younger than she, but he attended her quite tenderly. Temperance wondered suddenly if they were lovers. What odd morals the aristocracy had. Her gaze wandered to where Sir Henry sat beside a stout matronly lady, obviously his wife. She looked like a pleasant lady.

Temperance caught a flash of silver out of the corner of her eye, and her head turned to follow the movement. Her breath caught. The elegant young lady from the retiring room was strolling toward the chairs. She seemed to be all alone, her pale green and silver gown a perfect foil for her bright red hair and graceful, long white throat. All eyes were upon her as she neared the chairs, but she seemed unaware as she sank into a seat.

"Who is that?" Temperance whispered, forgetting for the moment that she wasn't talking to Lord Caire.

"Who?" the impossible man drawled.

How could he not know? Half the room was gawking at her. "The lady in silver and green."

Lord Caire twisted his neck to look and then leaned unnecessarily close. Heat seemed to radiate off his body. "That, my dear Mrs. Dews, is Lady Hero, the sister of the Duke of Wakefield."

"The sister of a duke?" Temperance breathed. Goodness! What a very good thing she hadn't known that when the lady had been helping her.

She'd once stood on a corner for three hours just to catch a glimpse of His Majesty's carriage in a procession, but that had been years ago. Besides, all she'd seen was a bit of white wig that may have—or may not have—been the king's head. Lady Hero was right here in the same room.

"Aye." Lord Caire sounded amused. "And the daughter of a duke as well, don't forget."

She turned and opened her mouth to set him down, but he placed a warm finger across her lips. "Hush. They are about to begin."

And she saw he was right. A gentleman in a splendid white wig and gold-trimmed coat had seated himself before the piano. A younger man stood by his side to turn the pages of the sheet music.

Lady Beckinhall stood at the front of the room and made some type of announcement, no doubt introducing the pianist, but Temperance hardly paid her mind. Her gaze was fixed on the gentleman at the piano. He sat quietly, unsmiling even when Lady Beckinhall gestured to him. He merely nodded once curtly and waited as she seated herself. He stared at the piano keys before him, seemingly oblivious to the guests who still chattered behind him. Then abruptly he began to play.

Temperance caught her breath, leaning slightly forward. The piece was unfamiliar to her, but the fine chords, the flying notes, lifted something inside of her. She closed her eyes, savoring the sweet swelling in her chest. Moisture pricked at her eyes. It had been so long since she'd heard music like this.

So long.

She drifted, her entire being focused on the music until at last it drew to a close. Only then did Temperance open her eyes and sigh.

"You liked it," a deep voice said next to her.

She blinked at Lord Caire and realized that her hand was grasped in his. She looked down at their intertwined fingers, puzzled. Had she taken his hand or had he reached for hers? She couldn't remember.

He tugged gently. "Come. Walk with me."

"Oh, but..."

She glanced at the piano, but the pianist had already left. Around them the other guests were standing or strolling, none of them appearing at all affected by the music.

She turned back to Lord Caire.

His blue eyes were intent, his high cheekbones ruddy. "Come."

She rose and followed him silently, paying no attention

to where he led until he opened a door and ushered her into a small sitting room, lit by a fire.

Temperance frowned. "What—?"

But Lord Caire closed the door behind her, and she turned to see him advancing toward her. "You liked the music."

She looked at him in confusion. "Yes, of course."

"There is no *of course*." His sapphire eyes seemed to glitter in the firelight. "Most who come to a musicale pay little or no attention to the music. But you... you were entranced."

He was so intent upon her that she backed up a step and found herself against a settee.

Still he came closer, heat blasting from him like a furnace. "What did you hear? What did you feel in that music?"

"I... I don't know," she stuttered. What did he want of her?

He caught her shoulders. "Yes, you do. Tell me. Describe your emotions."

"I felt free," she whispered, her heart beating hard. "I felt alive."

"And?" His face was angled, his eyes examining her.

"And I don't know!" She placed her palms on his chest, pushing, but though he stiffened at her touch, he didn't budge. "How can one describe music? It's an impossible task. One either feels the wonder or one doesn't."

"And you're one of the few who does feel it, aren't you?"

"What do you want of me?" she whispered.

"Everything."

His mouth was on hers. Hot, insistent, working as if he

meant to draw from her bodily what he couldn't in words. She gripped his arms, unable to defend herself from this onslaught so soon after the ecstasy of the music.

Eagerly she opened her mouth, wanting to taste, wanting to feel without guilt, just this once. He thrust his tongue into her mouth, withdrawing and thrusting again until she moaned and caught his tongue, sucking on it, tasting wine, tasting him. She wanted to pull the coat from his shoulders, to rip off his shirt and feel again the smooth skin beneath. To place her mouth against his nipple and lick him.

Dear God, she'd lost her mind, her balance, and her morals, and she no longer cared. She wanted to be free again, to feel without thought or horrible memory. She wanted to be born anew, pure and without sin. She ran her hands up his arms, squeezing, testing the hard muscles beneath until she reached his shoulders, then—

"Damnation!" The word was a groan as Lord Caire ripped his mouth from hers.

"Oh!" She'd forgotten his injured shoulder. "I'm so sorry. I've hurt you."

She reached for him, not sure what she could do, perhaps only wanting to offer comfort.

But he shook his head, beads of sweat on his upper lip. "Don't worry yourself, Mrs. Dews."

He straightened from where he'd leaned against the settee back, but then swayed.

"You need to sit," Temperance said.

"Don't fuss," he murmured irritably, but his voice was weak. Something dark stained the shoulder of his coat.

Temperance felt a thrill of fear. His face was too red, the heat of his body too hot. She swallowed, keeping her voice calm. In her experience, gentlemen never wanted to admit weakness. "I...I find myself weary. Would you mind terribly if we left?"

To her relief, he didn't argue over her obvious stratagem. Instead, Lord Caire straightened and offered her his arm. He led her back to the musicale room. There he made his way far too leisurely through the guests, pausing to exchange banter with other gentlemen, before making his excuses for his early departure to the hostess. All the while, Temperance watched him anxiously, aware that sweat slicked his brow. By the time they retrieved her wrap, he was leaning heavily on her. She wasn't even sure he was conscious of it or not.

"Tell the coachman to drive to Lord Caire's town house," she told the footman as he helped Lord Caire up the steps to the carriage. "Tell him to hurry."

"Yes, ma'am," the footman said, and slammed the carriage door.

"Such drama, Mrs. Dews," Lord Caire drawled. His head lolled against the squabs, his eyes closed. "Don't you want to return to your foundling home?"

"I think it best that we get you to your home as soon as possible."

"You worry too much."

"Yes." Temperance braced as the carriage swung hard around a corner. "Yes, I do."

She bit her lip. Because despite her light words, she knew her worry was well founded. She very much feared Lord Caire's wound was infected.

And infection could kill a man.

Chapter Seven

*At Meg's words, all within the room gasped.
"Nonsense!" the king roared. "I am beloved by my
people. Everyone tells me this is so."
Meg shrugged. "I'm sorry, Your Majesty, but they
have lied to you. You may be feared but you are not
loved."
The king's eyes narrowed. "I will prove to you that
I am loved by my people, and when I have done so,
I will have your head to decorate my palace gates.
Until then, you may reside in my dungeons."
And with a wave of his hand, Meg was dragged
away. . . .*
—from *King Lockedheart*

Infection could kill within days—hours if the wound turned putrid rapidly.

Temperance couldn't keep the morbid thought from her mind as Lord Caire's carriage rumbled through the dark London streets. She didn't even know where he lived or if they had a long ride or one of only minutes.

Perhaps she should've insisted he stay at Lady Beckin-hall's town house, despite his obvious desire to conceal his illness.

"You're very quiet, Mrs. Dews," Lord Caire said slowly from across the carriage. "I vow, it makes me nervous. What plots have you worked for me in that Puritanical mind of yours?"

"I only wondered how soon we would arrive at your house."

He rolled his head, squinting out the window as night lights flashed by. After a bit, he closed his eyes again. "I can't tell where we are. Halfway to Bath, for all I know. But never fear, my coachman is a humorless man. He'll see us safely home."

"Of course."

"D'you like dancing as well?" he asked suddenly.

Was he delirious? "I don't dance."

"Naturally not," he murmured. "Martyrs dance only upon crosses. I'm surprised you let yourself enjoy even something as innocent as piano music."

"I used to have a spinet as a young girl," she said absently. Surely they must be nearly there?

"And you played."

"Yes." She remembered suddenly the feel of the smooth, cool piano keys beneath her fingers, the sheer joy of producing music. That time seemed so innocent and far away now.

His eyes cracked lazily. "But you no longer play?"

"I sold the spinet after my husband's death." She waited for him to make a cutting remark about Benjamin again.

"Why?"

The simple question startled her enough that she glanced at him. He was watching her through slitted eyes, the blue of his irises glittering even in the dim carriage.

"Why what?"

"Why sell the piano you so obviously treasured? Did you fear you'd be tempted by the small pleasure of the music? Or was it something else?"

Temperance clenched her hands together in her lap, but her voice was calm as she replied with a half-truth. "We needed the money for the home."

"No doubt you did," he murmured, "but I don't think that's why you sold your spinet. You enjoy punishing yourself."

"What a nasty thing to say." She turned her face away from him, feeling the heat in her cheeks. Prayed he couldn't see her in the dim carriage.

"Yet you don't deny the accusation." He grunted in pain as the carriage rocked.

She glanced swiftly at him, only to inhale as she met his sharp gaze. Even in his weakened state, she felt as if she were pinned by a predator.

"What imagined sin do you punish yourself for?" he asked softly. "Did you covet another female's bonnet once as a child? Gorge yourself on sweetmeats? Felt a naughty thrill at a lout brushing up against you in the street?"

Raw rage, sharp and unexpected, washed over her, making Temperance shake. She restrained herself from shouting a retort only with difficulty. Instead, she breathed deeply, staring at her fists in her lap. To let herself speak now would be the height of stupidity. She'd say too much, *reveal* too much. He was perilously close to her secret shame as it was.

"Or," Lord Caire's obnoxiously calm voice drawled, "perhaps the sin was more grave than those I cite."

She remembered that long-ago thrill when she'd catch sight of a certain man, his crooked smile making her heart leap so unbearably. The memories were shadows of her ancient emotions and desires, still lurking long after their progenitor had died.

Temperance lifted her head, staring into his wicked blue eyes, her jaw clenched. A slight smile played about his wide mouth, sensuous and seductive. Did he torture her out of curiosity? Did he enjoy her pain?

The carriage halted and Lord Caire broke their stare. "Ah. We've arrived. Thank you for accompanying me home, Mrs. Dews. Once I alight, the coachman will take you to your own home. I bid you good night."

She was terribly tempted to simply leave him here. He'd taunted and prodded her like a little boy poking sticks at a caged monkey, purely for his own amusement. And yet when he stood and swayed, half slumping against the carriage doorway, she jumped up.

"I loathe you, Lord Caire," Temperance said through gritted teeth as she took his arm.

"So you've informed me already."

"I am not finished." She staggered as he leaned heavily against her. A young footman opened the carriage door, and he immediately took Lord Caire's other arm to help him down. "You're an impossibly rude man, without morals or even manners, as far as I can see."

"Oh, stop, I beg you, Mrs. Dews." Lord Caire grunted. "You'll turn my head with this flattery."

"And," Temperance continued, ignoring his words, "you've behaved abominably to me since the moment we met—when you broke into my home, might I remind you."

Lord Caire had made it to the street, where he paused, panting, his hand on the shoulder of the young footman who gaped at the two of them. "Is there a point to this diatribe, or are you merely venting your spleen?"

"I have a point," Temperance said as she helped him up the steps to his imposing town house. "Despite your treatment of me and your own foul personality, I intend to stay with you until a doctor sees to you."

"Flattered though I am by your martyrish impulses, Mrs. Dews, I have no need of your help. Bed and a brandy will no doubt see me right."

"Really?" Temperance eyed the idiot man, swaying on his own doorstep. Sweat dripped down his reddened face, the hair at his temples was plastered to his head, and he literally shook against her.

In one swift move, Temperance elbowed him in his wounded shoulder.

"God's *blood*!" Lord Caire doubled over, choking.

"Send for a doctor," Temperance ordered the butler, who was standing wide-eyed at the door next to another footman. "Lord Caire is ill. And you two"—she jerked her chin at the footmen—"help Lord Caire to his bedroom."

"You," gasped Lord Caire, "are a vindictive harpy, madam."

"No need to thank me," Temperance said sweetly. "I'm merely doing my Christian duty."

The sound he made at her words might've been either a laugh or a grunt of pain; it was hard to tell. In any case, Lord Caire made no more argument as the footmen helped him up the stairs to his room.

Temperance followed behind, and although her motives for making sure that Lord Caire was properly seen to were almost entirely altruistic, she still couldn't help herself from noting his home. The staircase they mounted was marble, but even more grand than the one at Lady Beckinhall's town house. It curved elegantly into the upper floor. Huge portraits of men in armor and haughty women in fabulous jewels lined the walls, their eyes seeming to examine with disapproval her intrusion into this home. Beneath her feet, a lush crimson carpet lined the stairs, cushioning their footsteps. In the upper hallway, life-sized marble statues peered eerily out of niches along the walls. Tall double doors were thrown wide as their procession neared. A slight servant of middling years stood anxiously by as they entered Lord Caire's rooms.

Temperance turned to him as the footmen took Lord Caire to the massive bed in the center of the room. "You're Lord Caire's valet?"

"Yes, ma'am." He looked between her and Lord Caire. "My name is Small."

"Good." Temperance turned to the footmen. "Fetch some water, as hot as possible, and clean cloths, please. Also, a bottle of strong spirits."

The footmen left hurriedly.

"Just let me be, man!" Lord Caire's irritable voice rose from the bed.

Temperance turned to see the valet backing away from his master. Lord Caire sat on the side of the bed, his head hanging, his body listing against the green and brown embroidered bed curtains.

"But, my lord…, " the poor valet protested.

She sighed. What a very exasperating gentleman Lord Caire was!

She advanced on the bed with determination. "Your wound has grown foul, my lord. You must let Small and me help you."

Lord Caire swung his head sideways and glared at her out of the corner of his eye like a wild thing. "I'll let you take care of me, but Small must leave the room. Unless you enjoy an audience?"

"Don't be disgusting," she said, far too gently, as she raised his uninjured arm and drew the coat sleeve off him. She frowned at the stain on his right shoulder. "This will be painful, I'm afraid."

Lord Caire had closed his eyes but he smiled crookedly. "All touch gives me pain. And besides, I have no doubt that any pain you cause me will at least bring you vast amusement."

"What a terrible thing to say." Temperance was unaccountably wounded. "Your pain brings me no joy."

She gently eased the coat sleeve from his shoulder, but despite her efforts, he hissed.

"I'm sorry," she whispered as Small deftly unbuttoned Lord Caire's waistcoat. Caire seemed to have forgotten that he'd ordered the manservant to leave, and she was relieved—undressing him would be hard enough with just the two of them.

"Don't be," Lord Caire murmured. "Pain has always been my friend. It reminds me when I venture too near the edge of reason."

He sounded delirious. Temperance frowned as she examined his shoulder. His wound was seeping and the poisonous fluids had glued his shirt to his body.

She looked up to meet the gaze of the valet. From the man-servant's anxious expression, he'd seen the problem as well.

The footmen returned with the hot water and cloths at that moment, trailed by the short, stout butler.

"Set it there," Temperance directed, pointing to a table by the bed. "Has the doctor been sent for?"

"Yes, ma'am," the butler said in a sonorous voice.

Small cleared his throat, and when Temperance looked at him, he whispered, "We'd best not wait for the doctor, ma'am. He's unreliable after seven of the clock."

Temperance glanced at the elegant gold clock on the bedside table. It was nearing eight at night. "Why not?"

"He drinks," Lord Caire slurred from the bed. "And his hands shake. Don't know if I'd let the blighter near me in that state in any case."

"Well, isn't there another doctor we can send for?" Temperance asked. For goodness' sake! Lord Caire was wealthy. He should have plenty of people to look after him.

"I'll make inquiries, ma'am," the butler said, and left.

Temperance took up one of the clean linens, soaked it in the near-boiling water, and gently placed it on Lord Caire's shoulder.

He jerked as if she'd laid a white-hot poker against his bare skin. "God's blood, madam, do you mean to parboil the flesh from my bones?"

"Not at all," Temperance replied. "We need to loosen your shirt from the wound so we don't tear open the stitches when we remove it."

He swore rather foully.

Temperance chose to ignore that. "Is it true what you said before?"

"What?"

"That all touch pains you?" Terrible of her to take advantage of his condition to quiz him, but she was curious.

He closed his eyes. "Oh, yes."

For a moment, Temperance stared at him, this wealthy, titled aristocrat. How could the touch of another human being possibly hurt him? But perhaps the pain he spoke of wasn't purely physical.

She shook her head and looked at the valet. "Is there anyone we should send for? A relative or a friend of Lord Caire's?"

The valet hummed under his breath and his eyes slid from hers. "Ah...I'm not sure..."

"Tell her, Small," Lord Caire rumbled. His eyes were closed, but his hearing apparently was quite acute.

Small gulped. "No, ma'am."

Temperance frowned, rinsing out the linen and applying it afresh. "I know you're estranged from your mother—"

"No."

She sighed. "Surely there's someone, Caire?"

Both men were silent. Oddly the valet seemed more embarrassed than Lord Caire. Caire merely looked bored.

"What about, er"—Temperance kept her eyes on the hot linen she was holding to his shoulder, the heat rising in her cheeks—"a...a female you might be close to?"

Lord Caire chuckled softly and opened his eyes. They were far too bright. "Small, when was the last time you saw a female other than a maidservant step foot in this house?"

"Never." The valet's eyes were fixed on his shoes.

"You're the first lady to cross my threshold in ten years, Mrs. Dews," Lord Caire drawled. "The last one was my mother, the day I ushered her from my home. On the whole, I think you ought to be flattered, don't you?"

LAZARUS WATCHED AS pink suffused Mrs. Dews's face. The color was becoming, and even in his weakened state, he felt a stirring in his loins, a longing that was more than sexual. For a moment, there seemed to be a twinge in his breast, a strange wish that his life, his person, could in some way be different. That he could somehow deserve a woman such as her.

Mrs. Dews took away the cloth from his shoulder, wrung it out, and replaced it, the sharp sting of the heat rousing him from his reverie. His head ached, his body felt weak and hot, and his shoulder was on fire. He wished to simply lie down and sleep, and if he never awakened... well, would that be such a very great loss to the world?

But Mrs. Dews had no intention yet of letting him escape. "You have no one at all to take care of you?"

She touched, whether by accident or design, his hand, and he felt the familiar burning pain. He kept his hand still only with an effort of will. Perhaps with repeated applications, he might become used to the pain of her touch—like a dog so often cuffed he no longer flinched at the blow. Perhaps he might even come to like the sensation.

Lazarus laughed, or at least tried to. The sound emerged more like a croak. "On my word, Mrs. Dews, no one. My mother and I talk as little as possible, I count but one man I could call a friend, and he and I fell out recently—"

"Who?"

He ignored the question—damned if he'd send for St. John tonight. "And despite your romantic notions, even if I had replaced my mistress, I'd not call her to my sickbed. The ladies I employ thus have other, ah, uses. As I've said before, I do not bring them into my home."

She pressed her lips together at that information.

He eyed her sardonically. "I am at your tender mercy, I fear."

"I see." She frowned down at him as she took off the cloth and tested the shirt beneath.

He hissed as the material pulled away from his wound.

"It has to come off," she murmured to Small, as if Lazarus was an infant they were taking care of between them.

The valet nodded and they took off his shirt—an excruciating operation. By the time they'd finished, Lazarus was panting. He didn't need to look at his bare shoulder to know that the thing was gravely infected. It pulsed and boiled against him.

"Ma'am, the doctor," one of the footmen said from the door.

Behind him the quack swayed, his greasy gray bob wig sliding off the back of his shaved head. "My lord, I came as soon as possible."

"Lovely," Lazarus murmured.

The physician approached the bed with the overly careful gait of a man drunk. "What have we here?"

"His wound—can you help him?" Mrs. Dews began, but the doctor brushed past her to peer closely at the wound.

The stink of cheap wine washed over Lazarus's face.

The doctor straightened abruptly. "What have you done, woman?"

Mrs. Dews's eyes widened. "I...I..."

The doctor snatched the bit of rag she'd been using from her fingers. "Interfering with the natural healing process!"

"But the pus—" Mrs. Dews began.

"*Bonum et laudabile.* Do you know what that means?"

Mrs. Dews shook her head.

"Good and laudable," Lazarus muttered.

"Quite right, my lord. Good and laudable!" the doctor cried, nearly tipping himself over with his vigor. "'Tis well known that the pus is what heals the wound. It must not be interfered with."

"But he is feverish," Mrs. Dews protested.

Lazarus closed his eyes. What mattered the method of physicking as long as it ended soon. He'd let his martyr and the quack argue it out.

"I shall let some blood and thus draw away the heat in his body," the doctor pronounced.

Lazarus opened his eyes to watch as the doctor fished in his bag. He produced a lancet and turned toward Lazarus, holding the sharp instrument in a palsied hand. Lazarus swore, struggling weakly to stand. Bloodletting was one thing, but to allow a drunk to wield a knife against his person was tantamount to suicide.

Damn it, the room was spinning about him. "Send him away."

Mrs. Dews bit her lip. "But..."

"Might as well throw me to the lions yourself as put me in his tender mercies!"

"Now, my lord…" The doctor had turned conciliatory.

Mrs. Dews met Lazarus's eyes, her own worried and unsure.

"Please." He was too weak, too feverish to enforce his will. She had to do it for him. "I'd rather die by your hand than a drunken quack's."

Abruptly she nodded and Lazarus sagged against the bed in relief. Mrs. Dews took the doctor's arm and with a mixture of firmness and bewitching sweetness got the quack out of the room. She handed him over to the butler and then returned to Lazarus's bedside.

"I hope you've made the right decision," she said quietly. "I have no training, only the practical skills of a woman who has taken care of many children."

As he looked into her extraordinary gold-flecked eyes, it occurred to Lazarus that he might very well be entrusting his life to this woman.

He lay back on his bed, his mouth twisted in amused irony. "I have complete faith in you, Mrs. Dews."

And though his words were said in his usual sarcastic tone, he was surprised to discover that they were true.

TEMPERANCE STARED DOWN at Lord Caire's infected shoulder, aware that his avowal of trust had caused sweat to break out along her spine. The last man who'd trusted her had had his faith horribly betrayed.

Now was not the time to think of the past, though. Temperance mentally shook herself. The wound was red and puffy, the edges swollen and inflamed with streaks of red radiating from it.

"Have the footmen bring fresh hot water," she muttered

to the valet as she wrung out the cloth again. This time she placed it directly on the wound. Sometimes the infection could be drawn out by heat.

Lord Caire stiffened at her touch, but otherwise he made no sign that he felt what must be awful pain.

"Why does the touch of others cause you pain?" she asked him softly.

"Might as well ask why a bird is attracted to the sky, madam," he slurred. "It's just the way I am."

"What about when you touch someone else?"

He shrugged. "There is no pain as long as I am the initiator."

"And you were always thus?" She frowned at the cloth, pressing it into the wound. Despite the doctor's philosophy, she'd always followed her mother's teachings on wound healing, and Mama had not liked pus, "bonum" or not.

Caire gasped and closed his eyes. "Yes."

She glanced quickly at his face before taking up the cloth and wiping away the liquid that had oozed from the wound. "You said before that there has never been anyone who didn't cause you pain."

The words were a statement, but she meant them as a question, for she remembered his slight hesitation before.

He was silent as she rinsed the cloth in the lukewarm water and reapplied it. For a moment, she thought he wouldn't speak.

Then he whispered, "I lied. There was Annelise."

Her head jerked up and she stared at him, feeling an odd spike of something that might've been jealousy. "Who is Annelise?"

"Was."

"What?"

He sighed. "Annelise was my younger sister. Five years younger. She took after our father in looks—a plain little thing with mousy brown hair and gray-brown eyes. She used to follow me about even though I told her...I told her..."

His voice trailed away as Small silently replaced the basin of water with a fresh one. Temperance rinsed the cloth in it, the water so hot it reddened her hands. She laid the hot cloth against his wound and pressed, but he seemed not to even notice now.

"What did you tell her?"

"Mmm?" Lord Caire murmured without opening his eyes.

She leaned closer to him, staring at his long nose, his firm, almost cruel mouth. Surely such a sarcastic, nasty man could not be defeated by something as mundane as a putrid wound?

Fear made her belly clench. "Caire!"

"What?" he muttered irritably, half opening his eyes.

She swallowed. "What did you tell Annelise?"

His shook his head against the pillows. "She'd follow me, spy upon me when she thought I wasn't watching, but she was so much younger than me. I always knew. And she would take my hand, even when I told her not to. Told her not to touch me. Yet her touch never hurt...never hurt..."

Temperance reached out and did something she never would have done had he been in his right senses: She gently stroked back his beautiful silver-white hair from his forehead. It was soft, almost silken, beneath her fingers.

"And what did you tell her?"

His sapphire eyes suddenly opened wide, looking as

lucid, as calm, as they had the day before he was hurt. "I told her to go away, and she did. She caught a fever not soon afterward and died. She was five and I was ten. Do not endow me with romantic virtue, Mrs. Dews. I have none."

She held his gaze for a moment, wanting to argue the point, wanting to comfort a little boy who'd lost his younger sister so long ago. But she straightened instead, withdrawing her hand from his hair. "I'm going to bathe your wound with strong spirits. It will hurt a great deal."

He smiled almost sweetly. "Of course."

And somehow, with the help of Small, she accomplished the horrible job. She bathed his wound in brandy, dried it, and dressed it once again, all the while conscious that she was causing him excruciating pain. By the time she'd finished, Lord Caire was breathing heavily under his covers, unconscious. Small looked disheveled, and Temperance was fighting sleep.

"That's done at least," she whispered wearily as she helped the manservant gather the soiled cloths.

"Thank you, ma'am," the little valet said. He darted a worried glance at the bed and its inhabitant. "I don't know what we would've done without you tonight."

"He is something of a handful, isn't he?"

"Indeed, ma'am." The manservant's words were fervent. "Would you like me to have the maids make up a room for you?"

"I should go home." Temperance stared at Lord Caire. His face was still red, and though she'd washed his brow, it was beaded with sweat again.

"If you'll pardon me, ma'am," Small said. "He might need you in the night, and in any case it's very late for a lady to be traveling out alone."

"'Tis, isn't it?" she murmured, grateful for the excuse.

"I'll have Cook make a tray for you," Small said.

"Thank you," Temperance replied as the manservant slipped from the room. She sank into a tall chair pulled close to the bed and propped her head against her fist, meaning to merely rest her eyes while the little valet fetched her supper.

When Temperance next woke, the fire had died low on the grate. Only a single guttering candle on the bedside table gave light to the room. She stretched a little, wincing at the ache in her neck and shoulders from having slept in such an awkward position, and glanced at the bed. Somehow she wasn't surprised to find glittering blue eyes watching her.

"What was he like," Lord Caire asked softly, "your paragon of a husband?"

She knew she should refuse to answer him, that the question was far too personal, but somehow, here in the depths of night, it seemed reasonable and right.

"He was tall, with dark hair," she whispered, remembering that long-ago face. It had been so familiar once and was so faded now. She closed her eyes, concentrating. It seemed so wrong to forget Benjamin and all he was. "His eyes were a lovely dark brown. He had a scar on his chin from a fall as a boy, and he had a way of stretching his fingers and gesturing with his hands when he talked that seemed elegant to me. He was very intelligent, very proper, and very kind."

"How ghastly," he said. "He sounds a prig."

"He wasn't."

"Did he make you laugh?" he asked quietly, his voice roughened from sleep or pain. "Did he whisper things in your ear that made you blush? Did his touch send shivers down your back?"

She inhaled sharply at his rude, too-personal questions.

But he continued, his voice impossibly deep now. "Did you grow wet when he looked at you?"

"Stop it!" she cried, her voice loud in the room. "Please, stop it."

Caire merely watched her, his eyes much too knowing, as if he knew she'd grown wet—but at *his* look, not at the old memories of her husband.

She inhaled. "He was a good man—a wonderful man—and I didn't deserve him."

Lord Caire closed his eyes and for a moment seemed to have fallen asleep. Then he murmured, "I've never been married, but I think it would be quite awful to have to deserve one's spouse."

She looked away from him. This subject made her chest ache, brought a depressing melancholy to her brain.

"Were you in love with him," Lord Caire asked, "this husband you didn't deserve?"

And whether it was because she still half drifted in dreams or because they were curiously intimate in the near dark, she answered truthfully. "No. I loved him, but I was never in love with him."

The room suddenly brightened, all at once it seemed, and she realized that the dawn had arrived unnoticed while they talked.

"It's a new day," Temperance said stupidly.

"Yes, it is," Lord Caire replied, and the satisfaction in his voice made her shiver.

Chapter Eight

Well! This was a very unfortunate turn of events for poor Meg, for the dungeons of King Lockedheart were not very pleasant. The walls dripped with fetid water, and rats and other vermin skittered across the corridors. There was no light and no heat, and in the distance could be heard the cries of the other sad inhabitants of that place. Things looked very desperate, but as Meg had never had it very easy in her life, she resolved to face this crisis with as much bravery as she could summon.
And she vowed as well that whatever happened, she would tell nothing but the truth....
—from King Lockedheart

Temperance rode home in Lord Caire's carriage as the new day dawned on London. She fell asleep during the journey, waking only when the carriage halted at the end of Maiden Lane. In fact, she was so exhausted from tending Caire that the consequences of a night spent away from home never even occurred to her until they descended like a great heavy boulder on her head when she entered the home.

"Where," Concord, her eldest brother, inquired in a deeply disapproving voice, "have you been?"

Perhaps it was unfair to compare Concord to a great boulder, but finding him just inside the foundling home's doorway was something of a shock. He nearly filled the hallway, his displeasure palpable.

"I...uh," Temperance stuttered, not very eloquently.

Concord frowned heavily, his bushy gray and brown eyebrows meeting over his stern nose. "If you were held against your will by this aristocrat Winter has told us about, we will seek reparations."

"We'll beat his bloody face in is what we'll do," Asa, her next eldest brother, growled from behind Concord.

Temperance blinked at the sight of Asa. She hadn't seen him in months. Oh, dear, this was not good. Asa and Concord rarely agreed on anything and, in fact, had made pains to speak to each other as little as possible for years. This morning, however, they stood shoulder-to-shoulder in the narrow foundling home hallway, united in their anger toward Caire—and their unhappiness with her. Concord was the taller of the two, his graying brown hair clubbed back and, like all her brothers, unpowdered.

Asa's hair, in contrast, was a deep golden-brown, the color of a lion, and though he was several inches shorter than Concord, his broad shoulders nearly took up the width of the hall. His shirt and coat strained over his chest as if he did some physical labor every day of his life. Yet no one in the family knew exactly how Asa earned his living, and he was quite vague when asked. Temperance had long suspected that her other brothers feared to press him too closely in case his work was not entirely respectable.

"Lord Caire did not hold me against my will," she said now.

Concord scowled. "Then what were you doing at his house all night?"

"Lord Caire was ill. I merely stayed to help nurse him."

"Ill in what way?" Asa asked.

Temperance glanced down the hallway, toward the kitchen behind her brothers. Where was Winter?

"He had an infection," she said cautiously.

Asa's green eyes sharpened. "An infection of what?"

"A shoulder wound."

Her brothers exchanged a glance.

"And how was he wounded?" Concord rumbled.

Temperance winced. "He was attacked the other night by footpads. One stabbed him in the shoulder."

For a moment, both of her brothers merely stared at her, and then Concord's eyes narrowed. "You spent the night with an aristocrat who gets himself attacked by footpads."

"It was hardly his fault," Temperance protested.

"Nevertheless," Concord began pedantically.

Fortunately, Asa interrupted him. "She looks half dead, Con. Let's continue this discussion in the kitchen."

Concord glared at his younger brother, and Temperance thought he might refuse out of sheer contrariness. Then he pursed his lips. "Very well."

He turned and stomped off down the hall. Asa gestured for Temperance to precede him. His eyes were unreadable. Temperance inhaled, wishing she could have this confrontation when she'd had more sleep.

The foundling home kitchen was usually bustling in

the morning—it was only a little after eight of the clock—but today only a single figure sat at the long table.

Temperance stopped short in the doorway, staring at Winter. "Why aren't you at the school?"

He looked at her, his dark brown eyes shadowed. "I closed the school today after searching all night for you."

"Oh, Winter, I am so sorry." Guilt swept away what little vigor she still had. Temperance sank into one of the kitchen chairs. "I couldn't leave him last night, truly. He had no one to help him."

Concord snorted not very nicely. "An aristocrat? His home wasn't crawling with servants to tend him?"

"There were servants, yes, but no one to ca—" She almost said *care for him,* but at the last second Temperance bit back the words. "No one to take charge."

Asa looked thoughtfully at her, as if he knew the word she'd cut off.

But Concord merely pulled at his chin, a habit he had when distressed. "Why have you sought the company of this man in the first place?"

Her head felt achy and dull. She stared at Winter, trying to think of some probable excuse for her friendship with Lord Caire. But in the end she was simply too tired to prevaricate.

"He took me to a musicale last night," Temperance said. "I wanted to meet someone we could persuade to become a patron for the home. We are in need of funds to continue to keep the home open."

She glanced at Winter as she ended her explanation and saw him close his eyes. Asa's mouth had compressed while Concord was frowning thunderously. There was a heavy silence.

Then Concord spoke. "Why haven't you informed us of your distress?"

"Because we knew you would want to help, brother, even if you could ill afford to do so," Winter said quietly.

"And me?" Asa said softly.

Winter looked at him mutely. Though they had debated asking Concord for help, they had never once discussed going to Asa.

"You never seemed interested in the home," Temperance said softly. "When Father would talk of it, you almost scoffed. How were Winter and I to know that you might help us?"

"Well, I would help you, despite what you think of me, but at the moment I'm somewhat short of funds. In another three months perhaps—"

"We don't have three months," Winter stated.

Asa shook his head, a lock of tawny brown hair falling from his queue, and went to stand by the fire, separating himself from their family as he always seemed to do.

Concord turned back to Winter. "And you allowed this?"

"I did not like it," Winter replied shortly.

"Yet you let our sister whore herself for this home."

Temperance gasped, feeling as if her brother had slapped her across the face. Winter was on his feet, speaking in a grim voice to Concord and Asa was shouting, but all she heard was a muffled roar in her ears. Did Concord truly think her a whore? Was her greatest shame written on her face for all to see? Perhaps that was why Caire had made his suggestive comments. Perhaps he'd seen with one glance that she could be so easily corrupted.

She covered her mouth with a shaking hand.

"Enough!" Asa had raised his voice to flatten his

brothers' argument. "Whether Winter is at fault or not, Temperance is near fainting with fatigue. Let us send her to bed while we discuss this further. Whatever happens, it's obvious that she can no longer see this Lord Caire."

"Agreed," Winter said, though he would not look at Concord.

"Naturally not," her elder brother said ponderously.

Well, this was wonderful—all her brothers were in agreement for once. Temperance almost felt a pang of guilt. "No."

"What?" Asa stared at her.

She rose from the table, placing her palms flat against the surface to steady herself. Any sign of weakness on this point would be fatal. "No, I will not stop seeing Lord Caire. No, I will not give up my search for a patron."

"Temperance," Winter murmured in warning.

"No." She shook her head. "If my reputation has already been compromised as Concord says, then what is the point in giving any of it up? The home needs a patron to survive. You all may protest Lord Caire and my virtue, but you cannot argue that fact. Furthermore, none of you have a solution for the problem, do you?"

She looked from Winter's weary, lined face to Asa's watchful eyes, and finally to Concord's disapproving countenance.

"Do you?" she demanded again softly.

Concord abruptly stamped from the room.

She let out her breath, feeling almost giddy. "That's answer enough, I think. Now, if you'll excuse me, I'm to bed."

She turned to make a grand exit but was stopped by a figure in the doorway.

"Beggin' your pardon, ma'am," Polly muttered.

The wet nurse held a bundle in her arms, and Temperance caught her breath at the sight. No. No, she couldn't take another heartache. Not now.

"Dear God," Temperance breathed. "Is she . . . ?"

"Oh, no, ma'am," the wet nurse said hurriedly. "'Tisn't that at all."

She pulled back a corner of the blanket, and Temperance saw dark blue eyes staring back at her curiously. The relief hit her so hard she hardly heard the wet nurse's words.

"I've come to tell you that Mary Hope is feeding at last," Polly said.

SHE'D BURNED THE joint of beef.

Silence waved a cloth over the smoking meat that night, trying to dispel the acrid odor. Stupid. Stupid. *Stupid.* She should have been more alert to the dinner, instead of staring off into space worrying about their future, hers and William's. Silence bit her lip. The problem was that it was so very hard *not* to think about their troubles.

The door to their rooms swung open and William came in. She looked up eagerly but could see at once that he'd not recovered the shipment. William's face was lined with worry, his complexion gray even with his tan from the sea. His shirt was rumpled, and his neckcloth was askew as if he'd been pulling at it in his agitation. Her husband seemed to have aged years in the last few days.

Silence hastily went to him, taking his cloak and hat and hanging them on a peg by the door. "Will you sit?"

"Aye," William replied absently. He ran his hand over his head, forgetting he wore his wig. He swore an oath he'd normally never utter in her presence, and took the thing off, throwing it to the table.

Silence picked up the wig and carefully draped it over a wooden form on the dresser. "Is there any news?"

"None of use," William muttered. "The two sailors left to guard the ship are missing—either dead or run away with their bribe money."

"I'm sorry." Silence stood uselessly by her husband's side until the stench of burned meat reminded her of the dinner.

Hurriedly she set the table with their pewter plates. At least the bread was fresh from the baker this morning, and the boiled carrots looked appealing. She set out William's favorite pickles and poured his ale before bringing the beef to the table. She carved the small joint and placed some on his plate with nervous trepidation, but he didn't even seem to notice that the meat was charred on the outside while still red inside. Silence sighed. She was such a pitiful cook.

"It was Mickey O'Connor," William muttered suddenly.

Silence looked up. "What?"

"Mickey O'Connor was behind the theft of the cargo."

"But that's wonderful! If you know the thief, surely you can inform a magistrate?"

William laughed, a harsh sound. "None of the London magistrates would dare touch Charming Mickey."

"Why not?" Silence asked, perplexed. "If he's a known thief, surely it is their job to bring him before a court of law?"

"Most magistrates are in the pay of the thieves and other lawbreakers themselves." William stared down at his dinner. "They only bring in the ones too poor to pay their bribes. And the remaining magistrates are so fearful of O'Connor that they'll not risk their lives to bring him in."

"But who is he? Why are the magistrates afraid of him?"

Her husband pushed his plate away untouched. "Charming Mickey O'Connor is the most powerful dock thief in London. He controls the night horsemen—the thieves who steal at night. Every ship that docks in London pays a bribe to Mickey; he calls it a tithe."

"That's blasphemy," Silence whispered, shocked.

William nodded, closing his eyes. "Indeed it is. 'Tis said he lives in a falling-down house in St. Giles, the rooms furnished for a king."

"They call this monster charming?" Silence shook her head.

"He's very handsome and the ladies like him, so 'tis said," William said quietly. "Men who cross Charming Mickey disappear or are found floating in the Thames, a noose about their necks."

"And no one will touch him?"

"No one."

Silence stared at her own plate, no longer hungry. "What shall we do, William?"

"I don't know," her husband replied. "I don't know. The owners are saying now that I must have had a hand in the theft."

"That's ridiculous!" William was one of the most honest men Silence had ever known. "Why are they accusing you?"

He closed his eyes wearily. "I left the ship early the night we docked. Left it with only two guards. They say I must've been bribed to help."

Silence clenched her fists under the table. William had left the ship early to return to her. Guilt made her chest ache.

"They need a scapegoat, I fear," William said heavily. "The owners are talking about prosecuting me for theft."

"Dear God."

"I'm sorry, my dear." William had finally opened his sad green eyes. "I brought this catastrophe upon us."

"No, William. Never." Silence laid her palm on her husband's hand. "This is not your fault."

He laughed again, that horrible croaking sound she was beginning to hate. "I should've put more men on to guard the cargo, should've stayed to make sure the cargo was safe. If not my fault, then whose is it?"

"This Charming Mickey's, that's who," Silence said in sudden anger. "He's the one who makes his living off the backs of honest men. He's the one who stole this cargo out of greed."

William shook his head, withdrawing his hand from hers as he rose from the table. "That may be, but we have no way of seeking redress from the man. He has no care for us or anyone else."

He stood a moment looking at her, and for the first time, Silence saw hopeless despair in his face. "We are doomed, I fear."

He turned and left the room, closing the bedroom door behind him.

Silence stared at the pitiful meal she'd prepared. She wanted to sweep the old dishes, the burnt meat, and mushy carrots to the floor. She wanted to scream and cry, to pull at her hair and let the world know her despair. But she didn't do any of that. None of those actions would help the man she loved. If William was correct, no one she knew could help them. She and William were on their own. And if she couldn't find a way to get the cargo back from Charming Mickey, then William would either die in prison or be hanged as a thief.

Silence squared her shoulders. She would never let that happen.

IT TOOK A week for Lazarus to recover from his wound. At least it was a week until he felt well enough to seek out Mrs. Dews. He'd been out of bed for days before that, but he was damned if he'd let the little martyr see him so weak again. So he'd bided his time, patiently eating the pap Small insisted was fit for the sickroom. Another doctor was called for, but Lazarus shouted at him when the quack started mumbling about bloodletting. The man beat a hasty retreat, but not before leaving a bottle of noxious liquid "medicine." Lazarus threw the bottle out, uncaring that he'd no doubt be billed for the elixir later.

He spent the rest of his confinement chafing at the delay in seeing Mrs. Dews again. Somehow the woman had crept into his blood as surely as the poison from his wound. During the day, he reviewed conversations they'd had, remembering the look of hurt in her gilded eyes when he'd said something particularly crass. The pain he'd caused her provoked a strange tenderness. He wanted to heal the hurt and then hurt her again just to make it better. It was impossible to keep thoughts of her gentleness, her wit, and her acerbity from his mind. His dreams at night were far more basic. Even with his illness, he woke each morning with the flesh between his legs straining for her.

Perhaps he should've let the quack bleed him. Perhaps

then his body would rid itself of not only the poison, but also of Mrs. Dews.

He considered abandoning her help and not seeing her again, but the thought was fleeting. On the night Small deemed him recovered, Lazarus prowled the alley behind the foundling home.

He'd not sent word ahead for her to expect him, and he felt an uncharacteristic uncertainty of his reception. The night was dark and cold, the wind blowing his cloak about his legs. Lazarus hesitated in the fetid alley. He laid a hand against the wood of the kitchen door as if in this way he could feel the woman within.

Nonsense.

He contemplated stealing in as he had before, but in the end, prudence made him rap sharply on the door. It was thrown almost immediately open. Lazarus stared down into light brown eyes gilded with golden stars. Mrs. Dews looked startled, as if she'd not expected him at the door, and indeed her hair was down about her shoulders, curling damply in the heat of the kitchen.

"You were washing your hair," he said stupidly. The thought of such a mundane intimacy stirred a longing not only at his groin but in his chest as well.

"Yes." Pink was suffusing her cheeks.

"It's beautiful," he said, because her hair *was* beautiful, thick and nearly to her waist. It waved and curled with reckless abandon. How she must hate that.

"Oh." She glanced down and then over her shoulder. "Won't you come in?"

His lips twitched in amusement at her unease, but he said as gently as was possible for him, "Thank you."

The foundling home kitchen was humid and hot

tonight. The fire was banked below a blackened kettle. Mrs. Dews's regular acolyte, Mary Whitsun, frowned at him over a basin of water at the table, while beside her stood a small boy. A plump young woman with a cheery red face and white-blond hair sat in the corner nursing a tiny infant. She looked up at his entrance and casually pulled a scarf over her exposed breast.

"This is Polly, our wet nurse," Temperance said distractedly. "She brought Mary Hope and her children to spend the night."

"Thought it best since they're holding a wake in the rooms next to mine," Polly said. "It can get a bit loud and wild."

"Pleased to meet you, ma'am." Lazarus inclined his head. He eyed the kicking infant. "The babe is better, then?"

"Oh, she's doing lovely, sir, that she is."

"I'm glad to hear it."

Lazarus propped himself against a wall, watching as Mrs. Dews and the girl cleared the table. While their backs were turned, the boy inched closer. His face was freckled, and to Lazarus's unskilled eye, he looked a bit of a rapscallion.

"That's a big stick," the boy observed.

"It's a sword stick," Lazarus said cordially. He twisted the head and withdrew the sharp sword.

"Coo!" the boy exclaimed. "Have yer killed anyone with it?"

"Dozens," Lazarus said loftily. He pushed the image of the noseless attacker's staring, dead eyes out of his mind. "I prefer to first disembowel them and then chop off their heads."

"Arr!" the boy said.

Lazarus chose to take the odd syllable as a mark of high esteem.

"Lord Caire!" Mrs. Dews had evidently overheard the last of their exchange.

"Yes?" Lazarus widened his eyes in innocence.

The boy saw fit to giggle.

Mrs. Dews sighed.

Polly pulled the baby from under her scarf. "Can you hold her a moment, ma'am, while I set myself to rights?"

The wet nurse held out the sleeping babe, but Mrs. Dews quickly backed away. "Mary Whitsun can take her."

The girl accepted the baby without hesitation. Neither she nor Polly seemed to think Mrs. Dews's actions were unusual, but Lazarus watched her speculatively.

Polly straightened her clothing and stood. "I'll take Mary Hope now. She's due for a nap, I'm thinking."

So saying, she carried the babe from the kitchen.

Mrs. Dews nodded at Mary Whitsun. "Please tell Mr. Makepeace that I intend to go out tonight—and take Joseph Tinbox with you."

Both children obediently left the room.

"You never informed your brother of your intentions before." Lazarus prowled to the fireplace and glanced inside the kettle there. A puddle of some type of soup sputtered at the bottom.

"How do you know that?" she asked from behind him.

He turned in time to watch her stroke a comb through that wonderful hair. "You never invited me in before."

She opened her mouth, but at that moment, Winter Makepeace strode into the room. He didn't seem surprised to see Lazarus, but the sight didn't bring him any joy either.

"Mind you take your pistol," he told his sister.

Mrs. Dews nodded, not looking at Makepeace. "I'll just put up my hair."

She slipped from the room.

The brother was suddenly beside Lazarus. "I would have you make sure that nothing happens to her."

Lazarus arched his brows at the order from the younger man. "Your sister has never been hurt in my company."

Makepeace grunted, looking sour. "Well, see to it that your luck continues. Temperance needs to be home before first light of day."

Lazarus inclined his head. He had no intention of keeping Mrs. Dews out in St. Giles any longer than necessary.

She reappeared at that moment, her hair safely confined and hidden under a white cap. She looked sharply between Lazarus and her brother, and he could only hope the younger man had wiped the expression of animosity from his face.

"I'm ready," she said, and took up a cloak.

Lazarus glided to her side and plucked the ragged thing from her fingers. He held it out. She looked at him uncertainly before donning the garment. Lazarus opened the door.

"Be careful," Makepeace called behind them.

The night was damp, a grimy mist immediately slicking his face. Lazarus pulled his cloak about his shoulders. "Stay close to me. No doubt your brother would have me drawn and quartered should I bring you back with even a hair on your head misplaced."

"He worries for me."

"Mmm." Lazarus glanced around and then down at her. "As do I. That attack we suffered last time was apurpose."

Her gold-flecked eyes widened. "You're sure?"

He shrugged and began walking. "I saw one of the

assassins at Mother Heart's-Ease's shop. That's quite a coincidence."

She stopped suddenly, making him stop as well or risk outpacing her. "But that means someone tried to kill you!"

"Yes, it does." He hesitated and then said slowly, "Twice now, I think. The night we first met, I was attacked by what I thought was a common footpad."

"The man we saw you kneeling over!"

"Yes." He looked at her. "Now I wonder if he was after my life instead of my purse."

"Dear God." She looked down at her toes thoughtfully. "If the man without a nose was at Mother Heart's-Ease's, then it stands to reason that the murderer was there as well."

He inclined his head, watching her.

She met his eyes, her own fearless. "Then we should return to Mother Heart's-Ease and see if she knows the man."

"That is my hope," he said as he set out again. "But I want to impress upon you the seriousness of this business. Before, I merely had to deal with the everyday dangers of St. Giles. Now it seems I may actually have caught the attention of a ruthless murderer." He glanced sideways at her. "If you wish to quit this hunt, Mrs. Dews, I will still honor my side of the bargain."

The hood of her cloak obscured most of her profile, but he could still see her lips purse primly. "I'll not renege on our bargain."

He leaned over her, bending his head to hers. "Then you had better stay close to my side."

"Humph." She looked up at him, and he saw that her eyebrows were knit. "Who had you spoken to the night we met—the night you were first attacked?"

"One of Marie's neighbors, a prostitute." His lips twisted. "Or at least I'd tried to talk to her. The woman slammed her door in my face, once she found out what I sought."

"I don't understand."

"What?"

"They must be linked somehow—the prostitute and Mother Heart's-Ease's gin shop, but I don't see how."

He shrugged. "Perhaps it's only the area—the murderer found out I was questioning Marie's neighbor and also knew I'd questioned Mother Heart's-Ease."

She shook her head. "He'd have to be very quick to take fright, then, if he sent an assassin after you merely for asking questions. No, I think you must've found something out."

She looked at him in question.

"If I did, I don't know what it is myself." He laughed a little grimly.

They walked the rest of the way to Mother Heart's-Ease's shop in silence. Lazarus kept an alert eye out but saw no followers unless one counted a mangy cur, mostly skin and bones, that shadowed them for a minute or more.

When he ducked into the low doorway of the gin shop, the heat and smell hit Lazarus in the face. He caught Mrs. Dews's arm, scanning the crowded room. A fire roared on the hearth in the back, and a group of sailors were singing drunkenly at one long table. The one-eyed barmaid scurried between tables, avoiding all eyes, especially his own. Mother Heart's-Ease was not in sight.

Mrs. Dews tugged at his arm and stood on tiptoe to shout in his ear over the noise of the room. "Give me some coins."

He looked at her, his eyebrow arched, and then took out

his purse and shook some shillings into her hand. She nodded and without a word began weaving her way through the throng, patiently stalking the barmaid. Lazarus wasn't about to leave her side in this company. He trailed behind, watching her movements, glaring when a sailor tried to catch her hand.

Mrs. Dews finally ran the one-eyed barmaid to ground near the fireplace. The girl reluctantly turned, looking a bit more interested when Mrs. Dews pressed a coin into her palm. There was a whispered conferral and the barmaid slipped away.

Mrs. Dews turned back to Lazarus. "She says that Mother Heart's-Ease is in the back room."

Lazarus glanced at the curtained doorway. "Then let's seek her out."

He lifted the curtain and led the way. Behind the door was a short, dark passageway. A young man leaned against the wall, cleaning his fingernails with the wickedly pointed tip of a knife.

He didn't bother glancing up at their entrance. "This 'ere's private like. Go on back to th' bar."

"I wish to speak to Mother Heart's-Ease," Lazarus said evenly.

The man wasn't very big, but he looked like he might be quick. Before he could reply, Mother Heart's-Ease opened a door behind him. A young girl slipped out, tottering on her heeled slippers. She glanced at the guard dismissively but slowed when she saw Lazarus. He turned sideways to let her pass, and she thanked him with a cheeky grin and a wink. He was quite sure that had he shown any sign of interest, she'd be amenable to a quick tête-à-tête in a corner of the gin shop. He shot a glance at Mrs. Dews and was unsurprised to see her lips pursed primly.

"Mrs. Dews," Mother Heart's-Ease called from her door. "'Aven't you enough to busy yourself with at that little home you run? 'Tis twice now in but a fortnight you've visited my part of St. Giles. And with Lord Caire, I see. I wasn't expectin' you back, m'lord."

Lazarus smiled. "Because you thought I would be killed at Martha Swan's house?"

The woman tilted her head and smiled coquettishly—a rather repulsive sight. "I'd 'eard you met with some trouble there. Poor Martha Swan! It's dangerous, walking the streets."

"Then you don't find it suggestive that she was gutted in the same way as Marie Hume?"

She shrugged bony shoulders as wide as a man's. "Many a lass 'as come to a bad end in St. Giles."

For a moment, Lazarus studied the old bawd. She was undoubtedly playing some kind of game, but whether it was for money, simply to protect her own mysterious interests, or because she had a more sinister intent, he wasn't sure. "Be that as it may, the man who attacked me was sitting in your gin house the night I came to question you. He wore a patch over his nose."

She nodded. "Aye, I've seen 'im about."

"Do you know who might've hired him to kill me? Who doesn't want Marie Hume's killer to be found?"

"Kill you?" She hawked and spat into the filthy straw on the floor. "Look 'ere, it's not my business what folk do after they leave my place. 'E probably caught sight of that purse you were wavin' about that night and thought you were a soft mark."

"Do you know if he has any friends? Men he drank with?"

"Don't know, don't care." She shrugged again and turned away. "I 'ave a business to run, my lord."

Lazarus watched as she shut the door behind her. Mother Heart's-Ease had seemed eager enough for his payment the first night they'd come, but tonight she'd not even hinted at money. Was she afraid? Had someone warned her off?

Mrs. Dews sighed beside him. "That's it, then. I don't think she'll tell you more."

The young man who had been leaning against the wall all this time cleared his throat. Lazarus looked at him, but the boy's eyes were on Mrs. Dews. "You want to know about Marie Hume?"

His mouth barely moved, his words all but inaudible. Still Mrs. Dews nodded silently and placed the rest of the coins Lazarus had given her into the man's hand.

"There's a house in Running Man Courtyard. D'you know it?"

Mrs. Dews stiffened, but she nodded.

"Ask for Tommy Pett and *don't* tell anyone where you got 'is name. Understand?"

"I do." Mrs. Dews turned and left the back hall.

Lazarus waited until they'd climbed the stairs and walked into the cold night air. "You know the way to this Running Man Courtyard?"

She pressed her lips together as if not well pleased. "Yes."

Lazarus glanced up and down the dark street. "Do you know that young man? Can we trust him?"

"I don't know. I've never met him before." Mrs. Dews

pulled her cloak about her shoulders. "Do you think it's a trap?"

"Or a wild-goose chase." Lazarus frowned. "Mother Heart's-Ease may've ordered him to whisper that information to us."

"Why would she do that?"

"I don't know, damn it." He blew out a breath. "That's the problem. I don't know the players in any of this. I'm too much the outsider."

"Well, if it helps, I thought his fear of her overhearing him was genuine."

Lazarus felt a sudden smile tug at his lips. He bowed low, sweeping his hat from his head. "In that case, Mrs. Dews, lead on."

She almost smiled—he would've sworn it on his life—but she schooled her expression and set off, walking briskly, her shoes echoing off the cobblestones. Lazarus trailed close behind, keeping an alert eye out. The mist furled about the corners of buildings and dimmed what lanterns had been set out. This would be a good night for an ambush, he thought grimly.

"When I returned from your house last week, I was met by my elder brothers," she said suddenly. Her head was turned away, so he could not read her face.

"What did they say?"

"That they didn't want me to go with you, of course."

"And yet here you are." They rounded a corner into a wider street. "Should I be flattered?"

"No," she said shortly. "I do this for the home, nothing else."

"Oh, naturally."

A party of three men staggered out of a doorway farther

down the street, obviously drunk. Lazarus reached forward and pulled her back toward him, ignoring her squeak of surprise. He halted in the shadows and wrapped her in his cloak until she was nearly hidden.

Lazarus bent his head to murmur in her ear, "The sad thing about being virtuous is that when one tries to lie, it doesn't work very well."

She opened her mouth and he caught the glint of anger in her eye, but the drunkards were passing by.

"Hush," he breathed across her ear. This close, he could smell the sweet herbs she'd used when she washed her hair. He wanted to draw her even closer, to press her hips to his, to lick that delicate ear.

But the toughs had passed them by and he let her go instead.

She immediately leapt back and glared up at him. "I have no desire to be with you. I only do this for the home and the children."

"How very noble, Mrs. Dews. You sound quite the saint." He felt himself smile, not very pleasantly. "Will you tell me now what this house is in Running Man Courtyard?"

"It's Mrs. Whiteside's house," she muttered before turning quickly and marching off.

Lazarus felt his eyebrows wing up in honest surprise as he hurried to catch up to his guide. This should be very interesting, indeed.

For Mrs. Whiteside ran the most notorious brothel in St. Giles.

Chapter Nine

*Very early the next morning, Meg was roused from
her sleep by four burly guards. They hustled her up
a winding staircase until she was once again in the
king's room. He sat sprawled on a golden throne,
his black beard and hair shining in the morning
sunlight. Before him were several dozen guards
standing at attention in strict rows.*

*"There you are!" the king snapped. "Now, then,
I shall prove to you my people's love." He turned
to the assembled guards. "My guards, do you
love me?"*

*"Aye, sire!" cried the guards with one strong voice.
King Lockedheart smirked at Meg. "You see? Admit
now your folly and I might grant you your life."...*
—from *King Lockedheart*

Temperance felt her cheeks heat as she continued walking. She knew about most of the houses of ill repute in St.
Giles—they were where many of her charges came from,
after all—but she'd never set foot in one after dark. And

Mrs. Whiteside's house was rather notorious for the types of amusements one could find there.

"Ah," Lord Caire murmured from behind her. "I believe I have knowledge of this place."

She bit her lip. "Then perhaps you have no further need of me tonight."

He caught hold of her suddenly, making her gasp. "You swore you would not renege on our compact, Mrs. Dews."

She frowned, truly puzzled. "And I won't, but—"

"Then lead on."

Temperance gathered the edges of her cloak together and did just that. The wind was bitter tonight, numbing her cheeks. She didn't know what to make of this man anymore. He'd teased and kissed her, probed for her most shameful secret, and then held her against his warm body to shield and protect her. She still trembled from the scent of his throat, the steel of his arms.

They crossed into another alley, this one smaller. Signs swung overhead, creaking in the wind. She heard laughter, sudden and close, and then it moved away. They passed a thin woman in a worn cloak carrying something in a bucket. The woman avoided their eyes as she hurried past. The alley widened abruptly into a courtyard with overhanging upper floors, making the square space seem close and cramped. Light flickered behind the shutters on each floor, and odd, muffled sounds leaked through—a cutoff laugh, a muttered word, rhythmic banging, and what sounded like moans.

Temperance shuddered. "This is Mrs. Whiteside's establishment."

"Stay close to me," Lord Caire murmured before raising his stick to knock upon the only door in the courtyard.

It swung open to reveal a hulking guard, his broad, plain face marked with pox scars. His narrow little eyes showed no expression. "Boy or girl?"

"Neither," Lord Caire said smoothly. "I wish to speak to Tommy Pett."

The man began to close the door.

Lord Caire stuck his stick in the doorway with one hand and pressed his palm flat against the door with the other. The door halted, causing the guard to look faintly surprised.

"Please," Lord Caire said with a hard smile.

"Jacky," a deep voice rasped from behind the guard. "Let me see our visitor."

The guard stepped aside. Lord Caire entered immediately, pulling Temperance behind him. She peered around his shoulder.

The hall inside was a small, square space, hardly big enough for the stairs leading to the upper levels. Immediately to the right was an open door that revealed a neat sitting room beyond. In the doorway was a woman in a pink satin gown, strewn with ribbons and bows. Her head barely came past Caire's waist, and her body was thick and squat, her brow heavy and deformed.

She flicked clever eyes at Caire. "Lord Caire. I've often wondered when you might visit our house."

Lord Caire bowed. "Am I speaking to Mrs. Whiteside?"

The dwarf threw back her head and laughed in a voice as deep as a man's. "Dear me, no. I am merely an employee of that lady. You may call me Pansy."

Lord Caire nodded. "Mistress Pansy. I would be very grateful for a moment's conversation with Tommy Pett."

"Why, may I ask?"

"He has some information I need."

Pansy pursed her lips and cocked her head. "Why not? Jacky, go and see if Tommy is free."

The guard lumbered off and Pansy gestured to the sitting room behind her. "Will you sit, my lord?"

"Thank you."

They entered the little sitting room, and Lord Caire sank into a worn velvet settee, pulling Temperance down beside him. Across from them was a wide, low chair padded in sumptuous purple and pink. Pansy hitched one hip up and hopped backward into the chair. Her feet, shod in elegant heeled slippers, dangled inches from the floor.

She laid her pudgy hands on the chair's arms and looked at Caire with a smile playing about her mouth. "You really ought to stop awhile with us, my lord, after you finish your business with my boy Tommy. I can offer you a special price."

"I thank you, no," Caire said with no inflection in his voice.

Pansy cocked her head. "We make a specialty of providing for the, ah, unusual requirements of gentlemen such as yourself. And, of course, your friend may participate as well."

Temperance's eyes widened as Pansy tilted her chin at her. She had no idea what Caire's *unusual requirements* were, but she knew she should be disgusted at the mere suggestion that she would indulge in them with him. Except she was still trying to figure out her feelings when a pretty young man entered the room. He was slim with golden hair that fell in silken waves to his shoulders. He hesitated inside the doorway, eyeing Lord Caire uneasily.

Pansy smiled at him. "Tommy, this is Lord Caire. I believe—"

Whatever Mistress Pansy had been about to say was cut short by Tommy darting from the room. Lord Caire surged off the settee, flying after the boy silently. There was a scuffling sound in the hall, a thump and a curse, and then Lord Caire reentered the room, holding Tommy firmly by the collar of his coat.

"All right! All right!" the boy panted. "You got me fair and square. Let me go an' I'll talk."

"I think not," Lord Caire drawled. "I'd rather keep a firm grip on you while you talk."

Pansy had watched this byplay with narrowed but unsurprised eyes. She stirred now. "Tommy's night isn't over yet, my lord. I do hope you'll bear that in mind when you handle him? His price goes down if he's bruised."

"I have no intention of hurting your employee as long as he tells me what I want to know," Lord Caire said.

"And what is that?" the dwarf asked softly.

"Marie Hume," Lord Caire said. "What do you know about her death?"

For a boy who made his living in a St. Giles brothel, Tommy was a terrible liar. He looked away, licked his lips, and said, "Nothing."

Temperance sighed. Even she could see that Tommy had some knowledge of Lord Caire's mistress's death.

Lord Caire merely shook the boy. "Try again."

Pansy raised her eyebrows. "I'm afraid your use of Tommy's time is costing me revenue, Lord Caire."

Without a word, Lord Caire reached into his coat pocket and withdrew a small purse. He tossed it at Pansy and she caught it deftly. After peering inside, she closed the purse again and hid it on her person.

She nodded at Tommy. "That'll do nicely. Now talk to the gentleman, my lamb."

Tommy sagged in Lord Caire's grip. "I don't know anything. She was dead when I found her."

Temperance looked quickly at Lord Caire at this news, but if he was surprised to hear that Tommy, not Martha Swan, had found Marie, he gave nothing away.

"Were you the first to find her dead?" Lord Caire asked.

Tommy shot him a confused look. "Weren't no one else there, if that's what you're asking."

"When did you find her?"

Tommy screwed up his face. "It was a while back— two months or more."

"What day?"

"Saturday." Tommy darted a look at Pansy. "Saturday morn is my day off."

"And what time did you arrive at Marie's rooms?"

Tommy shrugged. "Maybe nine of the clock? Or ten? Before noon anyway."

Lord Caire shook him again. "Describe it."

Tommy licked his lips, glancing at Pansy as if for permission. The little woman nodded her head.

He sighed. "Her rooms were on the second floor at the back of the house. 'Twern't no one about when I went to climb the stairs, save a charwoman scrubbing the front step. I was going to knock at her door—Marie's—but it gave under my hand. It wasn't latched, so I went in. The front room was neat as a pin; Marie liked to keep her things orderly, but the bedroom…"

Tommy halted his narrative, staring at the floor. He gulped visibly. "There was blood all about. On the walls and floor and even the ceiling. Lord, I've never seen such blood in my life. Her mattress was black with it and Marie…"

"What about Marie?" Lord Caire's voice was soft, but Temperance didn't mistake it for gentleness or pity.

"She were slit open," Tommy said. "From throat to her privates. I could see her insides peeking out like gray snakes."

He gulped once more, his face having turned ashen. "I cast up what I had inside me then, all over the floor. Couldn't help it. The smell was that terrible."

"And what did you do then?" Lord Caire asked.

"Why, I ran from the room," Tommy said, but his eyes slid away again.

Lord Caire shook him. "You never thought to search the room? She had jewels—a diamond hair pin and pearl earrings—as well as diamond chip buckles for her shoes and a garnet ring."

"I never—" Tommy began, but Lord Caire shook him so hard he couldn't speak.

"Tommy, my darling lamb." Pansy sighed. "Answer Lord Caire truthfully or I won't have any use for you."

Tommy hung his head sullenly. "She didn't need them no more. She was dead right enough. And if I'd left them there, they would've just been stole by her landlord. I had more right to them than anyone."

"Why is that?" Temperance asked.

Tommy lifted his head, staring at her as if seeing her for the first time. "Why? Because I was her brother."

Temperance glanced at Lord Caire. He was expressionless, but he'd frozen as if in surprise. She returned her attention to Tommy. "You were Marie Hume's brother."

"Aye, haven't I just said so," the boy sputtered. "Had the same mother, we did, though Marie was ten or more years older than me."

Temperance frowned. She caught a fleeting glance between Lord Caire and Pansy. Something didn't make any sense. She felt like she was missing some information that everyone else had in the room. "Then you knew her well?"

Tommy shrugged uncomfortably. "Fairly well, I guess."

"Did she have any other visitors other than Lord Caire and yourself?" Temperance asked.

"As to that, I don't know," Tommy said slowly. "I saw her but once a week."

Temperance leaned forward. "But surely you talked about each other's lives? She must have told you about her days?"

The boy looked at his toes. "Mostly I asked for money from her."

Temperance blinked, appalled at his lack of fraternal love. She would've thought that the boy was prevaricating to avoid giving more information were he not such a terrible liar.

"Can you guess who might've killed her?" Lord Caire asked suddenly.

The boy's eyes widened. "She was tied to the bed, her arms stretched above her head, her legs spread apart, and her face was covered with a hood. I knew at once who had killed her."

Lord Caire stared down at the boy. "Who?"

Tommy smiled, but somehow his lips twisted in a way that took away all his beauty. "Why, you, my lord. Isn't that how you liked to enjoy my sister?"

LAZARUS STARED AT the pretty boy. Truly he hadn't expected this charge—although he should have. He let the boy go, careful to keep from glancing at Mrs. Dews. What would she make of the boy's revelation? What *could* she make of it, other than horror and disgust?

"I have no further need of you," he said, dismissing the boy.

A look of disappointment crossed Tommy's face. No doubt he'd expected an argument or even flustered denials.

Damned if Lazarus would give the boy that.

Tommy glanced at Mistress Pansy. She nodded at him, her odd face expressionless, and Tommy left.

When the door had closed behind the boy, she turned to Lazarus. "Is that all?"

"No." He crossed to the small fireplace and stared into the flames, trying to think. This was a dead end in his investigations. If the boy—Marie's brother, of all people—didn't know who'd killed her, where could he turn now? He absently twisted his stick in his fist. And then the realization dawned. He knew he hadn't tied Marie up in such a manner; therefore, some other man had—a man who in this, at least, shared his proclivities.

He turned to Mistress Pansy. "You said this establishment catered to the whims of men like me."

The little woman raised her dark eyebrows. "Yes, of course. Would you like to see a selection of our wares?"

He was aware that Mrs. Dews had drawn in her breath

sharply. Though he still hadn't looked at her, he knew she stood as if frozen in a corner of the room. Perhaps she was frozen in disgust.

He shook his head. "No. What I want is information."

Mistress Pansy cocked her overlarge head, her eyes intelligent and sparkling now with the possibility of profit. "What kind of information, my lord?"

"I want to know the names of the men who like to use the ties and hood."

She stared at him, her dark eyes considering. Then she abruptly shook her head. "You know I can't give out the names of our customers."

He took out a purse from his pocket—larger than the one he'd given her before—and tossed it to the table at her elbow. "There's fifty pounds in there."

She raised her eyebrows and picked up the purse, spilling it into her lap to count the coins one by one. She paused when she was finished as if considering; then she put them back into the purse and tucked it into her bosom.

She sat back in her low, wide chair and looked at him. "Some gentlemen find it enjoyable to watch the play of others."

He cocked an eyebrow, waiting.

"Perhaps you'd like to indulge?"

Lazarus nodded once, his pulse speeding.

Pansy raised her voice. "Jacky!"

The lackey appeared at the door.

She gestured with her fingers. "Please take this gentleman to the peepholes. I think you'll be most interested in room six, Lord Caire."

Jacky turned without a word, and Lazarus strode over to grasp Mrs. Dews's wrist.

She pulled against him, but he held her firm as he hauled her to the door. "What are you doing? I have no wish to see any 'play.'"

"I can't leave you alone," he growled under his breath. It was the truth, but not quite all of it. He wanted to show her what lurked deep within his soul. She'd be repulsed by his truth, he knew that, but he had a morbid urge to find out for himself what her reaction would be. To lay his secrets bare before her and await her sentence.

Jacky led them up the narrow wooden stairs to a dim hallway above. Doors lined the hall, each marked with a crudely carved number. But instead of entering one, the man led them to the end of the hall to an unmarked door.

Jacky opened the lock with a key and gestured them inside. "Go to th' end and turn. One hour. No more."

And he closed the door behind them.

Mrs. Dews started against Lazarus, and he could feel the tremble of her body. He bent to whisper in her ear, "Hush. The door is unlocked. We may leave whenever we wish."

"Then let's go at once," she hissed back.

"No." His heart was beating fast, and he tightened his grip on her wrist.

They were in a low, narrow passage. He felt with his hand along one wall as he obeyed Jacky's instructions to go to the end. The passage made an abrupt turn here, and he squinted down it. At first it had seemed pitch-black, but as his eyes adjusted, he could make out tiny pinpricks of light at regular intervals along one wall. He neared the first and saw it was a peephole. Underneath, just visible in the light from the room beyond, was the number nine.

Mrs. Dews tugged on his wrist. "Please let us go."

He glanced through the peephole and turned to her, drawing her close. "No. Take a look."

She shook her head, but her resistance was weak as he guided her to the wall. He knew the moment she saw what was within, for her whole body went taut. She faced the wall, away from him, and he moved behind her.

He bent his head close to her ear. "What do you see?"

She trembled but was mute.

Not that he needed her words to know what was in the room beyond. He'd seen it all when he'd looked: a man and a woman, the man entirely naked, the woman still wearing a chemise. The woman knelt at the man's feet, his tool between her lips.

"Do you like it?" he whispered. "Does it arouse you?"

He felt her tremble against him, a hare within the hawk's grasp. She was so proper on the surface, but he knew, in a part of him beyond mind and spirit, that she had carnal depths that she struggled to hide. He wanted to explore those depths. Bring them to the light of day and revel in them. They were as much a part of her as the gold flecks in her eyes, and he longed to feast upon her cravings.

"Come, let us see what else there is to see." He took her hand, less resisting now, and led her to the second peephole. A quick glance proved the room was empty.

But the next certainly was not.

"Look," he murmured, pressing her to the wall with his body. "What do you see?"

She shook her head, but she whispered nonetheless, "He's...taking her from behind."

"Like a stallion covering a mare," he said low, his body hard against hers.

She nodded jerkily.

"Do you like it?"

But she refused to reply to that.

He drew her away, checking at the next little hole, the one Mistress Pansy had sent them to view. The sight within made him swallow convulsively. He turned and guided Mrs. Dews to the hole without a word. He knew the moment she understood. Her body stilled and the hand clutching his squeezed hard.

He moved behind her, covering and pressing her to the wall so that there was no escape possible. She was warm and soft beneath his larger body.

"What do you see?" he breathed against her ear.

She shook her head, but he took both her hands, spreading them wide against the wall, his own hands covering hers. He felt his cock, thick and throbbing, pressing against the fall of his breeches, pressing into her soft backside.

"Tell me," he demanded.

Her swallow was audible in the quiet of the dark passage. "The woman is beautiful. She has red hair and white skin."

"And?"

"And she's naked and tied to the bed."

"How?" He smoothed his mouth against her neck. Her scent was strong this close, the scent of a woman. He wished he could cast off the plain white cap she wore, tear the pins from her hair, and bury his face in her tresses. "Tell me how."

"Her hands are above her head, tied together to the top of the bed." Her voice was throaty, low and sensuous. "Her legs are spread apart, her ankles tied to the posts at the end of the bed. She's quite naked and her...her..." She gulped, unable to voice the word.

"Her cunny?" he drawled against her cheek. His hips surged instinctively against her at the word, as if seeking out that part of her.

"Yes, that. She's completely exposed." She whimpered as he licked the side of her throat.

"And?" he prompted.

"Oh!" She took a breath as if to steady herself. "She has a scarf tied over her eyes."

"The man?"

"He's tall and dark, and he's completely dressed; even his wig is still in place."

He smiled against her skin, grinding his hips into her bottom. He would raise her skirt right now, seek that soft, wet place at her center, if he was not sure it would draw her from her trance.

"What is he doing?" He bit gently on her ear.

She gasped. "He's kneeling between her legs and he's—Oh, God!"

He chuckled darkly. "He's worshipping her cunny, isn't he? He's tonguing her, kissing her, licking right through her pink lips, tasting her essence."

She moaned and pressed back against him—but not in escape. Her bottom rubbed his hard cock, and triumph leapt within him.

He tongued her ear, licking around the delicate outer edge. "Would you like that? Would you like my mouth against your center, my tongue against your bud? I'd lick you there, tasting you, savoring you, until you bucked beneath me, but I wouldn't let you go. I'd hold you down, your thighs widespread, your cunny open to me, and I'd lick you until you came over and over."

She struggled against him then, half turning in his

grasp, and he bent and kissed her hard, his mouth grinding hers open, thrusting his tongue into her mouth as savagely as he wanted to thrust his cock into her body. God! He was in danger of coming in his breeches, and he didn't give a damn. She was finally breaking, his little martyr, and her surrender was sweeter than any honey.

He jammed his leg between hers, high so that she was forced to ride him. He caught at her skirts, yanking them up, his entire being on but one goal. He no longer cared where they were, who she was, and who he was and his own damnable past. All he wanted was her warm, wet flesh around him. Now.

But she dug her nails into his hair and pulled suddenly, surprising an exclamation of pain from him.

It was all she needed. She darted, a fleeing hare before a hawk, wildly dashing down the dark corridor.

HE'D BEWITCHED HER.

Temperance panted as she rounded the corner of the dark passage. Panic was a live thing in her throat, fluttering and threatening to choke off her air. To drive reason itself from her mind.

How had he known? Was her shame a blaze upon her face for all men to see? Or was he a wizard who could discern the sensual weaknesses of women? For she'd been weakened. Her legs had quivered under him; her center had turned liquid with shameful want. She'd gazed through that awful peephole and described the scene within, and dear God, she'd *liked* it. The terrible words he'd whispered in her ear as he thrust against her bottom had left her hot and lusting. She'd wanted him to mount her like a rutting stallion in the sordid little passage of a brothel.

Perhaps she'd already lost her mind.

The door to the outer hallway was unlocked. It sprang open at her touch, and then she was flying down the stairs, the heavy tread of Lord Caire's boots right behind her. She made the square little hall and heard him curse and stumble. Thank goodness! Whatever his delay, it gave her a few extra seconds. She flung open the door to the brothel and fled into the night.

The wind took her breath, and something small and mean and four-legged scuttled from her path. She ducked into a tiny covered alley, her footsteps echoing against the ancient stone walls. She ran without direction or thought, panic beating at her breast. If he caught her, he'd kiss her again. He'd press his length to her, and she'd taste his mouth, feel his touch, and she wouldn't be able to break away a second time. She'd succumb, wallowing in her own sinful nature.

She couldn't let that happen.

So when she heard him call her name behind her, she made herself slow down, made herself move more stealthily. The covered alley opened into a tiny courtyard. She glanced behind her and darted across it. Her breast was burning, and she wanted to gasp, but she made herself breathe slowly, softly, and look behind her. The courtyard was empty. His voice had been distant. Perhaps she'd lost him.

Temperance crept through an alley, ducked into a side street, and then turned down another passage. The moon was out, giving her some feeble light. She'd run so fast and in such a rush that she had no idea where she was now. The buildings to either side were dark. She crossed a street, running fast again, a thrill of fear bolting up her back. She paused for a moment in the shadows of a house, peering behind her. She couldn't see Lord Caire. Perhaps he'd given up the chase? Except that didn't seem very like—

"You fool!" he hissed into her ear.

She yelped, an ignoble sound, but he'd scared the wits out of her.

He took her upper arms and shook her, his voice rasping with rage. "Have you no sense? I promised your brother I'd take care of you, and then you go running willy-nilly into the worst part of St. Giles."

She gaped up at him, stunned, her only thought that he was enraged because of fear for her. She'd thought he'd chased her out of sexual frenzy when all the time he'd been concerned for her safety. Temperance couldn't help it. She threw back her head and laughed, the wind taking the sound from her lips and spinning it high.

Lord Caire frowned down at her. "Stop that. It's not funny."

Which, of course, only made her laugh harder.

He sighed in male frustration and shook her again, but it was halfhearted. He began to pull her toward himself, and her fears of his attraction flooded back, sobering her. She placed her palms against his chest in weak protest.

And then he shoved her roughly behind him.

She stumbled at the sudden movement, then caught herself and looked up. A group of men had walked into the street, all of them armed with cudgels. Caire twisted and broke apart his walking stick. The short sword was in his right hand, the remainder of the stick in his left, and he didn't hesitate but flew at the attackers.

"Run!" he bellowed to her as he charged the men.

They hadn't expected such an abrupt offensive. Two of the men fell back, one hesitated, but the remaining two closed on Caire. Temperance felt for her pistol. She'd tied the sack she usually carried it in to her waist under her skirts, and she began hauling up the material.

There was a short scream, horribly cut off. She looked up in time to see one of Caire's attackers fall back, his face awash in blood. Caire was whirling gracefully, his cape flying out about him, as he thrust at another man.

"Temperance! Obey me now. Run!"

Abruptly, a thick arm wrapped around her neck, choking off her scream.

"Throw down yer sword," a rough voice said near her ear, "or I'll break 'er neck."

Caire turned, his eyes narrowing as he saw her plight, and then the man holding Temperance grunted and went limp. She scrambled away as he fell to the ground. She gasped and looked up and saw...

An apparition, moving silently and swiftly past her. The attackers never even knew he—*it?*—was there until one was run through. Was she dreaming? Had she been killed and not even known it? For the thing that fought silently and deadly beside Caire now was like nothing she'd ever seen.

He was tall and lean and wearing a black and red motley tunic. His breeches, jackboots, and wide-brimmed hat were all black. A black half-mask covered the upper part of his face, the nose grotesquely long, and eerie lines carved around the eyes and protruding cheeks. He held a glittering sword in one hand and a long dagger in the other, and he used both at once with deadly agility, skipping nimbly over the cobblestones as he fought.

Caire stood back-to-back with the apparition, both figures fighting with grim precision. Caire blocked a blow with the stick in his left hand and followed through with a jab from the sword in his right. The remaining attackers circled the two men like a pack of rabid dogs. But Caire and the harlequin moved together as if they'd fought like this all their lives. No matter how the attackers tried to breach their defenses, they could find no hole. The apparition slashed a man across the chest even as Caire stabbed one in the thigh. One of the attackers gave a shout, and suddenly they fled, disappearing into the St. Giles night. Even the man who'd caught her from behind had recovered enough to run away.

In the silence, Temperance could hear her own breath rasping in her throat. The pistol in her hands shook violently.

The apparition turned gracefully, his boots whispering against the cobblestones. He swept the hat from his head as he bowed low. A scarlet feather fluttered in his hat as he replaced it on his head.

Then he was gone as well.

Temperance stared at Caire. "Are you badly hurt? Who was that?"

"I have no idea." He shook his head. His silver hair had come down from its customary tie during the fight, and it fanned against his black cloak. "But it would appear that the Ghost of St. Giles is no rumor."

Chapter Ten

Meg shook her head. "That, Your Majesty, is not love."

"What?" The king looked ominous. "If not love, then what is it?"

"Obedience," Meg said. "Your guards tell you what you wish to hear out of obedience, Your Majesty."

Well! You could've heard the drop of a pin within the throne room. The little blue bird chirped, and the king let out a sigh.

"Return her to the dungeons," he ordered the guards. He added to Meg, "And when next you are in my presence, see to it you are properly washed."

Meg curtsied. "To wash, I'll need water, soap, and cloth, if it please Your Majesty."

The king waved a hand. "See that it is done."

And the guards led her away....

—from *King Lockedheart*

"I knew the Ghost of St. Giles was real!" Nell exclaimed later that evening.

Temperance turned to stare at the maidservant, aware that Winter, across the kitchen table from her, had turned at the same time.

Nell flushed at their combined stares. "Well, I did! Did he have bloodred eyes?"

Temperance smiled wearily at Nell's excitement. Caire had escorted her home after the attack, and she'd been set upon by Winter and Nell shortly thereafter. She'd spent the last quarter of an hour answering Winter's disapproving questions, interrupted now and then by Nell's exclamations.

"I couldn't see his eyes well," she answered truthfully. "He wore a black half-mask with a long, curving nose."

Winter snorted.

She glanced at him. "And he was wearing red and black motley, like a harlequin."

Her brother raised his eyebrows at that, looking vaguely interested. "A theatrical costume? He sounds like a madman."

"A mad actor." Nell shivered with delight.

"He fought very well for a madman," Temperance said doubtfully.

"Perhaps he's merely a footpad with a flair for the dramatic," Winter said drily.

"Or he really is a ghost, come back to avenge his death in St. Giles," Nell said.

Temperance shook her head. "He was no ghost. It was a flesh-and-blood man I saw tonight, tall and lean." She smiled whimsically. "Actually, his figure was rather like your own, brother."

Nell stifled a giggle.

Winter merely sighed.

"Well, whoever he is," Temperance said hastily, "I owe my life to him."

"Which is why it is only prudent that you not see Lord Caire again," Winter replied.

Temperance winced, knowing she'd just supplied ammunition for this argument. If only she weren't so terribly tired! She rubbed at her temple. "Winter, please, can we save this discussion for the morrow?"

He looked at her a moment, his sad, brown eyes grave; then he nodded and stood. "I'll spare you the debate tonight, sister, but a night's sleep won't change my mind. Your association with this man has brought you into danger, made you neglect your duties to the home and the children, and, I fear, imperils your good sense and virtue. I don't want you seeing Lord Caire again."

He nodded politely and left the kitchen.

Temperance let her head sink into her hands.

Nell cleared her throat after a moment of silence. "A cup of tea always sets me right, especially afore bed."

Temperance had to blink back the tears that had welled in her eyes. "Thank you."

She'd never exchanged heated words with Winter. Asa and Concord could be quite maddening in their stubborn inability to see other people's viewpoints, but Winter had never raised his voice to her. He was a thoughtful man, not easily roused to anger, and the realization that she'd done just that tonight was extremely upsetting.

Nell placed a pot of tea on the table along with two cups, and sat opposite her. She poured the steaming tea into one of the cups. "Mr. Makepeace didn't mean to be so...so...ah..." Nell trailed away, apparently unable to think of a word without disparaging her employer.

Temperance smiled wryly. "Yes, he did."

"Oh, but—"

"And he's right." Temperance reached across the table and took the full teacup, pulling it toward herself. "I shouldn't leave him to go gallivanting about the East End with Lord Caire. I am neglecting my duties."

Nell poured a second cup of tea silently, stirring in a huge lump of sugar. She took a delicate sip and then placed her cup carefully back on the table, her eyes on the tea. "Lord Caire is a very...fair man, quite easy on the eyes, I find."

Temperance looked at her.

Nell bit her lip. "It's that hair, I think, so long and thick and shining. And silver! It's just so very striking."

"I like his eyes," Temperance admitted.

"Do you?"

There was a drop of tea on the table, and Temperance placed her fingertip in it and drew a circle on the table. "I've never seen eyes so blue. And his eyelashes are so dark in contrast to his hair."

"He has quite a nice nose," Nell said with consideration.

"And his lips are wide and curved at the ends. Have you noticed?"

Nell sighed, which seemed answer enough.

Temperance bit her lip. "And they're so firm, yet so soft. They quite take my breath away."

She realized that she might've said too much with that last confession and hastily took a sip of tea.

When she placed the cup back on the table, Nell was looking at her thoughtfully. "He seems to have a special...consideration for you."

Temperance's eyes dropped to the table again. Her tea

circle had dried up. "How can you tell that? You've never even met him."

"Ah, but I've heard from the children and Polly," Nell said. "Polly says that the way he looks at you gives her thrills."

How did he look at her? Was Nell mistaking lust for caring? And why did it matter so much to her?

Temperance shook her head, placing her hands flat on the table. "His wants are unnatural. And even if they were not, what kind of a woman would I be to let my urges guide me?"

"Perhaps an ordinary woman," Nell said gently.

Temperance was silent, remembering the red-haired woman with the scarf over her eyes. Remembering how excited she'd been by the sight. She was *so tired* of trying to contain her urges, and here was Lord Caire who didn't try to contain them at all. He seemed to revel in them instead.

Nell cleared her throat. "I once had a friend who liked a bit of adventure in the bedroom."

"Really?" Nell hardly ever spoke of her previous profession.

Nell nodded. "He was an ordinary gentleman in other regards—he made watch faces—but in the bedroom, he liked to tie up the lady he was with."

Temperance kept her gaze carefully focused on the bit of table between her hands, even as she felt the heat rise in her cheeks. To have this discussion at all was horribly embarrassing, but to do so with Lord Caire in mind...oh, goodness!

"Did..." Temperance stopped and licked her lips. "Did he hurt you?"

"Oh, no, ma'am," Nell said. "Make no mistake, there are gentlemen who like to hurt the girls they're with, but my gentleman wasn't one of them. He just seemed to enjoy the whole thing more with me unable to move."

"Oh," Temperance said in a small voice.

She shouldn't be thinking of this at all; it incited the worst impulses in her. But she felt rebellion rise in her breast. Was it so horrible to merely contemplate a sexual union with Caire? To wonder what the scarf would feel like? To guess at what he might do first if she was bound, helpless and open to him? To imagine giving in to her urges without guilt—the way Lord Caire seemed to do?

She repressed a shudder. "I thought you disapproved of Lord Caire?"

"I don't know the man," Nell said carefully. "I know only his reputation among the ladies of the night in St. Giles."

Temperance frowned. "The fact that he has any reputation at all among those ladies should be cause enough for disapproval."

"I suppose you're right." Nell sighed. "I know a man should remain pure if he's unwed. He shouldn't visit whores if he has impulses."

Temperance nodded jerkily. Of course not. Sexual congress outside the bonds of marriage was sinful.

"The thing is, ma'am," Nell said quietly. "I just don't see how it hurts."

Temperance looked up quickly. "What do you mean?"

Nell shrugged. "Well, bedsport. I reckon all men and most women like it, even outside of marriage. Why is it so bad?"

Temperance stared, unable to reply.

Nell leaned forward. "If bedsport brings joy, even for a little while, why condemn it?"

ST. JOHN WAS in his study the next morning, frowning over a speech by Cicero, when Molder cleared his throat phlegmily at the door. "Lord Caire to see you, sir."

He would've perhaps claimed to not be home, but Caire, damn him, was right behind the butler. St. John clenched his jaw, set down his pen, and waved Caire in.

Caire strolled in carrying a huge bouquet of daisies. "You won't credit who I met in St. Giles last night."

"A whore?" St. John asked acidly.

"No. Well, yes." Caire scratched his chin. "At least I assume they were whores, but that is nothing new. No, I made the acquaintance of the infamous Ghost of St. Giles."

"Did you, now?" St. John busied himself rearranging the papers on his desk.

When he glanced up again, Caire was looking at him thoughtfully. He placed his posy on a table. "A man in a harlequin's tunic, a floppy hat with a scarlet feather, and a black half-mask. Oh, and he was brandishing both a long and a short sword. Rather overly flamboyant, in my opinion."

St. John snorted. "As if you're one to critique the flamboyance of others."

Caire ignored him. "I think it was the scarlet feather that was too much."

St. John sighed. "And what was the Ghost doing?"

"Saving my hide, if you must know."

"What?"

"I was attacked by five thugs last night. The ghost rather fortuitously intervened."

"Was Mrs. Dews with you?" St. John asked softly.

Caire turned and looked at him silently.

"Damn it!" St. John pushed away from the desk. "Why do you persist in pursuing that lady? You're placing her in danger."

"I dislike that fact as much as you. I've decided that I can no longer take her into St. Giles without a guard of some sort." He shook his head. "I haven't yet decided how to continue my inquiries with her."

"You should leave her be entirely."

Caire's mouth twisted humorlessly. "I find I cannot."

"Why?" St. John shook his head. "She isn't even your type."

"What is my type?"

St. John glanced away. They both knew well enough the kind of women Caire favored.

"Whores?" Caire asked softly. "Women who can be bought by jewels?"

St. John looked at him helplessly.

Caire was pacing the room. "Perhaps I tire of my type. Perhaps I wish to be in the company of a different sort of woman."

St. John sat forward, his voice low and intense. "Then why *her*? There are innumerable ladies of our own social rank, intelligent, witty, and beautiful, who would be more than happy to have you call upon them."

"And each would be mentally assessing my annual income and my ancestry." Caire smiled a bit sadly. "Perhaps I want a woman who cares naught for either. Perhaps I want a woman who, when she looks at me, sees nothing but a man."

St. John stared.

"There's something about her," Caire said in a low voice. "She cares for everyone about her, yet neglects herself. I want to be the one who cares for her."

"You'll ruin her," St. John said.

"Will I? The lady is not unwilling no matter your protests. Cut line, Godric. Why does she bother you so much?"

St. John was silent, a long-held sorrow welling in his chest.

"She reminds you of Clara, doesn't she?" Caire asked quietly.

"Damn it." St. John's eyes were stinging. "Does she remind you of Clara?"

"No." Caire touched the bouquet of daisies with one fingertip. "Clara was always yours, right from the very start. I never thought of her as anything but a dear friend. I confess I cannot say the same for Mrs. Dews."

St. John stared at his hands, clenched on his desk. "I'm sorry."

"What for?"

"I think I've acted out of jealousy." St. John closed his eyes. "You have a healthy, strong lady."

"No, it is I who should apologize. Your burden is heavy."

St. John bent his head, unable to speak.

"You know I would give my own life if I could take away her disease," Caire whispered.

Caire's steps moved away and St. John heard the door close gently.

St. John inhaled, opening his eyes. They were wet and he blotted them irritably upon his sleeve. Then he rose and crossed to the flowers Caire had brought. There were at least two dozen, bright white and gold daisies.

He picked them up and carried them out of his study.

Daisies were Clara's favorite flower.

IT WAS LATE that afternoon when Silence set out. If this Charming Mickey person was a thief who worked at night, it stood to reason that he'd not be in the best of moods in the morning.

And she wanted to see him when he was in a good mood.

She walked quickly along the narrow street, taking care not to meet the eyes of any of the other people who roamed this area of London. Most were street hawkers, returning home after a long day calling their wares in more prosperous parts. They pushed wheelbarrows with wilting vegetables or carried trays empty now of pies and fruit. These people she did not fear. But there were others she did—short men with shifting, mean eyes. Women in gaudy dresses, standing in doorways and at the entrance of alleys, lifting one side of their skirts as the men passed by to advertise their profession. These last two groups Silence hurried away from.

She was aware that her plain woolen skirt and simple lace cap were of far better quality than that worn by the other people around her. She'd dressed neatly for this interview, wanting to impress without standing out, but even her second-best skirt drew looks from the whores on the corners. She pulled her cloak more firmly about her and ducked her head, walking quickly.

She was beginning to wonder if keeping this mission from her husband had been the best idea. But what other choice had she had? She couldn't sit by and watch William be condemned to prison. This was the only possible action, and since he would no doubt disapprove of it, she'd seen no point in telling him in advance.

Silence drew a breath as she rounded the last corner. The building she'd been directed to was an old structure, tall and narrow, the brick face crumbling. It stood between a cobbler's shop and a tenant house, looking no more distinctive than its neighbors. Except that two burly, big men loitered in the doorway outside while a third paced the street across from the building. Silence marched up to the door, her shoulders back, her chin lifted.

She kept William's dear face firmly in her thoughts as she looked at the guards. "I'm here to see Mr. O'Connor."

One of the men completely ignored her, acting as if he'd not heard or seen her standing right in front of his nose. But the second man, who sported a huge mashed-in broken nose and a too-tight bottle-green coat, seemed amused by her request.

He looked her up and down in a too-familiar but not unkind manner. "Yer not really 'is type, luv."

"No doubt." Silence willed herself not to show embarrassment at the man's blunt assessment. "But I need to talk to him anyway."

"But, see, that's not likely, is it?" Broken Nose replied.

His companion spoke for the first time, revealing a row of missing teeth in his upper jaw. "What 'ave you got?"

Silence blinked. "I beg your pardon?"

Broken Nose tilted his head at the other man. "'E wants to know 'ow much you can pay us, luv."

"Oh!" Silence pulled the tiny purse hanging at her waist through a slit in her skirts. She opened it and looked back up at the two men. "Tuppence apiece?"

Toothless snorted. "Not less than a 'alf crown each."

Silence drew in her breath, but before she could protest, Broken Nose had turned on his companion.

"'Alf a crown? 'Ave you gone mad, Bert?"

"No, I 'ave not, 'Arry," Bert replied. "In my opinion, 'alf a crown is quite fair."

"If'n she's the Countess of Suffolk herself, it is," Harry exploded. "Does she look to you like the Countess of Suffolk?"

"Now, jus' a mo'," Bert began heatedly.

"Excuse me!" Silence said, rather loudly, for she was afraid the two men were about to come to fisticuffs.

Both Harry and Bert swung their faces toward her, but it was Harry who said, "Aye?"

"Would a shilling each do?"

Bert snorted again, loudly and with obvious contempt for the offering, but Harry was more generous. "A shillin' each is quite fair."

Bert muttered under his breath something about soft hearts and soft heads, but he stuck out his hand readily enough when Silence opened her purse.

"She's your pet," he said to Harry. "Better take 'er to 'imself."

Harry nodded agreeably to Bert. "I 'spect that's best. This way, miss." He held the door open for her.

Silence stepped inside the house and almost immediately stopped, gaping despite herself.

Behind her, Harry chuckled. "Bit unexpected, innit?"

And she could only nod numbly. The walls were lined with gold.

The hall wasn't wide, but it arched high overhead and the gold rose from the floor to gild the ceiling as well.

Beneath her feet was a mosaic of marble tiles in a rainbow of colors, laid randomly. Above, crystal chandeliers hung from the gold ceiling, and the lights were reflected in the glorious yellow metal over and over again until the whole was a dazzling display of wonder and wealth.

"Doesn't he fear thieves?" she blurted without thinking.

Good Lord, she'd never heard of anything as extravagant as this hallway. Even the king himself surely didn't have golden walls!

But Harry laughed. "It'd be a right fool who'd try and steal from Charming Mickey, miss. One who didn't mind meeting 'is maker on the morrow."

Silence gulped. "Oh."

Harry sobered. "You sure you want to see Charming Mickey, miss? I can let you back out that door, no 'arm done."

"No." Silence squared her shoulders. "I'm not leaving until I see him."

Harry shrugged his big shoulders as if to say he washed his hands of the matter. He turned without further ado and led her through the fabulous hall. There was a curving staircase at the back, carved from the same multicolored marble as the floors, like something from an emperor's dream. Harry mounted the staircase ahead of her—there wasn't really room for two abreast—and led her to the upper hall. Here, two great double doors stood directly opposite the head of the stairs.

Harry knocked on one.

A tiny square window opened in one of the panels of the doors and an eye blinked out at them. "Aye?"

"Lady to see 'imself," Harry said.

The eye swiveled to stare at Silence. "'Ave you searched the wench?"

Harry sighed. "Does she look like an assassin to you, Bob?"

Bob blinked. "Might. Best kind o' assassin would be the kind you *didn't* think were one, if you get my meaning."

Harry merely looked at the eye.

"All right, then," Bob the Eye said after an awkward pause. "But it's on yer 'ead should she try anything."

Harry looked at Silence. "Don't try anything, 'ear?"

She nodded mutely. The realization of what she was about to do had closed her throat tight.

The great golden doors were opened by Bob, who turned out to be a skeletally thin man wearing a badly fitting white wig. He had a brace of pistols stuck in a broad, worn belt over his coat. But Silence hardly noticed the doorkeeper.

The room within was magnificent.

The glorious colored marble floor continued inside the large square room, but the golden walls were replaced with walls of sparkling white marble. Silence looked closer and gasped. The white marble was inlaid with jewels. Above, the ceiling was gold and a multitude of crystal lights hung from it, shining as bright as morning sunshine. And every corner, every inch of the room was jammed with riches. Bolts of bright silks were stacked on marble-topped tables. Inlaid secretaries were shoved against carved mahogany sideboards. Crates spilled straw, revealing china dishes and thinly carved jade. Exotic spices in oriental chests perfumed the air, and graceful marble statues stared dispassionately on the scene. At the far end of the fabulous treasure room stood a dais with a huge, tall-backed chair.

It was overstuffed with red velvet, the arms carved and gilded; really, it could only be called a throne.

Which would make the man who sat upon it a king—Pirate King.

He lounged, one leg thrown over a chair arm. His black hair was unclubbed, inky curls tumbling about his shoulders and brow. He wore a linen shirt, unbuttoned, fine lace framing the bare olive skin of his chest. His breeches were black velvet, and he finished his costume with polished jackboots that came to midthigh.

She might have laughed at such a ridiculously flamboyant figure, if it weren't for the fact that the men about him obviously took him very seriously. To his right stood a thin little man, wigless, his bare head nearly bald, and wearing small, round spectacles. To his left were a half dozen or so rough men, lounging about, every one of them armed to the teeth. At his elbow was a small boy holding a silver tray of sweets. And directly in front of Charming Mickey, a hulking man kneeled before the throne, looking as if he feared for his life.

"I'm sorry!" The man clenched fists as big as hams on his thighs. "As God is my witness, I'm so sorry, sir!"

The thin little man to Charming Mickey's right bent and whispered something in the river pirate's ear.

He nodded and looked at the supplicant before him. "An' you'll be understanding me, Dick, if I don't quite find your apology worth as much as a pile of dog shit."

The big man, Dick, actually shivered.

Charming Mickey regarded him for a moment, his right elbow propped on the chair's arm, lazily rubbing his thumb and middle finger together. Jeweled rings sparkled on his fingers.

Then he flicked his fingers at two of his men.

Immediately they came forward, even as the kneeling man began to howl.

"No! God, no! Please, I have children. My wife is expectin' our third!"

The man screamed as he was dragged through a far door. The door closed and his scream was abruptly cut off. The sudden quiet echoed in the great hall.

Silence felt the breath she'd held escape her lungs. Dear God, what had she let herself in for?

Harry took her elbow and they began to walk to the throne. As they neared, he hissed out of the corner of his mouth, "Don't show fear. 'E 'ates a coward."

And then she stood in front of Charming Mickey O'Connor, in the exact same spot where the unfortunate Dick had kneeled just seconds before.

Charming Mickey gestured to the boy holding the tray of sweets. The boy brought it forward, offering him some. Charming Mickey's ringed hand hovered over the tray as he made his selection—a pink iced bonbon.

He held the sweet up between his elegant, ringed fingers and examined it. "Who is she?"

Harry nodded his head, unperturbed by the abrupt question. "Lady who wants to talk to you."

Charming Mickey's eyes flicked up, and Silence saw that they were a brown so dark that they might as well be black. "That I can see, Harry, luv. What I'm a-askin' is more along the lines of *why* she's in me throne room."

Silence glanced at Harry, who was looking uneasy for the first time, and decided to intervene for her champion. "I'm here about my husband, Captain William

Hollingbrook, and the cargo you stole from his ship, the *Finch*."

Beside her, Harry drew in his breath sharply. The boy holding the tray of sweetmeats flinched, and the thin man by Charming Mickey's side looked at her inquiringly over his round spectacles.

It occurred to Silence that perhaps she should've spoken with better tact. But it was too late now. Charming Mickey's dark eyes were upon her, examining her in minute detail. He popped the pink sweet into his mouth and chewed slowly, the muscles of his jaw flexing and relaxing as his eyelids half lowered in enjoyment.

He swallowed and smiled, and suddenly Silence understood where he'd gotten the epitaph of "charming." When he smiled, Mickey was the handsomest man she'd ever seen. He couldn't be more than thirty years old, his skin smooth and olive-toned, his black brows tilted up at the outer corners. His nose was long and almost aristocratic, his lips full and curved and elegant. A dimple played about his cheek, near his mouth. When he smiled, Charming Mickey looked almost innocent.

Except Silence knew she couldn't fall into that trap. No matter what his smile said, this man was no innocent.

"*Stole* is such an ugly word, I find," Charming Mickey drawled. His Irish brogue made the words almost a caress. "I must warn you, Mistress Hollingbrook, that I don't let many utter it in me presence."

Silence bit back the urge to apologize. This man's actions had imperiled her husband.

Mickey cocked his head, a long silky curl of ebony hair sliding across his shoulder. "What might you be wantin' from me, darlin'?"

She lifted her chin. "I want you to return the cargo."

Mickey blinked as if bemused. "An' why on earth would I do such a foolish thing?"

Her heart was beating so loudly she feared he must hear it, but she said steadily, "Because returning the cargo is the right thing to do. The Christian thing to do. If you don't, my husband will be sent to prison."

Mickey raised one black eyebrow, looking quite satanic. "Does your husband know you're here, luv?"

Silence bit her lip. "No."

"Ah." He beckoned the sweetmeats boy over again and selected another.

Silence began to open her mouth, but Harry nudged her, so she took his warning and shut it again.

Mickey ate the sweet slowly while those in the throne room waited. Silence noticed that a black marble statue of some Roman goddess stood slightly behind him. She wore a tiara, and long strands of pearls were draped over her naked bosom.

"Well, this is the way of it, luv," Mickey said so suddenly that Silence jumped. He smiled that innocent smile again. "The owner of the ship your husband captains and I have had a bit of a falling out, see. He thinks it well and good to not be payin' me my proper tithe from his cargos, and I . . . well, I can't agree with that tack. Shows a lack of respect, in me own humble opinion. So I've taken the liberty of confiscatin' the *Finch*'s cargo, sort of to get the man's attention, like. You might call it a drastic move, and I'd have to agree, but there it is, all the same. The man made his bed and now he must lay upon it."

And Charming Mickey shrugged gracefully as if to say the matter was out of his hands.

That was it, then. Her audience was at an end. Harry had laid his hand on her arm to lead her away, and Charming Mickey was already tilting his head to hear something the thin little man was whispering to him. But she couldn't give up. She had to at least try one more time. For William.

Silence took a deep breath, and even as she did so, she felt Harry's hand tighten on her arm in warning. "Please, Mr. O'Connor. You have said yourself that your grievance is with the ship's owner, not my husband. Can you not return the cargo for his sake? For my sake?"

Mickey slowly turned his head to look at her, no longer smiling now. His dark eyes were oddly dispassionate, and without his smile, his lips had a cruel edge. "'Ware, darlin'. I've let you play about me claws once and run away unharmed. If you skip back into them again, you'll have naught to blame but yourself."

Silence swallowed. His whispered warning made the hairs rise on the back of her neck, and for the first time she realized that she was truly in mortal danger. She wanted nothing more than to turn tail and run.

But she didn't. "Please. I beg of you. If you will not do it for my husband's sake or mine, then do it for yours. For the sake of your immortal soul. Do me this favor and I promise you, you will never regret it."

Charming Mickey stared at her, cold, remote, and expressionless. The room was so silent that each breath Silence took sounded in her ears. Beside her, Harry seemed to have stopped breathing altogether.

Then Mickey slowly smiled. "You must love him very much, this Captain Hollingbrook, this wonderful husband of yours."

"Yes," Silence said with pride. "Yes, I do."

"And does he love you in return, me darlin'?"

Silence's eyes widened in surprise. "Of course."

"Ah," Charming Mickey murmured, "then there might be another way for us to work this matter out to our mutual benefit, yours and mine."

Beside her, Harry stiffened.

She knew. She knew that whatever Charming Mickey proposed, it would be very bad. She knew that she might not escape this room, this wild, gorgeous house, with her soul entirely intact.

"That is, of course," Mickey murmured like the devil himself, "if you *truly* love your husband."

William was everything in the world to her. There was nothing she would not do to save him.

Silence looked the devil in the eye and lifted her chin. "I do."

Chapter Eleven

*Meg spent the rest of the day contentedly washing
her person so that when she went to sleep that
evening, she felt considerably neater. The next
morning she was brought before King
Lockedheart. He looked a bit surprised when he saw
her—perhaps he did not recognize her without her
layer of soot?—but his habitual scowl soon returned.
In front of him stood a great company of courtiers,
clad in rich furs, velvet, and jewels.
He asked the assembled dignitaries, "Do you
love me?"
Well, the courtiers did not speak in one voice
as the trained guards had the day before,
but their answers were the same: yes!
The king sneered at Meg. "There! Confess
now your foolishness."...*
—from *King Lockedheart*

"Then you mean to see him again?" Winter asked quietly
that night.

"Yes, I do." Temperance finished braiding Mary Little's fine flaxen hair and smiled down at the girl. "There, all done. Now off to bed with you."

"Thank you, ma'am."

Mary Little curtsied as she'd been taught and skipped out of the kitchen. Later, when all the children were settled in their beds, Winter would come up to hear their prayers.

"Now you, Mary Church." The girl turned her back and Temperance took up the brush, concentrating on taming the thick, brown curls without pulling too much.

The remaining three Marys sat before the fire in their chemises, their hair drying as they bent their heads over their samplers. Bath day was always quite a chore, but Temperance enjoyed it nonetheless. There was something wonderfully soothing about all the children being clean and neat at once.

Or at least this time *should* be soothing.

She sighed. "I need to go tonight."

All the girls could hear their argument, even though both she and Winter took pains to keep their voices even and polite, but the main child she worried over was Mary Whitsun. That Mary sat beside her, combing out the curls of two-year-old Mary Sweet. Mary Whitsun kept her eyes on her task, but she had a frown between her brows.

Temperance sighed. Pity she couldn't have this discussion in private, but if she was going to attend the ball Caire had promised to take her to tonight, she would have to get the children safely to bed and then rush to dress in Nell's lent gown. She wished it were merely for the home that she looked forward to the evening. Already her heartbeat had quickened at the thought of seeing Caire again. She glanced worriedly at the old clock on the mantel. She'd be cutting things perilously close as it was.

"I'm sorry, but I hope to see a certain gentleman tonight."

Winter turned from staring into the fireplace. "Who?"

Temperance frowned over a tangle in Mary Church's hair. "He's a gentleman Caire introduced me to at the musicale, Sir Henry Easton. He seemed quite interested in our home—he asked me about apprenticing out the boys and the clothing we provide. Things like that. I'm hoping to convince him to help the home."

Winter glanced at the girls, all avidly listening. "Indeed? And what assurance do you have that he'll do as you hope?"

"None." Temperance pulled overhard on Mary Church's hair and the girl yelped. "I'm sorry, Mary Church."

"Temperance—" Winter began.

But she spoke, quick and low. "I have no assurances, but I must go nonetheless. Can't you see that, brother? I must at least grasp at possibilities, even if they prove to be false hopes."

Winter's thin lips compressed. "Very well. But be sure to stay by Lord Caire's side. I dislike the thought of you at one of these aristocratic balls. I've heard"—he glanced at the girls and appeared to modify his words—"about events that can take place at such balls. Be careful, please."

"Of course." Temperance smiled at Winter and then transferred the smile to Mary Church. "All done."

"Thank you, ma'am."

Mary Church took Mary Sweet's hand, for the toddler was properly braided as well, and led her from the kitchen.

"Well, then, only three little heads and six little braids to go." Winter smiled at the remaining girls by the fire.

They giggled at him. While Winter was always gentle, he didn't often speak in such light tones.

"I'll go up and begin reading the Psalm for the night," Winter said.

Temperance nodded. "Good night."

She felt his hand, briefly laid on her shoulder as he passed, and then she breathed a sigh of relief. She hated his disapproval more than that of her other brothers. Winter was the brother closest to her in age, and they'd become closer still by running the home together.

She shook her head and quickly finished braiding the other little girls' hair and sent each on their way until only Mary Whitsun remained. It was something of a ritual between the two of them that Mary Whitsun was the last to have her hair braided at night. Neither spoke as she worked the comb through the girl's hair, and it occurred to Temperance that she'd been doing this for nine years— since Mary had come to the home. Soon they'd find an apprenticeship for Mary, though, and their nights together by the fire as she braided the girl's hair would be over.

Temperance's breast ached at the thought.

She was tying a bit of ribbon to Mary's braid when a knocking came at the front door.

Temperance rose. "Who can that be?" It was still too early for Lord Caire.

She hurried to the door, Mary Whitsun at her heels, and unbarred it. On the step was a liveried footman, holding a large covered basket.

"For you, miss," he said, and thrust it into her hands before turning away.

"Wait!" Temperance called. "What is this for?"

The footman was already several yards away. He half turned. "My lord says you're to wear it tonight."

And then he was gone.

Temperance closed and barred the door, and then took the basket into the kitchen. She set it on the table and pulled back the plain linen covering it. Underneath was a bright turquoise silk gown embroidered with delicate posies of yellow, crimson, and black. Temperance drew in her breath. The gown made Nell's wonderful scarlet dress look like a sack in comparison. Underneath the gown were fine silk stays, a chemise, stockings, and embroidered slippers. Nestled in the silk was a small jeweler's box. Temperance picked it up with trembling fingers, not daring to open it yet. Surely she couldn't accept such a gift? But, then, if she was going to a grand ball with Lord Caire, she didn't want to shame him with the modesty of her toilet.

That decided her.

She turned to Mary Whitsun, wide-eyed beside her. "Fetch Nell, please. I need to dress for a ball."

LAZARUS FELT THE hackles rise on the back of his neck when he entered the ballroom that night with Temperance on his arm. She was magnificent in the turquoise gown he'd sent to her. Her dark hair was piled atop her head and held with the light yellow topaz pins he'd included in the basket. Her breasts pressed against the shimmering silk bodice, mounded and tempting. She was beautiful and desirable, and every man in the room took note. And he was damnably aware of the other men taking note. He actually felt a growl building at the back of his throat, as if he'd stand guard over her like some mangy dog over a scrap.

What a fool he was.

"Shall we?" he murmured to her.

He could see the movement of her throat as she swallowed nervously. "Yes. Please."

He nodded and began their perambulation through the overdecorated room. Temperance's quarry was by the far windows, but it wouldn't do to approach too eagerly.

Every notable presently residing in London was here, including, inevitably, his own mother. The Countess of Stanwicke was known for extravagant balls, and she'd outdone herself tonight. A platoon of footmen, attired in orange and black livery, attended the gathering, each attesting to the money needed for both their gaudy clothes and their time. Hothouse flowers were mounded on every surface, already wilting in the heat of the ballroom. The scent of dying roses and lilies mingled with that of burning wax, sweating bodies, and perfume, the whole both nauseating and heady.

"I intend to return this gown to you after tonight," Temperance said, taking up the argument that had begun in the carriage ride here.

"And I've already told you I'll simply have it burned if you do," he replied smoothly, baring his teeth to a gentleman staring at her bosom. None of them would have ever noticed her in her usual drab black gowns. He was a fool for taking her out of her obscurity and bringing her into contact with these overdressed wolves. "I must confess my disappointment in your waste, Mrs. Dews."

"You are an impossible man," she hissed under her breath while smiling at a passing matron.

"I may be impossible, but I've gained you entry into the most fashionable ball of the season."

There was a short silence as he guided her around a pack of elderly ladies in far too much rouge.

Then she said softly, "So you have and I thank you."

He glanced swiftly sideways at her. Her cheeks were pink, but the color was not from any rouge pot. "You have no need to thank me. I'm merely fulfilling the bargain we made."

She looked at him, her gilded eyes mysterious and far too wise. "You've done more than that for me. You've given me this beautiful gown, the hairpins, slippers, and stays. Why shouldn't I thank you for all that?"

"Because I've brought you into this den of wolves."

He felt more than saw her startled glance. "You make a ball sound overly dangerous, even for one as inexperienced as I."

He snorted. "In many ways, this company is as dangerous as the people we've met on the streets of St. Giles."

She looked at him skeptically.

"Over there"—he tilted his chin discreetly—"is a gentleman—I use the word in only its social sense—who has killed two men in duels in the last year. Beside him is a decorated general. He lost most of his men in a vain and stupid charge. It's rumored that our hostess once beat a maid so badly she had to pay the woman over a thousand pounds to hush up the matter."

He glanced down at Mrs. Dews, expecting shock, but she stared back, her expression open and frank and a little sad. "You're merely proving that money and privilege do not go hand in hand with good sense or virtue. That, I think, I already knew."

He bowed, feeling heat stealing up his cheeks. "Forgive me for boring you."

"You never bore me as well you know, my lord," she replied. "I only wish to point out that while money can't buy those things, it can buy food for the stomach and clothes for the body."

"So you think the people here are happier than those in St. Giles?"

"They should be." She shrugged. "Being hungry or cold does terrible things for the temperament."

"And yet," he mused, "are the wealthy here any happier than a poor beggar on the street?"

She looked at him with disbelief.

He smiled down at her. "Truly. I think a man may find happiness—or discontent—no matter if he has a full belly or not."

"If that is true, it is very sad," she said. "They should be happier with all their needs fulfilled."

He shook his head. "Man is a fickle, ungrateful creature, I fear."

She smiled at that—finally! "I don't think I can understand the people from your class."

"Best not to," he said lightly.

"You, for instance," she murmured. "I'm not sure you have any more need of me in St. Giles, but you take me with you still. Why?"

He looked ahead of them, examining the crowd, watching the other men watching her. "Why do you think?"

"I don't know."

"Don't you?"

She hesitated, and though he didn't look at her, he was aware of her every movement. Of her restless fingers tracing the neckline of her bodice, of her pulse fluttering at her throat, of the moment she parted her lips again.

He leaned closer to her and repeated low, "Don't you?"

She inhaled. "At Mrs. Whiteside's house, you made me watch..."

"Yes?" They were in a damnably crowded room, the press of bodies almost suffocating. Yet at the same time he felt as if they existed in a closed glass sphere of their own.

"Why?" she asked urgently. "Why did you make me watch? Why me?"

"Because," he murmured, "you draw me. Because you are kind but not soft. Because when you touch me, the pain is bittersweet. Because you cradle a desperate secret to your bosom, like a viper in your arms, and don't let go of it even as it gnaws upon your very flesh. I want to pry that viper from your arms. To suckle upon your torn and bloody flesh. To take your pain within myself and make it mine."

She trembled beside him; he could feel the quivers through the arm she kept on him. "I have no secret."

He bent and whispered against her hair, "Sweet, darling liar."

"I don't—"

"Hush now." A shiver ran up his spine, and he knew without even turning that his mother was approaching. They'd neared Sir Henry, who stood with two other gentlemen. Deftly he inserted Temperance into the circle, made a slight excuse, and turned just as Lady Caire tapped him rather hard on the arm.

"Lazarus."

"Madam." He inclined his head.

"I see you're still escorting that woman."

"I'm so glad your memory is intact," Lazarus said smoothly. "So many begin to lose recollection as they age."

There was a short, frigid silence, and for a moment he was sure he'd said enough to drive her away. He watched as Temperance leaned toward Sir Henry, and the man's eyes dropped to her bosom.

Then Lady Caire drew a trembling breath. "What did I ever do to you to deserve this terrible sentiment you show toward me?"

He looked back at her, blinking in honest astonishment. "Why, nothing."

She sighed. "Then why this constant hostility? Why this—"

Something snapped in him. He took a step toward her, using his height to tower over her smaller frame. "Don't ask questions when you don't truly want to know the answers, madam."

Her blue eyes, identical to his own, widened. "Lazarus."

"You did nothing," he said quietly and hard. "When Father abandoned me at the wet nurse, you did nothing. When he returned five years later and tore me screaming from her arms, you did nothing. When he whipped me for crying for the only mother I knew, you did nothing. And when Annelise lay dying of a childish fever—"

He cut himself off, staring blindly toward Temperance. Sir Henry had his hand upon her arm, and there was a slight frown between her brows.

His mother laid her hand on his arm. "Don't you think I mourn Annelise's death as well?"

He turned back to her, swallowing, his mouth twisted in a sneer. "When Annelise lay dying, desperately ill from fever, and my goddamned *father* refused to send for a physician because a five-year-old girl should learn strength, what did you do?"

She merely stared at him, and he noticed for the first time the fine lines that radiated from her blue eyes.

"I'll tell you what you did. *Nothing.*" Out of the corner of his eye, he saw Sir Henry draw Temperance away from the other gentlemen. Toward the back of the ballroom. "Nothing is what you always do, madam. Don't be surprised when I, in return, feel *nothing* for you."

He took her hand off his sleeve and threw it away from himself.

Lazarus turned swiftly, but Temperance and Sir Henry had vanished. Goddamn it! He began weaving through the ballroom, making for the far corner where he'd last seen her. He should never have left her alone with the man. Should never have let himself be distracted. Someone caught his arm as he passed, but he shook off the hand and heard an exclamation of surprised displeasure; then he was at the corner where he'd last seen her. He shoved aside a pyramid of dying flowers, expecting to find a passage or nook for lovers. But there was nothing. Only the blank wall behind the flowers.

Lazarus turned in a circle, searching the ballroom for a flash of turquoise, the proud tilt of her head. But he saw only the idiot faces of the cream of London society.

Temperance had disappeared.

*   *   *

TEMPERANCE KNEW ALMOST at once that she'd made an unfortunate mistake in judging Sir Henry's character. As he led her into a darkened room, her pulse beat with alarm, but hope died hard. If she was mistaken, if he really was interested in the home, she'd be a fool to insult him. On the other hand, if his interest wasn't in the home at all, she might be in very grave danger indeed.

Which was why she made sure to put a large armchair between herself and Sir Henry as they entered the room.

"I sympathize with Caire your need for privacy, sir," she said as sweetly as possible, "but might we want to find a better-lit room at least?"

"Can never be too sure, my dear," Sir Henry replied, not reassuring Temperance at all. "I dislike to discuss my business where others might overhear."

He closed the door behind him, making the room quite black.

Temperance inhaled. "Yes, well, as to that. The Home for Unfortunate Infants and Foundling Children has only three staff at the moment: myself, my brother, Mr. Winter Makepeace, and our maid, Nell Jones."

"Yes?" Sir Henry said, his voice sounding nearer.

Temperance thought it prudent to abandon her armchair and shift a bit to her left and closer to the door. "Yes. But if we had sufficient funds, we would be able to hire more staff and thus help more children."

"You've fled, my little mouse," Sir Henry singsonged in a nauseating voice.

"Sir Henry, are you at all interested in my foundling home?" Temperance asked in exasperation.

"Of course I am," he replied, much too close.

She made a startled movement to her right, and male arms immediately closed about her. Horrid wet lips slid across her cheek. "The home will be a perfect cover for meeting you."

And then his lips were mashing hers against her teeth.

Sadly, the first thing Temperance felt at this assault was disappointment rather than outrage. She'd spent the time since the musicale imagining how the home could benefit from Sir Henry's patronage. Now she'd have to start the whole bloody process of finding a patron over again. In disgust, she shoved against his chest, but naturally he didn't give an inch. Instead he attempted to insert his thick tongue into her mouth, a truly revolting prospect.

Temperance had been disciplining males for a half score of years now. True, the males she dealt with were usually much shorter and less hairy than Sir Henry, but the principle, surely, was much the same.

She reached up, took a firm hold of his left ear, and twisted hard.

Sir Henry screamed like a little girl.

At the same time, the door to the room crashed open. Someone moving low and fast rushed in, shoving Temperance aside and slamming into Sir Henry. The two men went down. Temperance squinted in the dark. She heard the thud of fists, then Sir Henry's choked-off scream.

There was a pause.

Caire took her arm and escorted her roughly out the door. Temperance blinked as he began hauling her back down the passage. As they neared the ballroom, the sound of the crowd inside grew.

She attempted to withdraw her arm from his grasp. "Caire."

"What the hell were you doing going to a dark room with that ass? Have you no sense?"

She glanced at him. There was a reddened spot on his jaw, and he looked livid. "Your hair has come undone."

He stopped suddenly, pushing her up against the wall of the passage. "Never go anywhere with a man not of your family."

She arched her brows up at him. "What about you?"

"Me? I am far, far worse than Sir Henry." He leaned close, his breath brushing against her cheek. "You ought never to be near me again. You should run right now."

His bright blue eyes blazed and a muscle in his hard jaw twitched. He was truly a frightening sight.

She stood on tiptoe and brushed her lips against that tic. He jerked and then stood still. She felt the muscle jump once more beneath her mouth and then subside. She slid her lips toward his mouth.

"Temperance," he growled.

"Hush," she whispered, and kissed him.

It was strange. Another man had just kissed her on the mouth, but this pressing of lips with Caire was entirely different. His mouth was firm and warm, his lips stubbornly closed against hers. She placed her hands on his wide shoulders for leverage and leaned a little closer. She could smell some kind of exotic spice on his skin—perhaps he'd rubbed it on after shaving—and his mouth tasted of heady wine. She licked the seam of his lips, once, gently.

He groaned.

"Open," she breathed across his lips, and he did.

She probed delicately, licking the inside of his lips,

across his teeth, until she found his tongue. She stroked across it and retreated. He followed her tongue into her mouth, and she suckled him softly, raising her palms to frame his lean cheeks.

Something in her shifted, crumbling apart and re-forming into a new and wonderful shape. She didn't know what that shape was, but she wanted to keep it. To stay here in this dim hallway and kiss Caire forever.

The murmur of voices came from the far end of the passage, drawing nearer.

Caire lifted his head, looking toward the ballroom.

A door opened and closed and the voices stopped.

He took her hand. "Come."

"A moment."

He turned to look at her, one eyebrow raised, but she darted around him. His black velvet tie was nearly out of his hair. Carefully, she unknotted it and combed through the silver strands with her fingers before retying the ribbon.

When she came back around him, he still had that eyebrow cocked. "Satisfied?"

"For now." She took his arm and he led her back to the ballroom.

"I'll need to begin anew," she said as they began circling.

"So it seems."

She glanced up at him. "Are you willing to take me to another party or musicale?"

"Yes."

She nodded. He'd said it matter-of-factly, as if there'd never been a question. "And when will you be going into St. Giles again?"

She'd expected him to reply at once, but he was silent

for a moment as they walked. She looked at him. His eyebrows were slightly knit.

"I don't know," he said finally. "I'm worried that we've been attacked twice now. On the one hand, it must mean I'm getting closer to Marie's murderer. On the other, I don't wish to put you at risk. I must think on the matter and decide how best to make further inquiries."

Temperance looked down, smoothing her hand down the lovely turquoise gown. She'd never felt material so fine and had gasped when she'd seen her reflection in the little mirror in her room. Caire seemed so cynical, but in many ways his actions were thoughtful. She took a breath. "Did you love her?"

He stopped, but she didn't look at him. She couldn't.

"I've never loved anyone," he said.

That made her look up. He was staring ahead stiffly. "No one?"

He shook his head. "Not since Annelise died."

Her heart contracted at the admission. How could one go through life without love at all? "But you've spent months searching for Marie's killer," she said softly. "She must have meant something to you."

"Perhaps I search because she should have meant something. Because I should've loved her." He grimaced. "Perhaps I'm chasing a will-o'-the-wisp of phantom emotion. Perhaps I'm merely fooling myself."

She had an urge to take him into her arms, to comfort this cold, isolated man. But they stood in a crowded ballroom. Instead, she squeezed his arm. The contact might cause him pain, but no man could survive without another's touch, not even he.

They stopped at the side of the dance floor, and she

watched as the beautiful figures moved past. Lady Hero, the sister of the Duke of Wakefield, was a striking figure in a silver tissue gown.

"Would you like to dance?" Caire asked.

She shook her head. "I don't know how."

He angled a glance down at her. "Truly?"

"There isn't much call for it in a foundling home."

"Come." He began towing her again.

"Where are you taking me?"

"Not to a dark room, I assure you."

They reached the back of the ballroom, where a double door stood cracked to let in some of the chill night air. Caire pushed through them and drew her out onto a long balcony that ran the length of the back of the house.

"Now, then." Caire stood next to her and raised their joined hands.

"Oh." She suddenly realized what he was going to do. "Not here."

"Why not here?" he asked. "No one is about."

That was true. The night was too cold for others to be out on the balcony.

She bit her lip, feeling foolish that she'd never learned to dance when everyone else at the ball could dance as well as they could breathe. "But..."

He smiled at her suddenly, handsome and wicked. "Are you afraid I'll see how clumsy you are?"

She stuck out her tongue at him.

"Careful," he said low, though the smile still played around his lips. "I might abandon this lesson for one far more to my taste."

Her eyes widened, unsure how to take his teasing tone.

"Come, it's not so very hard."

His voice was gentle now—and he was far too perceptive.

She inhaled, looking away from him, touched by his tenderness.

He took her hand. "The main thing is to always look as if you have a poker up your"—he cast a sideways glance at her—"er, back. Watch."

And he patiently demonstrated the steps to the dance, coaching her to follow him as the music floated through the open balcony doors. Temperance studied his graceful movements, trying to imitate them, but what seemed inborn to him was a confusing series of steps to her.

"Oh, I shall never be able to do this," she exclaimed after several minutes.

"So dramatic," he murmured. "You're doing quite well, I think."

"But I keep confusing the steps," she said. "You make it seem so natural."

"It is natural—to me," he said flatly. "I spent hours upon hours practicing these steps as a boy. If I misstepped, my dance master had a cane he would bring down on the back of my calves. I learned quickly not to misstep."

"Oh," she said rather inadequately.

His world was so different from hers. While she'd been learning to cook, mend, and pinch pennies as a child, he'd learned to master these silly, intricate steps. She pictured him, a proud little boy, dancing all by himself in a large, elegant ballroom, his only company a cruel dance master.

She shivered.

His brows knit. "You're cold. Let's go in."

She nodded gratefully.

They stepped back into the ballroom, which seemed more crowded than ever.

"Would you like some punch?" Caire asked.

Temperance nodded again. He found an empty chair for her near a huge vase of flowers, and she sat while he went off in search of refreshment. The hour was growing late now, the scent of half-burned candles pervading the room. Temperance saw several ladies employ their fans and wished rather wistfully for one of her own. Then she was chiding herself for wanting more when Caire had already given her so much for this night. Perhaps he was right: perhaps no matter how much a person had, they could still be unhappy.

A movement out of the corner of her eye caught her attention, and she saw Sir Henry making his way through the crowd. Oh, goodness! How awkward if he should see her. Temperance turned her head away and lifted her hand to her coiffure as if checking to see if her jeweled pins were still in place.

"Have you dropped something?" a feminine voice said nearby.

Temperance looked up, startled, and met Lady Hero's wide gray eyes. She had taken the seat next to Temperance's, and while the lady didn't smile, her expression was quite pleasant.

Temperance realized she was staring and remembered that she'd been asked a question. "Oh. Oh, no, my lady."

"Someone has told you who I am," Lady Hero said.

"Yes."

"Ah." Lady Hero looked at her lap. "It was to be

expected, I suppose." She glanced up and caught Temperance's eye, smiling a little crookedly. "I find people treat me differently when they know my name."

"Oh." Temperance wasn't sure how exactly to respond to that, because, of course, Lady Hero was quite correct: A duke's daughter was treated differently. "I am Temperance Dews."

Lady Hero smiled more fully. "How do you do?" This close, Temperance could see a fine sprinkling of freckles across her nose. They only served to highlight Lady Hero's smooth, white complexion.

Sir Henry chose that moment to walk past them. She met his embarrassed eyes before quickly looking away.

Lady Hero followed her gaze. "That man is a toad."

"I beg your pardon?" Temperance blinked. Surely she hadn't heard correctly. Did the daughters of dukes call gentlemen toads?

Apparently they did. Lady Hero nodded. "Sir Henry Easton, yes? He looks agreeable enough, I'll grant you, but he has definite toad tendencies. I say"—her brows knit slightly—"he hasn't done anything to you, has he?"

"No." Temperance wrinkled her nose. "Well, yes. He tried to kiss me."

Lady Hero winced. "Horrifying."

"It was, really. And rather disappointing, too. You see, I thought he might be interested in my foundling home, but he wasn't. I'm afraid it was rather foolish of me."

"Ah," Lady Hero said, sounding wise. "I don't think you should blame yourself, you know. Toadlike gentlemen generally try to kiss ladies entirely unprovoked. Or at least that is what I have been led to believe. No gentleman has ever attempted to press his unwanted attentions upon me, of course. Duke's daughter and all that." Lady Hero sounded just a tad disappointed.

Temperance smiled. She would never have guessed that a duke's daughter would be so delightful to talk to.

"But tell me about this foundling home," Lady Hero said. "I've never met a lady who managed one."

"Oh!" Temperance felt a pleasurable rush of confusion. "Well, the Home for Unfortunate Infants and Foundling Children is in St. Giles, and we take care of eight and twenty children at the moment, but we could take care of ever so much more if only we had a patron for the home." Her shoulders slumped. "That's why I was so hopeful of Sir Henry."

Lady Hero shook her head. "I'm sorry. Do you have both girls and boys at your home?"

"Yes, we keep them in separate rooms, of course, but we accept all children up to the age of nine. They're apprenticed out at that age."

"Really?" Lady Hero said. Her hands were folded gracefully in her lap, and she made no movement, but she seemed somehow to be genuinely interested. "But then how—oh, bother."

Her gaze had gone beyond Temperance's shoulder.

Temperance glanced quickly and saw a rather stout matron gesturing imperiously.

"It's Cousin Bathilda," Lady Hero said. "She probably wants me to go in with her to dinner, and she'll only become more irate if I pretend not to notice her."

"Then you had best go."

"I fear so." Lady Hero inclined her head. "It was a pleasure meeting you, Miss Dews."

"Mrs." Temperance said quickly. "I'm widowed."

"Mrs. Dews, then." Lady Hero rose. "I do hope we meet again."

Temperance watched her make her way to "Cousin Bathilda."

When she turned back, Caire was standing in front of her, a glass of punch in his hand. "You've been in rarefied company in my absence."

Temperance smiled at him. "You wouldn't credit how nice she is."

He glanced in Lady Hero's direction, then back at her, his expression indulgent. "Is she? Come, drink up your punch and then I shall feed you some scandalously decadent dinner before I take you home. Your brother is bound to be pacing by the door as it is."

Indeed, it was nearly an hour before they finally made their way to Caire's carriage. Temperance was yawning widely after the rich food and richer wine. Caire settled her on a seat, knocked on the carriage roof, and then sat beside her, drawing her into his arms. He threw a fur across them both, and she drifted in and out of sleep as his carriage rumbled across London.

It was like a dream world. She felt so safe and warm in his arms, and she could hear the strong beat of his heart under her ear. He was different from her, an aristocrat from a marvelous spun-sugar world, but his heart beat just like any other man.

The thought comforted her.

When next she was aware, the carriage had drawn to a halt and he was gently shaking her shoulder. "Up, my sleeping beauty."

She opened her eyes and yawned. "Is it dawn?"

He glanced to the window. "It soon will be. I have a

feeling your brother will take a strip from my hide if I don't have you home before the first light."

That woke her up a bit more. She scrambled upright and felt to make sure her hair was still in place. "Oh, I've lost a slipper."

She bent to look on the floor, but he'd already knelt and felt along the base of the seat. "Here 'tis."

He took her stockinged foot and gently slid the slipper back on. She stared, dazed, down at his silver head.

He must've felt her look for he glanced up, his eyes darkening. But he merely said, "Ready?"

She nodded, unable to trust her voice.

He helped her from the carriage and walked her to the door of the foundling home. The light had turned gray as they'd approached, but no one yet stirred on the street. She turned as they reached the door, placing a hand on his chest.

"Caire..." She wasn't sure what she was about to say, but it didn't matter anyway.

He bent his head and brushed her lips with his, murmuring, "Good night, Mrs. Dews."

He turned away.

She watched his broad back blend into the gray mist; then she opened the door to the foundling home with her key. She yawned as she barred the door behind her, then hopped on first one foot and then the other as she removed her heeled slippers. Afterward, she wandered into the kitchen.

Four male heads swung around at her entrance. Temperance stared. Surely her brothers hadn't waited up all night just for her? But there was something else wrong. For the fourth male was her brother-in-law, William, and his eyes were red.

Her gaze flew to Winter. "Silence."

Winter looked drawn and years older than his true age. "Silence has been missing since yesterday afternoon."

HE'D TOLD HER to unlace her bodice and to take down her hair, so she had.

Silence walked from Charming Mickey O'Connor's bedroom with her hair trailing down her back. His bedroom was on the floor above the throne room, and in the hall outside, she came upon a maid—the first female servant she'd seen here. The woman stared at her and then looked quickly away again, back to her work of polishing the multicolored marble floor. For a moment, Silence wondered if the maid had any help in her chore, or if perhaps that was all she did? Polish yard after yard of amazing marble floor? If so, it was a task she did not envy the woman.

"This way, miss," a male voice called.

She looked up and saw that Harry waited for her. His eyes were filled with pity.

Silence straightened her shoulders. "Thank you."

The guard hesitated. "Would you like to put yourself to rights?"

He kept his gaze firmly away from the tops of her breasts, revealed by her open bodice.

"No," Silence whispered. "No, thank you."

Charming Mickey had made it plain that straightening herself was not allowed.

Harry looked at her helplessly for a moment and then nodded. He turned and led the way down the curving marble stairs. Other people were up by now, for it was well past dawn, and the expressions as they saw her varied. Some were pitying like Harry. Some—mostly women—looked envious. But the majority were merely contemptuous; one bold fellow even dared to wink at her before Harry shoved him hard into the wall. After that, most turned their faces away as she passed.

They came to the front door, and Harry held it open for her.

"If'n you need anything, miss, just ask," he muttered as she passed.

"Thank you," she replied politely, "but I have everything I came for."

And she walked into the bright, merciless sunshine.

Charming Mickey had been quite explicit in his instructions, so she placed one foot in front of the other and walked up the middle of the dingy St. Giles street, her long hair blowing in the wind. She didn't look left or right but kept her eyes focused straight ahead, even when the whores returning home called crude things to her.

She closed her ears and heart and heard nothing, saw nothing, until directly in front of her she saw Temperance's face, tears streaming down her cheeks.

Then Silence gasped once and felt the sting of tears at her own eyes.

But by then she'd made it to the end of the street, so it was quite all right. She'd followed his instructions, done everything he'd said, and he'd honor his part of the bargain as well.

Except her life would never be the same again.

Chapter Twelve

⁂

Meg sighed. "This is not love, Your Majesty."
King Lockedheart froze in the act of feeding a small
morsel of cake to the little blue bird. "Then what
is it?"
"Fear," Meg said simply. "Your courtiers fear you,
Your Majesty."
The king grunted and seemed pensive.
"Take her back to the dungeons," he ordered the
guards. "And, Meg?"
"Your Majesty?"
"Take care you comb your hair when next I see you."
"But I need a comb and pins to dress my hair," Meg
said softly.
The king only nodded impatiently and once again
Meg was led away....
—from *King Lockedheart*

Temperance held Silence close and gently laced her bodice as the rented carriage rattled back to Wapping. Silence
was limp, but her breath was rough and Temperance could

feel her tears dropping to her fingers as she worked at the gown.

"Do you need a doctor?" Temperance finally asked.

"No. No, I'm fine," Silence whispered.

That was so obviously not the case that Temperance felt fresh tears start again. She swiped at them fiercely with her wrist. Now was not the time to succumb to her own horror and regret. She had to be strong for Silence.

"What"—she had to stop and inhale—"what did he do to you, dearest?"

"Nothing at all," Silence said tonelessly. "He never even touched me."

Temperance started to protest but then reined herself in. Quite obviously Charming Mickey had done *something* to Silence, and just as obviously she couldn't talk about it right now. For the next several minutes, Temperance concentrated on finger-combing her sister's long russet hair. She parted and braided it and, using a few of her own hairpins, wrapped it in a crown about her head.

Silence lay against Temperance's breast while Temperance stroked her forehead as if she were a little child.

She broke the quiet after a bit. "Dearest, whyever did you go to that man?"

Silence sighed, the sound lost and lonely. "I had to save William."

"But why didn't you come to me first? We could have discussed it, perhaps found another way to help William." Temperance tried to keep her voice even, but she knew some of her despair leaked through.

"You were so busy," Silence said quietly. "With the home, with the children, with Lord Caire and your hunt for a new patron."

Her words were like a knife to Temperance's breast. How could she have become so involved with other things that her own sister had not thought to come to her for help?

"It wouldn't have mattered anyway," Silence whispered, closing her eyes. "I had to go to Charming Mickey alone. I had to make the bargain I did with him alone. And it worked, you know."

"What worked, dearest?" Temperance murmured.

"My going to Charming Mickey. My bargain with him. He says he'll return the *Finch*'s stolen cargo."

Temperance closed her eyes as well. She hoped that the pirate king would keep his word, but even if a miracle happened and he did, that would not change things for Silence.

Her baby sister was ruined—now and forever.

LAZARUS HAD RISEN only moments before when the argument started outside his bedroom door that afternoon. He looked up from his desk, where he'd been sitting in his banyan and breeches, and watched his bedroom door burst open.

Temperance marched in the room. Behind her hovered Small.

Lazarus took one look at the evidence of tears on Temperance's face and snapped to his valet. "Leave us."

Small bowed and drew the bedroom doors shut.

Lazarus stood slowly. "What has happened?"

She looked at him, tragedy in her gold-flecked eyes. "Silence...Oh, God, Lazarus, Silence."

He noted absently that she'd never addressed him by his given name before. "Tell me."

She closed her eyes, as if to steady herself for the recitation. "She decided to try and get back William, her husband's, cargo herself. She went to the dockyard gang lord, a man named Mickey O'Connor...."

He'd heard vague rumors of a flamboyant dockyard thief in his wanderings in St. Giles. The man was dangerous. Caire frowned. "And?"

A silver tear slipped from beneath her eyelid and dropped, sparkling, in the afternoon light, to the floor. "He agreed to return the ship's cargo...but at a price."

A lifetime of cynicism made him know what the price was, but he asked anyway. "What was it?"

She opened her eyes, shining gilded brown. "He made her spend the night with him."

Lazarus exhaled at the confirmation. He'd never met this Silence, knew nothing of her, and even if he had, he would probably care not a whit for her. Except that she was Temperance's sister.

And that made all the difference in the world.

It was a strange thing, this feeling of empathy. He'd never experienced it before. He realized that what hurt this woman hurt him as well, that what made her bleed caused a hemorrhage of pain within his soul.

He held out his arms to her. "Come here."

She dived for his arms and he caught her against his chest, shards of exquisite pain prickling his bare skin where the banyan parted and exposed him. She smelled so sweet, of dawn and woman.

"I'm sorry," he crooned, the words foreign on his tongue. "I'm so sorry."

She sobbed once. "When I came home this morning, William said Silence had never returned the night before. He suspected she'd gone to O'Connor, but it was too dangerous to venture into the gang lord's territory at night."

Lazarus thought silently that if it had been Temperance, if he'd had knowledge that she were in a den of thieves, her person and soul imperiled, he would've retrieved her no matter what the cost.

"We waited until light and then rented a hack," she whispered into his shoulder. Her breath sent shivers of unease across his skin. "We'd just come within sight of O'Connor's house when Silence emerged from it."

He stroked her hair. She still wore the yellow topaz pins he'd bought for her, though she'd changed her gown.

She shuddered as if remembering. "Her hair was down, Caire, and her bodice undone. He made her walk that way up the street, as if to brand her a whore. When she saw me, she started to cry."

He closed his eyes, absorbing her pain, and repeated the only thing he knew to say. "I'm sorry."

"She said nothing happened, that O'Connor made her stay the night in his bedroom but didn't touch her. Oh, Caire, her protests were so pathetic that I didn't dare press her for the truth. All I could do was hold her."

He tightened his arms about her. "I'm sorry."

She pulled back, looking into his eyes. "But the worst part was when we returned to the foundling home. William was waiting for us—"

"He didn't accompany you in the hack?" Lazarus frowned.

Temperance shook her head. "He said if he was seen near O'Connor's house, it would give credence to the claim that he was in league with the river pirate."

Lazarus ran his hand soothingly over her back without comment. Hollingbrook sounded like a fool.

"And when we arrived, he took one look at Silence and

then turned his face away. Oh, Caire"—her eyes closed wearily—"it near broke my heart."

He bent his head then because he couldn't not do so. His lips brushed hers gently. "I am so sorry."

Her head sank wearily against his shoulder as she accepted his kisses. Her lips were soft and tasted of tears. He brushed his mouth over her cheeks, tasting the tears there as well, licking up her grief.

"Caire," she sighed.

"Hmm?"

"I'm so tired," she said, almost like a little girl. He guessed she'd not slept since he'd brought her back to her home the night before.

"Then lie with me a while," he whispered.

He picked her up like a child and brought her to his still-unmade bed, laying her gently there before climbing in beside her. He pulled her close until her head was snuggled against his banyan-covered chest, pricking him with almost-pain.

She sighed again. "'S funny."

"What is?" he murmured, threading his fingers through her hair. He took the yellow topaz jewels out of her coiffure and laid them on the table by his bed.

"William sent word. After he went home with Silence. After my brothers argued and Asa stormed out."

"What did he say?" He plucked bent little pins from her hair, one by one, releasing her tresses from their confinement, combing them gently with his fingers.

"The ship's cargo," she said. "Mickey O'Connor kept his word. It was all there on the ship this morning. As if it had never disappeared in the first place."

Lazarus stared at the canopy over his bed and thought about a thief's perfidy and his honor and the price a woman might pay for the man she loved. When he looked down again, he saw that Temperance breathed slowly and evenly against him, her lush mouth slightly parted. Her mahogany hair was spread like a blanket of silk upon his shoulder and bed, and the sight gave him satisfaction deep in his soul.

He lifted one lock and watched as the strands curled adoringly around his fingers. He smiled slightly. How a man might deceive himself with such a sight.

Then he let his arm drop. He pulled her a little closer against his chest and closed his own eyes.

And slept.

SHE AWOKE IN a darkened room with the realization that something awful waited for her just as soon as she opened her eyelids.

So she didn't.

She drifted, not thinking, not waking, trying to hold on to the peace of sleep. There was another body next to hers, large and warm and comforting, and she concentrated on that. He breathed deeply as if still asleep, and she liked the sound of his soft exhalations. It meant that she wasn't alone. She wished she could stay here forever, in the gray warmth of half-sleep. But inevitably, wakefulness and knowledge intruded and she opened her eyes on a pained gasp.

Caire's arm tightened about her.

She turned her face into his side, inhaling his musk, ashamed that tears still threatened. Silence was the youngest, the most innocent of their family, and her downfall seemed too terrible to bear, as if all light had been extinguished in the world.

He sighed heavily, one hand trailing down her back to her bottom and squeezing. "Temperance."

He was hot. She slid her arm over his back, vaguely surprised to realize that only a thin layer of silk separated her fingers from his bare skin. "Caire."

His mouth found hers, lazy with sleepiness. He kissed her and she was comforted, here in the darkness. She wasn't Temperance at this moment; he wasn't an aristocratic lord far above her. Here in the limbo between night and day, they were simply a man and a woman.

And as a woman, she opened her mouth to his.

He made a satisfied sound, deep in his chest, and thrust his tongue into her mouth, asserting his authority. She let him, drawing him deep. Right now she didn't want to face the world outside those bedroom doors. She only wanted to feel.

To let herself feel as she hadn't in years.

Desire hit her, hard and fast. She'd always been particularly vulnerable to physical lust, had to guard against it every day of her life to make sure others didn't know how it controlled her. Now she let it run free.

She opened her hands over his back, feeling the slick silk slide beneath her palms. He was muscled, his shoulders wide, the indent of his spine very defined.

He broke the kiss on a gasp, plucking at her bodice. "Take this off."

It was awkward, here in the dark, but she skimmed and wriggled, and in the end, when her stays twisted about her middle, he simply inserted his fingers under the laces and tore them from the holes. Each lace made a popping sound as it was released from its prison, and she felt her breasts jiggle in freedom. He ripped the ruined stays from her body and then pushed her chemise over her head.

And then she was naked.

"Remove this," she whispered, pulling at his banyan.

"I can't. I'm sorry," he murmured, and she remembered his sensitivity.

She met his eyes. They stared regretfully down at her. "It will hurt you?"

"Not hurt." He brushed his lips against the corner of her mouth. "No longer hurt with you. Just...discomfort. And only if you touch my bare skin."

"And if you touch my bare skin?"

He smiled slowly. "That, I assure you, will cause me no pain at all."

This frustrated her, but then she moved against him, rubbing her breasts against his chest, feeling the silk against her nipples.

He growled, reaching for her, and she broke free of her reins. She threw a leg over him and ran her bare calf up and down his leg. He wore breeches, and she felt the rough material against her skin before she came to his bare lower legs. He stiffened. She knew she was causing him discomfort, but she couldn't stop. She delighted in the contrast between her softness and his hard strength.

He moved suddenly, rolling her beneath him.

"Yes," she gasped. "Yes."

But he didn't do the expected. Instead he captured her hands, pressing them above her head, shoving his weight down on her until she could hardly move.

"Please, now," she panted. She didn't want to leave this drugged state, to return to normal life and guilt and sorrow.

"There's no rush," he murmured against her throat.

"Yes," she replied angrily, "yes, there is."

But he only laughed, his breath tickling her skin as he trailed his mouth over her collarbone. What was he about? Didn't he have the same urges as other men? That part of him—the part that made him a man—was most definitely interested. It pressed against her belly, hard and hot through his breeches, sliding to her hip as he moved down her body.

She was distracted, dazed and confused, her attention split between his wandering mouth and the cock that pressed now at the top of her mound. She tried to raise her hips, to push against him, but he chuckled and shifted one thigh, ensuring her immobility.

"What are you doing?" she cried in frustration.

"Why, Mrs. Dews," he drawled, "I thought you'd been married."

"I *was* married," she said waspishly. The last thing she wanted to think about now was her dead husband.

"Then I would think you'd be somewhat familiar with this process," he whispered just before he took her nipple into his hot mouth.

Her mind went blank, and then a rolling wave of sensation made her literally shake. Dear God, it'd been so long since a man had touched her there. Since she'd felt that strong suckle. The eroticism was almost overwhelming.

He lifted his head to lazily lick at the breast, each languid swipe of his wet tongue harrowing in its own way.

"I must admit I'm a novice at this myself," he drawled.

"What?" She blinked into the darkness. "What do you mean?"

"Making love," he said, quite matter-of-factly, and bit gently on her other nipple.

She sobbed, feeling that pleasure-pain, feeling the growing ache in her center. He would not move to relieve her.

Instead he babbled.

"I've been told it's an extraordinary experience," he said calmly, "but you must forgive me if I seem unsure. I've bedded many women, but the act of making love is one I've never ventured. In this, I think, you must be the master."

His voice had a slight question, but even if she'd been in her right senses, she wouldn't have commented. Why was he playing this game when all she wanted was his flesh between her thighs?

"Gently," he crooned in a hushed voice, chiding her for a groan of frustration. He shoved apart her thighs and settled himself into the space he'd made. "There. Is that better?"

It wasn't perfect, but it was unquestionably better. The length of his hardness lay against her wet folds, the material of his breeches a wonderful abrasion. She closed her eyes in bliss at his heat, at the slight, but not quite hard enough, pressure.

"There," he repeated soothingly. "Now, what if I add this?"

And he drew her nipple into his mouth again, his teeth scraping just barely as he suckled.

She wanted to touch him as well, to run her fingers through the hair on his chest, to grip his shoulders and reach beneath his breeches to knead his buttocks. But his hands still chained hers and she was forced to simply wait.

To submit.

"Widen your legs," he whispered, his voice deep and clear in the still dark.

She complied.

"Lift them a little."

She obeyed. He grunted in what sounded like pleasure. Her movement had caused him to settle closer to her, his cock now lodged between the folds of her sex.

She swallowed, waiting for his next move.

"I think…yes, this." He shifted, his hand between them, opening his falls, letting himself out. When he again let his weight settle against her, his naked penis rubbed quite explicitly on her clitoris, and while she was distracted by that, he brought his mouth down on hers.

He kissed her openmouthed, and it was almost too intimate, here in the dark. He lay on her—his chest pressed into her vulnerable, naked breasts, his hot cock burrowed against her softness—and thoroughly, leisurely, kissed her.

He caught her bottom lip between his teeth, nibbling delicately, then whispered against her lips, "Open."

She accepted the sweep of his tongue into her mouth, sucking for long moments helplessly. So erotic was the kiss that she almost didn't notice when he began to move against her. But she did. She stilled, her entire concentration on that part of his body becoming intimate with that part of her body. Until he nipped the corner of her mouth.

"Pay attention." His voice was ragged now.

Something wild and feminine thrilled at the roughness of his voice, at the knowledge that she was affecting him, despite his sophistication. She opened her mouth beneath his, biting back at him, and he inhaled sharply. Then his mouth was crushing hers, roughly, almost out of control, a male creature dominating a female. His female.

He shifted again, his penis drawing back, finding her entrance and notching into her. He raised his head only far enough to whisper, "Now."

He shoved powerfully.

His hardness breached her soft depths, parting and burrowing, invading where she'd been empty for years. She gasped at the movement, at the sensation both physical and mental, but his mouth was on hers again, and he inhaled her breath. He shoved and shoved again until he was seated fully, her thighs stretched wide, his hips hard against hers.

She had a moment of panic. Who was this man? Why was she under him, letting the worst part of herself dictate her actions? Then he began to move and all thought fled her mind. He moved like a wave pounding against a beach, like the wind flying across the cobblestones, like a man on a woman. It was the oldest, most common movement in history, and at the same time it was new and pure. Because it was him and her and they'd never done this together before.

She arched under him, feeling his flesh part and merge with hers as he continued to kiss her deeply.

He ran his mouth over her cheek, never breaking his smooth, slow rhythm, and whispered in her ear, "Wrap your legs around my hips."

She did and then they were locked tightly together. He hitched himself up a little on her and she gasped. On each downward thrust, on every slow, dragging withdrawal, he rubbed his flesh against the apex of her sex. She turned her head, suddenly too exposed, too vulnerable, even in the dark, but he followed her, pressing his mouth softly at the corners of her lips. It was unbearable, this slow, controlled, repeated invasion, this sure attack on her senses. She wanted to scream, to make him stop. To urge him to go faster. And as if he understood her anxiety, he increased his pace, thudding into her core with a strong tempo.

Driving her insane.

She tore her mouth away from his, panting, her wrists twisting under his hold. "Stop."

"No," he whispered, an unseen ghost. "Let go."

"I can't."

"You can." He levered himself up a little more and began a slow twist of his hips as he drove into her, and somehow, the pressure, the pleasure, the heat, and the expectation all released at once.

She flew apart, sobbing, gloriously free, no mind, no soul, only a single throbbing point of shining beauty. Dimly she heard his breath catch, felt his rhythm falter and jerk, and then suddenly lose control. He thrust into her body savagely as she floated, and the movement sent her even higher.

He exhaled roughly.

His body made one or two more thrusts, and then he stopped, his head dropping as he kissed her tenderly. She had a wild urge to say something entirely inappropriate. To tell him what this had meant to her.

He released her wrists, but she was too worn out to lower her arms.

"Extraordinary indeed," he murmured, his voice calm and deep, only slightly out of breath.

She knew she should analyze that, should make some reply.

But she drifted to sleep instead.

HE'D NEVER WOKEN beside a woman before.

It was Lazarus's first thought the next morning. His usual lovers were, by definition, more in the way of business partners. They sold a commodity; he bought it. Simple, clean, and impersonal. So impersonal he'd sometimes not known their true names, even the ones like Marie, who he'd kept for years. Marie in whose name he searched for a killer in St. Giles.

Yet he'd never lain next to Marie. He'd never felt her sweet warmth beside him, never listened to the soft exhale of her breath as she slept.

He opened his eyes and turned his head to watch Temperance. She lay with her arms still thrown over her head. Her lips were a deep red, her cheeks flushed, and the dawning sun gave her skin a golden glaze. She was almost too beautiful, lying next to him, to be real. Only the tangle of her dark hair saved her from perfection. Thank God. He'd bought and used perfection before, and it no longer interested him. His blood stirred now for a real woman.

One untidy lock of hair trailed across a cheek, down her neck, sticking a bit sweatily, and curled at the top of one exposed breast. Round and full, the nipple a soft rose. He touched that nipple, wondering at the velvet texture of her skin, the instant tightening at the tip.

She gasped and his gaze flew toward hers. She looked at him wonderingly as if surprised to find herself here in his bed.

Well, perhaps she was.

"Good morning," he began. Banal, perhaps, but what the deuce else was he to say?

But she threw back the covers and bounded out of the bed like a startled fawn. "Where is my chemise?"

He crossed his arms behind his head. "I have no idea."

She turned a glare at him—entirely charming since she was nude. "You took it off me. You must know."

"I had, er, other matters on my mind." Pity. He had no need to look at his lap to know that his cock would've been more than happy to repeat their activities of last night.

He glanced at her. She was on her knees, her bottom in

the air as she searched under a chair, presumably for the missing chemise. The view was astounding, but he had the feeling she wasn't in the mood.

And, indeed, when she suddenly straightened and caught his stare, she glared. "I need to go home. I told Winter I was coming to see you, but I never expected to spend the night! He'll be worried."

"Naturally," he said in what he hoped was a soothing voice. "But it's just dawn. Surely you can stay long enough to break your fast?"

"No. I need to get home," she muttered. "I can't have my brothers thinking we're lovers."

He opened his mouth, but some sense of survival kept him from pointing out that they *were* lovers.

Instead he said patiently, "I'll ring for a maid to help you—"

"Oh, no!" She held up the remains of her stays.

He winced. "Ah. Allow me to send one of my maids to purchase you a new one."

"That will take hours!" She was back to glaring at him again.

He sighed. He'd never particularly enjoyed rising early, but it was quite evident he wouldn't be allowed to lie abed this morning.

Lazarus threw back the covers and rose, permitting himself only a moment's satisfaction when she took one look at the tent in his breeches and blushed violently. He crossed to the cord and rang for Small. After a sotto voce conference at the door to his room—Temperance had retired to his bed—the valet acquired a set of stays from a maid, and in half an hour, Mrs. Dews was properly attired again.

Lazarus lounged in a chair, watching as she tied her cloak quite firmly under her chin. Every hair was in place, a white cap sat primly on her head, and she looked every inch the respectable matron of a foundling home.

He hated the look.

"Wait," he said as she put her hand on the doorknob.

She turned impatiently but looked wary as she saw him prowling near.

"I need to make some investigations tonight," he said. "I had word of a man I should question when I returned home last night."

She bit her lip. "Of course."

He nodded. "Then be ready at eight o'clock."

"But..."

He bent and kissed her hard, his mouth forcing hers open, thrusting in his tongue as she gave way.

When he raised his head, she was looking at him in alarm. He smiled. "Good morning, Mrs. Dews."

And he watched as she turned and left his bedroom. Her spine was straight, and she never looked back. Perhaps she'd already decided to put their night together behind her.

If so, he pitied her. For he had every intention of bedding her again.

Chapter Thirteen

*Meg spent the rest of the day quite happily combing
out the tangles from her long flaxen hair. Early the
next morning, she braided her hair and wound it
about her head in a golden crown. She'd hardly
put the last pin in when the guards came to bring
her before the king. This time the throne room was
filled with a bevy of lovely ladies. Each was more
graceful than the last, their faces painted delicately
to highlight their dazzling beauty.*
*In the midst of this feminine bounty, the king
lounged, large and masculine and isolated. His gaze
immediately went to Meg.*
*Without preamble, he asked, "Do you love me, my
concubines?"*
*As one, the ladies turned and, with various
simpering expressions, said, "Yes!"…*
—from King Lockedheart

What had she done?

Temperance stared blindly out of Caire's carriage
as it rolled through the bright London sunshine. She'd

succumbed to the temptations of the flesh, had lain with a man not her husband—for the second time in her life. She should feel guilt and sorrow and perhaps panic, and she did feel all those things. But at the same time, there was a spark of joy deep within her breast that stubbornly refused to be quenched by all her doubts.

She'd lain with Caire and she was happier for it.

Still, she was bracing herself to meet Winter's disapproval when the carriage stopped near the home. And, indeed, when she descended, she saw that Winter stood outside the home's front door. Oh, dear.

He watched her approach, his dark brown eyes intent, but when she drew near, he merely said, "Come inside, sister."

Temperance followed him, subdued. She half expected him to quiz her on her absence the previous night, but he simply led her into the kitchen instead. There, Nell was supervising the cooking of the morning meal, Mary Whitsun in attendance. Nell rolled her eyes at Temperance's entrance, obviously agog with questions she couldn't ask at the moment.

Winter turned as if to go, but Temperance laid her hand on his arm. "Silence?"

He shook his head, turning his face from hers. "Neither she nor William have communicated since he sent word that the cargo was returned."

Temperance released a breath. "And Asa?"

"I don't know. He and Concord aren't speaking. I fear he's disappeared again."

She nodded dismally. Their family had splintered apart in only a matter of days.

"I must go to the school," Winter said.

"Of course," she replied, dropping her hand.

He hesitated. "Are you truly well, sister? I worry for your welfare."

She nodded, her eyes on her shoes. What must he think of her?

She felt the brush of his hand on her hair, light and comforting, and then he was gone from the kitchen.

"We missed you last night, ma'am," Mary Whitsun said softly. She was busy stirring the porridge over the fire and would not meet Temperance's eyes.

Temperance sighed and considered avoiding the issue. But that wasn't fair to either Mary Whitsun or herself. "I'm sorry. I neglected you and the other children. I should never have left you so abruptly last night."

Mary gave her an inscrutable look, much too old for a twelve-year-old child. "It's all right, ma'am."

Temperance winced.

"It's just…" Mary had slowed her stirring until the big wooden spoon was nearly motionless in the pot. "Mr. Makepeace said that a lady was making inquiries about girl apprentices yesterday evening. He said it might be a good position for me."

Temperance's heart squeezed. She wasn't ready yet to let go of Mary Whitsun, but she must face the reality of her position.

"I see." She found she had to clear her throat. She smiled brightly to cover the pause. "Well, that's good news, isn't it? I'll discuss this with Mr. Makepeace and make sure the position is a good one for you, Mary."

Mary ducked her head, her little shoulders slumping. "Yes, ma'am."

And Temperance had to turn away to hide the shine of tears in her eyes.

The rest of the day was spent in the usual labors of the home—cooking, cleaning, ordering the children and gently chiding. By evening, Temperance was at once exhausted and on edge, anticipating seeing Caire again. Yet, when his knock came at the kitchen door, she was still not prepared to see him.

Temperance opened the door and looked at him, standing there in the waning dusk. His silver hair was pulled back into a sleek tail, but her fingers remembered the silkiness of the locks. His sapphire eyes watched her from beneath the brim of his tricorne, and he wore his usual black cloak, but now she knew what it felt like to have him lie between her thighs. Knew how the lines about his mouth deepened when he was at his point. Knew how his penis jumped and jerked within her as his semen washed into her.

She inhaled, fighting to keep the polite, everyday expression on her face.

A corner of his sensuous lips curved just slightly as if he had an idea of the battle she fought within. "Mrs. Dews. How are you this evening?"

"Quite fine, my lord," she replied, perhaps a touch too sharply. She had an overwhelming urge to touch him, and yet she could not.

His mouth hid a definite smile now, and the sight made her want to both slam the door in his face and grab him and kiss him all at once.

It was a rather frustrating sensation.

She cleared her throat. "Would you care to come in for tea before we depart?"

"I thank you, no," he replied, as formally as she. "The business I have tonight cannot wait."

She nodded. "Very well."

Her cloak was ready and she swung it around herself before nodding to Nell, who was pretending not to be eavesdropping at the kitchen table, and left. Caire immediately set off. She hurried to catch up, but they hadn't gone half a dozen steps before he pulled her suddenly into a darkened doorway.

"What—"

His mouth cut off her startled exclamation. He kissed her thoroughly and possessively before raising his head slowly. "That's better."

He sounded very satisfied with himself.

"Humph."

He set off again, more moderately this time. Unlike their other evenings in St. Giles, she did not know where they were headed. Caire was the one leading now. They followed the back alley out to the crossroads, and Temperance saw his carriage waiting.

She glanced at him, surprised. "Where are we going?"

"To visit the man we saw at Mrs. Whiteside's house," he said matter-of-factly.

She halted. "Oh, but surely you don't need me for that."

"You have no idea the ways that I need you," he murmured, and helped her into the carriage.

Well, she really had no choice. At least that was what Temperance told herself as she sat on the carriage cushions. Perhaps the truth was that she liked being with him no matter the pretext.

He sat opposite her, and she tamped down a twinge of regret.

The carriage lurched forward, and she looked down at her hands in her lap, aware of his gaze upon her.

"Are you all right?" he asked softly after a moment.

"Fine," she replied.

"I meant after our coupling last night."

"Oh." She felt heat creep up her neck. He would talk bluntly about the matter! "I'm well. Thank you."

"And your sister?"

She frowned, the tears too close to the surface. "We haven't heard anything else."

"Ah."

She peeked through her lashes, trying to read his expression in the dim light. He sounded as if he might be worried for her. Did he intend to repeat the events of the night before? Or was it a one-time thing best forgotten? But surely if he was not interested in her, he would not have dragged her along on this ride. Temperance felt heat pool low in her belly at the thought of his hands caressing her breasts again. Of his lips against her neck.

The carriage shuddered to a halt and she looked up quickly. "Where—"

She didn't have time to finish the question, because the carriage door opened at that moment and a tall man in a gray wig and half-moon spectacles entered.

"Mrs. Dews, perhaps you remember my friend Mr. St. John?" Caire asked smoothly.

"Of course," she replied, trying to hide her confusion.

Mr. St. John inclined his head. "Ma'am."

"St. John has kindly consented to join us in our investigations this evening," Caire said.

St. John snorted softly, making Temperance wonder how his *kind consent* had been obtained. She stared curiously between the two men. Caire and St. John didn't seem likely friends. Caire was so carefree—but with an air of danger—while St. John looked grave and scholarly.

"May I inquire as to how you two became friends?" she asked.

It was Caire who replied. "St. John and I met at Oxford, where I was spending my time drinking bad wine, and he was attempting to translate obscure Grecian philosophers and arguing politics with other boring fellows."

St. John interjected another snort here, but Caire continued, oblivious to the interruption. "One night I came across him in the midst of six vulgar toughs who were in the process of pounding him into a sort of puree. I'm afraid I took offense at their chosen pursuit."

Temperance waited, but both men merely looked at her as if their story was done.

She blinked. "So you met in a tavern brawl?"

Caire looked at the ceiling consideringly. "More a street fight."

"Or melee." St. John shrugged.

"And you became friends," she finished for them.

"Yes," Caire said while St. John shrugged again, as if the outcome was self-evident.

"I don't understand," Temperance muttered under her breath.

Caire must've had acute hearing. "I think it was the blow St. John received to the crown of his head," he said kindly. "Blood all over the place. It has a kind of bonding effect."

She blinked again. "And you were untouched?"

That presumption was too much for St. John. "He had his nose broken and both eyes blacked," he said with what sounded very much like satisfaction. "And his lip swelled so much he talked with a lisp for a month."

"A sennight," Caire interjected.

"Six weeks at the very least," St. John shot back without heat. "You were still lisping on May Day when we, ah..."

"Rowed down the Isis dead drunk at dawn," Caire said. "With the don's stolen pug."

"Quite," St. John murmured.

Temperance's eyes widened. "Oh."

Caire's mouth cocked up. "So you see why I brought him when I thought we might need another."

"Oh, yes," Temperance said weakly.

"I spent the next two years at Oxford trying to get him to drink more wine and study less," Caire.

"And I spent those two years attempting to keep you from succumbing to your worst urges," St. John said far less lightly. He glanced at Caire. "At one point, I was certain you had a death wish."

"Maybe I did, " Caire whispered. "Maybe I did."

The carriage jolted and stopped.

Caire glanced out the window, immediately sobering. "And here we are."

AFTER THAT LAST attack in St. Giles, Lazarus had vowed never again to put Mrs. Dews at risk. Yet, at the same time, he needed an excuse that required her continued presence in his life. His inquiries, while dangerous, were perfect.

Hence St. John's appearance tonight.

Lazarus admitted to himself wryly that a male duenna—whom he'd provided himself—made his pursuit of Temperance somewhat comical. But he'd not compromise either her safety or his...courtship of her.

The word gave him pause. Was that what this was? A courtship? Perhaps. It was the first time that he'd pursued a female without the lure of money. It was a strangely humbling thought: She'd come to him with no regard for what he could give her. He had to use his charm alone.

And that was often in short supply.

"Who is the man we see tonight?" St. John asked as they descended the carriage. He might be a scholar, but Lazarus knew from those days at Oxford that the man could fight if need be.

"George Eppingham, Lord Faulk," Lazarus said, looking at the crumbling town house in front of them. They were in Westminster. The area had once been fashionable, but now most of the wealthy former citizens had fled west. "He's fond of blindfolds."

Lazarus felt St. John's quick glance, but he ignored it as he rapped on the door. There was a long pause.

"How did you find this man?" St. John asked stiffly.

Lazarus smiled humorlessly. "A brothel madam recommended him to me."

He caught St. John studying Temperance, but before he could voice a possible concern, the door to the house was opened.

A slatternly maid stood gaping at them.

"May we see your master?" Lazarus asked.

She gulped, scratched at one arm, and turned without replying. The maid led them into a house that obviously had once been better maintained. The worn wooden floor was dull. Dust had settled into the dark corners. A room was off the hall, and she opened the door without preamble. Faulk was seated inside at a desk, attired in a frayed brown banyan and soft cap to keep his shaved head warm. He wore fingerless gloves on his hands to write, and Lazarus noticed that his fire was meager. In fact, the whole house was chill.

"Who was it, Sally?" Faulk asked before belatedly looking up. He stared at them for a moment, and Lazarus thought his eyes iced over. "I have no monies to give you."

Lazarus arched an eyebrow. "We're not bill collectors."

"Ah." Faulk showed no sign of embarrassment. "Then what is your business, if I may ask?"

"I wished to ask you about a mutual friend."

Faulk arched a single eyebrow. He was younger than Lazarus had first taken him for—perhaps no more than forty. He was handsome, but want or hard living had etched lines in his face, and his jawline sagged. In another year or so, his good looks would be gone.

"Do you know Marie Hume?"

"No," Faulk replied promptly. His gaze never wavered, but his hand fisted on top of the desk.

"A fair woman with a round, red birthmark by the corner of her right eye?" Lazarus asked gently. "She was found dead in St. Giles almost two months ago."

"Many whores die in St. Giles," Faulk said.

"Yes," Lazarus said, "but I never said she was a whore."

Faulk's expression blanked.

In the silence, Lazarus took Temperance's arm and pulled her to sit next to him on a listing settee. St. John remained standing by the door.

Faulk flicked his eyes to Temperance and St. John and then seemed to disregard them.

"What is this about?" he asked Lazarus.

"Marie was a friend of mine," Lazarus replied. "I'm interested in finding the man who murdered her."

Faulk's sallow skin turned waxen. "She was murdered?"

Could a man pretend a change in skin color? Lazarus thought not. "She was found bound to a bed, her belly cut open."

Faulk stared at him and then abruptly shifted his weight in his chair, slumping back. "I didn't know."

"You saw her?" Lazarus asked.

Faulk nodded. "A half dozen times or more. But I wasn't the only man she entertained."

Lazarus waited, not saying anything.

Faulk's color—what there was of it—was returning to his face. "She had several callers. She was willing to do, ah, unusual things."

He looked knowingly at Lazarus, as if they shared a dirty secret. Except Lazarus had held his "secret" so many years he'd lost any shame he'd once had in it.

He stared back stonily at the man. "Do you know the names of any of her other callers?"

"Perhaps."

Lazarus studied the man a moment, and then said without looking at St. John, "Take Mrs. Dews to the carriage, please."

Temperance tensed beside him, but she went without protest as St. John led her from the room. He shut the door behind them.

Lazarus hadn't taken his eyes from Faulk the entire time. "Now. Tell me."

＊　　＊　　＊

"SHOULD WE LEAVE him alone with that man?" Temperance whispered anxiously to Mr. St. John.

He didn't break stride as he descended the town house steps. "Caire knows what he's doing."

"But if Lord Faulk should call more servants? What if he overwhelms Lord Caire?"

Mr. St. John handed her into the carriage and then sat across from her. "I expect Caire can handle himself. Besides, it didn't look like Faulk had any more servants than that half-witted girl."

Temperance gazed nervously out the window, not exactly convinced by this vague reassurance.

"You worry about him," St. John said softly.

She looked at him in surprise. "Well, of course I worry about him."

She saw suddenly by the satisfaction on his face that *worry* had a far more significant meaning for him.

She looked down at her hands and repeated more softly, "Of course I worry for him."

"I'm glad," he said. "No one has worried about him for a very long time, I think."

"Except for you," she said quietly.

He frowned a little, and she noticed for the first time that his thoughtful gray eyes were rather lovely in a remote sort of way. "I worry about him, but it isn't the same, is it? I have my own family." He blinked suddenly and his head jerked as if he'd remembered something. "Or I had one, at least."

There was an awkward silence then, for he was obviously suffering from some kind of grief and just as obviously didn't want to discuss it.

After a bit she inhaled. "He still hasn't come out."

St. John crossed his arms. "He will."

"Did you know her?" she asked suddenly. "Marie?"

Mr. St. John's cheekbones were high and sharp, and she saw them pinken slightly now with flags of color. "No, I never met her." The color deepened. "He kept—keeps—that part of his life well hidden."

"And he's never married?"

"No." He frowned, thinking. "As far as I know, he's never even been interested in a respectable woman." He looked up at her. "At least not until now."

It was her turn to examine her hands while her cheeks heated.

She felt more than saw St. John sit a little forward. "Look here. He may seem hard and cynical and, well, *brutal* sometimes. But remember, there's a part of him that's vulnerable. Don't hurt him."

Her head jerked up, appalled at the very thought. "I would never hurt him."

But he was already shaking his head. "You say that now, it's natural, but keep it close to your heart. He *can* bleed. Don't make him."

The carriage rocked as Lord Caire threw open the door and entered.

St. John shot her a warning look, then sat back against the squabs. "Did you get what you wanted?"

"Indeed." Caire thumped against the roof and settled himself beside St. John. "Faulk knows of at least three other men."

St. John raised his eyebrows doubtfully. "It's not much to go on."

"But it's more than I had before," Caire replied.

St. John scoffed. "And how do you propose going about finding these fellows?"

"I'll inquire," Caire said loftily.

"Dear God, *inquire*."

They were bickering, but Temperance had the idea that both men enjoyed it, thought they'd die a thousand deaths before admitting it. She looked out the window and half drifted as she thought about what St. John had said earlier. Surely he must be mistaken? How could a man like Caire have any vulnerabilities at all? She glanced at him from under lowered lids. His attention was on some point he was making to St. John, but he caught her look nevertheless. His eyelids drooped and a corner of his mouth curled sensually even as he argued with his friend.

Temperance caught her breath and hastily looked away. Dear God. If he could affect her with a mere look, surely it was she who should be warned?

They pulled up at St. John's house shortly thereafter.

"Good night, Caire, Mrs. Dews." St. John nodded.

Temperance inclined her head.

"Good night and thank you," Caire said.

St. John shrugged. "Any time."

The door closed behind him and then the carriage jerked into motion again. Temperance half expected Caire to cross and sit beside her, but he seemed content to watch her from across the carriage. She fidgeted a moment under his eyes, and then a question that had been hovering at the back of her mind for days now tumbled out.

"Did you know she saw other men?"

The question was abrupt, she knew, but he had no trouble following her train of thought. "No."

"But"—she frowned down at the folds of her cloak,

rubbing at a spot on the edge—"she was your mistress. Surely you expected fidelity?"

"Yes."

"Well?" Her voice verged on the strident, but she didn't moderate it. How could he not care?

"She was my paid mistress," he said coldly, "nothing more."

"For how long?"

"Nearly two years."

"And how often did you see her?"

He stirred impatiently. "It was my habit to visit her twice a week."

She stared at him, a rising tide of some emotion swelling in her breast, threatening to break the barrier of her silence. "You saw Marie for twice a week for two years. You made love to her hundreds of times—"

"What we did was not making love," he cut in sharply.

She waved away the interruption. "You once said you didn't love her, but you must have felt *something* for her."

He simply looked at her.

"You've gone to great trouble and risked your life on more than one occasion to find her killer." She smacked her open palm against her seat. "She must've meant more to you than a mere mistress."

"So you believe I must have loved her?" he asked softly.

She leaned forward, enraged for no discernible reason. "I believe that you wanted to love Marie—that you're enamored by the idea of love—but that you have no concept what love is. I think that's what you're searching for in St. Giles—some source of emotion, some inkling of what human feeling really is."

"How terribly perceptive of you, Mrs. Dews," he drawled horribly. "You've known me less than a month and you've already plumbed the depths of my soul."

All her anger left her instantly. "Lazarus..."

"What?" A muscle twitched on his jaw. "What do you want me to say?"

She closed her eyes. "Something. Anything. Tell me she was the love of your life. Explain to me how it is she was your mistress, but you had no idea she had other lovers or even a brother. Tell me something, Caire. *Feel* something."

"Perhaps there's nothing to tell," he murmured, apparently unmoved. "Perhaps my actions are on a whim only. Perhaps I've never loved another human being in my life. Perhaps I can't."

She stared at him, feeling wounded, feeling weary. "I don't believe you. All people can love."

He threw back his head and laughed, not at all nicely. "All? What a very childish thing to say. Do whores love? Do murderers? Tell me, does the man who raped your sister feel love?"

She was across the carriage before she thought about it, flailing at his neck, shoulder, and face, anywhere she could reach. "Stop it! Stop it! Stop it!"

He caught her flying wrists deftly. "I'm sorry. I know what you want me to say, but I can't give you that. I can only give you *this*."

And he wrapped his black cape about her like the wings of a bird and kissed her.

Chapter Fourteen

*King Lockedheart turned to Meg, his eyebrow cocked
in challenge.
But Meg merely said, "This is not love."
"And what is it, then, fair Meg?"
Meg's lips twitched as she hid a smile. "Lust, Your
Majesty. Your concubines lust after you."
The king swore loudly, making the blue bird flutter
on her perch. "Away with you again, Meg. And be
sure to wear a gown more befitting a throne room
when next I call for you."
Meg curtsied. "I'm sorry, Your Majesty, but I only
have the clothes upon my back and no others."
"See to it that she is properly attired," King
Lockedheart commanded, and once again Meg was
led back to the dungeons....*
—from *King Lockedheart*

Temperance struggled against Lazarus even as he shoved
his tongue into her mouth. Her rage was desperate, baf-
fling, and she wanted to scream and weep at the same

time. Why couldn't he feel? Why couldn't he love? Why couldn't he give her what she needed?

But his mouth was heavy on hers, his lips drugging. She found herself grasping at him instead of trying to free herself. If he would not let her go, then she'd take from him as he took from her.

She knocked his hat to the floor of the carriage, speared her fingers through the silver threads of his hair, dislodging his ribbon. She loved his hair, gloried in the shining silken strands. She fisted her hands in his hair and tugged, pulling his head back. He groaned as their kiss was broken, then groaned again as she slid her open mouth down his throat. She didn't care if she was causing him pain. His skin was cool from the night air, salty and sweet. She licked him, tasting, wanting to bite. Wanting to devour this man she could neither let go nor fully possess.

She opened her mouth over the tendon at the side of his neck and bit down hard.

He cursed, the sound loud in the carriage. He took her head between his palms as if to forcibly dislodge her, but then abandoned the attack. Instead his hands were suddenly at her skirts, pushing, shoving them upward as he continued to curse steadily.

She clutched at his shoulders to keep her balance as he jostled her, bringing her legs to either side of his hips. She could feel her skirts up around her waist, but she had her eyes closed, savoring the taste of his flesh in her mouth. He fumbled between their bodies, his hands knocking against her bare inner thighs, and one corner of her mind wondered if he really thought he could accomplish anything in this close space.

And then she felt his naked erection probing.

She opened her eyes and reared back, staring at him in shock.

He watched her, his eyes silently locked with hers as he guided himself between their bodies. She felt as he rubbed her lips, felt as he found her entrance, felt as he lodged his head there.

Felt as he paused.

She looked at him, balanced atop his cock, only the barest tip inside her. She was empty and waiting.

"You do it," he rasped.

She blinked, as if coming out of a daze, glancing about them. They were in a moving carriage, for goodness' sake.

"No." He laid one palm against her cheek, turning her face to look at him again. "It's far too late for doubts. Stay with me. Put me in you."

"But..."

He slid his hand up until his fingers were right against her feminine flesh.

Her eyes widened.

He held her gaze as he deliberately circled the part of herself that was holding him, then moved up and pinched her clitoris between thumb and forefinger.

She gasped.

"Temperance," he whispered, a dark, sexual devil. "Temperance, make love to me."

She arched her back, feeling his cock, large and insistent, those fingers, assured and relentless. This was wrong, so wrong, and it felt so very, very good.

"Temperance," he whispered, sliding his left thumb across her mouth as he rubbed his right against her clitoris.

She opened her mouth, licking his thumb.

"Temperance."

Her hips bucked, once, twice. Her head fell back even as she drenched his penis in her orgasm. She opened her eyes as she came, watching him beneath lowered lids. His face was drawn, his mouth a tight, tortured line.

"Don't keep me in suspense," he said.

But she was wild now, a being without thought other than to fulfill her body's desires. She watched him, half smiling, as she swiveled her hips, teasing him and herself.

He moaned. "Temperance."

The carriage jolted over a rut in the road, and she let the movement bear her down on him, let him enter her an inch or two.

But then she immediately lifted so that only his head teased her folds.

He swore, his upper lip beaded with sweat.

And she laughed low, the sound like no other she'd ever made in her life. She was possessed, here in this dim carriage, traveling between worlds, on a journey without a clear destination. She arched, bringing him inside again, just a little, and then let him slide entirely from her body.

"Damn it, Temperance." His voice, normally cool and dispassionate, was ragged.

She smiled and leaned forward, rubbing herself against him, using his hard, hot flesh to arouse herself. She bent, tilting her hips, and took his bottom lip between her teeth.

He might've sworn then—the words were unintelligible—but his purpose was certainly clear. He grabbed her hips in a firm hand and brought her up, shoving his cock in place with the other hand and bringing her down hard.

Oh, ecstasy! He filled her, stretching her wide in this position. The feeling was exquisite. She arched, clutching at his shoulders, grinding herself against him, but he wanted something different.

He slapped her bottom through her skirts. "Ride me."

She pouted. "No." She liked this, this subtle grinding, this wonderful rubbing.

"Ride me, damn it." He pressed his thumb against her, and for a moment she saw stars.

Then he took it away again.

"Nooo," she moaned.

"Then ride me. Please."

She looked down at him, this aristocrat, this lord, begging her to bring him pleasure, and decided she would take pity. She rose up on her knees, his length sliding from her, and then brought herself down again.

He watched her, thumbing her secretly under her skirts as she rode him, jolting hard into him, swiveling, panting, riding him as the carriage bumped through the darkened streets. Each rough jolt, each swaying swerve added to her pace until she was moving on him fast, openmouthed and gasping for air. Galloping toward a finish.

His face was sheened by sweat, his mouth drawn and strained. The muscles of his neck stood out in ropes of tension, and she saw him swallow as he pressed against her.

She wanted to tell him—to cry aloud to him—how very much he meant to her. But then she lost her pace, faltered, and fell against him, her body convulsing uncontrollably. Dimly she was aware that he clutched her hips with both hands now, that he was bucking beneath her, driving his length again and again into her open flesh. She sobbed into his shoulder, waiting, her muscles turned to liquid, her center a furnace. He pumped into her without mercy, and she turned her head to watch him, saw when he tilted his face to the ceiling, his mouth open, his teeth bared in a silent bellow.

His semen flooded her.

He was arched, his hips tilted up, her knees nearly off the seat as he held himself in her, pumping out his essence.

And then he suddenly relaxed.

Her knees bumped down onto the squabs again. His arms came up slowly, as if he were worn out, and crossed behind her back, holding her close. They were still locked together, his softening flesh in her as she laid her head against his shoulder and listened to the sounds of the London night passing by outside.

SHE WAS A warm weight on his lap, holding his cock still within her soft, slick body.

Lazarus closed his eyes, inhaling the perfume of their mating. It was an earthy scent, a humble scent, one he would forever associate with her. He ran his palm down her back, feeling the rough wool of the cloak she still wore. They'd made love in a carriage. A corner of his mouth twitched up at the absurdity. He wasn't a young lordling given to flights of wagered daring, but she seemed to arouse him no matter what the venue.

She lifted her head and tried to push away from him, but he held her a moment longer. "Hush."

"We'll arrive home soon," she whispered.

She was right, but he was reluctant to let go. To separate from her. But his flesh was weak. She moved again and he felt himself slide from her depths. He sighed and opened his arms.

She scrambled from his lap, almost falling as the carriage tilted around a corner.

"Careful." He steadied her with a hand, but she soon moved across the carriage and sat on the opposite seat.

She looked away from him.

Ah. Mrs. Dews, that reserved matron, was back. He laid his head wearily on the seat.

"You need to set yourself to rights," she said, gesturing at his lap without looking. As if the sight offended her.

He glanced down. Well, he certainly wasn't at his proudest, lying limp and damp against the outside of his breeches.

"Please," she murmured.

"Have you a kerchief?" he asked politely.

She fished in her sleeve and produced one, holding it out.

He took it, slowly wrapped the bit of linen around his member, and wiped himself off. He handed the handkerchief back. "Thank you."

Her mouth dropped open, as horrified as if he'd taken a piss in Westminster.

He would've laughed, save that the situation was more tragic than amusing. Why must she be so provincial in her attitude toward lovemaking? He narrowed his eyes. Perhaps her husband had been a prude or otherwise inadequate. It came to him that she'd hardly mentioned the man at all, though she professed to have loved him. He opened his mouth to ask her about the dead man, but the carriage shuddered to a halt. He glanced out the window and saw that they'd drawn up at the end of Maiden Lane.

She was already scrambling to leave him.

He rose.

"That's quite all right," she said hurriedly. "I can get out by myself."

He stretched his lips into a thin smile. "I have no doubt that you can, but I intend to walk you to your door."

"Oh, but..." Her protest died when she saw his face. "Oh."

After that she descended quietly.

He took her arm as soon as he made the street, not confident that she wouldn't simply flee ahead. They walked to her door silently, and by the time they made it, he was in a rage, though he couldn't pinpoint why. She turned as soon as they were abreast of the home, intending, it seemed, to enter without even bidding him good night.

Something snapped. He muttered a curse before hauling her around and slamming his mouth down on hers. This was what he wanted; this was what tamed the beast within him: her soft lips, the quiet sound of her moan as he licked across them. There was a desperate, animal need within him, one he couldn't fully identify. One he couldn't understand rationally. It was tearing him apart from within, this need. It wanted her—something from her—though he didn't know quite what. He only knew that if this terrible need was not assuaged, he very much feared he might lose something within himself. It was a confusing thought, and as he raised his head, he saw that her face revealed her confusion as well. Perhaps she, too, was in the grip of something terrible that she could not define. She opened her mouth as if wanting to say something.

But in the end, she turned away without saying anything.

"Temperance," he pleaded, for what he wasn't sure.

She stopped, her back to him. "I...I can't. Good night."

And she rapped on the door to her home.

Christ's bloody body! He turned away, kicking at the

uneven paving stones. They couldn't go on like this. One of them would break, and he wasn't sure which would be worse: him or her.

The return carriage ride was long and wearisome. By the time he made his own town house, the clocks had already chimed the midnight hour. He gave his hat, cloak, and stick to the butler and was already walking toward the stairs when the man cleared his throat.

"My lord, you have a visitor."

Lazarus turned and stared at his butler.

The butler bowed. "Lady Caire is in the library."

Lazarus strode to the library, some nameless trepidation making his heart beat quickly. He opened the door and saw her at once. She lounged on a settee, her shimmering lake-blue skirts spread about her, her head slumped onto her shoulder. She'd fallen asleep waiting for him.

He approached the settee on the balls of his feet, oddly hesitant to wake her. When was the last time he'd examined her unobserved? Years, perhaps, or more likely decades. She was beautiful; she always had been and she always would be. The bones of her face were fine and aristocratic, but he noticed now a slight softening of her jawline, a tiny drooping of her upper eyelids. He bent closer to look for other changes and inhaled the scent of oranges. Her scent. She'd always worn it, and it brought back memories of the nursery. Of her coming to visit when he ate his tea when he was seven or eight. Of her kissing his cheek before she left.

She stirred and he hurriedly stepped back.

"Lazarus." She opened those sharp blue eyes. "I'd ask you where you've been if I did not fear to hear the answer."

"Madam." He propped a shoulder on the mantel. "To what do I owe this visit?"

She smiled, arch and flirtatious, but he thought he saw her lips tremble. "Can't a mother drop in on her son?"

"I'm tired. If you've only come to play, you'll excuse me if I seek my bed instead." He turned toward the door, but her voice stopped him.

"Lazarus. Please."

He looked at her. The smile was gone now, and her lips did definitely tremble.

She inhaled as if bracing herself. "Have you any wine?"

He stared at her another moment and then sighed. Perhaps it was the lateness of the hour or his own weariness, but he could use a drink as well, though not of wine. He crossed to the decanter and poured them each a glass of brandy.

"I seem to remember you preferring this instead." He handed her a glass.

"Do you?" She took the glass with both hands, looking startled. "How did you know?"

He shrugged, taking a seat across from her. "I think I saw you one night in Father's study."

She raised her eyebrows but did not comment. For a moment, they both sipped their brandy in silence.

Finally she cleared her throat. "You took that woman to Lady Stanwicke's ball."

He gazed at her over his glass. Her tone had been very neutral. "Her name is Temperance Dews. She runs a foundling home in St. Giles."

"A foundling home?" She glanced up quickly. "For children?"

"Yes."

"I see." She was gazing at her glass now with pursed lips.

"What did you come for, Mother?" he asked softly.

He expected her usual dramatic outrage. Perhaps some cutting sarcasm. Instead she was silent for a time.

Then she said, "I loved her, you know."

And he knew that she was talking about Annelise, dead a quarter of a century.

"I miscarried three times," his mother said low. "Once before you were born and twice before Annelise was born."

He eyed her sharply. "I didn't know."

She nodded. "Of course not. You were a child, and we were not a particularly close family."

He didn't bother replying to that.

She continued. "So when Annelise was born, she was very dear to my heart. Your father, of course, had no need of a girl child, but that was just as well." She glanced up quickly at him and then down again at her glass. "He'd taken you away from me when you were but a baby, made you his own, as it were. His heir. So I made Annelise my own. Her wet nurse lived in the house, and I visited her every day. Several times a day if I could."

She took a long sip of brandy, closing her eyes.

Lazarus didn't say anything. He didn't remember this, but then he'd been a child and only interested in matters that impacted his own small world.

"When she became ill…" She stopped and cleared her throat. "When Annelise became ill that last time, I begged your father to send for a doctor. When he refused, I should've sent for one myself. I know that. But he was adamant…and he was your father. You remember how he was."

Oh, yes, he remembered well how Father was. Hard. Mean. Completely assured of both his own invincibility and his own correctness. And cold, so very cold.

"Anyway," she said softly, "I thought you should know."

She looked at him as if waiting for something, and he stared back, mute, because he wasn't sure if he was ready—if he'd ever be ready—to give it to her.

"Well." His mother drained her glass and set it on a table before rising. She smiled brilliantly at him. "It's very late and I must be getting home. Tomorrow I have a fitting for a new gown and then an afternoon tea to attend, and I must get some sleep if I'm to look my best."

"Naturally," he drawled.

"Good night, Lazarus." She turned to the door, but then hesitated before looking at him over her shoulder. "Please remember that just because love isn't expressed doesn't mean it isn't felt."

She swept from the room before he could reply.

Lazarus reseated himself and watched as he swirled the last of the brandy in his glass, remembering a little girl's brown eyes and the scent of oranges.

SHE COULDN'T GO on like this.

Silence pretended sleep as she watched her husband rise. They'd slept in the same bed last night, but it might as well have been separate houses. William had lain as still as a corpse on the far side of the bed, so near the edge she'd thought he might fall off in the night. When she'd carefully inched over to lie against him in the dark, his entire body had stiffened, and fearing he really would fall, she'd rolled back to her own side, hurt.

But it had taken her many hours to finally sleep.

Now she watched as he shaved and dressed without ever looking her way. Something shriveled and died inside her. His ship's cargo had reappeared just as suddenly as it had disappeared. The ship's owner was overjoyed, William was no longer in peril of being sent to prison for theft, and he'd finally received his pay.

They should have been happy.

Instead, despair hovered over their little home like an insidious mist.

William buckled his shoes and left the bedroom, closing the door softly behind him. Silence waited a moment and then rose herself, hurriedly tiptoeing about the room to dress. Yesterday he'd left without saying good-bye. And, indeed, when she came out of the bedroom, he already had his hat on.

"Oh," she said.

He walked to the door.

"I...I'd hoped to make you breakfast," she said in a rush.

He shook his head without looking at her. "No need. I have business this morning anyway."

He'd been at sea for over six months. Probably he did indeed have business, but at seven of the clock?

"He never touched me," she said low. "I vow on my mother's grave, he never touched me. I swear...I swear on..."

She looked wildly around the room and ran to pick up the Bible her father had given her as a little girl. "I swear, William, on—"

"Don't." In two strides he was beside her, finally. He gently took the Bible from her hands. "Don't."

She looked at him helplessly. She'd told him again and again, but each time he merely looked away from her.

"It's the truth," she said, her voice trembling. "He took me to his bedroom and told me that if I spent the night in his bed, then in the morning he would return the cargo. He promised he would not touch me, and he did not. He did not, William! He slept on a chair by the fire the entire night."

She fell silent, mutely urging him to acknowledge her, to turn and kiss her and pat her on the cheek and say what a silly misunderstanding this all was. To be her William again.

Instead he turned his face away from her.

"Oh, why can't you believe me?" she cried.

He shook his head, his weariness more chilling than anger would've been. "Mickey O'Connor is a notorious scoundrel without a scrap of decency or pity, Silence. I don't blame you. I just wish you had let me handle this." He looked at her finally, and to her horror, she saw that his eyes swam with tears. "I wish to God you'd never gone there."

He strode to the door and jerked it open.

"He asked me if you loved me," she cried.

He halted, still and silent.

"I told him you did," she whispered.

He walked out without answering and shut the door behind him.

Silence stared at her hands and then around the small, old room. She'd thought it homey once. Now it merely seemed dreary. She sat abruptly on a straight-backed chair. When she'd told Charming Mickey that her husband did indeed love her, he'd simply smiled and replied, *If he loves you, he will believe you.*

What a fool she was.

What a fool.

HE'D NEVER REALLY allowed himself to examine why he sought Marie's killer, Lazarus reflected as he paced through the darkening streets the next night. St. John had told him he was obsessed, and Temperance had accused him of believing he was in love with Marie when he had no idea what love was, but was either right? Perhaps he simply was on a quixotic quest for no discernible reason. Perhaps his life was so barren that the violent death of a mistress was a welcome excitement.

Depressing thought.

She'd been seeing other men while living at his expense. The knowledge should've shocked him, made him angry, but his only emotion was curiosity: Had she needed more money than his generous allowance? Or had she needed the sexual coupling?

He stepped around a near-skeletal man, passed out or perhaps dead in the street. He was nearing St. Giles. The street was becoming narrower, more filthy and wretched. The channel in the middle of the street was clogged with noxious debris, the stench a miasma that seemed to cling to the skin.

He'd already found one of the men Faulk had named, a thin weasely fellow who'd never once met his eyes as they'd talked. He couldn't help but think the man needed to tie up his women in order to get the courage to become aroused. The thought was repugnant. Was that what he was? A coward unable to look a woman in the eye as he bedded her?

Except he could look Temperance in the eyes. He didn't need the ropes and hood with her. She was a kind of freedom for him. A pleasant sort of normalcy.

Perhaps that was why his feet guided him to her even now.

Night had fallen fully, black and ominous, by the time he entered St. Giles proper. Lazarus grasped his stick more firmly, aware that he'd been attacked three times now in this area. He'd been intent on the hunt, on following the trail of blood, but perhaps he should look more closely at where and when he'd been attacked.

On *why* he'd been attacked.

Up ahead, a gang of men emerged around the corner. Lazarus faded back into a side alley and watched their approach warily. They were arguing over a gold watch and a curled wig—they'd obviously already preyed on at least one unlucky gentleman tonight.

Lazarus waited a moment after their voices had died into the night and then continued.

Ten minutes more and he stood outside Temperance's kitchen door. The hour was late. He hesitated a moment, straining to listen for any sounds from within. When he could make out none, he twisted apart his stick, drawing out his short sword. He inserted the blade in the crack between the door and the frame. A moment of careful maneuvering and he'd lifted the bar.

Easing the door open, he glided inside and rebarred it. The kitchen fire was banked for the night. Perhaps she'd already gone to bed. He could sneak up the stairs, but he had no idea which room was hers. The risk of alarming the house was too big. Besides, a teapot sat on the table, a small, pitiful tin of tea beside it. Perhaps she meant to return for her midnight cup of tea.

He entered her little sitting room as he had on that first night he'd met her. The grate was cold, and he knelt to lay a fire, returning briefly to the kitchen for a spill. Then he sat and waited like a lovelorn swain. Lazarus laughed lightly under his breath. Wasn't that what he was? A suitor waiting in bitter hope that his lady would grace him with her presence? It wasn't even about the sex. He simply wanted to be with her. To watch the expressions flit across those extraordinary golden eyes. To listen to her voice.

Oh, he was pitiful.

He heard rustlings from the kitchen and he tilted his head, closing his eyes to listen. Was it her out there? He imagined so, seeing in his mind's eye her pulling the kettle from the hearth and pouring the water over the tea leaves. He sat inert and called to her silently, his whole body longing for her.

The door creaked and he opened his eyes to see her staring at him. He smiled like a fool; he couldn't help it.

"Oh," she said, quite obviously nonplussed. "What are you doing here?"

"Calling on you," he replied. "I fear I need to go into St. Giles tonight, and I need you with me."

She stared at him a moment and then turned back into the kitchen. He followed to find her already putting on a cloak. "Why do you need me?"

"Because I plan to go back to Mother Heart's-Ease."

"Why?" She frowned at him over the ties to her cloak. "We've been there twice; surely we've learned all we can there?"

"It would seem so." He ran a finger along the worn wooden kitchen table. "Except that I went to see one of Marie's lovers. He says he met Marie at Mother Heart's-Ease's gin house."

"What?" She stared at him. "But Mother Heart's-Ease acted as if she'd never met Marie."

"And perhaps she hadn't." He shrugged. "Still, I find it very odd that Marie would have patronized her gin shop. Marie catered to gentlemen. Had you asked me before she died, I would've said she wouldn't be caught dead in a place like Mother Heart's-Ease's shop."

"It's very odd." She walked to the bottom of the stairs and called softly, "Mary Whitsun."

A thump and then the patter of feet came from above.

"And then there's Martha Swan," he said.

She looked a question at him.

He smiled whimsically. "I know it sounds daft, but think: Why were we attacked at Martha Swan's place?"

She shrugged. "To keep us from talking to her."

"But she was already dead."

Her brows knit together, but Mary Whitsun appeared at that moment in her night rail. "Ma'am?" The girl looked uncertainly between him and Temperance.

"Bar the door behind me, please," Temperance said. "And then go back to bed."

The girl nodded and in another moment they were in the alley.

The wind caught the edge of Temperance's cloak and sent it billowing about her. "If not to keep us from talking to Martha Swan, then why the attack?"

"I don't know." He set a quick pace, making sure to keep her close to his side. "Perhaps someone at Mother

Heart's-Ease's saw us there. Someone who didn't want us to investigate. Perhaps Marie met whoever this person is at Mother Heart's-Ease's shop."

She shot him a doubtful look. "Or perhaps this is all just coincidence."

They walked the rest of the way in silence. Lazarus was damnably aware of Temperance's heat next to him, of her vulnerability. Perhaps he shouldn't have brought her along, but the more he thought about it, the more sure he was: The answer somehow lay at Mother Heart's-Ease's gin shop. And Temperance was his key to getting people to talk there.

Fifteen minutes later, they entered the dingy room, and at first the shop seemed the same as the first two times they'd been there. The gin shop was crowded and hot, the fire wasn't drawing well, and smoke hung about the blackened rafters. Lazarus began pushing his way to the back, toward Mother Heart's-Ease's rooms.

Temperance caught his arm, halting him. He bent down so she could murmur close, "Something's not right. The room is too quiet."

He lifted his head to see that she was right. There was no drunken singing from the table of sailors in the corner, no arguments or loud discussions from the rest of the company. In fact, the customers huddled together. No one met his eyes.

Lazarus looked at Temperance. "What's happened?"

She shook her head, her beautiful golden-flecked eyes puzzled. "I don't know."

The one-eyed serving girl emerged from the curtained back hall. Before the curtain fell, Lazarus counted three men in the hall. What had made Mother Heart's-Ease triple her guard? The girl's head was down, her face tear-streaked. She caught sight of them and ducked her head, sidling to the side.

Temperance hurried to her without any urging from Lazarus. He watched as she seemed to plead with the girl, following as she shook her head and turned away. Temperance laid a hand on the barmaid and the girl shook it off, saying something sharply. Temperance straightened abruptly, her eyes wide.

Lazarus was at her side in a second. "What is it?"

She shook her head. "Not here."

Temperance led him back outside the gin shop, looking fearfully around. He drew her close, under his cloak, wrapping his arms about her. "Tell me."

She looked up at him, her face a pale oval in the night. "She wouldn't even discuss Marie. There's been another murder—a prostitute. She was found bound to her bed and her belly . . ." She gasped, unable to finish the sentence.

"Shh." His heart was beating fast, his senses alert to every tiny movement, every small sound in their vicinity. "I have to get you back to the home."

She clutched at him. "They're saying it was the Ghost of St. Giles."

"What?"

"Some think him a phantom, some think him a real man, but in either case they believe he's the murderer."

He shook his head and began walking. "Why?"

"They don't know. There's speculation that he's seeking revenge of some sort, that he's been sent to punish the sinful or that he simply enjoys killing." She shivered again. "It doesn't make any sense, does it? If he was the murderer, if he wanted us dead, he wouldn't have joined you in defeating those attackers."

"No," he murmured, "it doesn't make sense."

It was another ten minutes before they were at her door again, and Lazarus was never so happy to see the home. When she unlocked the door, he followed her into the kitchen.

He watched as she filled her little kettle and hung it over the hearth before stirring up the banked fire. "What evidence is there that the Ghost is the murderer? Did the barmaid say?"

She shot him a perplexed look as she set out her tea things. "She didn't seem to know. She was just repeating what everyone else said."

"Hmm." He tapped his fingers on the kitchen table. "I wonder, then, if someone is spreading this rumor."

"But who?"

He shook his head. "In any case, I can no longer take you into St. Giles. Not while this murderer is at large."

She nodded silently, her brows knit at his pronouncement. Was she that docile to his command, or would she disobey him later? The thought made him restless—that he had no real power over this woman. She could do as she pleased no matter what he thought or how he worried.

The kettle came to a boil after a bit and she filled her teapot. He followed her into her little sitting room, squatting to make up the fire there as she sat on her stool. Then he lounged in the chair and watched, ridiculously content, as she poured herself a cup of tea and added sugar. It occurred to him that he wouldn't mind spending every evening for the rest of his life thus, watching her take her first sip of hot tea, considering the way she half closed her eyes in relaxation.

"How is your sister?" he asked after a bit.

She looked up quickly, perhaps surprised, and that irritated him.

He raised his eyebrows. "Silence, I think? Has she recovered from her confrontation with O'Connor?"

"I don't know," she sighed. "I haven't heard from her at all. Winter won't talk to me; he simply goes about his work without discussing anything. Concord is quite angry—or perhaps *disapproving* is a better word."

"And the children?" he asked. "How fare they?"

She cradled her cup between her hands. "Mostly they seem the same as usual. Mary Whitsun follows me about the house like a shadow, though, as if she fears I'll disappear if she loses sight of me."

He nodded, unsure of what to say to all this. His experience with families—indeed, with feelings—was woefully inadequate.

She inhaled. "And you? How is your shoulder?"

"Almost as good as new."

She was silent for several seconds, and then she asked quietly, "Why do you think Marie never told you about her brother?"

"Perhaps because I never asked her about her family." He shrugged. "The fact of the matter is that we hardly talked at all. There wasn't a need to in our relationship."

"So, when you saw her, you'd simply..."

"Fuck. Yes." He watched her, waiting for her revulsion. "I didn't want or need anything else from her."

"And me?" she whispered.

He inhaled. "From you I want much, much more."

Chapter Fifteen

Now Meg sat all alone in her tiny dungeon cell that day, for no one came to visit her. She busied herself tidying the cell and then washed herself in the bucket of water and combed out her long golden hair. She'd almost resigned herself to going to bed when there was a tap at the door to her cell. In came three lady's maids and one very elegant hairdresser, and before she knew it, Meg was arrayed in a sparkling blue gown, her hair dressed with pearls, and fine heeled slippers on her feet.

"Why, what is the meaning of this?" she cried in astonishment.

The hairdresser bowed and replied,

"Tonight you are to dine with the king himself." …

—from *King Lockedheart*

Temperance watched him, this exotic creature, this man from a foreign world, saying that he wanted *more* from her. How much more? She wanted to ask but feared the answer.

So instead she set down her teacup. "Very well."

He nodded, staring into the flames of the fire. He seemed content with their pact, whatever it was, but she felt heat unfurling in her belly. She wanted *more* as well.

"You haven't told me about your family."

He shook his head irritably. "That's not true. I've told you about my sister, about my mother."

"But not about your father," she said in a low voice. She didn't know where it came from, this sudden need to know all his secrets. Perhaps it was the knowledge that a murderer stalked the streets of St. Giles; perhaps it was the subtle brush with death. All she knew was that she wanted to know him, this man she'd taken into her body.

He stiffened. "My father was an aristocrat. There's nothing more to tell of him."

She cocked her head, watching him. His eyes were back on the fire, and there was quite obviously much more to tell.

"What did he look like?"

He glanced at her, startled. "He was...a big man."

"Taller than you?" she asked.

"Yes." He frowned. "No, that's not true. I was taller by the time I returned from Oxford. He just seemed...large."

"Why?"

"I don't want to talk about this," he said abruptly.

"But you want more from me," she said. "Shouldn't I, in turn, want more from you?"

He smiled crookedly. "You drive a hard bargain, Mrs. Dews. What do you want to know of me?"

"Maybe I want to know everything," she said boldly.

"Ah, can anyone ever know everything about another person?"

"Probably not," she said, rising.

He stilled, watching as she took two steps to stand in front of him.

"Probably we remain separate, lonely individuals for all of our lives," she murmured, perching on his spread knee. She touched the folds of his neckcloth and then began unwrapping it. "We can never know another truly. Isn't that what you want me to say?"

He cleared his throat. "I hadn't really thought about it."

"Of course you have," she mocked gently. "You're a gentleman of intellect, a very cynical one. I think you spend inordinate amounts of time thinking about the world and how very alone you are in it."

He swallowed, his Adam's apple moving beneath her fingers. "Aren't I?"

"Perhaps." She flicked a look at him, then concentrated on slipping off his neckcloth. "Is that why you tie them?"

"Who?"

"Tsk. I never thought you a coward, Lazarus."

He sighed and closed his eyes. "Maybe. I don't know."

She began on the buttons of his waistcoat. "You don't know why you tie them, or you don't want to admit it?"

"How very stern you are, madam." His voice held a hint of warning.

"Yes." She nodded, her eyes on her work. "But I think I would never get any answer from you otherwise. Does their nearness give you pain? Does the thought of how apart you are from them—from everyone—cause you the anguish you feel when others touch you?"

"Your perception terrifies me." He helped her remove his waistcoat. "I don't know why I feel pain."

"Is the pain physical or mental?"

"Both."

She nodded as she began to unbutton his shirt. She could feel the heat of his skin, and his dark chest hair was shadowy beneath the fine linen. She felt her insides clench. "Then perhaps you tie them so they will not cause you pain."

"Perhaps."

"Or"—she lifted her eyes to meet his—"perhaps you tie them so that you have no need to acknowledge their humanity."

He arched an eyebrow. "Wouldn't that make me the devil?"

"Would it?" she asked softly.

His eyes slid away from hers.

"Are you afraid of their gaze? Is that what the blindfold is for? So you can't see their eyes?"

"Perhaps I don't wish them to see *my* eyes."

"Why?"

"Perhaps I don't want them to see the black at the center of my soul."

She stared into his amazing blue eyes a moment, and he let her as if he was telling her something silently.

Then she looked away.

"You don't tie me." She felt her pulse speed. She wanted to take off his shirt, but then again, she had no wish to cause him pain. She smoothed her hands over the linen, feeling his warm muscles beneath. He had a lovely chest, broad and fine, the mounds of his shoulders flowing smoothly into the bunched muscles of his arms.

"No, I don't."

"Is it because I'm more important than those others or less?"

"More. Most definitely."

She nodded, watching her hands on him. The thought that she was important to him made tears prick in her eyes.

"Am I more important to you?" he asked softly.

Of course he was. But she brushed aside the question. She was interested in his vulnerabilities, not her own. "Does this pain you? If I touch you through the cloth?"

"No."

She leaned forward and softly kissed his shoulder. "I'm glad."

"I answer your questions, but you don't answer mine."

She shook her head. "I can't. Not yet. Don't push."

"What—" His question was cut off as she leaned forward and delicately licked one nipple through his shirt.

He inhaled. "I'll need to know someday."

"Perhaps." She traced around his nipple with her tongue. The wet fabric was nearly transparent, and she could see the brown nipple beneath his shirt.

"Ahh."

She smiled against his shirt.

"Temperance."

"Don't push." She held the shirt flat against his chest to more clearly see him. His puckered nipple made a tiny peak.

"As you push me?"

"Am I pushing you?"

"Most assuredly."

She tugged on a strand of his hair in reprimand.

He grunted. "Do you ask yourself why you have a need to push me?"

"No." She traced downward to lay her hands flat against his belly. It felt firm and hot.

"Maybe you should."

"Hmm." She was distracted for a moment by the waist-band of his breeches and the fall beneath.

"Temperance..."

"No." She slid off his lap and to her knees between his legs. She flicked open the buttons of his breeches. "Do you feel pain now?"

"Hmm?" he murmured. He seemed enthralled by the sight of her fingers working at the opening to his breeches. Beneath, his erection strained at the cloth. Her mouth was dry, anticipating the sight.

But she wasn't going to let him go that easily. "Lazarus? Am I hurting you?"

"If you are, it is exquisite."

"Good," she said as she laid his breeches open. His cock was tenting the front of his smallclothes. "Lazarus..."

"Yes?" he answered. "Ah..."

She wrapped her hands about his penis inside his smallclothes. She glanced up at him under her eyelashes. "Would you like to tie me sometime?"

He blinked as if awakening from a daze, his eyes growing wary. "No. No, of course not."

"Now who lies?" she murmured as she gently squeezed, testing his hardness. "Would it hurt you if I took this out and touched it?"

He inhaled. "I think I could bear it."

"Could you?"

"Please."

His husky plea decided her. Carefully, delicately, she unbuttoned his smallclothes and pulled back the flaps. And then she simply looked.

He was truly magnificent, sitting in her worn armchair, his legs spread, his penis enormously erect. The fact that he still wore his shirt and breeches, hose and shoes, made the sight of his black pubic hair and ruddy cock all the more arousing. The sight was shockingly intimate. He looked like a king, arrogant and sure of his power.

"I love to look at you," she said.

"Indeed?" he whispered, his voice a deep male purr.

She glanced up at him and at the same time wrapped her hand about his cock. "You're sure you wouldn't want me spread upon your bed? Powerless, helpless to your desire?"

His eyes had half closed, his cheeks flushed with sexual hunger. "I...I...perhaps."

"Perhaps?" she murmured, her attention drawn back to the prize in her hands. Truth be told, her interest in the game had waned. "I've never known you to be uncertain as to your wants. Your desires."

She squeezed very carefully, feeling the softness of his skin, the iron hardness underneath.

He gasped, arching his hips so that his cock thrust into her hands. "Damn it. Put it in your mouth."

She bit her lip, a little shocked. She'd never done such a thing before. She stroked her finger over the tip of his penis, where a tiny slit leaked liquid. What would that liquid taste like in her mouth?

"Temperance," he said, his voice very deep and very clear in the quiet room. "Suck me."

She bent her head and stuck out her tongue hesitantly. And licked. She wrinkled her nose. It was salt and musk, not unpleasant, but not what she'd expected either.

Above her, he moaned. "Please."

Oh, to hear him beg. There was something in her, something wicked and base that lapped up that plea in his voice. She opened her mouth and placed the head of his cock inside.

Sucked.

His hips jerked, jamming his cock farther into her mouth. She almost backed off, but then she held him more firmly and flattened her tongue against him, sucking gently. His hands came up, stroking her head. She felt him take the pins from her hair, wrapping his hands in the locks, pulling gently. She wasn't sure he even knew what he did. She leaned back a little, letting him slide from her mouth so she could look up at him.

He was watching her.

The knowledge made her wet. She laid her tongue against him and, locking her eyes with his, licked all the way around the head of his cock.

"Jesus." His jaw gritted, flexing in the firelight.

She stroked down on his penis and opened her lips about him, sucking gently on the very tip.

His face was strained, the muscles standing out on his arms. "Take it deeper."

And she did, swallowing as much of him as she could, her eyes still on his even as his hips moved under her. He covered her hand with his own to help her stroke faster.

He was gasping now, his cheeks furrowed, his face flushed. "Do you want it?" he whispered. "Stop now if you can't take it."

She couldn't talk—her mouth was full of his cock—but she wanted to see this. Wanted to bring him to the inevitable end. She watched him as she felt his cock swell in her mouth. Watched him as his hand jerked powerfully on his length. Watched him as he bared his teeth.

"Ah, God!"

She tasted salt and warmth. Felt tears fill her eyes as he spasmed helplessly. He was big and strong, but she'd brought him to this point.

She licked him as he softened, feeling tender, feeling somehow lost.

"Come here," he ordered, and pulled her into his arms.

He tucked her head under his chin, and they lay there for long moments as he stroked her hair. Then he began to pull her skirts up. Wordlessly, relentlessly, he uncovered her limbs until she lay sprawled on him, the fabric of her skirts around her waist.

He looked down and she followed his gaze. Her dark curls were a shocking contrast to the whiteness of her skin. She wasn't used to this, to a man examining her in the firelight, and she started to pull down her skirts to cover her nudity.

"Don't." He stayed her hand, his eyes meeting hers in command. "I want to see you."

She shook her head, but the movement was weak.

He moved his hand to the juncture of her thighs, and she turned her head, hiding her face in his shoulder. She felt him pet her, stroking through her curls.

"Open your legs," he said quietly.

She complied, swallowing shallowly, waiting for his touch.

It was so delicate when it came that she almost missed it. He skimmed her inner thighs, up close to where her center waited for him. But then he skirted up, around her mound, touching only the edges of her hair.

"Watch," he said.

She shook her head. "I can't."

"Yes, you can."

She inhaled and raised her head.

His big hand lay over her mound, his fingers spread possessively.

"Don't look away or I'll stop," he murmured.

She swallowed, watching as his fingers slowly slipped down to her far lips. He widened them, spreading her lips, revealing the deep rose within and her own embarrassing moisture.

"So soft," he said, and ran his forefinger through her folds.

She was panting now, watching as his finger reached her apex and circled around her nub. Gently, he tapped her clitoris.

"Do you like that?" he whispered.

She wanted to shake her head, to look away, but if she did, he would stop and the mere thought was enough to make her think she'd die.

"Temperance," he whispered, deep and intimate, "tell me if you like this." He pressed gently, not quite hard enough. "Temperance?"

"Harder," she breathed.

"What?"

She swallowed. "Harder. Touch me harder."

He pressed again. "Like this?"

Oh, glorious bliss! Her hips rose of their own accord. She nodded jerkily.

He circled against her, using that exact amount of pressure. "Now watch. Keep your eyes open and on my hand or I'll stop. Do you understand?"

She nodded again, mesmerized by that finger, growing steadily slicker with her own moisture. He ministered to her in the quiet of her sitting room, the only sounds her ragged breathing and the small liquid noises his hand made against her flesh. He rubbed faster and faster until her eyelids were heavy, until it was a herculean struggle to keep them open. She was afire, warmth and sweet pleasure radiating from her center.

And suddenly his hand twisted.

Her eyes opened wide as she watched him insert two fingers deep into her, and she gasped at the feeling and the sight. He brought his thumb down on her at the same time and she broke apart. The fire spreading through her limbs, her head thrown back, her vision blurring even as she still watched him work her flesh. Dear Lord, she'd never felt so wanton. She was trembling in his arms, her legs flexing, and still he shoved his fingers into her, spreading them apart, twisting them inside of her.

His other hand turned her head, and he was kissing her suddenly. His mouth open and wet as those clever fingers of his slowed.

"Temperance," he gasped against her. "I need you. I need you now."

He was lifting her, bringing her legs around, positioning her like a rag doll for his own pleasure, because she certainly could no longer move.

He rose, holding her, and reversed their positions, laying her back in the big armchair, her bottom on the very edge of the seat, her feet on the floor. He crouched before her, and she saw that his erection was enormous. She watched as he took it in one hand and brought it between her legs. He pushed his shoulders underneath her spread legs and straightened, bringing them up so that she was helplessly draped across him.

He positioned his cock at her entrance, his mouth open

and panting, and she watched him as he shoved himself inside her. His head was arched back as if he suffered some unbearable pain. As if he were about to expire.

"Oh, God," he panted. "I can't…I can't…"

And he began pounding into her, shoving her back into the chair, clutching her legs against his chest so that she had no purchase, no way of defending herself against his assault.

Not that she wanted to.

The feel of him filling her repeatedly, just after her exquisite release at his hand, brought the warmth rushing back immediately. She crashed, wave after wave of pleasure beating against her, overwhelming her senses. She was only dimly aware of him straightening on his knees, still locked to her, bringing her bottom entirely off the chair as he slammed himself into her fully. He held her there as he spilled himself into her.

His big hands were on her bottom, spread and holding her. He ground himself into her as if he couldn't get enough of her, as if he wanted to stay locked with her forever. But he was only a man after all. He slumped forward, somehow managing to bring her down gently. He disentangled her legs from his shoulders and then laid his head next to hers in the chair seat.

"Temperance," he murmured, big and heavy and satiated on her. "Temperance."

She looked at the ceiling of her little sitting room and knew she had to find the words to tell him what he meant to her. Knew she would lose him if she couldn't let the words leave her lips, however painful and hard it was for her. She stood at a crossroads, and to make no decision was to lose everything instead. Tomorrow. Tomorrow she would find the way.

Tonight she simply closed her eyes.

*   *   *

TEMPERANCE WOKE EARLY the next morning and lay staring at the ceiling in her tiny lonely bedroom. She didn't want to rise. Her bedroom was up under the eaves. This high in the home, there were only three rooms—hers, Winter's, and the one Nell slept in when she wasn't watching over the nursery at night. The rooms were cramped with low, sloping roofs. When it rained, a corner of her room leaked. In winter she was cold, and in summer it was abominably hot.

Dear God, sometimes she wished she could simply fly away. Perhaps that was why she'd indulged in those dangerous interludes with Caire, risking not only pregnancy and a bastard child, but also her very soul. He was a temptation she seemed to have no defense against. Perhaps after all these years of fighting her very nature, it had finally become a moot point. Perhaps the fight itself was never really winnable. Perhaps—

A thump came from the room next to hers—Winter's room. Temperance frowned and started to rise.

Something crashed next door.

She ran from her room. Winter's door was shut, of course, so she rapped on it. "Brother?"

No answer.

She rapped harder and when there was still no sound from within, she balled her hand into a fist and pounded. "Winter! Are you all right?"

She tried the door handle, but it was locked. His bedroom was the only room in the house where Winter might find a measure of privacy. She was just beginning to wonder how she might break the door down when it swung suddenly inward.

"It's all right." Winter stood in the doorway, but despite his soothing words, all was manifestly *not* right. Blood streaked his pasty face, running from a gash on his forehead, and he swayed where he stood.

Temperance wrapped her arms about her brother's waist to keep him from falling. "What happened to you?"

He raised his hand to his face and then seemed startled when he saw the blood on his fingers. "I...I believe I fell."

His hesitant tone alarmed her more. "You don't know?"

"I can't seem..." He trailed off and looked about his tiny, cell-like room. "Perhaps I should sit down."

She helped him to sit on his bed—there was no room for even a chair—then stood over him anxiously. "Are you ill? When did you last eat?"

She tried to lay the back of her hand on his forehead, but with uncharacteristic irritation, he brushed her away. "I'm perfectly fine; I just—"

"Fell down and can't remember why?" she said in exasperation. "What did you eat for dinner last night?"

His forehead creased. "Ah..."

"Oh, Winter! Did you eat anything at all?"

"Perhaps some broth," he said, not meeting her eyes.

Temperance sighed. Winter had never learned how to lie effectively. "Stay here and I'll fetch some breakfast and bandages."

"But the school," he said fretfully. "I must open it."

"No." She pushed him back onto his bed, for he'd tried to rise again. "The school can close for one day."

"We'll lose the tuition," he said.

Temperance stared at him. It was true; if the school was not opened, then the students did not pay tuition for that day. "Surely we can afford one day closed?"

He shook his head, his complexion almost as white as his pillow. "We've used nearly all the money Lord Caire gave us."

"What?" she asked, shocked.

"We owed the butcher and baker," he whispered, "and we hadn't paid the cobbler for the boys' shoes this last November."

Temperance looked about the small room, but there was no one else to make the decision for her. "We'll be fine. Just don't try to get up. Promise me, Winter?"

"Yes." He nodded, and, indeed, his eyes were already closed when she left the room.

Dear God, she'd known they were in desperate straits, but she'd had no idea the depths to which they'd fallen. Temperance hurried down the stairs, trying to order her priorities, but she kept coming back to the fact that Winter was ill, and she just couldn't run the home without him.

She walked into the big old kitchen, her mind in turmoil, but stopped when she saw who was within.

Polly stood next to Nell, and both women's faces were fearful. Mary Whitsun huddled in a corner, her little face white. Polly held a still bundle in her arms.

"What is it?" Temperance whispered.

"I'm sorry," Polly said. "She was suckling fine and then last night..." She pulled back a corner of the blanket. Mary Hope was within, her tiny face red and shining with moisture.

Polly looked up, her face white. "She has the fever."

Chapter Sixteen

That night, Meg was led into a magnificent dining room. A feast was laid there, but the only one who sat at the table was the king with his little blue bird in its golden cage at his elbow.
The king dismissed the guards and indicated a chair at his right hand. "Come sit by me, Meg."
Meg sat very carefully so as not to harm her lovely dress.
"Now, Meg," King Lockedheart said as he took a gold plate and set meat and sugared fruit upon it. "I have a question for you."
"What is that, Your Majesty?"
The king set the plate he had filled with his own hands before her. "I wish to know what love is."…
—from *King Lockedheart*

"The lighter wood, I think," Lazarus said consideringly early that afternoon. "With the ivory inlay."

He and Mr. Kirk, the piano maker, were in his study.

Mr. Kirk had brought half a dozen different wooden boards, each intricately decorated. Lazarus ran his hand over the sample he'd chosen. It was feminine without being overornamented.

Like Temperance.

"A very nice choice, my lord." Mr. Kirk gathered his samples into an especially made case. "I believe we have something nearly finished. Shall I deliver it to you in a fortnight?"

"No. It's to be a present. I shall give you the address to deliver it to."

"As you wish, my lord." Kirk bowed, backing from the room obsequiously.

Lazarus leaned back in his chair feeling oddly light, almost carefree. He'd given presents to other women—payments for services rendered—but he'd never taken the trouble to pick out the gift himself. Frankly it hadn't mattered, either to him or the woman. She would regard the trinkets and jewels he bestowed as insurance against the inevitable time when they would part, something easily converted to money. He hoped that Temperance would regard his gift in a more permanent light, that perhaps their relationship itself might one day become—

His dreamy thoughts were interrupted by the door to his study opening again. Lazarus looked up and for a moment wondered if his thoughts of Temperance had conjured her out of thin air.

He stood. "Temperance. What are you doing here?"

"I…" She glanced about his study as if dazed. "I…I thought to visit you."

His brows drew together. "Are you all right?"

"Yes, perfectly." But her bottom lip trembled.

Why was she lying to him? "Would you like to sit? I'll ring for some wine—"

"No!" She started for him. "No, please don't call anyone. I simply wanted to be with you."

Her face was pale. The wide-brimmed hat she held in one hand fell to the floor as she came toward him.

"How did you get here?" he asked.

"I walked," she said breathlessly.

"From St. Giles?" He shook his head. "Temperance, you must tell me what the matter is. I—"

"No." She took his face between his palms. "I don't. I don't want to think about that for a while. I don't want to think about anything."

And she pulled his head down and kissed him. Her mouth was desperate on his, not soft and luring, but hot and hungry. His body reacted as if trained to service her and her alone. He found himself with his arms about her, his tongue already in her mouth. She made a sound of satisfaction beneath his lips as he crowded her against the desk. His hands were on her skirts, gathering them even as his mind reminded him that there was no lock on his study door.

"Damn it." He tore his mouth from hers, sweeping her into his arms.

Swiftly he bore her out of the study, past his startled butler and up the stairs to his bedroom. Small was inside when he kicked the door open.

"Out," Lazarus said in a voice he no longer recognized as his own.

The valet disappeared silently.

Lazarus laid Temperance on his bed, then began to climb in beside her.

"No," she said breathlessly.

He froze, watching her.

"I want..." She licked her lips. "I want to do this your way."

Despite her veiled words, he knew immediately what she meant. Animal desire slammed through him, hardening his cock to the point of pain, drawing his balls tight. Dear God, *yes*. In a second, he was half mad with the mere thought. He could take her in the way he liked best; she'd *asked*. But a small part of him withdrew, shaking its head in disapproval. Temperance was different. He couldn't use her like this.

"Are you sure?" he demanded.

"Yes."

He leaned over her, a hawk guarding prey before the strike. "Be sure. Once a certain point is crossed, I won't be able to back away. And you won't be able to make me."

Her throat worked as she swallowed. "Please. I want to know what you do. I want to feel it."

He stared at her a moment longer, trying to read her mind, before shoving off the bed again. His hands were trembling.

"Very well." He took a step back, afraid to touch her. Afraid to lose control. "Take off your clothes."

She drew in a breath, her cheeks pinkening, but her hands moved to the laces of her bodice readily enough. He watched, his fingers flexing by his sides, as she stripped off bodice and stays, her skirt and shoes. When she extended a slim foot forward and slowly unrolled her stockings, he began to think she was teasing him. When she pulled the chemise gracefully over her head and threw it to the floor, he knew. She reached up and took the pins from her hair, fluffing it and combing her fingers through the locks. She sat on his bed, entirely nude, her breasts high and proud, one calf under the other leg, and she simply looked at him, waiting for his next command.

He swallowed. God. Could he do this? But she'd wanted it. She'd asked for it.

He turned before he could change his mind and quickly crossed to his chest of drawers. Inside the top drawer was a pile of neckcloths, neatly folded. He grabbed a handful and returned to the bed.

"Lie down," he said, his voice husky.

She complied, placing her wrists over her head without prompting, near the spools of his headboard. He tied them there, trying to keep his eyes away from her breasts, drawn high by her lifted arms, away from her parted mouth.

"Spread your legs."

She parted her thighs, spreading her legs wide, for his bed was not narrow, and he fastened each ankle to the posts at the end. He straightened, looking at her as he held the last neckcloth. She was like some feast for a god. Her body pink and white against the green and brown of his coverlet, her hair long and silky, spread upon his pillow.

Her eyes were not afraid, but they were wide.

He walked to the head of the bed, drawing the neckcloth through his fingers. "And now I blindfold you."

TEMPERANCE WATCHED AS Caire bent over her with the neckcloth. His face was grave, his sensuous lips drawn tight with strain, and his sapphire eyes had darkened to near black. She knew she should feel fear, but all she felt was anticipation.

Exquisite anticipation.

He placed the soft folds of linen over her eyes, and all was black. She listened to the sound of her own breathing, louder somehow, as she felt him tie the neckcloth firmly. His hands left her and she cocked her head, listening for his movement. He had paced around the bed, she thought, near the foot, but he stopped. She nervously fingered the carving at the head of the bed. What was he doing? What did he wait for? Her thighs were parted widely, air cooling her most intimate flesh.

"You are so lovely." His deep voice was near her left side and she started.

"Shhh," he murmured, and she felt something—a fingertip?—on her left shoulder. The touch was so light she wasn't even sure it was there.

"Your skin is like silken velvet," he said, close to her ear. His fingertip skimmed down to her breast, slowly circling. "A pearly pink, so fine, so sweet."

He withdrew his fingertip from her skin, and for a moment she was untouched.

Something wet touched her nipple.

She inhaled at the suddenness. It was his tongue, it must be, but it was the only part of him that touched her. He circled her nipple and then closed his mouth about it, suckling. Shivers of sparkling sensation ran from her nipple straight to her center. She squirmed without conscious thought, but the binds at her wrists and ankles kept her from moving much. She must simply wait and submit to his attentions. Submit to what he wished to do next.

Was this the allure, then? This helpless wanting, this anxious anticipation?

He let go of her nipple suddenly, and she felt cool air

blow against her damp skin. She shivered, both nipples now at a peak.

"So sweet," he whispered, and she felt his breath against her belly.

The bed depressed between her spread feet, and she realized he must be down there, sitting or lying, so close to where she was embarrassingly wet. There was a moment of silence, and she imagined him simply looking at her, exposed and waiting.

She grew wetter.

"I wonder"—his fingertip landed lightly just behind her right knee—"are you sweet everywhere?"

She caught her breath as his touch wandered up her thigh, delicately, seemingly in no hurry.

"Shall I taste?" he asked idly.

She bit her lip, trying to catch her breath, though she made no exertion.

"Temperance?" he asked, his voice deep. "Shall I?"

Dear Lord, if the cloth wasn't over her eyes already, she would've hidden her face. He wanted her to *ask* for it.

"Perhaps here," he whispered as he grazed her inner lips with one finger. "Or maybe here?" He circled her clitoris.

"Please," she choked.

"I'm sorry?" he asked politely, his finger still lightly—too lightly—touching. "Did you say something?"

"Please taste me," she gasped.

"Certainly. Whatever you wish."

And she felt his tongue, wet and sure and, thank God, so firm. He licked her in strong strokes. He missed no part of her, thoroughly laving her quivering, sensitive flesh. When he at last got to her clitoris and bore down on it with the flat of his tongue, she went a little mad. She twisted in her bonds, panting and muttering who knew what, feeling the warmth building inside of her until it turned liquid and ran all through her veins. She arched, pressing her pelvis into his face shamelessly, seeking more, and he gave it, thrusting two fingers into her as his tongue rapidly flicked over her peak.

She'd had enough—she was done—but he would not retire. He brought that tiny bit of flesh into his mouth and sucked and sucked until she wailed her surrender, her body concussing with the explosions of her pleasure.

She was weak and warm and still tied open for his desire.

"I think," he said, his voice husky and low as it blew across her wetness, "I think you may be ready for me now."

He lifted from her and then she felt the brush of his breeches on her inner thighs, the weight of his body, and the probe of his penis. It was smooth and hard at her entrance. He swirled it against her moisture and then with one quick thrust seated himself within her. She felt the depression of the mattress on either side of her shoulders, as if he held his upper body up off her with his arms. Then his mouth was against her left nipple as he set a leisurely pace. He thrust and withdrew firmly, but without any haste, as if he had all the time in the world. As if she were his private plaything that he might amuse himself with for as long as he wished.

He tongued her nipple, then moved to the other, his penis moving in and out of her without pause. It was maddening. She tried to thrust up, but the bonds prevented her.

"Please," she whimpered.

"What is it?" he whispered like some devil in her ear.

"Please."

"Tell me." He kissed her ear.

"Harder."

There was a split second's pause and then a low, muttered curse. He hitched himself up her and slammed himself into her as if he'd lost all control. Fast and hard, as she'd asked, and it was pure bliss. White light burst behind her eyelids, hot and blinding, and she would have cried out had he not covered her mouth with his. He kissed her deeply as he continued to pound into her, taking his pleasure on her helpless body.

And when he jerked and broke their kiss, rubbing his face into her neck, she knew he'd found his bliss as well. He thrust once more, and again, and then his entire weight slumped against her.

For a moment they lay like that, and then the neckcloth was removed from her face. She blinked up into his sapphire eyes.

"Now will you tell me what the matter is?" he asked.

MAKING LOVE TO Temperance like this had been like a dream come true. But there had been something missing. Something small, nagging at the back of his brain, and the moment Lazarus took the neckcloth off her face, he knew what it was: Temperance's eyes. He'd wanted to see the golden stars in her eyes as they made love. And he'd wanted for her to see his eyes.

To see *him*.

Those extraordinary gilded eyes shifted away from his gaze now. "I don't know what you're talking about."

He should've felt anger at her obvious prevarication, but instead tenderness flooded him. He pushed the hair back from her face. "Cut line, Temperance. Tell me."

She pulled at the bonds on her wrists. "Untie me."

He nuzzled her cheek. "Not until you tell me."

She closed her eyes and whispered, "Mary Hope, the baby I brought home that first night we met, is dying."

Relief was a liquid lightness in his chest. She'd told him; she'd let him in a little. "I'm sorry."

"She's so small, so weak. I should've known she would not make it. But then she rallied for a bit and I hoped…"

He was silent, absorbing her pain.

She sobbed and shook her head. "She's dying there at the home. I couldn't bear to watch her struggle to breathe, so I left Nell to nurse her."

"It's all right." He lifted his head to look at her. "You bear so much already."

"No." She grimaced, as if in physical pain. "I don't bear enough. Winter collapsed this morning. The home is killing him, I fear. I should never have left there today. I should never have come here."

"No, you probably shouldn't have left, but everyone needs a rest sometime. Don't worry yourself so."

She merely shook her head.

He kissed her forehead, thinking. An uneasy emotion he couldn't quite identify was growing in his chest. "That home is like a prison for you."

Her eyes flew open. "What?"

He reached to work at the ties at her wrists. "I've wondered for some time why you insist on working there. Do you like it? Do you enjoy the work?"

"The children—"

"The work is no doubt very admirable," he said. "But do you enjoy it?"

She didn't reply and he looked down at her. She was staring at him wide-eyed. He'd succeeded in shocking her into silence, it seemed.

"Do you like it?" he asked again gently.

"Liking has nothing to do with it."

"Doesn't it?"

"No. No, of course not. The home is a charity. One doesn't have to enjoy charity."

He half smiled. "Then there is no shame in admitting you don't like it."

"I've never thought about it one way or the other. I like the children, naturally, and I do sometimes feel satisfied when we place one in a good position. I must enjoy it, mustn't I? I'd be a monster if I didn't." She appealed to him, as if she couldn't answer the question herself.

He shrugged. "It's neither good nor bad—how you feel about the home and working there—it just is."

"Well, then, of course I—"

"No," he said sternly. "Tell me without lies or evasions."

"I don't lie!"

He smiled at her affectionately. "Oh, my little martyr, you lie every day, to yourself, I fear, most of all."

"I don't know what you mean," she whispered.

"Don't you?" He gave up on the bindings for the moment; she seemed comfortable enough anyway. "You refuse to admit love for Mary Whitsun or even tiny Mary Hope—I've seen you refuse to touch the baby. You hold yourself back, deny yourself pleasure—unless pressed. You make yourself work at a hopeless job that is killing you, and all for some ridiculous sense of unworthiness.

You are the most saintly woman I know, and yet you think yourself a sinner."

Abruptly, white lines appeared around her mouth.

"Don't you..." She gasped for breath. "Don't you *dare* tell me I'm saintly. That I don't know what sin is."

She was truly angry; he could see that. She yanked wildly at her bonds.

"Explain," he demanded.

"Let me go!"

"No."

"You don't know me!" she screamed. Her mouth was wide, and tears had started at her eyes. "I'm not good; I'm not a saint. I *need* to work at the home."

He pressed his nose to hers. "Why?"

"Because it's a good and true thing to do. It doesn't matter a whit how I feel about it."

"You're doing penance, aren't you?" he whispered.

She shook her head, red-faced, the tears running into her tangled hair. "I don't deserve—"

He leaned close, capturing her face between his palms. "Tell me."

She gasped, closing her eyes. "When my husband died...when Benjamin died..."

He waited patiently as she sobbed. He'd known that something was here. Had she not loved her husband? Perhaps even wished him dead? He was prepared for such mundane confessions, but not the one that came from her mouth.

"I was with another man."

He blinked, so startled that he let her go. "Truly?"

She nodded jerkily. "He was...Well, it doesn't matter who he was, but I let myself be seduced by him. I was at his rooms, with him carnally, at the exact moment Benjamin was run down by a brewer's cart. I came home, trying to decide how I would keep my sin from him, and he was dead." Her eyes suddenly flew open. "He was *dead*."

He looked at her a moment, as a horrible realization began to form at the back of his mind. Abruptly he stood and went to his desk to find a penknife.

"How long had you known your lover?" he asked as he cut through the binds at her ankles.

"What?" She knit her brow in confusion. "Not long. It was the first time I'd been with him. What does it matter?"

He laughed shortly, but the sound was not amused. "It matters only in the irony, I suppose. The first time you sinned, you were punished overhard, I think."

He cut her wrists free.

She stared at him. "Don't you understand? This isn't a simple wrong. It isn't eating too many sweets or desiring another woman's bonnet. I slept with a man not my husband. I committed adultery."

He sighed, suddenly weary. "And you expect vilification from me for such a human failing."

"It wasn't a *failing*." She sat up and wrapped herself in his coverlet. She was beautiful—he could see that in a dispassionate way—the most beautiful woman he'd ever known. "I betrayed my husband."

"And yourself," he said quietly.

She blinked. "Yes, and myself."

"Sexual congress was your downfall," he said. "Sexual congress with a man not your husband was the worst thing you'd ever done in your life."

"Yes," she whispered.

He closed his eyes for a moment, wishing irrationally

that he hadn't pressed her. "You'll never forgive yourself, will you?"

"I..." She seemed taken aback by his unemotional articulation of her dilemma.

"Sexual congress is the most unpardonable sin to you," he said. "And when you decided you needed to punish yourself, you used your worst sin."

He opened his eyes and looked at her, so beautiful, so strong. Everything, he suddenly realized, that he would wish for in a woman, had he ever thought to wish, and he finally identified the emotion in his heart. Hurt. She'd hurt him as thoroughly as if she'd shoved an arrow through his chest.

"You've used me to punish yourself, haven't you?"

He watched dawning realization spread over her face, a confirmation more positive than anything she could ever say, and that arrow twisted deep in his chest. Yet still he had to ask the last question.

"Am I anything to you but a punishment?"

Chapter Seventeen

Meg looked at the most powerful man in the kingdom. "Your Majesty, may I ask why you wish to know what love is?"
The king frowned. "I know what it is to face death in battle. I know about ruling a vast kingdom, about meting out justice and showing mercy, but despite all this, I do not know what love is. Can you tell me?"
Meg thought about his question as she ate. How was she to explain love to a king? At last she looked up and saw the king feeding a date to the little blue bird. "Open the cage door," she said....
—from King Lockedheart

"Punishment?" Temperance stared at Caire.

He was dressed while she was entirely nude. He'd not even removed his coat to make love to her. She felt at a terrible disadvantage. She'd just told him of her greatest shame—a thing she'd told no other person, not even Silence—and he'd accused her of ... what?

She shook her head, confused. "I don't think of you as punishment."

"Don't you?" He was quieter than she'd ever seen him, withdrawn from her somehow. "Then explain your sudden request for me to bind you."

She pulled the coverlet up to shield her bare shoulders from his gaze. "I . . . I simply thought it was something you liked. Something I was curious about. I don't know why I asked tonight."

"I do." He'd turned his back to her, his hands clasped behind him. "It was degrading for you, wasn't it?"

"No!" she exclaimed without even having to think.

But he wasn't listening.

"You wanted—needed—sex, but it's a sin for you, isn't it? The very worst of sins. The only way you could approach the act was by making it something foul."

"No!" She struggled from the covers, unmindful now of her nudity. How could he possibly imagine—

"Something degrading." He turned and looked at her, and she froze, half-risen from the covers. "Because otherwise, well, it would be nothing but pleasure, wouldn't it? And that you couldn't allow yourself."

She sat back slowly, not even defending herself anymore. Was this true? Had she really used him in such a despicable way?

"It shouldn't matter to me," he said dispassionately. "What you feel. After all, I never considered the emotions of my partners before. Quite frankly, their feelings were of no account to me in our transactions. But oddly, what you feel does somehow matter to me."

He paused, looking down at his hands for a moment

and then back up at her, his face exposed now, sad and hurt and resigned.

The sight made something twist in her chest—made her want to say something—but still she could not bring herself to speak.

"You matter to me," he said. "And although I am a disgusting creature in many ways, although I have needs not of the ordinary, perhaps even evil needs, I believe that I do not deserve to be used in this way. I may be a man without conscience, but you, my dear martyr, are better than this act."

He turned and left the room, closing the door quietly behind him.

For a moment, Temperance simply stared at the door. She wanted to run after him, to apologize, to explain somehow, to say the words she couldn't before, but she was nude. She looked down at the coverlet fallen to her lap.

Hurriedly she rose and began dressing, but her chemise tangled over her head and she couldn't find her second stocking. By the time she'd poked enough pins into her hair to hold it off her neck, it was half an hour later and he'd still not returned.

Temperance opened the door and crept into the corridor. The house was eerily quiet, and she realized she had no idea where he might have gone. Perhaps his study? Did he have a private sitting room or library? She began walking down the hall, peering into rooms. Eventually she realized that a library would surely be on another floor, and she wandered down the stairs.

There was light in the main hallway, and as she entered, she saw that Small was standing by the butler.

"Have you seen Lord Caire?" she asked, knowing her face was reddening. What must the servants think of her—a lone woman, her hair falling from its pins, in an unmarried gentleman's house?

But her embarrassment fled at Small's reply. "My lord has gone out, ma'am."

"Oh." Temperance stared blankly. Had he loathed her company so much that he'd vacated his own house?

"Lord Caire left instructions that the carriage be brought around for your use, ma'am." Small's face was the expressionless mask of the good servant, but his eyes were sympathetic.

Temperance had a sudden urge to weep. Was that it, then? Was all that had been between her and Caire over now?

She bit her inner cheek. She would not break down—not now, at least. "Thank you. That was most...kind of Lord Caire."

Small bowed as if she were a true lady instead of the daughter of a brewer, recently discarded by an aristocratic lover. She swept out into the late afternoon daylight and down Caire's front steps with as much dignity as she could muster. Inside the big carriage, though, after the door had been slammed shut and she was all alone with no curious eyes to stare, her spine collapsed. She huddled in a corner of the seat, rocking against the soft leather as the carriage drove through the London streets.

All her life she'd thought of herself as an essentially good person. Her downfall with the man who'd seduced her had been shocking. She'd known that she'd been led astray because of a flaw within herself, and she'd thought that flaw had been her overwhelming sexual urges.

But what if that had merely been a symptom of a far greater sin?

What if her true flaw was pride?

She watched with sightless eyes as London rumbled by and thought about her marriage, so long ago now. Benjamin had been Father's protégé, a quiet man, grave beyond his years. He'd studied at one time for the church, but when he'd met Father, Benjamin had been an impoverished schoolmaster. Father had offered him work at the home and a room in their house. Temperance had been sixteen then—so very young! Benjamin had been mature and pleasant of face, and Father had approved of him. It had seemed the natural thing to do to marry him.

She'd been happy enough in her marriage, hadn't she? Surely she had because Benjamin was a good man, a likable man. And he'd been gentle in their marriage bed— the few times he'd been passionate. Benjamin believed that physical love was a holy act between a man and wife. Something to be done thoughtfully and not too often. In fact, the only time he'd come close to sounding vexed with her was when she'd suggested that perhaps they might practice their physical bond more often. He'd made it quite plain that a woman who sought out sex was to be pitied.

She'd known, even then, that something was wrong about her makeup. That she had urges that needed to be watched. And yet when temptation had presented itself, she'd fallen with hardly a struggle. John had been a young lawyer renting a room next to their house. Temperance frowned. Now when she tried to recall what he'd looked like, all she could remember was how hairy the backs of his hands had been. At the time, to her younger self, that had seemed like an exciting sign of male virility. She'd thought herself passionately in love, with a tragic fateful-ness that had been all-consuming at the time and now was only dimly remembered. The afternoon she'd fallen, Temperance remembered thinking that she would die—physically fall ill and die—if she did not lay with John.

So she had and her life had crumbled apart.

She'd returned from the dingy room John had rented to find Benjamin—grave, handsome Benjamin—breathing his last. His chest had been crushed by the wheels of a huge brewer's cart. He hadn't even regained consciousness before dying. Temperance didn't remember much after that. Her family had taken care of Benjamin's funeral, had cared for and comforted her. Weeks later, she found out that John had left his rented rooms without ever say-ing good-bye to her.

She hadn't cared.

Ever since, she'd worked to hide her sin—and the temptation of lust. Had she in the process become a hypo-crite? She'd wanted the comfort of Caire's arms, but she was so wrapped up in her own demons that she hadn't even thought about his feelings.

Caire was right. She'd used him. The thought made her squirm, made her want to lash out—blame Winter for his collapse, blame John for seducing her so long ago, blame Silence for her foolish bravery, blame Caire for his advances—blame, in fact, anyone but herself. She hated the knowledge that she was so base. He was right. She'd used him for sexual pleasure and hadn't even the courage to acknowledge the fact to herself.

And somehow in the process of using him, she'd so hurt him that he believed she thought sex with him was degrading.

It was a temptation to make excuses for herself. But she fought down all her prevarication, her lies and evasions. She swore to herself two things: one, that she would save the home. And two, she would find a way somehow to heal the hurt she'd caused Lazarus. She'd find a way to open herself to him, even at the risk of hurting herself, because she owed him that. Because if she didn't, she would never be able to get him back. Could she admit how she felt to him? She was no longer sure. The mere thought of expressing aloud her feelings made sweat start at the small of her back.

But there was something she knew she could do.

Standing, Temperance knocked hard against the carriage roof. "Stop! Stop, please! I wish to go to a different address. I wish to visit Mr. St. John."

LAZARUS HAD NEVER thought of himself as lovable. Therefore it should come as no shock at all that Temperance did not, in fact, love him. No, not a shock...but it would have been nice had she had some small feeling for him.

Lazarus pondered his own sickening craving as he guided his black gelding through the London morning throng the day after he'd walked out on Temperance. It appeared that his own nascent emotions had provoked a new desire as well: the urge to be loved. How banal. And yet, banal or not, he could not change the way his heart felt.

A corner of his mouth quirked up humorlessly. It seemed he must be like other men after all.

The black shied and Lazarus looked up. The address he sought this morning was not so very far from his own town house. The square he now guided the horse into was new, the houses genteel and so elegant they must've cost a fortune to rent. Lazarus swung down from the gelding and gave the reins to a waiting boy, along with a shilling for his troubles. He mounted the pristine white steps and knocked.

Five minutes later, Lazarus was shown into a study both luxurious and comfortable. The chairs were wide enough for a man's girth and covered in a deep red leather. The books were in enough disarray to suggest actual use, and the massive desk, taking up an entire corner of the room, shone with polish.

Lazarus strolled the room while he waited for his host. When the door at last opened, he had a copy of Cicero's speeches in his hands.

The man who entered wore a full-bottomed white wig. The outer corners of his eyes, his lips, and his jowls all sagged downward as if pulled by an invisible string, giving his countenance the agreeable look of a hunting dog.

He glanced at Lazarus, raised a bushy gray eyebrow at the book in his hands, and said, "May I help you, sir?"

"I hope so." Lazarus closed and set aside the book. "Am I addressing Lord Hadley?"

"You are indeed, sir." Hadley gave an abbreviated bow and, sweeping aside the skirts of his coat, sat heavily in one of the leather chairs.

Lazarus inclined his head before sitting across from his host. "I am Lazarus Huntington, Lord Caire."

Hadley arched an eyebrow, waiting.

"I was hoping you could help me," Lazarus said. "We have—or rather *had*—a mutual acquaintance: Marie Hume."

Hadley's expression didn't change.

Lazarus cocked his head. "A blond lady specializing in certain forms of entertainment."

"What forms?"

"The rope and hood."

"Ah." Hadley didn't seem at all embarrassed by the outré turn of conversation. "I know the gel. Called herself Marie Pett when she was with me. I was under the impression she had died."

Lazarus nodded. "She was murdered in a house in St. Giles almost three months ago."

"A pity," Hadley said, "but I don't see how it matters to me."

Lazarus inclined his head. "I wish to find the murderer."

Hadley showed the first sign of emotion since Caire had arrived: curiosity. He took a small enameled box from a pocket, tapped out a pinch of snuff, inhaled, and sneezed. He blew his nose and shook his head as he put away his handkerchief. "Why?"

Lazarus raised his eyebrows. "Why what?"

"Why d'you want to find this gel's murderer?"

"She was my mistress."

"And?" Hadley fingered the snuffbox still in his hand. "You know about her specialty, so I assume you used her for the same purpose as I. A pity, as I said, that she's dead, but there are other women to fulfill our particular needs. Why bother seeking her killer?"

Lazarus blinked. No one had ever asked him the question phrased in such a way. "I . . . spent time with her. With Marie."

"You loved her?"

"No, I never loved Marie. But she was a person. If I do

not find her killer, seek retribution for her death, then no one held her in regard. Then..."

Then what?

But Hadley finished his sentence for him. "And if no one holds Marie in regard, then perhaps no one holds you in regard? No one holds *us* in regard. We are merely solitary creatures enacting our bizarre form of human contact without anyone caring about us at all."

Lazarus stared at the other man, a bit stunned.

Hadley's mouth curved, creating a whole array of sagging wrinkles in his cheeks. "I've had a bit more time to think it out than you."

Lazarus nodded. "Do you know any other who visited her?"

"Besides that worm she called a brother?"

"Tommy?"

"Aye, Tommy." Hadley pursed his lips, not an attractive expression for him. "Tommy was there, lurking about, nearly every time I visited fair Marie. Once he came with an older woman. She wore a soldier's red coat. Seemed a bad sort, but as I said, I didn't bother much with Marie's personal life."

"Indeed?" Lazarus frowned. The brother had said he only visited his sister rarely. Apparently he lied. And how was Mother Heart's-Ease involved with this? She and her shop seemed to pop up at every turn.

"Does that help?" Hadley inquired courteously. "I never met any of her other clients."

"It does help." Lazarus stood. "I thank you, my lord, for your time and your frankness."

Hadley shrugged. "It was no trouble. Would you like to stay for a glass of wine, sir?"

Lazarus bowed. "Thank you, but I have another appointment this morning. Perhaps some other time?"

It was merely a polite gesture and both men knew it. A fleeting emotion crossed Hadley's face, but it was gone before Lazarus could decipher it.

"Of course." Hadley stood. "Good day, sir."

Lazarus bowed again, crossing to the study door. But a thought gave him pause there. He turned to look at the older man. "Might I ask one more question, sir?"

Hadley waved a hand, indicating assent.

"Are you married?"

That same expression trod across Hadley's face, deepening each wrinkle and sag. "No, sir. I have never married."

Lazarus bowed yet again, conscious that he'd crossed the bounds of civility. He let himself out of the elegant, expensive town house. But as he emerged into the morning sun, he wondered: Had loneliness left its stamp upon his features as well?

SILENCE STOOD IN front of the foundling home the next morning and smiled. No, that wasn't quite right. She looked at her feet and tried again, feeling the muscles move in her cheeks. How odd. Something that had been as natural as, well, *smiling* just days ago was now so foreign that she wasn't sure she was doing it properly.

"Have you got a toothache, ma'am?"

Silence looked up into the rather grubby face of one of the orphans. Joseph Smith? Or perhaps Joseph Jones? Goodness! Why had her brother and sister chosen to name all the boys Joseph Something and all the girls Mary Whatever? Had they been quite mad?

But the boy was still staring at her, one dirty finger stuck in his mouth.

"Don't do that," she said sharply, startling them both. She'd never reprimanded one of the children, sharply or otherwise.

The child immediately removed his finger, watching her rather warily now.

Silence sighed. "What is your name?"

"Joseph Tinbox."

Silence wrinkled her nose. "Whyever were you named that?"

"Because," the boy said, "when I comed here, I had a tin box tied to my wrist."

"Of course," Silence muttered, giving up on the smile altogether. "Well, Joseph Tinbox, I'm here to see Mrs. Dews. Do you happen to know where she is?"

"Yes'm," Joseph replied.

He turned and opened the door to the home—apparently unlocked this afternoon—and led her into the house. There was a great commotion coming from the kitchen, and when Silence stepped in, she saw Temperance, her hair coming down about her ears, managing sheer chaos. A group of boys stood in the corner, alternately singing in high, angelic voices and poking each other when Temperance or Nell turned their back. Nell was supervising the weekly wash, while three small girls tended a large pot of something steaming on the hearth.

Temperance turned just as Silence entered and shoved back a lock of curling hair. "Silence! Oh, thank goodness. I could use your help today."

"Oh." Silence stared about the kitchen rather dazedly. "Really?"

"Yes, really," Temperance said firmly. "Winter is still ill. Could you take this tray up to him?"

"Winter is ill?" Silence picked up the tray automatically.

"Yes." Temperance frowned at the singing boys. "From the beginning again, please. And Joseph Smith, do stop shoving Joseph Little. Yes," she said again, turning back to Silence. "I forgot to tell you, didn't I? Oh, so much has happened in the last day. Just take him his food, and under no circumstances should you let him rise from his bed."

Temperance's look was quite stern, and Silence was tempted to salute, though she wisely refrained from the gesture. She hurried from the kitchen instead and made her way to Winter's room up under the eaves. Perhaps Temperance had had some sort of foresight, for as Silence pushed open the door, she caught Winter putting on his breeches.

Or trying to in any case.

Her youngest brother was pale and sweating and fell against the bed as she shut the door behind her.

"Can't a man have some privacy?" Winter said in uncharacteristic ill humor.

"Not if you're attempting to escape." Silence set the tray on a small table by the bed, balanced precariously atop a pile of books. "Sorry."

"She told you, didn't she?" Winter asked darkly.

"That you're ill? Yes."

Silence wrinkled her nose in sympathy. Temperance could be rather bossy sometimes, although in this case Silence was in full agreement with her sister. Winter looked quite terrible. He'd taken off his nightshirt to get dressed, and she could count the ribs on his bare torso. He bent to retrieve his nightshirt from the floor, and she sucked in her breath.

He straightened hastily, but she'd already seen the long cut on his back. "Dear God! Where did you get that?"

He pulled his nightshirt on over his head. When he reappeared, he grimaced. "It's nothing, really. Please don't tell Temperance; she'll only worry more."

Silence frowned. "But where did you get it? It looks like a knife cut."

"Nothing of the sort. I fell." He looked sheepish. "In the street the other day. I'm afraid I came down on a wagon wheel and the iron cut right through my coat."

"How strange. It looks exactly as if someone had cut you with a knife—or a sword, I suppose." Silence tried to look over his shoulder, but he sat back against the pillow with a slight wince. "Have you cleaned it?"

"It's fine. Truly." He smiled, crooked and endearing. "I admit that I may've let the wound go when I first got it and that may have led to my fainting spell, but it's healing properly now."

"But—"

"Really, Silence," he said. "Now. Tell me how things are with you."

"Oh." She carefully transferred the tray to his lap, making sure it was settled enough that it wouldn't spill. "Well, William has sailed again."

Winter glanced up from a spoonful of soup. "So soon?"

She looked away, busying herself with straightening the bed linens. "There was a ship whose captain fell suddenly ill. William assured me that he would be paid well for going back to sea early."

"Ah," Winter said noncommittally.

"And I went to Concord's house for dinner the other

night, and he was quite cold. Asa was supposed to be there as well, but he didn't come. Didn't even send his regrets." Silence picked up a pillow to plump. "You won't credit it, I'm sure, but Concord implied that I'd been seduced by Mr. O'Connor, even after I told him that that simply wasn't the case. I don't think he believes me, Winter. I don't think Temperance believes me either."

She must've hit the pillow overhard because a small cloud of feathers puffed from a corner.

"I see," Winter said slowly, eyeing his damaged pillow.

"I'm sorry." Silence placed the pillow back on the bed and gave it a gentle pat. "But you believe me, don't you? You know that Mr. O'Connor never touched me, that he only asked me to spend the night. And I did. I did spend the night in his room, but nothing—nothing at all!—happened. Do you believe me, Winter?"

She stood, arms crossed protectively over her breasts, and stared at him anxiously.

"I believe," Winter said slowly, "that you are my sister and that no matter what happened, I will continue to love you and stand by you."

"Oh," she whispered, and stupid tears started in her eyes. For it was the sweetest thing Winter could possibly say—and also the most horrible. He obviously didn't believe her either.

"Silence..."

"Well, then," she said without looking at him; she couldn't or she just might either burst into tears or hit him, neither of which would be very good. "I'll just go down and see if Temperance needs my help in the kitchen."

"Silence," he called as she made the door.

She didn't turn, staring down at her hand on the knob as she said gruffly, "What?"

"Have you ever thought about helping us here on a more permanent basis?"

The question was so startling that Silence turned to look at Winter.

He was regarding her gravely. "We could use your help, you know."

"Why?" she whispered.

He blinked and looked down at his plate of soup. "I think it might be of benefit both to you and to us."

He thought she was ruined. The realization was sudden and so entirely unwelcome that Silence was struck dumb.

Winter raised his eyes to hers, and they were filled with regret and sorrow. "Please at least think about it."

She nodded jerkily and left quickly without replying. She couldn't.

No one believed she'd walked out of Mickey O'Connor's bedroom untouched. Not her neighbors, who whispered as she walked by. Not the shopkeepers, who turned their backs and pretended to be busy when she came into their stores. Not William, who had been mute as she'd watched him pack and leave. Not Asa or Concord or Verity or even Temperance or Winter. Even her own family thought she lied to cover some horrible sin.

No one believed her in all the world.

Chapter Eighteen

❧

King Lockedheart looked bemused. "But if I open the
cage door, the bird shall fly."
"If you want to learn what love is, you must open the
door," Meg said.
So the king opened the little blue bird's cage door.
Immediately the bird took flight and darted out an
open window of the room.
The king looked at Meg with his eyebrow cocked. "I
think that all I have learned is how to lose a bird."
"Is it?" she asked. "What do you feel?"
The king frowned. "Loss. Emptiness." . . .
—from King Lockedheart

"Then you think we can do it?" Mrs. Dews leaned forward,
her face bright, her extraordinary brown eyes eager.

St. John nodded, amazed by her vitality. How could he
not be? She was in such extreme contrast to Clara's still
form upstairs.

He shoved the awful thought aside and focused on
answering her instead. "Yes. Yes, of course. I've already

had my secretary send out the invitations to view the foundling home."

Mrs. Dews bit her lip. "How many did you invite?"

"A little over a hundred people."

"Oh!" She sat very still, her eyes wide, but her hand crept out to seize the wrist of her maidservant, a woman named Nell.

St. John had been taken aback by the presence of the maid on this, Mrs. Dews's second visit to his house. On the first, she'd arrived alone and nearly vibrating with the excitement of her idea: to open the Home for Unfortunate Infants and Foundling Children for viewing in the hopes of catching the interest of a prospective patron for the home. It was a daring scheme, but one that was shrewd as well. Viewing the unfortunate, whether at prisons, hospitals, or houses for the hopelessly mad, was fashionable in London at the moment. Most came merely to stare and titter at the antics of those poor souls, but many would also pledge monies to the charities they viewed.

"That's quite a lot of people," Mrs. Dews said, letting go of her maid.

"Yes, but they are all of the best families—ones to whom charity is now in fashion." St. John arched a significant eyebrow.

"Quite. Yes, of course." Mrs. Dews smoothed her black skirts with one hand. It trembled slightly, and St. John had a wild urge to cross the room and comfort her.

"Do you think you'll be ready in time?" he inquired, clasping his hands behind his back.

"I believe so," she said, looking a bit relieved at the change of subject. "We've already scrubbed the walls and floors, Winter has been listening to the children recite various poems by heart, and Nell has been busy mending the children's clothes."

"Good, good. I'll have my cook make a quantity of punch and some gingerbread the day before to be delivered quite early on the set morning."

"Oh, but you've done so much already," Mrs. Dews exclaimed. "I don't wish you to go to the expense on my account."

"It's for the children," St. John reminded her gently. "I'd feel quite the lackwit if I didn't contribute to our little plan. Please, don't mention it."

"In that case..." She smiled shyly at him, her eyes so alive.

How Caire could've let this woman slip through his hands was beyond him. He turned quickly, pretending to study the china clock on his mantelpiece. "If that is all today?"

"Oh! Oh, of course," she said from behind him, sounding a little hurt. "I don't mean to take up your time, Mr. St. John. You have been of such great help to me and our home."

He clenched his jaw to prevent himself from stuttering apologies. Instead he bowed a bit stiffly. "Good day, Mrs. Dews."

She left then, after a graceful curtsy, and only the maid shot him a curious look over her shoulder. He waited until the door to his library shut before walking to the window that overlooked the street below. He watched as she crossed the street, her stride light and graceful, one hand on her bonnet, for it was a windy day. The maid walked by her side instead of behind, and they seemed to be conversing. Her black-clad figure grew small, and in another moment she'd disappeared into the London crowd.

St. John let the curtain fall from his fingers.

He looked about his library, but despite the books and news sheets and clutter, it seemed barren and lonely after her visit. He left the room and mounted the stairs, climbing two floors up. He didn't visit Clara often at this hour; she usually slept in after what was invariably a restless night. But today he found himself unable to keep away. In the back of his mind, he knew that there would come a day—perhaps soon—when he would no longer be able to climb the stairs and see her.

St. John tapped at her door and then cracked it open. The old maid who was Clara's constant companion looked up from her chair by the bed, then rose and crossed to tend the fire.

He approached the bed and looked down. Clara must've just had her hair washed, for it was spread, a bright banner, over her white pillow. The locks were a deep brown with bits of red in them, now streaked with strands of gray. He found himself stroking her hair. She'd once told him it was her best feature, and he'd been amazed that ladies categorized their person thusly. Amazed and fondly amused.

"Godric," she whispered.

He looked down and saw her brown eyes watching him. Once they had been as beautiful as Mrs. Dews's. Now they were always pain-filled.

He bent and brushed a careful kiss across her wide forehead. "Clara."

She smiled, her pale lips curving just slightly. "To what do I owe this visit?"

He whispered in her ear, "A deep and abiding longing to see the most beautiful woman in the world."

She laughed, as he'd intended, but then the gentle

sound turned to a hacking cough that shook her frame. The nurse hurried over.

St. John stepped back, watching with painful patience as Clara's spasm gradually subsided. When it was over, sweat had dampened her hair and her face was more pale than her pillow, but she looked at him and smiled.

He swallowed past the constriction in his throat. "I'm sorry to disturb you. I merely wanted you to know that I love you."

She held a shaking hand out to him.

He took it and watched as she mouthed, "I know."

St. John made himself smile before turning and leaving his wife's bedroom.

IT WAS LATE afternoon nearly a week later when Temperance knocked on Polly's door. Now that Winter was recovered, she and Mary Whitsun had been running errands in preparation for the home's viewing, but it was important that she stop by Polly's rooms today.

Polly answered the door with a sleeping Mary Hope in her arms and a shawl thrown over her shoulder. "Come in, Mrs. Dews, Mary Whitsun. It's that glad I am to see you."

"Is Mary Hope any better?" Temperance whispered the question as she stepped into the crowded little room. A glance showed her Polly's own babies sleeping together on the bed. Mary Whitsun tiptoed over to replace the blanket one of the children had kicked off.

"Aye, she is." The wet nurse beamed as she looked down at the baby. "The fever's left and she's sucking strong. I think she might just live, ma'am."

"Oh, thank God." Temperance closed her eyes in relief.

The babies died so often. It was a welcome surprise to find one who struggled through fever so young.

Not that Mary Hope was entirely out of the woods yet. "And your own babies?"

"They never got the fever, thank the Lord," Polly replied. "Healthy as young puppies, they are."

"Thank you, Polly." Temperance made a mental note to reward the wet nurse.

"Will you hold her?" Polly asked. "She's just now fallen to sleep, and I haven't had a moment to put myself to rights."

She held out the babe, and Temperance remembered Lazarus's words—that he'd seen her refuse to touch the baby. She hesitated only a second before taking the warm little bundle into her arms. Mary Whitsun peered over her arm, and they both looked down with wonder at the tiny delicate fingers that splayed against one pink cheek. Temperance's eyes stung with tears.

"Are you all right, ma'am?" Polly asked with concern as she tucked her shawl into her bodice.

"Yes," Temperance murmured as she wiped her cheek against her shoulder. "It's just that it was so close."

"That it was," the wet nurse said comfortably, taking back the baby.

"There's no use not loving them, is there?" Temperance whispered. She glanced at Mary Whitsun, who was still enthralled by the baby's tiny face.

"Aye, I'm afraid 'tis silly to even bother," Polly replied. "One look in their wee faces and we're all lost, aren't we?"

"Yes, indeed."

Temperance bid Polly good night and closed the door to her room gently behind her. When she looked up, she saw Mary Whitsun watching her.

"Will the baby live, ma'am?"

Temperance smiled. "I think so, Mary."

"I'm very glad," Mary said somberly.

They clattered down the rickety stairs and out the front door of Polly's rooming house. Temperance glanced uneasily at the sky. The sun was beginning to set. "We need to hurry home before dark."

Mary hurried beside her. "Is it true that the Ghost of St. Giles comes out after dark and hunts girls?"

"Where did you hear that?"

Mary ducked her head. "The butcher's boy. Is it true?"

Temperance frowned. "Some girls have been hurt, yes. But you needn't worry so long as you stay at the school, especially at night."

"Will you stay home?"

Temperance glanced at Mary. The girl had her eyes fixed on the ground as they walked. "I need to do errands, naturally—"

"But if another baby needs help at night?" Mary was biting her lip.

"My job is to help orphaned babies in St. Giles," Temperance said gently. "Where would Mary Hope be if I hadn't gone after her?"

Mary said nothing.

"But I hardly ever have to make trips after dark," Temperance said briskly. "Really, there's no need to worry."

Mary nodded, but she still looked troubled.

Temperance sighed, wishing she could set Mary's mind at ease, but as long as the murderer was loose, that would be hard to do.

When they reached the home, yet more work waited

and Temperance sent Mary Whitsun to supervise the lit-
tler girls in washing the hall walls.

By the time Temperance climbed the stairs to her room
that night, it was quite late. The preparations for opening
the home for viewing were exhausting. Every time she
thought they were nearly done, another job would rear its
head and she'd have to somehow see to it.

She turned the corner on the rickety stairs, examining
the banister. It was in need of a polish, but would making
it look better merely persuade any potential patron that
the home wasn't really in need of funds? This was the
dilemma with all the decisions she made to neaten and
clean the home. Every decision she second-guessed, even
when Winter told her in his quiet voice that she was doing
a fine job and not to worry so much. And beneath all her
worries was a nagging sadness. Put simply, she missed
Caire. She found herself wondering what he'd think of her
decisions, wanting to discuss her problems and small joys
with him. She wanted to be with him.

But she'd pretty well fouled those waters, hadn't she?
Her shoulders slumped at the thought as she rounded the
final twist in the old staircase, coming at last to the upper-
most floor of the home. He thought she'd wanted him only for
a crass sexual relationship, and while she certainly longed to
embrace him again, there was so much more to her emotions.

She halted, there at the top of the stairs, a single candle wavering in her hand to give her light, as she finally
acknowledged what she'd known all along. She felt much
more for Caire than lust.

A sob caught in her throat before she could stifle it. She'd
been so lonely before he'd come into her life. His absence
now only highlighted just how alone she was. Oh, she had

her brothers and sisters, the children and Nell, but even with her own family, she was apart. Only with Caire was she herself, flaws and all. He saw her sexual need, her sometimes un-Christian urges and emotions and, wonder of wonders, liked her just the same. *Wanted* her just the same. It was so freeing, simply being with him! Knowing that she could be herself—all of herself—and he would not turn away.

She looked about the dim, squalid hallway. Alone. She was so alone.

IT WASN'T UNTIL half an hour into the viewing that Temperance decided that the event was going quite well, all things considered.

They'd had a rather rocky start when their first visitors—a lady with an enormous plume in her hair accompanied by a stout gentleman in a full-bottomed wig, improbably dyed an inky black above his elderly face—arrived a bit early at just before five of the clock. Joseph Tinbox had been the only one to hear the knock at the door, and when he'd answered it, had at first refused them entry on the grounds that they were "too early and ought to go away and come back at the proper time."

Fortunately, Nell had gone looking for Joseph Tinbox at that moment and found him about to shoo their visitors away. Profuse apologies, and the application of two cups of Mr. St. John's punch, had done much to soothe the couple's indignation. After that, a steady stream of gentlepersons had arrived. So many, in fact, that at one point their grand carriages had clogged the end of Maiden Lane, much to the interest of the usual inhabitants. Some had, in fact, taken out chairs and sat along the street to watch the parade of nobility go by.

Yes, all was going quite well, and if the punch held out

and she could keep Winter from engaging in a political discussion with a rather loud young gentleman in an atrocious yellow coat who insisted on saying the most idiotic things, they might actually live through this day.

Temperance smiled and shook the hand of a vivacious lady in a plum-colored dress as the lady exclaimed about the "poor little wretches." She was leaving and, despite her rather unfortunate choice of words, seemed genuinely moved by the orphanage.

"Who is that?" Nell muttered behind Temperance.

"I don't know, but she's quite enthusiastic," Temperance whispered back.

"No, not her. *Her.*"

Temperance looked over their guest's head to see Lady Caire picking her way across the cobblestones, her mouth twisted in distaste. She wore an entirely inappropriate gold and blue brocade dress and held the hand of a gentleman in a ginger wig and lavender coat. The Maiden Lane spectators were quite taken with her, many elbowing their neighbor as she passed. Fortunately, Mr. St. John had seen her approaching and intercepted her, apparently pointing out the home's rather sad architecture. He couldn't hold her off forever, though.

"Oh, no!" Temperance groaned.

"What? *What?*" Nell hissed, all agog.

"It's Lady Caire," Temperance murmured. "She's quite horrible."

A muffled giggle came from behind them.

Temperance turned and to her horror saw that they weren't alone. Lady Hero, in a striking silvery-blue dress, had somehow entered the little hallway and, what was worse, had obviously heard her.

"Oh. I'm sorry," Temperance muttered, beginning a curtsy and then changing her mind halfway down and popping back up too fast. "I didn't mean...that is...uh..."

"She *is* rather horrible," Lady Hero said, smiling faintly. "But if you will credit it I've heard her discuss the plight of poor children before."

"Really?" Temperance asked faintly. She darted another look at the street. Lady Caire had stopped to argue about something with her escort. She turned back to Lady Hero. "So she might actually be interested in our home?"

"I think so, yes. As am I," Lady Hero said almost diffidently. "I was orphaned at the age of eight, you know."

"I'm so sorry, I didn't."

Lady Hero waved aside her apology. "It was a long time ago now. But there are any number of ladies who are interested to one degree or another with the welfare of poor infants."

"Oh," was Temperance's not very eloquent reply. It hadn't occurred to her to seek a patroness. Somehow she had been thinking all along about a patron who would be like Sir Stanley Gilpin—older, wealthy, and male— when perhaps she should've been focusing merely on the *wealthy* bit. She smiled at Lady Hero. "How wonderful!"

Lady Hero smiled. "Perhaps you'll be so kind as to show me about your home."

"Of course," Temperance said, but Winter descended the stairs at that moment.

"Sister, have you seen Mary Whitsun?" Winter had a line between his brows.

"Not since this morning." She turned to look at Nell.

The maidservant shrugged. "Shall I look for her?"

"If you don't mind, Nell," Winter said.

Nell hurried up the stairs.

"You must be Mr. Makepeace," Lady Hero said.

"This is Lady Hero Batten, Winter," Temperance said.

"An honor to meet you, ma'am." Winter bowed.

"I was just telling Mrs. Dews—" the lady began, but Nell came rushing back in the room again. She held Joseph Tinbox by one arm.

"Tell her what you've told me," Nell demanded of Joseph. "Tell her where Mary Whitsun went!"

"She left," Joseph said succinctly. His brown eyes were wide, his face so pale the freckles stood out. "She said it was all right. She said everyone was too busy."

Temperance felt ice form in her breast. "Too busy for what?"

"A woman came and said there was a babe what needed fetching," Joseph said. "Mary went with her."

Temperance glanced out the door. The sky had already begun to darken, night slinking into St. Giles like an alley cat.

Dear God. Mary Whitsun was out in St. Giles at night with a mad killer on the loose.

LAZARUS DRIFTED THROUGH the late afternoon streets of St. Giles. The sun was beginning to set, the feeble rays withdrawing swiftly from tall buildings, overhanging eaves, and a myriad of swinging signs. Lazarus leapt over the corpse of a cat in the gutter and continued on his way.

He was close, very close, to finding Marie's murderer. Again and again he'd come back to St. Giles, and this trip he felt might very well be the last one—for better or worse. Danger was lurking here, sharpening its claws, waiting for him to make a false move.

Danger or not, something deep inside him felt it only right to balance the scales. He needed to see that Marie's murderer was punished before he could move on with Temperance. And he needed to see Temperance again. Badly. He had no doubt that the breath would stop in his chest if he could no longer touch her, speak to her, and watch those amazing golden-flecked eyes reflect her true emotions.

But first he had to find Marie's murderer.

To that end, he'd tried speaking to Tommy Pett thrice in the last week—the boy must know something about the connection between Mother Heart's-Ease and his sister. But each time Lazarus had called at Mrs. Whiteside's establishment, Tommy had been unaccountably absent. Perhaps a late daytime call would find him in.

In another fifteen minutes, he turned into Running Man Lane, following its twists and turns until it spilled into the courtyard where Mrs. Whiteside's whorehouse was. But as he neared, he could hear bawling and raised voices. His last few steps were made at a run.

The sight that greeted him in the courtyard was an odd one: the ladies—and boys—of the night all seemed to be standing in the courtyard, many holding candles or lanterns. Some argued, some wept, and some simply stood stunned. At that moment, Pansy walked out of the whorehouse with her hulking guard, Jacky, behind her. Lazarus began pushing through the crowd, even as Jacky raised his massive hands above his head and clapped them together, effectively silencing the courtyard.

"The house has been searched. No one lurks within. The danger is gone," Pansy said in her deep voice. "Now I want all of you to go back inside."

Jacky clapped his hands together again, and one by one, the whores moved reluctantly inside.

A big woman in purple silk braced her hands on her hips. "An' 'ow are we to know it's safe in there?"

Pansy shot her a stern look. "Because I say 'tis."

The woman turned red-faced and shuffled inside.

Lazarus stepped forward and Pansy caught sight of him. She jerked her chin. "You're not wanted here."

He was undeterred. Wanted or not, he had the feeling that what was inside the whorehouse was of importance to him.

"What has happened?" he asked.

"Nothing you need worry about," she muttered, and turned aside as if to leave him there.

Without thinking, he caught at her shoulder before she could disappear inside the house, then felt more than saw Jacky swing at him. The guard was a big man, but he had a big man's slowness. Lazarus easily ducked inside the blow and punched him hard in the gut. Jacky fell heavily to his knees.

Pansy made a distressed sound and wrapped her tiny arms about the big man's shoulders. "Stop it!"

Lazarus stepped back but kept his hands fisted. It wouldn't do to underestimate Jacky.

Pansy sighed, her misshapen face looking a little gray. "I'm as good as dead anyway. Come inside."

Jacky lumbered to his feet, shooting a nasty look at Lazarus, but he stood aside to let him in.

Lazarus entered the house with the hairs on the back of his neck on end. The guard wouldn't mind killing him. Only Pansy's will kept him from attacking.

She made no other comment but led the way up the

stairs. A few whores still lingered in the hallways, gossiping, but at the sight of the madam, they vanished into their rooms. Pansy stopped at a door midway down the upper hallway and cast an inscrutable glance at Lazarus before she pushed it open.

The smell hit him first, the stench of bowels and blood. The body on the bed had been gutted—just like Marie. He stepped closer, mindful of the dark smears on the floor, and gazed into the waxen face. It was Tommy, the boy's countenance oddly serene above the violence of his body.

Lazarus looked back at Pansy. She was staring fixedly at the horror on the bed, but at his look, she jerked her chin at him. "Come downstairs. I need a cup of tea."

She closed the door behind them, and they all tramped down the stairs silently and into her little sitting room. Pansy sat in her special chair, gesturing for Lazarus to sit opposite her.

"Tea, Jacky." When the big man didn't move, she nodded wearily. "It's all right. Lord Caire won't hurt me."

The guard grunted and left the room.

"He was killed the same way as Marie and the other prostitutes," Lazarus said softly. "He must have known the killer."

"Mmm." Pansy seemed to be in a meditative mood, her chin propped on a fist.

"Mistress Pansy."

She sighed heavily, looking up. "Yes. Yes, of course he knew the murderer."

Lazarus narrowed his eyes. "As do you."

She met his gaze squarely. "As do I."

"Who is it, Pansy?"

She held up her hand as the door opened. Jacky entered, carrying a delicate tea tray in his huge hands.

She smiled at him as he set the tray down. "Thank you, Jacky. Could you please guard the door for me?"

The big man shot a suspicious glance at Lazarus and trundled out.

Pansy waited until the door was closed. Then she looked at Lazarus. "It's the owner of this house. She controls all the prostitutes in her little corner of St. Giles. They each must pay a portion of their earnings to her, even if it's only a few pennies. Marie refused. And Tommy, that fool..."

She shook her head in disgust and poured herself a cup of tea.

Lazarus made himself sit patiently.

She took the full teacup, but then merely stared into the tea. "I think he tried to blackmail her. I think that's what set her off. She was here tonight visiting Tommy, and she left in a hurry. Tommy must've known all along who'd killed his sister, and once you started asking questions, he figured she would pay him to keep her secret. He was pretty, but not very smart."

Lazarus closed his eyes. He was so close. "Who, Pansy?"

"Mother Heart's-Ease."

His felt his pulse begin to race. *Finally.* "The bawd who runs the gin shop?"

Pansy's lips twitched. "She's much more than that. She's the most powerful woman in this part of St. Giles. And the most dangerous. You saw Tommy. She did that in a houseful of people. She's in a berserker rage. She's burning her bridges behind her now."

"But why kill Marie and the other prostitutes so dramatically?"

Pansy shrugged. "To scare away her competitors, her allies, her whores—anyone and everyone, in fact."

He frowned. "You're in danger."

"She'll kill me afore the sennight's out, I think," Pansy said dispassionately, and finally took a sip of her tea. "Me and whoever else she thinks has betrayed her or stands in her way. You'd better watch your step as well. She's already killed Tommy to keep him from talking to you— and to Mrs. Dews."

Lazarus raised his eyebrows, his alarm growing. "Mrs. Dews?"

Pansy set her teacup carefully on the tray. "I think Mother Heart's-Ease sees Mrs. Dews as a sort of rival for control of St. Giles. She doesn't like that Mrs. Dews rescues the children Mother Heart's-Ease would rather sell—or whore out."

"You think she'll go after Temperance Dews?"

"She already has."

"What?" Lazarus felt his muscles tighten in alarm.

Pansy looked at him with a terrible fatalistic tragedy in her eyes. "One of the girls here brought in a lass tonight— the one Mrs. Dews dotes on."

"Mary Whitsun."

"Yes. Mother Heart's-Ease took the girl with her when she left."

Lazarus sprang to his feet, dashing to the door as Pansy's last words floated after him.

"And I think Mother Heart's-Ease means to strike at Mrs. Dews through the girl."

Chapter Nineteen

"What you feel is the sorrow of loss," Meg said.
"What you feel is love. And," she continued as the
little blue bird flew back in the room and lit on the
king's hand, "that is love also."
"I do not understand," the king said.
"What do you feel now?" Meg asked.
King Lockedheart frowned as he gently stroked the
little bird's head. "Joy. Happiness."
"That is the joy of love." Meg smiled. "To experience
your love for the bird, you must be willing to let her
go. And in exchange, the bird displays her love for
you by returning." ...
—from *King Lockedheart*

Dear God.

Temperance felt her knees give way in horror. *Not Mary Whitsun. Not her darling Mary Whitsun.*

She felt Nell wrap an arm around her to brace her. Lady Hero was looking concerned. Mr. St. John ushered Lady Caire and her escort in and after a brief word with

Winter, shot Temperance a grave look before showing the lady up the stairs. Winter took the rest of them into the kitchen. Temperance sank into a chair. She needed to rescue Mary, but how could she when they didn't even know where Mary had gone?

"We need to search for her," Winter was saying. "Where was the baby Mary was fetching?"

Someone started pounding on the kitchen door. "Temperance!"

It was Caire's voice. Temperance jumped up and flew to the door, fumbling with the bar, her hands trembling.

She threw open the door and fell into Lazarus's arms, and for a moment she simply stood there, shaking against him. He was so large, so warm, and he was here when she most needed him.

He clutched her to his chest. "Are you all right?"

"No." She shook her head against him. "Mary Whitsun is missing."

He tilted her chin up. "I know. Mother Heart's-Ease has her."

"What?"

"I've just come from Mrs. Whiteside's house. Mother Heart's-Ease *is* Mrs. Whiteside. She seems to have lured Mary Whitsun there with the help of one of the prostitutes."

"We must go at once." Temperance grabbed her cloak, hanging on a peg by the door.

"Wait. There's something else." Caire caught her arm, but it was Winter he addressed. "Mother Heart's-Ease is the murderer."

Temperance stared at him. "Marie's murderer? The one who has been...?"

He nodded.

She sobbed once before pulling herself together. "Then the matter is even more urgent."

"Yes," he said gently, "but there's also a possibility of a trap. Mother Heart's-Ease has a particular dislike of you, it seems."

Winter stirred. "Then she should not go."

Temperance rounded on him in a fury. "Not go? It's Mary Whitsun! I can't leave her with that woman, trap or no."

Winter began to protest, but Caire looked at him. "I'll accompany her and keep her safe."

"You promise?"

"On my life."

"You can take my footmen as well."

They all turned at the voice. Lady Caire had entered the small kitchen with her beau. Two burly footmen stood behind her. She met Lazarus's eyes for a minute.

He nodded. "Thank you."

Caire took Temperance's hand and then they were out the door and into the night with the footmen following.

"What does she want with Mary Whitsun?" Temperance panted as they hurried.

Caire shook his head. "She may be merely a lure. In which case she's probably in no danger."

Temperance shivered. "But Mother Heart's-Ease hates me, you said."

"According to Pansy." He hesitated, glancing about them as they rounded a corner. "She's already killed Tommy Pett."

"Oh, God." Temperance tried to control her rising panic. Why had she never told Mary how much she loved her? Why had she kept her at arm's length? "Then she may kill her simply to spite me."

Lazarus didn't answer, merely squeezing her hand.

The journey seemed to take hours, but it was only minutes later when they and the two footmen made Mother Heart's-Ease's gin shop.

Lazarus eyed the door and broke apart his stick.

"Stay behind me," he said to Temperance. "You two"—he jerked his chin at the footmen—"to either side of me."

Temperance nodded, watching as he pushed the door open with his foot.

The sight within was a strange one. The gin shop was nearly empty, but the overturned tables and broken chairs told of a struggle. Two bodies lay upon the floor—Mother Heart's-Ease's guards. The one-eyed barmaid cowered under the remains of a table. In the center of the room stood the Ghost of St. Giles, his sword tip at the throat of the last guard. At their entrance, the Ghost glanced at them from behind his black mask but made no other move or sound.

"I don't know where she is!" the guard blubbered. "Mother Heart's-Ease 'eard you were comin' and ran out the back door. She could be anywheres now."

The Ghost merely pressed his sword to the man's throat. The guard yipped and a trickle of blood ran down his neck.

"Don't!" called the barmaid. "Oh, don't hurt Davy!"

The footmen looked uneasily at Caire.

"Tell him where Mother Heart's-Ease is, then," Lazarus said in a calm voice.

Temperance saw the Ghost's mouth twitch up at the corner as if in sardonic approval.

"She was going after you." The girl pointed at Temperance.

"Where?" Temperance asked.

"To yer home," the girl said. "Said she'd make sure you'd leave St. Giles once and for all."

Temperance frowned, exchanging a puzzled glance with Lazarus. "Was she alone? Did she have a girl with her?"

"She 'ad one of yer lasses," the barmaid said. "Now leave my Davy alone. She's not 'ere, I tell you!"

"We'd best get back to the home," Lazarus said grimly.

"But what is she about?" Temperance cried. The fact that Mother Heart's-Ease had taken Mary with her when she fled sent chills down her spine.

"I don't know." Lazarus looked at the Ghost. "Are you with us?"

The harlequin nodded and with a graceful spin was out the door and running lightly down the street.

"Hurry!" Caire called to the footmen. He took her hand again and they retraced their steps.

Night had fallen fully. Signs swung overhead, creaking eerily in the wind. Now and again, they could see the moon, floating bloated and weak behind drifting clouds. The Ghost of St. Giles ran ahead, his footfalls nearly silent. As they neared the home, Temperance could see an odd orangey-red light flickering over the rooftops, teasing and coy, but becoming bolder as they ran.

And then she smelled the smoke.

"Dear God!" She couldn't even put into words her fear.

They rounded the corner and saw. The home was on fire. For a dreadful moment, the sound seemed to stop in Temperance's ears and all she heard was a kind of rushing noise. Oddly she focused on Lady Caire, standing by herself in the middle of Maiden Lane. Lazarus's mother had one hand to her mouth, and she was gazing up—at the top of the foundling home. That sight was what brought Temperance back suddenly and all at once. People were shouting. Nell was there, shaking her arm, and she could smell the smoke now, a dreadful hint of the chaos within.

"Are they out?" she shouted at Nell. There were children milling about her. "Are all the children out?"

"I don't know!" Nell replied.

"We need to take count!" Temperance shouted.

Maiden Lane was in chaos. People screamed and ran back and forth, the aristocrats who had come to view the home mingled with the everyday folk of St. Giles. A bucket line had formed. The ragged cobbler who lived in the cellar next door handed a bucket of water to a footman in full livery who handed it to the fishmonger's wife who handed it to a lord in a snowy white wig and so on. It was a bizarre sight. Temperance turned and looked behind her at the home.

And caught her breath.

Flames were shooting out the upper windows, smoke billowing in a gray-black cloud. At that moment, Winter and St. John staggered from the house.

"Winter!" Temperance called.

He carried a small boy in his arms. "No one else is in the nurseries. I think we got them all. Did you count the children?"

Temperance turned to Nell.

"Six and twenty—all but Mary Whitsun."

Temperance clutched at Lazarus's arm. "Where is she? Where could Mother Heart's-Ease have taken her?"

But when she looked at him, he was staring up at the building. "Christ's blood."

She followed his gaze. Atop the roof, a tall, gaunt woman in a tattered man's scarlet military coat was picking her way across the shingles.

The harlequin flashed by them silently and disappeared into the house next to the foundling home.

"Where is Mary Whitsun?" Temperance fisted one hand at her breast. No, it couldn't be. No one would be so terrible as to leave a child in that inferno.

But Mother Heart's-Ease was clearly alone.

Temperance burst into tears. Dear God, Mary Whitsun was in a burning building, dying.

"God's bloody stones," Caire muttered, and before she could speak, he was gone.

Gone inside the burning home.

THE LOWER FLOORS were relatively clear, but as Lazarus ran up the wooden stairs, the smoke rapidly built. He threw his cloak over his head, holding part of it against his mouth, but it provided little barrier against the smoke. He choked, fighting his body's urge to return to clean air. Dear God, he could hardly see, let alone breathe. Everything was gray with smoke. He looked about the floor where the children slept.

"Mary!"

His bellow turned to a hacking cough and was lost in the roar of the fire. She might not even be here. He might be on a fatal fool's mission. But the sight of Temperance's despair had been too much for him to bear. If the child was here, he would find her.

The inferno moaned like a live thing, lurking in the

floor above—the floor where Temperance and her brother had rooms. He narrowed his stinging eyes against the smoke as he climbed the rickety staircase. If he survived this hell, he'd be damned sure the home was better built next time. Tears streaked his face but evaporated almost at once in the heat.

The upper hall boiled with smoke.

Where would a madwoman hide a child? Lazarus fell to his knees, crawling, the tears blurring his eyes. If the girl was at the far end of the hall, she was gone now, but Temperance's room was not yet engulfed. He had to at least check.

He reached up to turn the doorknob, shoving the door open with his shoulder. "Mary!"

An answering cry.

He was blind now, so he felt with his hand, finding and clutching at a small foot. She was bound, lying on the floor next to the bed. She crowded against him as if she might burrow her small body into his, and he felt the wiggling fur of the cat she held. He broke apart his stick and used the sword to cut the rope about her legs and hands. Then he tucked her under one arm and dragged her toward the stairs. The flames were blasting in his face, licking down his throat, trying to set him afire from within. His lungs ached. There was a terrible roaring in his ears, and he realized, suddenly and fatefully, that the house was giving way. The cat leapt from the girl's arms.

Temperance loved this child, even if she'd never admitted it.

He shoved Mary's little body ahead of him. Dear God, let her at least live. "Run! Run now!"

He might've said more, but at that moment, hell opened up and swallowed him whole.

*   *   *

THE HOME WAS dying, and Caire and Mary Whitsun were still inside.

Temperance watched as a section of the roof suddenly slid and came tumbling down to the cobblestones. For a moment, two figures were silhouetted against the flames: Mother Heart's-Ease's cadaverous form and the quick shadow of the Ghost of St. Giles. Then they were both gone. Temperance couldn't muster the energy to wonder what had happened to them. All her will, all her hopes and prayers, were centered on Lazarus and Mary.

Fire licked up from a broken window, the room beyond entirely golden with flame. The crowd had quieted, as if in awe, as the roar of the fire had grown louder. The bucket line was still struggling heroically, but their efforts had no visible effect on the flames.

There was a sudden shriek, and Temperance watched, detached, as the Ghost of St. Giles dragged Mother Heart's-Ease from inside the neighboring house. It was a bizarre sight. Mother Heart's-Ease fought like a maddened wolf, but the Ghost had his hand locked about her upper arm and easily contained her. He shoved her at Mr. St. John, pointing with a gloved finger first at the burning home and then at the screaming woman, as if any of them needed an explanation. St. John's face hardened, and he called over two loitering footmen to help him hold the murderess.

Then the Ghost of St. Giles simply walked away into the crowd. No one gainsaid him.

Temperance didn't care.

"I must go in," she said to no one in particular, and started forward, only to find her arm in Winter's firm grip.

"Let me go." She turned her face to his, pleading.

She could see tears in his eyes. "No, sister. You must remain here."

"But he'll burn," she whispered, turning back to the fire. "He'll burn and I don't know if I can bear it."

Winter said no more, even when she collapsed to her knees. She was bereft, here on the muddy cobblestones, watching her love die. He was her love, she knew it now that it was far too late to tell him. Caire was both stronger and more vulnerable than any man she'd ever known before. He saw her flaws, saw her anger and sexual need, and her pretense of being someone better than she really was, and he didn't care. It was odd; she'd always thought she'd love someone who saw only the best in her when all along it was the man who saw everything—the good and the bad—who she loved.

And now it was too late.

Her throat was raw, and Temperance realized she was screaming, trying to crawl forward, Winter's hold on her arm preventing her.

And then a small form appeared, walking from the smoke and flames. Mary Whitsun emerged from the burning home like a miracle. She saw Temperance and ran to her. Temperance hugged her close, crying and kissing her face, squeezing her much too tight in her sorrow and joy.

Until Mary Whitsun raised her tear-streaked face. "He's still inside, Lord Caire. He came for me, but he shoved me down the stairs. He's still inside."

Something crunched and then gave way, and the entire front half of the house collapsed in on itself.

Chapter Twenty

*King Lockedheart was very pleased with this
demonstration. To reward Meg, he offered to give her
anything she asked for—anything at all.
Meg smiled. "I thank you, Your Majesty, but all I
wish for is a little pony and a pack of provisions, for
I long to see what the wide world is like."
The king frowned at this, for he'd become rather fond
of Meg. But no matter how he argued, Meg was quite
firm: She would leave on the morrow to go exploring.
This put the king into a foul mood, and he was
terribly curt with her for the rest of the wonderful
meal. Meg for her part was cheerful, ignoring the
king's more sarcastic comments.
And at the end of the evening, she left the king sitting
all alone in his dining room....*
—from *King Lockedheart*

The rain was gentle at first. It drifted down, as soft as
a mother's kiss on a sleeping child. Temperance didn't
notice the drops falling from above until the fire began

to hiss. And then, all at once, the clouds above opened up, pouring rain down like a waterfall, the drops so hard that they ricocheted off the cobblestones, splashing back up as they hit. The fire fought back, hissing and spitting its defiance, great waves of steam rising up. But the rain was stronger, more relentless, and the flames began to fall back.

And in the midst of all this, a figure in a black, swirling cloak emerged from the clouds of steam, limping but walking steadily.

Temperance rose to her feet, a cry strangled in her throat. His silver hair was tarnished by the smoke, but it was him. It was Caire. She pulled away from Winter and ran, slipping on the wet cobblestones, blinded by the rain and her own tears, rushing toward her heart. As she neared, a black singed cat struggled from under his cloak and streaked straight to Mary Whitsun.

Caire coughed. "I loathe cats."

Temperance sobbed once.

He caught her hard, pulling her under his cloak, kissing her with a smoke-filled mouth, there in the rain in front of everyone.

"I love you," she sobbed, rubbing her hands over his face, his hair, his chest, making sure he was solid and real. "I love you, and I thought you were dead. I couldn't bear it. I thought I would die too."

"I'd walk through fire for you," he rasped, his voice hoarse and broken. "I *have* walked through fire for you."

She choked on a laugh, and he kissed her again, his mouth hard, tasting of smoke and fire, and she'd never tasted anything so wonderful before, because he was alive.

He was *alive*.

He broke their kiss, resting his forehead against hers. "I love you, Temperance Dews, more than life itself."

He would've said more, but she kissed him again, softly this time, trying to convey everything she felt with just her lips.

"Ahem." Someone cleared their throat nearby.

Lazarus pulled back from the kiss enough to mutter, "Yes, Mother?"

Temperance blinked and turned her head. Lady Caire stood beside them, her elegant white coiffure ineffectively shielded by a coat held over her head by her shivering companion. She looked wet and cold and hurt.

"Caire," Temperance whispered.

He lifted his head to glance at his mother. "What is it?"

"If you're done making a public display of yourself," Lady Caire said, "the children need to be seen to, and there's an insane woman Godric St. John says started the fire and murdered three women."

"Your concern is touching as always," Caire began, but then Temperance pinched his earlobe. "Ouch." He looked down at her.

Goodness, aristocrats were idiots at times! "Your mother was very worried for you."

Caire lifted an eyebrow.

"I love you, Lazarus." Lady Caire's voice was clear and certain. But then her lower lip trembled. "You're my son. I may not express my love effectively, but that doesn't mean I don't love you."

He turned his head and stared at her in wonder. And he probably would've continued to stare, dumbstruck, if Temperance hadn't pinched him again.

"Ow." He shot a glare at her.

She arched a brow at him pointedly.

"Mother, mine." Caire leaned down gingerly and kissed his mother's cheek. "A wise woman once told me that just because love isn't expressed doesn't mean it isn't felt."

Lady Caire's eyes welled with tears. "Does that mean you love me as well?"

A corner of Lazarus's mouth quirked up. "I think it must."

"I didn't think you listened to me."

"Every word you have ever uttered," Caire whispered, "is engraved upon my heart."

Lady Caire closed her eyes as if she'd received a benediction.

Then her eyes snapped open. "Yes, well. What shall we do with all these children?"

Temperance glanced at the home. The fire looked nearly out, but there was not much left beyond smoldering ruins. Dear God. It only now occurred to her that they had nowhere to take seven and twenty children, and although she'd set out this morning to find a patron for the home, now she no longer even had a *home*.

"Perhaps they can come to my town house," Caire started doubtfully.

His mother snorted. "The home of a bachelor gentleman? I think not. The majority will come to my town house for the moment."

"And I can find places for some as well." Lady Hero had approached quietly. "My brother has a house standing nearly empty. He's in the country for the summer."

"Oh, thank you!" Temperance hardly knew what to say to such generosity.

"I can help with the little ones," Mary Whitsun said. Her lower lip trembled. "Until I find an apprenticeship, that is."

Temperance laid her hand gently on Mary's sooty hair. "How would you like to remain at the home—wherever the home might be—and help as long as you'd like?"

Mary Whitsun's eyes shone. "I'd like that, ma'am."

"Good." Temperance blinked back yet more tears.

Lady Hero smiled at the two of them. Her titian hair was wet and straggling about her shoulders, and yet she still seemed dignified and every inch the sister of a duke. "When you are settled, I would like to discuss building a new home."

"As would I," Lady Caire said. For a moment, both ladies eyed each other.

"Larger, do you think?" Lady Hero murmured.

"Definitely."

"And with room for the children to play?"

"Oh, quite," Lady Caire replied decisively, and smiled at the younger woman.

They seemed to have come to some sort of unspoken pact.

"Thank you," Temperance said, dazed.

"You're in for it now," Caire murmured irreverently in her ear. "With my mother and the sister of a duke attending to your affairs."

But she ignored his teasing, hugging him in her glee. The home had not one but *two* patronesses!

"And if you don't mind, I'd like to contribute something to the home as well." His tone was oddly diffident.

She looked up at him and said, "Thank you. We'd be most honored to have you as a patron as well."

He kissed her quickly and then Caire sighed. "I need to attend to *that*." He nodded his head to where St. John held Mother Heart's-Ease with the two footmen. "Will you stay here?"

Temperance smiled up at him. "No."

He sighed. "If you'll excuse us, Mother, my lady." He made an abbreviated bow to both ladies.

"Certainly," Lady Hero said. "I think we need to organize these children." She raised her eyebrows at Lady Caire.

That lady nodded and as one, the women wheeled to descend on Nell and the group of children.

Caire shivered with mock apprehension. "Those two are going to be formidable."

"And just what we need," Temperance said with satisfaction.

He hugged her to his side as they approached St. John and the struggling Mother Heart's-Ease.

St. John looked at Caire. "What is this about? Why would this women set fire to the home?"

"She killed Marie," Caire said grimly. "And Marie's brother, too, when he tried to blackmail her. She realized that we were getting close to discovering her, and she came here to kill Mrs. Dews, I think."

Temperance looked at the gaunt woman with loathing. "All the children were inside the home as well. She would've killed many more than just me."

"Yes. She didn't care." Caire nodded at St. John. "If we search her gin shop, we might find evidence of the murders."

"No need," St. John replied. He flipped back the ragged red man's coat that Mother Heart's-Ease wore. Beneath, rusty stains splashed across the bosom of her dress and down the front.

"Dear God," Temperance whispered, covering her mouth with her hand.

It was apparently too much for Mother Heart's-Ease. She lunged, shrieking obscenities like a madwoman, which, it was quite apparent, she was. Both footmen were hauled forward at the strength of her attack. Caire swung Temperance behind him and backed several steps, putting them both well out of Mother Heart's-Ease's reach.

"I'll bring her to gaol in my carriage," St. John shouted above the woman's ravings.

Caire nodded. "Bind her well."

"I will," St. John replied. "I'm taking no chance of her escaping."

The men set about their grim task.

"Come," Caire whispered in Temperance's ear. "You're wet and cold and so am I. Let's find a carriage to take us home."

"But Winter..." Temperance glanced about and spotted her brother helping to herd the children.

Winter caught her look and raised his hand, jogging over. "I'm to help Lady Caire and Lady Hero to settle the children, especially the boys. They'll be staying at the Duke of Wakefield's house, and they'll need supervision there."

"I must help," Temperance began.

Winter laid his hand on her shoulder. "No need. There's enough people between the servants and Nell and me."

Caire nodded above her. "I'm taking her home and giving her a warm bath."

Winter eyed Caire without speaking. And then he stuck out his hand. "Thank you."

Caire took his hand, shaking it firmly. "No need to thank me."

Winter looked between Caire and Temperance, his brow arched, but he merely said, "Take care of her."

Caire nodded. "I will."

Winter bussed Temperance on the cheek and ran back to the children.

"Now to find a carriage," Caire muttered, then grimaced. "Damn it, I forgot to thank St. John for capturing Mother Heart's-Ease."

"But he didn't," Temperance exclaimed.

He turned to look at her.

And she couldn't help but laugh; it was such a silly thing after all that had happened. "The Ghost of St. Giles appeared with her while you were inside the house."

"What, in front of everyone?"

"Yes. He marched right up to St. John and gave Mother Heart's-Ease to him. I think we were all too stunned to detain him."

"And St. John was there at the same time?"

"Yes." She looked at him curiously.

Caire shook his head. "I wish I'd been there. I'd enjoy very much finding out who it is that hides behind that mask."

Temperance wrapped her arm about his side as they started for the carriages. "I think that's a mystery that we'll have to save for another day."

TEMPERANCE WOULD HAVE fallen asleep on the carriage ride to Caire's house if she weren't so nervous with anticipation. She had told Lazarus that she loved him, but there was still something yet—she needed to *show* him.

So when the carriage stopped outside his town house, she took his hand and led him silently inside.

"I smell of smoke," he protested as they climbed the grand staircase together.

"I don't care," she replied. "I nearly lost you today."

Her heart was leaping in her chest so violently that she thought she might well faint. She had a second chance. Dear God, *Caire* was giving her a second chance.

Whatever she did, she mustn't mess it up. She carefully closed his bedroom door behind them and then stood before him.

"I want to...no, I *need* to show you how much I love you," she murmured. "I've been thinking about it for the last week. How you thought I felt I was degrading myself by making love to you."

He started to speak, but she placed her forefinger across his lips.

He raised his eyebrows.

"Let me." She inhaled to fortify her courage and deliberately trailed her finger across his lips, over his jaw, and down his neck. "Please let me."

He held very still, barely breathing. She knew this caused him pain, but she did it anyway. She needed to teach him that touch—especially *her* touch—need not bring him pain, that it could be pleasurable as well, and the only way she knew to demonstrate the lesson was to show him.

"I want to see if I can find a way"—she held his gaze as she untied his cloak—"to do this without it hurting you."

He shook his head. "It doesn't matter."

"It does to me."

The cord rasped softly as it slid apart. She took the cloak from his shoulders, carefully placing it along with his hat next to the candle atop the chair. When she turned back to him, he was still standing, watching her curiously. He'd made no move to take off any more of his clothing.

"You healed me." She swallowed and placed her hands on his shoulders. His jerk this time was softer, as if he either strove to contain the pain or it had receded a bit. She hoped it was the latter. "You made me whole again after years of suffering. I'd like to do the same for you."

Slowly, gently, she took off his coat, waistcoat, and neck-cloth. When she began unbuttoning his shirt, she could feel him shivering under her fingertips. For a moment, her courage failed her. What if forcing her touch on him merely made him more sensitive to it? Gave him more pain?

Then she looked into his face.

"Very well," he said. "But don't be disappointed if this doesn't work. I'll still love you no matter what."

She felt tears prick her eyes at his calm acceptance of her and what she wanted to do. Whatever happened, they were in this together and that at least made her feel better.

Bit by bit, one article of clothing at a time, she undressed him in near-complete silence. By the time they got down to his smallclothes, she was out of breath and he was already erect under the cloth. Her hands shook as she divested him of his last article of clothing.

She stood back and looked at him.

He was magnificent nude. His silver hair spread over his shoulders, long enough to brush his dark nipples. In contrast, the hair on his body was nearly black. Dark curls swirled between his nipples in a diamond-shaped pattern on his chest. His hard belly was bare, but just below his navel, the dark hair began again, in a thin line that trailed to the curls around his manhood. His legs were long and strong, his shoulders broad and muscled. And his eyes—dear God, his eyes!—watching her silently, sparkling sapphire blue, as he waited for her next move.

"Tell me if I go too far," she whispered. "If it hurts too much, if you want to stop."

His deep sapphire eyes were trusting. "I will."

She placed her palms flat against his bare chest, firmly, and gently pushed him to sit on the bed. She was expecting his flinch by this point, but she didn't give in to it, keeping her hands against his warm skin as he inhaled deeply. When he had settled, she slid her palms slowly down his torso, feeling the smoothness of his skin, the tickling abrasion of his body hair. She watched his eyes as they darkened to midnight blue; she paused and then slid her hands back up his chest.

"You're so beautiful," she murmured. "I've wanted to simply look at your bare body for so long."

His mouth twisted, but he didn't comment. He inhaled, his chest swelling and deflating beneath her palms. He was so alive, so vital, and for the moment he was all hers.

She gave a gentle shove, making him lie back on the bed.

His eyes narrowed, but he lay obediently.

She went to his chest of drawers and searched until she found his neatly folded neckcloths. She drew five out and turned back to his great bed. "When you tied me, I was forced to accept your lovemaking without giving in return. I'd like to do the same for you."

His eyes widened, but he nodded once, firmly.

She began tying his right ankle to the post at the bottom of the bed. She finished that foot and looked at him. He was breathing faster, but his eyes were calm. She tied his other foot and both his wrists. The knots were loose, and in any case, she was fairly certain he could tear himself free from the bonds if he truly wished. But that didn't matter. The point was merely to give him the feeling of helplessness.

And to that end, she approached the bed with the last neckcloth between her fingers.

His sapphire eyes glittered as she laid the neckcloth

across them and tied it firmly to the back of his head. She brushed her fingers over his cheek. "All right?"

He cleared his throat. "Oh, yes."

His voice sounded sensuous. Anticipatory.

She stood back and looked at her handiwork. He filled the huge bed. She'd tied his wrists to one post. His fisted hands were stretched over his head, the muscles bulging in his upper arms. The neckcloth covered his face from his brow to the middle of his nose. His lips were parted as he waited for her next move, his face turned to her as if he tracked her movements by sound. She shivered, remembering how it had felt when he blindfolded her—her senses primed by the dark. His broad chest heaved. His penis lay thick and ruddy against the paler skin of his flat belly.

Dear God, she was growing wet merely looking at him. For the first time in her life, she welcomed her own arousal. She half closed her eyes, glorying in the sensation of her heavy breasts, of her thighs rubbing together. This was who she was, whether she liked it or not, a woman who wanted and needed sex. Who loved sex. And tonight she would use that part of herself—the part she'd always despised—to heal this man she loved.

Quietly, she removed her clothing, bodice, stays, dress, underskirts, stockings, and shoes. When she took off her chemise, his nostrils flared. Could he scent her arousal? She could smell it herself, faint and tangy. She would usually be wildly embarrassed at her own body's scent and moisture, but she willed the embarrassment away.

She needed to be bold and without fear to do this.

For a moment, she stood by the bed, not touching him, not moving, merely breathing in and out, feeling her own body, watching his. Then she touched one finger to his nipple—as he had once done to her. His chest heaved at the touch, but he made no sound.

"I love you." She circled his nipple, small and dark against his pale skin. It pebbled as she touched him. She inhaled as well, her chest suddenly tight. He was at her mercy, this powerful, lonely man, both physically and emotionally. If she made the wrong move, she might hurt him terribly, for she knew now that she could hurt him, and the realization was wondrous and strange.

Somehow, by some miracle, she mattered to him.

"All of you." She leaned forward and placed her mouth against his chest, kissing him, stroking him with her lips, trying to convey all she felt. She licked his nipple, circled it with her tongue, tasting man, tasting *Caire*. She took that small bit of flesh between her lips and bit gently, carefully, listening as his breath quickened.

"I think I've loved you since that first night when you surprised me in my sitting room."

Her breath quickened as well, but it wasn't enough. It wasn't nearly enough. She climbed on the bed and straddled his hips, but when he pressed up, she ignored him, sliding lower, her legs on either side of his thighs.

"Or perhaps it was when you talked to me so shamefully in your carriage that first time." She lay flat on him, her breasts crushed just above his hot penis, her forearms along his sides, touching him with as much of her body as she could. "Do you remember?"

"Ye-es," he hissed.

She felt his body shudder, knew she was hurting him with just her gentle touch, but she pressed on. She licked down his chest, feeling the tears start in her eyes as his heartbeat thudded under her lips. She was causing him pain and she hated it, but at the same time, she hurt him with all the love in the world.

"Do you remember what you talked about? How you described me kneeling before you?"

He shuddered.

She took down her hair, letting it spread over his chest as she kissed around his navel. A soft sound left his lips, perhaps a moan, but she didn't stop. She tongued her way to that special spot by his groin where his thigh met his hip, licking like a cat. She wriggled farther down him, stretching her legs full length along his, her feet hanging off the end of the bed, her breasts resting now atop his hard thighs.

"And what I would do when I knelt before you?"

His whole body stilled. Carefully, thoroughly, she licked over his hard cock, feeling it leap beneath her tongue. She bathed him with her tongue but didn't take his penis into her mouth. His breathing was rough now, and she didn't know whether it was from arousal or pain.

Perhaps it didn't matter anymore.

"I was so aroused by your words," she whispered. "So shamed and at the same time so excited. You were opening up a new world for me. A world in which I could be free. I want you to be free too."

She placed her head between his thighs and kissed his sac, gently, tenderly, inhaling his male musk. Then she turned her head and ran her mouth down first one thigh, then the other, leaving no spot untouched, leaving no bit of flesh unloved. By the time she reached his feet—big, but with surprisingly elegant arches—she was drenched with her own need. He no longer trembled, but when she looked toward the head of the bed, she saw his fists clenching the spindles of the headboard so tightly she feared he might break them.

Now.

She flowed up him, bracing one hand on his shoulder, using the other to guide him into her. They both gasped at the penetration.

"I love you," she moaned.

Her tears overflowed as she took him deep within her. She raised her bottom, letting him slide out once, twisting herself back down on him. Then she laid herself on him like a blanket, covering as much of his flesh with hers as she could. She found that she had to curl her legs next to his hips to keep him lodged within her depths, but she could spread herself over nearly all of his torso. Then she lay still, her head on his chest, his hot cock within her, listening to his leaping heartbeat under her ear.

He was gasping beneath her.

She raised her head a little and brushed her lips over his exposed jaw, trying to comfort him. "Is it all right?"

But he wouldn't answer. His hands were still fisted, the muscles in his upper arms bulging with his restrained strength. She watched his hands flex around the neck-cloths, waiting to see if he'd tear himself free, feeling his hard length within her, pulsing with life.

When after a while he still let her lay on him, she moved. A gentle circling of her hips, a mere rising and falling, like waves upon a great rock.

She licked his throat, humming under her breath, comforting as she made love to him. He hardly moved within her. She wanted—needed—this to last. At the same time, her desire was rising. She ground herself against him, using his body to pleasure herself, even as she tried to convey all he meant to her.

He made a sound, perhaps a sob, and she closed her eyes, rubbing her wet face against his jaw.

"Temperance." He moved his face then, catching her lips. "Dear God, Temperance!"

She kissed him gladly, letting him thrust his tongue into her mouth, letting him take control in this small way.

Her movements slowed until she was merely pulsing against him, concentrating on his cock filling her completely, on his hips against the inside of her thighs, on his tongue within her mouth. It began gradually, naturally, like the dawning of the sun, a warmth starting at her center and spreading throughout her body. She hardly noticed until she was clenching inside, sobbing noiselessly against his mouth. She felt him jerk inside her, felt all of his muscles tense beneath hers. She knew he was reaching his peak as well and continued to kiss him. Gently. Softly. Telling him all she felt with just her body.

He relaxed, his spasm spent, while she still lay on him, her flesh wet with both their fluids, delicately sensitized. She had enough presence of mind to reach up and untie his hands.

Then she tucked her head under his chin and lay quiet, his cock still lodged within her, and whispered, "I love you, Lazarus Huntington. I love you."

"DOES IT STILL hurt when I touch you?" Temperance asked sometime later.

She and Caire had bathed and supped and made love again, and now they sprawled nude upon his bed. She lay on her side, her legs tangled with his, rubbing her palm over his chest. She couldn't seem to touch him enough.

Caire turned his head, his sapphire eyes meeting her

own. "No, your touch no longer pains me. I think you have indeed cured me. It tingles a bit, but the sensation is not painful." He caught her hand, rubbing her fingers over his nipple. "Quite the opposite, in fact."

Happiness streaked like a golden light through her, but she kept her face grave. "Are you sure? Perhaps we should test your endurance further."

His lips curved rather wickedly, and he brought her fingers to his mouth, kissing each one slowly and carefully until Temperance nearly squirmed. "Is that a challenge, madam?"

She lowered her eyelashes demurely, her heart pounding at their flirtation. "Perhaps."

"Then I shall endeavor not to disappoint." His voice had turned serious, and when she looked up again, his face had lost its former teasing look. "I never want to disappoint you."

"You won't," she whispered.

He closed his eyes as if pained. "I am not the man you would've chosen on your own, I think."

She laid a palm on his cheek. "Why do you say that?"

His eyes snapped open, and he suddenly rolled to bring her beneath him. "Because I am selfish and vain and venal—nothing, in fact, like you or the men in your family. Don't think I'm unaware of that fact. I don't deserve you, Temperance, but it doesn't matter. You have told me you love me, and I'll not let you change your mind, now or ever."

He lay on her heavily, his legs between her spread thighs, and she was aware that he was erect and ready again. It was a position of dominance, one meant to enforce his will.

But she looked up at him and smiled gently. "What makes you think I didn't choose you?"

His dark brows snapped together. "What?"

She threaded her fingers through his glorious silver hair. "You are exactly what I want, exactly what I need. You are honest and strong and fearless, and you make me fearless too. You don't let me hide behind excuses and prevarication; you make me face myself and you as well. I love you, Lazarus. I love you."

"Then marry me," he said fiercely.

She gasped, the prospect of happiness shimmering so close she could almost reach out and touch it. "But... what about your mother?"

He arched an arrogant eyebrow. "What about my mother?"

Temperance bit her lip. "I'm not an aristocrat—I'm not even close. Father was a beer brewer. Surely your mother and the rest of society will disapprove of marriage to me? After the fire, I don't even have anything to my name but the clothes I wore today!"

"Well, that's not entirely true," he drawled, and his sapphire eyes seemed to glow in the shadows of the curtained bed. "You have a very fine piano."

"I do?"

"You do," he said, and kissed her nose. "I ordered it only a couple of weeks ago as a surprise present, and as it wasn't delivered before the fire—it wasn't, was it?"

"No."

"There you are," he said loftily. "You have a piano and a full set of clothes, and that's plenty dowry to marry me."

"But you provided the piano!" Temperance couldn't

stop the smile that was spreading over her face. A piano? Lazarus might call himself selfish, but it was the sweetest gift she'd ever received.

"Where the piano came from is of no matter, Mrs. Dews," Lazarus replied. "The fact is you own it. As for society, it can go hang. I'll wager the thing the gossip mongers will be most scandalized by is that I found a lady to consent to be my wife."

"And your mother?"

"And my mother will no doubt be extremely happy that I've married at all."

"But—"

He nudged himself against her damp folds, and she lost whatever objection she was about to make.

"Oh!"

She looked up and saw he was so very close, his silver hair falling like a curtain to either side of her face.

"Will you marry me, Mrs. Dews," he whispered, "and save me from a life of loneliness and uncaring?"

"I will if you'll save me from a joyless life filled with only work and duty."

His blue eyes flamed, and then he was kissing her passionately. He pulled back only long enough to say, "Then you'll marry me, my sweet Mrs. Dews?"

"Yes," she laughed. "Yes, I'll marry you and love you until the end of both our days, my Lord Caire."

And she would've said more, but he was kissing her again and it didn't matter anyway. All that mattered was that he loved her and she loved him.

And that they'd found each other.

Epilogue

Now, a year passed and during that time, King Lockedheart grew more and more morose. One by one, he dismissed his courtiers until only a very few wise men remained. He grew weary of his beautiful concubines and he sent them, weeping, away. He sat alone in his great golden throne room on his velvet throne and wondered why he felt this way. All that was left to keep him company was his little blue bird, but a bird cannot talk or laugh or smile.

One day, a quiet knock came at the throne room doors, and when the king called for entry, who should come in but Meg the maid?

Well, the king sat up straight, but soon his broad shoulders slumped again and he looked a bit sulky. "Where have you been?"

"Oh, hither and yon and over all the wide world," Meg said cheerfully. "I had a wonderful time."

"Then I suppose you'll be going again?" the king asked.

"Perhaps. Perhaps not," Meg said as she sat at his feet. "How did you feel when I was gone?"

"Lost. Empty," the king said.

"And now that I've returned?"

*"Happy. Joyful," King Lockedheart growled as he
scooped Meg into his lap and kissed her soundly.
"Do you know what this is?" Meg asked in a
whisper.
"Love," the king replied. "This is love, true and
eternal, my sweet Meg. Will you be my queen?"
"Oh, yes," Meg said. "For I've adored you since first
you had me dragged before you. We will be married
and we'll live happily ever after."
And so they did!*

THREE WEEKS LATER...

The mornings were the hardest, Silence found. There just
never seemed to be any *reason* to get up. She lay in bed
and stared at the ceiling. William was gone, of course,
four weeks now at sea and still no letter. That wasn't so
unusual, but the nagging feeling that he wouldn't write
at all this voyage was. Concord wasn't speaking to her,
except for one short lecturing letter that she'd burned
because it might destroy any sisterly feeling she had for
him should she read the whole thing. No one had heard
from Asa.

Silence sighed and rolled to her side, idly watching a
fly buzz against the bedroom window. Temperance would
be happy to have her come and help plan the wedding. But
the sad thing was that Temperance's happiness with Lord
Caire contrasted depressingly with Silence's estrange-
ment from William. And jealousy of her own sister made
Silence feel small, ugly, and bitter.

Winter had come around twice asking in his easy, patient way for her help with the foundling children, but—

There was a thump at her door.

Silence turned in the direction of the outer room. It had been quite a loud thump for her to have heard it in the bedroom. Who could it be? She owed no tradespeople and wasn't expecting anyone. It might be Winter come to cajole her again. She scrunched down in the covers. If it *was* Winter, she didn't want to see him. She had just decided to pretend to not be at home when she heard it: a faint mewling.

Well, that was odd. Was there a cat at her door?

She got up and padded to the door, cracking it only slightly because she was still in her chemise. No one was there—or so she thought until she heard the sound again and looked down. A baby lay at her feet in a basket, like Moses, only without the rushes. She frowned at him and he frowned back, stuffing a fat fist into his mouth and growing rather red in the face. She didn't know much about babies, but she did know when one was about to bawl.

Hastily she bent, scooped up the basket, and closed the door behind her. She set the basket on the table and lifted out the baby, inspecting him—or rather *her,* as it turned out. The baby was dressed in a gown and stays and was quite pretty, with dark eyes and a wispy curl of dark hair peeking from her cap.

"I don't receive visitors before two of the afternoon," Silence muttered to the little girl, but the baby simply waved a fist, nearly catching her in the nose.

Silence looked in the basket and found a worn silver locket in the shape of a heart.

"Is this yours?" she asked the babe as she opened it awkwardly with one hand. Inside was a slip of paper with the word *darling* written on it. That was all. She searched the basket, even taking out and shaking the blanket the baby had lain on, but there were no more clues to the baby's identity.

"Why would someone leave a baby on my doorstep?" she wondered aloud as the baby gummed her fist. The child seemed happy enough now that Silence was holding her. Perhaps the unfortunate mother knew of her connection to the foundling home?

"Well, then I'd best take you to Winter," Silence said with decision. Suddenly she had a reason to get up this morning. She felt almost excited. "And since I found you, it seems only right that I be the one to name you."

The baby raised her eyebrows as if in query.

Silence smiled at her. "Mary Darling."

When the ton's favorite pleasure
garden burns to the ground, wildly
popular actress Lily Stump finds
herself without a theater to call home.
But among the charred ruins of
Harte's Folly, she meets a mysterious,
silent gardener who may be more
than he appears…

Don't miss the next enthralling book
in the Maiden Lane series.

Please see the next page
for a preview of

Darling Beast

The day hadn't been going well to begin with, Apollo Greaves, Viscount Kilbourne reflected.

At a rough estimate, fully half the woody plantings in the pleasure garden were dead—and another quarter might as well be. The ornamental pond's freshwater source had been blocked by the fire's debris, and now it sat stagnant. The gardeners Asa had hired for him were an unskilled lot. To top it off, the spring rains had turned what remained of Harte's Folly into a muddy morass, making planting and earthmoving impossible until the ground dried out.

And now there was a strange female in his garden.

Apollo stared into huge lichen-green eyes lined with lashes so dark and thick that they looked like smudged soot. The woman—girl?—wasn't that tall, but a swift glance at her bodice assured him she was *quite* mature, thank you. She was only a slim bit of a thing, dressed foolishly in a green velvet gown, richly over-embroidered in red and gold. She hadn't even a bonnet on. Her dark hair slipped from a messy knot at the back of her neck, waving strands blowing against her pinkened cheeks. Actually, she was rather pretty in a gamine sort of way.

But that was beside the point.

Where in hell had she come from? As far as he knew the only people in the ruined pleasure garden were the brace of so-called gardeners, presently working on the hedges behind the pond. He'd been taking out his frustration alone on a dead tree stump, trying to uproot the thing by hand since their only dray horse was at work with the other men, when he'd heard a feminine voice calling and she'd suddenly appeared.

The woman blinked and her gaze darted to his upraised arm.

Apollo's own eyes followed and he winced. He'd instinctively raised his hand as he turned to her, and the pruning knife he held might be construed as threatening.

Hastily he lowered his arm, which left him standing in his mud-stained shirt and waistcoat, sweaty and stinking, and feeling like a dumb ox next to her delicate femininity.

But apparently his action reassured her. She drew herself up—not that it made much difference to her height. "Who are you?"

Well, he'd like to ask the same of her but, alas, he really couldn't, thanks to that last beating in Bedlam.

Belatedly, he remembered that he was supposed to be a simple laborer. He tugged at a forelock and dropped his gaze—to elegantly embroidered slippers caked in mud.

Who *was* this woman?

"Tell me now," she said rather imperiously, considering she was standing in three inches of mud. "Who are you and what are you doing here?"

He glanced at her face—eyebrows arched, a plush rose lower lip caught between her teeth—and cast his eyes down again. He tapped his throat and shook his head. If she didn't get *that* message she was a lot stupider than she looked.

"Oh," he heard as he stared at her shoes. "Oh, I didn't realize." She had a husky voice, which gentled when he lowered his gaze. "Well, it doesn't matter. You can't stay here, you must understand."

Unseen, he rolled his eyes. What was she on about? He worked in the garden—surely she could see that. Who was she to order him out?

"*You*." She drew the word out, enunciating it clearly, as if she thought him hard of hearing. Some thought that since he couldn't speak that he couldn't hear as well. He caught himself beginning to scowl and smoothed out his features. "Cannot. Stay. *Here*." A pause, and then, muttered, "Oh, for goodness' sake. I can't even tell if he understands. I cannot believe Mr. Harte allowed..."

And it dawned on Apollo with a feeling of amused horror that his frustrating day had descended into the frankly ludicrous. This ridiculously clad woman thought *him* lackwitted.

One embroidered toe tapped in the mud. "Look at me, please."

He raised his gaze slowly, careful to keep his face blank.

Her brows had drawn together over those big eyes, in an expression that no doubt she thought stern but was, in reality, rather adorable. Like a small girl chiding a kitten. A streak of anger surged through him. She shouldn't be out by herself in the ruined garden. If he'd been another type of man—a brutal man, like the ones who'd run Bedlam—her dignity, perhaps even her *life*, might've been in danger. Didn't she have a husband, a brother, a father to keep her safe? Who was letting this slip of a woman wander into danger by herself?

He realized that her expression had gentled at his continued silence.

"You can't tell me, can you?" she asked softly.

He'd met pity in others since the loss of his voice. Usually it made him burn hot with rage and a sort of terrible despair—after six months he wasn't sure he'd ever regain the use of his voice. But her inquiry didn't provoke his usual anger. Maybe it was her feminine charm—it'd been a while since any woman beside his sister had attempted to talk to him—or maybe it was simply *her*. She spoke with compassion, not contempt, and that made all the difference.

He shook his head, watching her, keeping his face dull and unresponsive.

She sighed and hugged herself, looking around. "What am I to do?" she muttered. "I can't leave Indio out here by himself."

Apollo struggled to not let surprise show on his face. Who or what was Indio?

"Go!" she said forcefully, sudden enough that he blinked. She pointed a commanding finger behind him.

Apollo fought back a grin. She wasn't giving up, was she? He slowly turned, looking in the direction she indicated, and then swiveled back even more slowly, letting his mouth hang half open.

"Oh!" Her little hands balled into fists as she cast her eyes heavenward. "This is maddening."

She took two swift steps forward and placed her palms against his chest, pushing.

He allowed himself to sway an inch backward with her thrust before righting himself. She stilled, staring up at him. The top of her head barely came to his mid chest. He could feel the brush of her breath on his lips. The warmth of her hands seemed to burn through the rough fabric of his waistcoat. This close her green eyes were enormous, and he could see shards of gold surrounding her pupils.

Her lips parted and his gaze dropped to her mouth.

"Mama!"

The hissed word made them both start.

Apollo swung around. A small boy was poised on the muddy path just outside the thicket. He had shoulder-length, curly dark hair and wore a red coat and a fierce expression. Beside him was the silliest-looking dog Apollo had ever seen: a delicate little red greyhound, both ears flopped to the left, head erect on a narrow neck, pink tongue peeping from one side of its mouth. The dog's entire demeanor could be labeled "startled."

The dog froze at Apollo's movement, then spun and raced off down the path.

The boy's face crumpled at the desertion before he squared his little shoulders and glared at Apollo. "You get away from her!"

At last: her defender—although Apollo *had* been hoping for someone a bit more imposing.

"Indio." The woman stepped away from Apollo hastily, brushing at her skirts. "There you are. I've been calling for you."

"I'm sorry, Mama." Apollo noticed the child didn't take his eyes from him—an attitude he approved of. "Daff an' me were 'sploring."

"Well, explore nearer the theater next time. I don't want you meeting anyone who might be..." She trailed away, glancing nervously at Apollo. "Erm. Dangerous."

Apollo widened his eyes, trying to look harmless, even though that was most likely impossible. He'd hit six feet at age fifteen and topped that by several inches in the fourteen years since. Add to that the width of his shoulders, his massive hands, and a face that his sister had once affectionately compared to a gargoyle, and trying to appear harmless became something of a lost cause.

His apprehension was borne out when the woman backed farther away from him and caught her young son's hand. "Come. Let's go find where Daffodil has run off to."

"But, Mama," the boy whispered loudly. "What about the monster?"

It didn't take a genius to understand that the child was referring to him. Apollo nearly sighed.

"Don't you worry," the woman said firmly. "I'm going to talk to Mr. Harte as soon as I can about your monster. He'll be gone by tomorrow."

With a last nervous glance at him, she turned and led the boy away.

Apollo narrowed his eyes on her retreating back, slim and confident. Green Eyes was going to be in for a shock when she found out *which* of the two of them was tossed from the garden.